AMAZON/Libraries ONLY

Original Ebook/Print Cover: Carol Marques Design
Editing, Proofing, backgrounds, & Formatting: Dirty Sexy Words/ Storm shield Editing/Little Tailfeather Publishing
Cassandra's logos: Pretty in Ink Creations/Artlogo
Goosebusters Alpha team: Kat Silver, Becky Ross, Erica Taryn
Duckhunters Beta Proofing: Jackie Hanson
ARC Team(s): Literary inspired, Cassandra's Claws
Sensitivity Readers: Brit Mason, Gail Jericho
Translation Consultant: Mo Jacobs
Legal Services: Joshua Farley, esq.
Images/Fonts: Depositphotos, Shutterstock, Canva, & Photoshop

No GenAI was used within this book. All errors and greatness are by an ADHD muppet.

FAETAL ATTRACTION

JAMMER IN THE BOX

Content Information

This is a *paranormal whychoose romance with poly elements*—our FMC, Rogue, will not have to choose between love interests.

There are many situations included that are intended for mature audiences (18+).

In this book, there may be instances/references (be they small or lengthy) that could trigger some individuals such as:

- liberal use of appropriate consent
- biting
- BDSM
- raw sex
- shifted sex
- traumatic childhood
- MMF, MM, MFM, MF, MMFMM, and more
- drug use
- sex parties
- unhealthy coping mechanisms
- gambling
- accidental lion balls

- aggressive boundaries
- neurospicy MCs
- death
- body modifications
- fancy genitalia
- mate knots/barbs
- stepbrother romance
- bullying (in person and on social media)
- PTSD
- blood
- mating/marking/blood play
- emotional abuse from parents and friends
- alcohol abuse
- kidnapping of a sibling
- implied child abuse
- body dysmorphia
- bad language
- illegal racing
- emotional manipulation
- power play
- adorable nicknames
- physical intimidation
- mafia figures
- voyeurism
- rough sex
- a fricking spider shifter
- sex with wings and tails
- attempted murder
- marking
- crossover with *Blood on the Ice* and *Discordia University*
- brother's best friends
- family dysfunction
- betrayal (non-poly group)
- absolute disrespect for shitty parents
- pop culture references (so many)
- brief mentions of non-body positive dieting culture

- discussion of disability & neurodivergence
- mention of drug sales and distribution
- very liberal re-imagining of history
- discussion of other species as lower
- fights to the death
- official corruption
- name calling
- occasional misogyny
- inappropriate use of a bathroom
- exhibitionism
- hand necklaces
- adult bullying
- mean girls
- magical kinks
- impact play
- elitism
- bribery
- corpses
- fat shaming (not by MCs)
- drama
- physical threats to FMC and others
- species-ism
- discussion of shifter trafficking
- discussion of trafficking auctions

No sexual practices in this book should be taken as safe or appropriate for real life application.

Content information is important and I don't ever want to harm a reader with inaccurate information.

Author Ramblings

Readers,

The note I left you in *Hell on Wheels* was fraught with disaster in regard to the history of that book: failed cover designs twice, failed anthology, and other nonsense. However, *Jammer in the Box* hasn't had the rocky beginnings the first book did, and whew, am I glad for it.

As before, this book has been releasing on my serial platform as I wrote, and of course, was put through the usual editing/proof/ARC, etc, teams throughout the process. I am epically grateful to **all** of those folks—from my serial readers to my ARC teams—for their constant support and work on this book and others.

Rogue is finding her way in the midst of a major life change (losing her BFF, enemies galore, and finding the guys), but she's also now navigating a much larger conspiracy. Therefore, you *need* to have read book one *and* the bonus for this to make sense, but I **highly** recommend following the crossover diagram in book for everything (even the small crossover and Easter eggs) to hit just right.

You're going to enjoy the interaction with the other FMCs and their men (Discordia University & Secrets of State U), plus it all ties together eventually here and in the larger universe of *Legends of the Ouroboros*.

Faetal Attraction is a faster burn across the books and series than most of my books, and Rogue has her history with the guys to thank for her ability to jump in head first. Also, she's a wee bit older than FMCs like Kat or Dolly, and somewhat less damaged than Sydney or Delilah. It makes for a character who occasionally has doubts, but is able to take charge and lead when she needs to, even when it hurts. She's confident in that ability but still able to allow the guys to share the reins sometimes. Rogue is balanced, and her men aren't afraid of that.

Settle in for a trip to a huge meeting, a portal, new faces, injuries, attacks, and all sorts of chaos that makes Bay City a lot more stressful than other cities. You'll want to keep your drinks away from the reading device because you're in for some shocks and some adorable moments, plus some steamy scenes.

The stepbrother, the hockey player, the bartender, and the demon twins are going to give you all the feels... I hope you're ready.

Blood and guts,

Cassandra Featherstone

A FEW THINGS YOU SHOULD KNOW...

Jammer in the Box is the second book in the *Faetal Attraction* series. The world in which our characters live is set up in those books and I also recommend reading all the bonus scenes as well. It is part of the *Legends of the Ouroboros* universe, so it interconnects with various other series.

This is a multi-book series, so *everything will not be revealed in the first book*. Some plot lines will continue through series in a larger arc and not get resolved until the last book. (There are five planned.)

I write lengthy books with intricate world building, strong character development, and *lots* of tiny threads that stretch throughout a series that may not always seem important at first glance. However, I promise nothing I put to paper and leave in the book is unimportant; it may simply become *more* important later on. There is no 'throw-away' detail in my worlds, so every scene will mean something eventually.

I promise it will all get tied up and have a HEA; don't worry!

Jammer in the Box is a why choose/poly romance, which means our FMC will not have to choose.

I would consider it a fast burn, pre-built family group. It will get spicier throughout the series. If you're looking for porn with little to no plot, no judgment, but this isn't the series for you. It's also not closed door or FTB, so I believe the spice was worth the wait. I realize spice scales are subjective and everyone has different opinions on it, so forgive me if mine and yours aren't totally aligned.

There are some characters and creatures that speak in other languages. I made the *translations clickable end of chapter notes* to help.

Just an FYI:

There are scenes that connect to *Discordia University* and *Secrets of State U.*

There are some words that are slang, jargon, or foreign that may seem to be spelled wrong—*please email the author or find her on social media rather than report to Amazon* if you find a typo. This has been proofed and edited *several* times since release; if you believe you found errors, you may not be correct. It could be a stylistic choice or a dialect choice.

Please do not email critical feedback that is not a simple typo or formatting issue—this book is written and released. It will not be changed after publication to suit personal editing opinions or requests.

Note: If any artist/creator/real life individual/place/creative work/thing becomes problematic after the publication of this book, please note that I will likely not remove them in the future. This does not mean I support whatever shitty thing they have said/done, etc, but reflects several realities about being an author.

First, I may have a subrights contract with a third-party (ie, audio, translations, etc) that keeps me from amending the text without their approval. Typically, that involves cost and agreement from them, which is difficult to come by. Second, my writing schedule is often extremely tight, and I am not able to comb through every book in my catalog to amend small details like references, playlists, chapter titles, or other minutiae that might be affected by such a thing. Not removing it does not equate to support/agreement with whatever awful thing was revealed, nor does it mean that I am problematic as well. Third, since I am not aware of everything that happens in the world every day, I may not even know about this atrocity yet. Please be understanding.

If you see this book *anywhere besides Kindle Unlimited/libraries in ebook format,* please reach out to me via social media or email. Pirating kills my ability to write full time and I am so grateful for your help.

Contact my team for typos or to report piracy: teamcassandrafeather stone@cassandrafeatherstone.com

THANK YOU FOR SUPPORTING ME BY BUYING THIS BOOK!

YEAH, I KNOW. YOU THINK THE COVERS ARE COOL AND YOU REALLY WANT TO READ THIS SERIES.

NOPE.

I'M JUST NOT COMFORTABLE WITH THE NEXT GATHERING BEING ONE WHERE I HAVE TO EXPLAIN WHY MY FOLKS ARE TELLING PEOPLE I WRITE PORN ON VACATION.

I MEAN, I LOVE THAT Y'ALL ARE ADVERTISING FOR ME, BUT ROMANCE ISN'T SOMETHING YOU HAVE WHISPER ABOUT LIKE YOU'RE TALKING ABOUT GOODY PROCTOR, GUYS.

YOU'RE GOING TO HAVE TO GET REAL COOL, FAST, IF YOU WANT TO BE ABLE TO READ MY STUFF. #SORRYNOTSORRY.

CAVEAT: IF YOU CHOOSE TO KEEP READING, KNOW THAT AT NO TIME WILL I EXPLAIN TERMS, POSITIONS, THEMES,

TROPES, OR ANY OTHER PART OF THIS NOVEL AT FAMILY
EVENTS, IN GROUP CHATS, OR ON SOCIAL MEDIA.

DON'T ASK.

Start with:
Read this next!
Veiled FLAME
CASSANDRA FEATHERSTONE
BONUS SCENE #1
Veiled FLAME
CASSANDRA FEATHERSTONE
HELL ON WHEELS
CASSANDRA FEATHERSTONE
BLOOD ON THE ICE
CASSANDRA FEATHERSTONE
This timeline intersects with Veiled Flame
BONUS SCENE #1
HELL ON WHEELS
CASSANDRA FEATHERSTONE
BONUS SCENE #1
BLOOD ON THE ICE
CASSANDRA FEATHERSTONE
Bonus Scene
Bonus Scene
Crossover Reading Order

Zero Spark
Starts Here

Intersects at
Chapter "Devil"
Bonus may
include things

Intersects at
Chapter
"Battle"
+ bonus

This timeline
intersects with
Suspicions at
the end.

Bonus Scene

Jammer in the Box Playlist

CHAPTER TITLE SONGS

Jammer in the Box Playlist

SHIFTER TERRITORY
GENERAL POPULACE LIVING AREA
GENERAL POPULACE LIVING AREA
GENERAL POPULACE LIVING AREA
OUTCAST TERRITORY
GUILLERMO LAIR
NON-AFFILIATED TERRITORY
PRISON
SOLDIER LINE
STUHLI TERR
UPPER CLASS GATES
VAMPIRE TERRITORY
LEGAL RACEWAY
SPORTS LEAGUE HQ
SON
LIGHTNING FIELD
STORM FIELD
TOWN HALL
CITY CENTE
THUNDER RINK
OUTCAST TERRITORY
BOMBERS RINK
MAYOR'S HOUSE
OUTCAST TERRITORY

City
Soss Docks
Territory
Society Docks
Angelo & Damon's House
General Populace Living Area
Gemini Territory
Gemini Compound
Mythical Territory
Fae Temple
Demon Gate
Fae Territory
Storm
General Populace Living

This is for the women who are weary of being told what to do,

what not to do, and being held to ridiculous standards

we cannot possibly meet.

Go out there and find your real family—
even if it's your hot stepbrother and his friends.

You'll thank me later.

You're disposable as soon as they decide you are.
~Anonymous

Contents

Wait!

A FINAL REMINDER BEFORE YOU READ...

MY SERIES TYPICALLY HAVE PREQUELS, gap novellas/novels, and bonus material that are integral to your having a satisfying reading experience.

If you have not read the other pieces in this series, you may feel as though you have missed critical details, developments, plot points, and other information. This will cause the book to appear to have continuity gaps that it does not have.

If you have not read the bonus material for this series, it is available online here, in audio versions (if applicable), and in print special editions (if applicable).

I highly recommend consulting the bonus page prior to reading this new title so you're up to speed on all the things going on in this world.

Happy reading!

Let's Get This Party Started

"WHAT DO you think connecting us with those people got Tracer?" I ask my guys as we leave the 'secret meeting' tent. "Nothing I've seen from that shithead so far says he's motivated by altruism."

Damon snorts, nodding in agreement. "You're not wrong, Sparkles. Tracer might be the second least objectionable Finn I've met now, but that doesn't make him trustworthy."

"He did it because he's hoping to eventually inherit the *Sons*, and if there's multi-realm chaos upending everything, small fry gangs and mafias won't have a chance in the ensuing wars." Rebel frowns as we walk down the garden path, heading towards the demon territory slowly in the bubble he and I created for privacy. "Tipping off anyone he believes might be connected enough to stop it is his way of getting someone else to do the dirty work."

As we make our way around the paths, I study the various entry gates for the territories. I'm not eager to explore most of them right now, despite my curiosity about the Fae lands. I remember little from my early childhood; Graciella and Odhran were adamant that Reck and I never discussed it. They were even less willing to discuss our heritage after Reck was shipped off and they brought Reb in. It feels weird to avoid the one place I might have a connection to at this damn meeting, but I figure we're going to face enough bullshit when we hit the demon territory. I don't need to dredge up bad memories and get myself further on edge when I'll certainly be tested at our primary destination.

"You feel nervous, Princess," Angelo murmurs as he winds his arm around mine. "I have faith that you're going to be fine. Luca and Lola won't want to seem weak in front of the entire hierarchy and guests from other organizations. Jealous demons aren't likely to confront you like they did at the party."

"Mmm," I reply absently as I tangle our fingers together. "Appearances are important; I get that. That doesn't mean they won't attempt to use others to do their shifty shit. Just like Tracer, they're smart enough to realize if they stay hands off, they can do whatever they want."

"Not true." Archie grins as he bobs his brows. "A lot of these groups won't want to get caught with their hands in the demonic cookie jar at a treaty-bound event. It's not much, but it's something."

Rebel snorts, shaking his head. "We just learned there are underground groups from all over committing crimes all over the country and in the other realms, Arch. If our suspicions about the twins' parents are right, then they will have access to plenty of patsies for hire."

Squinting, I look at my stepbrother. "Are you *trying* to make me worried?"

"No. I'm trying to keep you on your toes, lil' sis. We've been trained to look for threats in every corner by trade, and if we were doing it in our personal lives, we might have seen your ex-friend coming."

Ouch. True, but painful in a way that only Reb can get away with.

"Okay. Everyone is a suspect and I'll keep my eyes peeled. Happy now?"

He shrugs, giving me a look that makes my insides flutter. "Getting there."

Not the time, Rogue; not the time.

THE INSANELY OSTENTATIOUS entry point to the demon territory makes me roll my eyes inwardly. There's no way it needs to be gilded *and* oddly dark, with curling ironwork and weird dead looking plants I suppose must be indigenous to Hell. Angelo and Damon don't seem to be surprised, so I leave it alone as they approach the gates and place their palms on flat plates in the center. A burning smell fills the air, like a barbecue in the summer, and the heavy doors swing open slowly. We all look at the twins and they sigh.

"All the lands will have them roped off somehow, and if we hadn't been able to open this without help, some sort of gatekeeper would have shown up," Damon replies as he holds his arm out for me. "Those who aren't from your lands have to be recorded as guests and—"

Before he can finish, a large angry looking demon appears with a burnt smelling tome floating in front of him. The demon is definitely not in humanoid form, and I'm not sure what kind he is, but he definitely does *not* look like he's happy to see us. "State your names and species in order to be recorded. Non-demon guests must declare themselves personally after demonic visitors. Lord Gemini reserves the right to refuse entry to anyone he sees fit."

Lord? Is Luca fucking kidding people with this shit?

Angelo snickers, walking up to the demon and eyeballing him. "You must be fresh out of the pits. What a lazy ass way to keep our brethren safe—placing cannon fodder with no idea who is who on the gate. Fuck, Luca needs to vet his lieutenants better."

"How *dare* you—"

Damon sighs as he cuts the moron off. "Presenting Damon and Angelo Gemini, heirs to the Gemini family, you fucking knob."

The demon's eyes go wide and he bumbles for a second as I grin. "Rogue Kelly, fated mate to Angelo and Demon Gemini, heirs to the Gemini family line. Unseelie dark Fae, Guardian, adopted, and very excited to watch you get your innards pulled out by your bosses."

"Rebel Kelly. Unseelie Fae, Guardian. Bored as fuck with this shit."

Javier and Archie laugh, elbowing Rebel as he rolls his eyes. They each introduce themselves snarkily, and by the time we're finished, the magical book slams shut. The dumbass demon is still trying to figure out what the fuck he's going to do when Angelo takes my other arm. They chuckle and lead me away, obviously not concerned with the flunky any longer.

"You know, I feel like there are a lot of better things all the assholes holding this thing could do with their excess of money than build entire mini-realms that will only get destroyed when it's over."

Turning to Javier, I smile fondly. "I agree, birdie. But since most of the organizations holding court here aren't exactly known for their generous natures, I suppose it's no surprise they're unconcerned with the little people."

He and Damon are the softest hearts of everyone, despite Archie looking the part more than them.

"Don't let anyone intimidate you. Rogue did exactly what she should have back there," Angelo says as we approach a dark, curling archway. "If we have to admit she's mated to all of us, we will. For now, we'll say you're part of our chosen family group or some shit."

Archie chuckles as he shakes his head. "It's always hard for the species who rarely form polycules to grasp this shit. When we're around the shifters like my parents, no one bats a lash."

"Demons often form caliphates with their closest friends and allies. Sometimes, those also include fated, but the rate of demons finding a fated is quite low," Damon replies. "Most of our kind enter advantageous business arrangement marriages or commitments like Luca and Lola. No one really knows why the success rate of finding a mate is so low in Hell."

"Maybe because they all stay down there and avoid nine other realms where they could be?" Rebel snarks as he arches a brow. "You two wouldn't have found Rogue if you weren't living up here because the King hates Luca. Demons not finding fated are a self-fulfilling prophecy, it sounds like."

Javier clears his throat, interrupting with a soft murmur, "We should be careful what we talk about inside. Those magic bubbles will probably be unreliable once we're surrounded by all the demonic power and whatever else is in there. Though, I agree with what you guys are saying. Phoenixes are similarly limited because they try to stay within their kind."

"I think it's stupid," I say with a shrug. "It's outdated nonsense, and we all know everyone puts hybrids like me on the bottom of the pile. Truthfully, we're doubly strong and not so tied to one species that we can't see when they're being ass clowns."

"Everyone ready?" Angelo asks. I nod, and the rest of the guys do as well. "Let's go rub elbows with a bunch of crusty outdated assholes and nasty new money demons."

I'm surprised when we can get into the raucous affair without being stopped by anyone. Angelo and Damon are escorting me with Reb, Javi, and Archie, walking behind us as we make our way through the oddly dressed crowd. There are people dressed as formally as us, but also a decent amount of demons outfitted for clubbing or bondage. I arch a brow at the twins, but they just shrug. I suppose it's normal to them, and that's something I tuck away as knowledge for the future. Most of the people are in either humanoid or partially shifted forms, much like Luca's party, except for the staff. They're all fully shifted into demon form, be it small and snively on the serving crew or huge and ugly against the wall.

The latter, I assume, are the security demons. There's no other explanation.

"What do we do now?" I murmur to Damon. "Is there a protocol? If so, are we following it or simply wandering about gathering intel?"

Damon grins as he leans in to reply, "A little of both. We can mingle briefly, checking out the attendees for suspicious faces or conversations as long as we make our way toward wherever Luca is holding court. It'll be obvious what the path to dear old dad is as we get farther into the territory."

I frown, not sure I want to imagine what it's going to look like as that approaches. We've already passed a dance floor full of techno grinding, a mini-BDSM stage with on-lookers, three bars, four drug dens, and a very weird seating area full of demons gambling with bones. None of this is particularly off-putting, but I have this uneasy feeling in the pit of my stomach. It's telling me this whole 'den of iniquity' thing is going to get less palatable when the atmosphere goes from 'guest' acceptable to full-on demonic.

"You know, I don't think I've had the pleasure of performing that kind of shit for a crowd before," Archie says wryly. "Think I'd be good at it, guys?"

"No." Damon and I growl simultaneously. I chuckle when the twin flushes bright red, and his brother groans.

"Good thing you agree," Rebel drawls as he sweeps the next area with his eyes warily. "I'd hate for Rogue to get the idea we're okay with her climbing the boards to do the same."

Whipping my head around, I glare at my stepbrother. "If I choose to perform at the club again, I won't be asking for *any* of your permissions, assholes. You don't own me, even if we are mated."

Angelo's eyes darken, and I feel the flare of his ire on my other side.

His voice is low, and he grits his teeth as he hisses, "That is a conversation for much later, preferably *never*, Princess."

Men are the goddamn worst.

"I don't think it's fair to limit Arch if you're allowed," Javi says mildly. "He'd make a fortune with that sculpted hockey bod, especially because he's well known. I mean, think about it. Supes of every gender would go for watching him get topped in restraints."

I blink, letting that wash over me for a moment. It makes my magic surge with jealousy, filling my veins with fury. "Fine. Point taken. No one performs naked for people."

Rebel just smirks at me as if he knew that was going to be the answer and I have to clench my fist so I don't punch him. "Mmmhmm. What's good for the goose, lil' sis."

There's a reason I was dating women before these jokers, and this is definitely it.

The Devil Went Down To Georgia

ANGELO

THE BICKERING amongst my family is amusing, but I'm only half paying attention to it. We're in a shark tank in this room, and I'm watching carefully for perceived foes. Damon isn't used to the absolutely disgusting shit our father gets up to because I'm the one he taps for the dirty work. I've never complained about it because D has always been softer, less hard edged than me. I'm not sure he could take the assignments I've been part of, nor would I want him to.

It's the one thing I could do to protect him and I will always strive to allow him that tiny modicum of innocence.

But his instant attachment to Archer is even cuter than his adoration of Rogue, and I don't want our parents to get even a whiff. They don't care about sexuality unless it affects their reputation, and until we're ready to announce our entire family as a unit, we have to keep the specifics under wraps. Damon barely paid attention to demonic customs and shit during our education at Discordia, so I doubt Luca will assume we've formed a caliphate. Technically, under demonic tradition, that's exactly what we're doing; Rogue is part Cubi and we're full demons. The others are connected by mating, so they'd be allowed to be inducted by law.

Luca and Lola would lose their fucking minds; caliphates are most often formed in elite demon families as a prelude to taking over their family empires. While Luca brags about me taking his seat at the head of the Geminis, I know he'll stay in that role until the day he draws his last breath. Having an heir is convenient and shields him from internal coups, but he has zero intention of ever letting go of the reins to our organization.

"Ang?"

I turn to look at our girl, smiling as she arches a brow. "Yes, Princess?"

"You're obsessing. There's a crease between your eyes that I *know* means you're worried about something." Rogue smirks when I scowl, leaning in to murmur against my ear, "And you're stiffer than a corpse in the Arctic, baby. Not in a fun way, either."

"Tell me about it," I grumble as my shoulders drop. "There's a lot of shit about demon culture that both you and D have little awareness of. You were raised completely outside of it, and he buried himself in books and computers to avoid Luca. I, however, spent many years being groomed for the throne."

She frowns as she follows my gaze to a corner where two demons are being whipped on racks in front of a crowd of drunken, hooting lower level on-lookers. "Stuff like this?"

I chuckle, nodding at her indication. "Well, yes. Pain with pleasure is a fairly common occurrence in our species, though I wouldn't say it's the only way. But the parties and events that are not attached to more formal occasions typically have a lot of hedonistic flavor. This isn't the worst of it, but notice it wasn't right at the front entry, either. Most events have rings like Hell itself, which keep the very depraved and dark stuff away from 'visitors' to our scene."

Her eyes squint and she shrugs. "That's fine. You'd have to do some pretty weird shit to find things I haven't seen at the club. I'm not saying degradation or high pain are my thing, mind you, but I won't be scandalized by it. Whatever floats people's boats is their business, Ang."

"Archie and maybe Javi will probably be uncomfortable by the time we find my parents," I reply as I shake my head. "I've seen some eye-bleach worthy shit at Luca's ragers in the past. Reb won't be ruffled, I don't think, but those two are much more normal than us dark side supes."

"Gotta lose the naiveté sometime," she says. "They've bonded to our bent selves, baby, and that means seeing things they wouldn't have ever had the chance to witness before. I'm sure they'll survive okay."

"Even if we run into Luca and Lola being… serviced by large, random groups of demons? Because unfortunately, that's more likely. I wasn't joking about seeing shit I'd like to have removed from my memory with a sharp object."

Rogue makes a face, shuddering as she holds onto my arm. "Fucking gross. I take it back; my jackass parents aren't remotely as bad as yours, even if they sold my brother on the black market. What kind of whacked out motherfuckers let their kid see them being rogered—or worse—in public?"

"Definitely 'or worse' applies," I mutter. "But Damon didn't have to go to that kind of shit, so he might have a wee bit of trouble as well. You know I've always tried to push him away from the in person parts of the Gemini lifestyle."

She sighs. "Well, tonight is going to suck no matter how we shake the globe, Ang. Maybe we can get a group rate on therapy?"

She has no idea how accurate that might be, but for now, I'll just smile.

IT TAKES a bit to wend our way through the upper levels of the space Luca had his minions build, and I want to scream at the ridiculous wastefulness of this monstrosity. I don't claim to be any kind of eco-warrior or someone who struggled financially at any point in my life. But I recognize the excess involved in all these organizations and species creating temporary territories for a three-day event is a bit much. I guarantee it's bothering Rogue, but she's more focused on making sure that Reb and I help her surround the softer members of our group.

"Wheels, you're gonna bruise me if you're not careful," Archie jokes as she holds onto him with one arm and Javi with the other. Damon is on his other side, and Reb is flanking our phoenix on the outside. "You guys have all gone super serious badass, and no one is telling the rest of us why."

"Shut up, Archie."

Reb's growl doesn't help, especially when Archie growls back. Rogue stops our progress through a room full of naked people fucking on every surface possible with a sigh. "*No* fighting or none of you are sleeping in my room when I finally scrub this place off of me."

Damon grins a little at her. "I'll help you get clean, Dragonfly. Don't worry."

"How much longer is it going to take to get through this shit?" Javier asks, as he frowns at the piles of demons in various levels of transformation writhing around us. "I feel like I should change my name to Dante."

Rogue snorts, squeezing his arm. "Aw, you're so cute when you're squicked out."

"I'm not squicked out—well, maybe I am a little. I'm just tired of watching pit demons rutting with their weird shit flopping all over the place."

I laugh at his petulant grumbling. Pit demons are pretty skeevy, and he's not wrong about having to see them... do their thing. "You're not wrong, but nothing we've passed so far is depraved enough for it to be close to our parents. The last time I had to attend one of his bacchanals... Well, hopefully, you guys don't have to see that shit, but it wasn't something I'd wish on anyone."

Damon frowns as he looks at me. "Is this what it's always been like when you did shit with him?"

I shrug. "Sometimes. I don't notice most of it anymore—unless it involves Luca or Lola. That's still weird and way over my line. They never seemed to think it was a big deal, and I honestly have no idea if that's normal for demons. I haven't had the guts to ask in the past— like at school—and I sure as hell wasn't going to take a poll once he moved us up here for good."

"Ewwwwww," D mutters as he shudders. "Sweet merciful fuck, if there's anyone watching over us, *please* don't let that be what we find at the boss level of this damn place. I'll never sleep again."

"Thanks, Ang. Horrifying *and* nightmare inducing. Glad you shared. Can we get a move on?" Rebel looks pained, and I'd bet my favorite poker chips he's got a nasty image in his head that doesn't do reality justice.

Nodding, I lead the group out of the orgy room, shutting the door behind us. The antechamber we end up in is surprisingly free of the party atmosphere; it only has a bank of elevators with different buttons and security pads next to them. This is unusual; in fact, I've never seen extra security like this at one of my asshole father's shindigs.

"What's this?" Rogue says as she drops to a crouch to examine the first of three panels by one of the elevators. "Buttons are in the demonic language, so that's you, D. I'm not sure about the other part of this set-up, though. It's not a fingerprint or cornea—I have no idea."

Rebel is similarly bent to look at the next one, his face scrunched in concentration. "The middle is soft? But she's right; it's not for finger- prints. Fuck if I know what the hell your dickhead sperm donor is pulling, man. This is fucking weird."

Something about it is familiar, but I can't remember where I might have seen the devices. My gaze cuts to Damon, who shrugs. He squints at the buttons, then says, "In order, they say: enter the third and fourth, fall to the fifth or sixth, and descend to the seventh and ninth. It's definitely Inferno bullshit—even though Dad hates it—but those things must keep guests or low-level demons from getting to the most objectionable floors."

Okay, I sort of know what this is hiding, but normally, it doesn't require extra security. What is Luca hiding?

"Do you think he's trying to keep the other families and groups from seeing the really twisted stuff?" Rogue asks curiously. "I've never heard of that, but who knows what horrors are going on in the super secret levels? Maybe some of it would offend the other supes."

I consider that for a moment, then shake my head. "Shifters and vampires run hunts, so do some mythicals. Death and violence will not make most criminals or supernatural species who would attend this sort of thing blink. Whatever Luca has going on here is probably violating laws in multiple realms. This system is probably to keep anyone who isn't accompanied by a demon from experiencing those illegal pleasures."

"He might host people who aren't supposed to be on the surface at the lowest levels," Damon says softly. "You know we saw Darkstar at that party. That son of a bitch is up to his ass in shady shit, which is why he got sentenced to running the school rather than being welcome at the courts."

"Plus, he's a fucking dick."

The tone of the being behind us is filled with snark and disrespect, so I whirl around to find out who thought it would be a good plan to eavesdrop on the Gemini heir. My jaw drops when I see the cadre of demons looking at me expectantly, their expressions full of entitlement that they certainly earned. Somehow, my family is surrounded by the royal caliphate of Hell—none of whom are supposed to be on the surface, much less at my father's stupid ass party.

"Prince Jasper..." I nudge Damon until he faces the group of hybrid demons who will inherit the throne of our realm with me. "I didn't mean to—"

"Relax, Gemini." The dark-haired heir to the greed line gives me a knowing smirk. "He's not here to smite you for your jackass father's sins."

"That's good to know," Rogue mutters. "Though it'd be nice if that was prefaced by a fucking introduction."

I'm about to shush her when a small guy emerges from the middle of the caliphate. I've never seen him before, but his floppy hair and small stature are almost as shocking as the royals in this realm. He grins a little, looking at our woman despite the half a foot difference in their height.

"That's what I've been saying! These assholes run around meeting people they know in every realm, wave their dicks at one another, and I'm left looking like the dumbass in the middle. This is the second time that dick waffle has gotten into it with someone while we all watch." I wince as he refers to the prince of Hell like some random dude, but the kid just steps closer and holds out his hand. "I'm Kit, by the way."

Rogue looks surprised for a second, then beams at the guy as she takes his hand. "I *like* this guy, Ang. He's got moxie and I *adore* watching puffed up men get put in their place. I'm Rogue Kelly, Guardian and mate to these twin idiots. That pretty one is Archie, the suave one is Javier, and the grumpy-looking guy is my step-brother, Rebel."

That's fantastic—our mate just became besties with someone tied to the people my father is looking to overthrow. I look at the rest of the guys and they shrug, unwilling to help me figure out what the fuck I'm going to do now.

What in the hell do I do now?

Friends in Low Places

ROGUE

The second his hand met mine, I knew the guy had a *big* secret. I mean, I knew it could have been something the rest of the demons were aware of until our eyes locked. That's when the surge of fear zipped between us and I realized he was definitely *not* doing this for an identity reason. I make a mental note to ask Angelo about that college, and give the poor kid a gentle smile I hope lets him know I will not spill the beans.

Now that I see it, I can't unsee it, but I definitely get why he's been able to successfully hoodwink them—you don't notice if you're not looking.

"Um, Jasper's rep has preceded him, I guess, which is no surprise." His crooked grin makes me want to laugh; there's definitely something very Buffy/Spike between the secret girl and the grumpy prince and I'm here for it. "The big guy is Slash—he's nicer than he looks unless you don't eat your lunch. The dark-haired one is Oriel, the two-toned guy smiling is Salem, the only one who isn't a giant is Zavida, and the two very suave looking demons are Anton and Xerxes."

"Little demon…"

I laugh when the big dude sighs and chastises Kit gently. My gaze rakes over the group carefully and I let my magic taste the surrounding air. The demon part of me—which I rarely access—tells me the truth of this situation immediately. Every single one of these men is attracted to the spunky, unemerged demon pretending to be a guy; not only that, he is as well, though I believe he's probably clueless about it. His aura has flavors of desire and confusion simultaneously, so I'm uncertain Kit even understands what he's feeling.

"Thank you, Kit," I say as I smirk at his companions. "I'm not sure why the others find it so hard to be normal when they meet people, but I'm glad you have such lovely manners."

The guy chuckles and shrugs. "I think it's because these dudes," he hitches his thumb over his shoulder, "never come to the surface. Since I was semi-lured into going to school in Hell after living my whole life up here thinking I was human... I've got a different set of social protocols."

That explains everything—including why demons that old haven't noticed why Kit smells like a female.

Angelo and Damon look at me curiously, and I shake my head slightly. I don't want them to accidentally out Kit, either, so I hurry to say, "That must have been an eye-opener. Reb and I are unactivated Guardians, which means someday, our job will be to protect a human who has the potential to be supernatural but hasn't gotten their powers. You should have had one, to be honest, but I'm not sure we worry about demons unless they're hybrids."

The Prince finally speaks, scoffing at me with unsurprising bluster. "Demons do not use the Society's Guardian program because we keep track of our progeny, even on the surface. We are self-regulating."

Rebel snorts, then gives the snarky royal an amused expression. "I'd say you don't, given this kid being yanked from the surface into a world he didn't know existed. Unless I'm misunderstanding his story, which I don't think I am."

There's a growl as the enormous guy Kit called Slash bristles at the offense and I cringe. My step-brother lives to piss people off and he never thinks about what the consequences are going to be. Shitting on the Prince of Hell definitely has repercussions, if you're not the little guy who introduced them. "Maybe he's not a hybrid, Reb—"

I'm cut off by another growl, this time from the two-toned dude who puts his hand on Kit's shoulder. "You have no idea *what* KK is. Don't presume to put him in a box without permission."

Okay, that one clearly knows he has feelings for the kid and doesn't give a fuck who else knows.

"Salem, Slash... It's okay. Rogue wasn't trying to be mean to me, and her brother... Well, likely he has the same giant cocknozzle disorder Jasper has. No need to be confrontational." The shorter guy winks at me and I cover my laugh with a knowing smirk.

"He's right. Reb's far too blunt for his own good—though he's *not* my brother by blood. I want to make that *very* clear before you think weird shit about me." I chuckle as their eyes widen, and Kit's face turns bright red. Quite cute, and certainly naïve about sex stuff. I'd almost pay to watch this shit unwrap, but alas, we have things to do. "It *is* very odd that you were never tagged as a lost one or by the demons until you were of age. I know of a few older lost ones through our program, but you're an exception to the usual rules. That's what he meant."

"Is there a point to this?" The tall, rainbow haired guy that is Xerxes or Anton squints at me. "I enjoy meeting new people, as does X, but we have specific things to do on this very unannounced visit to the surface."

"Unannounced?" Damon says as he moves forward. "The royal caliphate shows up at an Apalachin with nebulous origins with no notice, and Tracer brings those people from the college to ask about secret shit. What the fuck is going on around here?"

"What college people?" Oriel—I think—gives my demon a sharp look as he tilts his head. "A group with a professor, a siren, a badass gargoyle, a Prince, and a dragon with an attitude?"

What.

"Yes, *that* group. One of them is related to the leaders of an organization here. They visited that gang, but a liaison related to both parties wanted us to meet them. It sounds like you've had a run-in with Morgana and her guys as well." I frown, feeling pieces fly together in my mind like a picture is going to form eventually.

Kit turns and glares at the dude she called Salem, then faces me again. "We just came from the Fae territory. *I* can't tell you the entire story of the orc attack because *someone* hid me in a tent. However, I'm sure the other big, bad demons who dealt with it alongside our new friends can explain it."

Archie bursts out laughing, shaking his head as he grins at the smart-mouthed kid. "Man, I *really* enjoy your honesty, dude. You don't mince words for a second. It's hilarious to see how the demons all react to it, too. Shit, I could watch this all day."

"But you won't," the gorgeous demon Anton called Xerxes says. "My caliphate is full of poor communicators, save for KK, so I'm taking over this negotiation. There was an orc attack, and we worked with that group to protect the Fae. Many died or were injured, but both of our groups needed to leave prior to any 'official' authorities arriving. Neither of our families are on the invite list, if you get my drift, so we don't want people to know we're here."

Angelo arches a brow at Xerxes. "You're with the *Prince of Hell*, man. How in the fuck are you slinking around without being recognized?"

"Hey!" Kit puts his hands on his hips as he glares at my mate. "Xerxes goes by they/them. Be respectful now that you know."

I thought I couldn't like this faux guy more, but damn.

"Shit. Sorry, Xerxes," Angelo apologizes quickly and I'm instantly proud of him, too. "I didn't know. Damon and I were at DU many years ago, and we're never down below. I didn't know, though it's probably fairly common knowledge in Hell."

Xerxes smiles, the sparkle in their eyes brilliant as they nod. "No worries. The worst part about being a demon is that we're so divided regarding up and down. I think it leaves a *lot* of room for trouble, which is... well, it's why we're here."

"The Games," Damon murmurs as he looks at them. "You're here because they reactivated the Games for the first time since your families took the crown."

"Yes," Jasper says, his eyes dark as he looks at us suspiciously. "And if I'm honest, we believe *your* family is involved."

Oh, fuck. Is this going to go sideways?

Angelo and Damon look at one another, grimacing before they face the demonic group. After a moment, Angelo sighs. "Yeah, we've been kind of suspicious about that, too. Did you know Darkstar was up here recently? He was at our father's compound during a party recently."

"I *knew* it," the prince snarls as he looks at the huge silver-haired bruiser. "That son of a bitch is conspiring against us, and it's why he's doing all this bullshit."

I feel Rebel's eyes on me and suddenly, his voice echoes in my mind. *~Kiandra, orcs in this realm are very bad news. The Daybreak Prince and his family may be right about a bigger threat. ~*

He's not wrong, but I don't want the surrounding people to know what he said. "Luca Gemini is always up to something, and none of us are part of it, even Angelo and Damon. We *have* an invitation, but it was a mysterious one. No one has admitted to bringing us to the event yet, but we haven't seen their parents yet, nor have the meetings happened."

Kit frowns, his brow crinkling. "How does this thing work? None of the guys seem familiar with it, but when we went to the Fae area and met Morgana's group, they mentioned visiting Slade's family. Maybe understanding why and what this thing is will help me put some pieces together."

This time, Damon grins. "Good question, man. So, these meetings are mostly for the criminal organizations in Bay City and happen whenever one or more of the leaders call one. There's enough time between when the mysterious invites arrive and the meeting for everyone to set up. Often, there's more than just crime lords attending because other supes—like the Society—need to keep their eyes on shit, too. There's a bunch of party stuff, like now, then the meeting happens. It's a few days each time—or that's what I figured out when I had to dig up dirt before we came."

"Interesting," Anton says as he scratches his chin. "Like in a human mafia movie, right, Kit Kat?"

I stifle a laugh as Kit gives the colorful demon a proud look. He must be teaching them all about human culture and they've watched the *Godfather* or something. "Something like that, yeah. There's definitely supe mob here, plus motorcycle gangs, courts, demon families…. all the ne'er-do-wells in one place. But Bay City is practically ruled by these groups and it actually works here."

The red and white-haired demon pushes his glasses up and finally speaks as he looks at me. "If it's true that the twins don't support whatever scheme their parents have with our dickhead Headmaster, then why are you headed for the same private levels we are? Aren't you going to see the heads of the family now?"

Ah, he's the Damon of their group—the insanely intelligent, logical one. Bet he's a gamer, too.

Angelo nods. "We are, but not because we want any part of their shit. There are threats against my mate, random attacks on our family, and a lot of weird things going on here. Tonight, we've learned—much like your caliphate, I suspect—that something much bigger is going on all across the realms. Something big enough to make me want to witness shit I'd prefer to never see again, so I can spy on my dad."

The Prince shudders, and the look on his face makes me wonder if he's actually empathizing with my mate. Man, demons are fucking *weird* with their kids and everything I've learned today makes me thankful that I am *never* procreating. At least, that's my stance for the moment and I don't see it changing, no matter how hot my idiot mates are.

"If you're so eager to find out, why were you standing around in this atrium when we arrived?" The dark-haired demon smirks at us and Kit swats him lightly.

"Because we have no idea how to breach this weird security panel," I admit. My guys all groan and I roll my eyes. "Look, dummies. I know it hurts your manly bits to say that to people, but if the twins have never seen these, and none of us know how to make the elevators move, we'll stand here until we're petrified."

That's when our new friends, except for Kit, all smirk and shift into a half-demon form full of tails and horns.

I might have fucked up. Danger, Will Robinson.

Way Down We Go

DAMQN

WHEN THE ROYAL caliphate shifts into their demon forms, Angelo and I tense up. We don't have time to protest, though, because the guy Rogue is making friends with whirls around with a pinched look on his face. He glares at most of them, and when I look closer, his hands are clenched in fists at his side that seem to tremble a little. I don't get why he looks so mad, but several of the demons look sheepish as fuck once Kit is facing them.

Something weird is going on and I have no idea what the fuck it is.

"Un. Necessary," the guy grits out, and I grin a little as everyone but the Prince dip their chins in shame. "Salem and Oriel could have done... whatever the fuck this is."

The Prince's eyes narrow at him, fury flashing in his gaze until the enormous grey and white beefcake bares his teeth at him in warning. They stop paying attention to the little guy as they have a silent stand-off, and I worry that we're going to see a demon duel if the tension doesn't break soon. This definitely isn't what I expected when these dudes showed up, and I'm curious as hell about what's causing it.

"Put them away, boys," Rogue says as she smirks. "Whatever dramatic effect you wanted to have is ruined because somehow, you've pissed off the only one of you I actually like. Kit, are you okay?"

A heavy sigh punctuates his movement as the kid turns around, wrinkling his nose. "I'm okay. Thank you for asking, Rogue. They're just, uh, breaking a promise about holding their tempers while we're up here."

He's a fucking horrible *liar, but I don't think we need to call him out on it.*

"Pretty big ask for demons like them," I say as I jerk my head toward his group. "But I don't blame you for being frustrated. Sometimes, we have family members who can't control their tempers, too."

Kit's posture relaxes a bit as I joke, and I realize that he's struggling a bit. As I observe him, the telltale signs of anxiety become apparent, and I get why his aura is so spiky. The guy must really have it bad, too, because the silence of his caliphate as the leaders stare at one another angrily is ramping up his pulse.

I'm about to give humor another try when the golden scaled demon that Kit called Xerxes steps forward. "The testosterone in here is practically choking me to death."

The demon has a long, thick tail like a serpent, which makes me think they're reptilian in their other form. Everything about them is beautiful and alluring, including the lithe, muscled frame and curved fangs. Xerxes has emerald slitted eyes that confirm my snake theory and two long, curling horns that almost look like Rapunzel tresses. I don't know if I've ever seen a demon who looks quite so... gorgeous and statuesque. They have to be from the lust line; there's no other explanation.

"Boys will be boys, no matter what the species," Rogue mutters in annoyance. "Since you're not keen on the display, how about showing us why you all changed and ticked off my new friend?"

Kit's eyes widen, and he practically beams at our girl. "Really? That's cool as hell."

Does this kid not have any actual friends at Discordia?

I shudder at the thought of being down there again with no one to talk to besides this group of royal assholes. That would suck a *lot*. "Our mate is a loyal friend, Kit. If she says it, she means it. She took us and we had some... making up to do for our reticence."

The black and white demon looks at me curiously. "That's interesting. See, KK? She let them grovel a bit to make up for their bullshit. Everyone is redeemable."

"I think not, Salem." The kid snorts and I don't miss his eyes cutting to the proud Prince as he and his general square off still. "Some people can't get their head out of their ass because their fucking horns are too big to remove it."

Angelo bursts into laughter and before long, Archie and Javi join in. My lips quirk as Rogue gives Reb a pointed look, and he rolls his eyes, crossing his arms over his chest. My twin mutters, "Yeah, we have one of those, too, man."

The snickers spread to the demons, and it finally gets the attention of the two big guys glaring at one another. The gray one gives Angelo a sharp toothed grin and I tilt my head as I try to work out what he might be. Kit turns and moves closer, laying a hand on the enormous bicep of the second-in-command, which makes him immediately look down.

"Hey, big guy. I'm okay. Like X said, we should show them whatever you guys know about the system so we can all get out of this somewhat dangerous fishbowl we're crammed into."

"Good point, Kit Kat," the feathered demon says as he nods. "This is pretty strategically bad for everyone. Fish in a barrel, right?"

Rebel blinks and groans. "For fuck's sake. I should have thought of that."

"Okay, boys. Everyone was distracted and there's too much dick waving going on for anyone to be logical except maybe Kit, the pretty demon, and me. Let's fix that instead of moaning about it, yeah?" Rogue winks at the small guy and he gives her that happy grin again.

She's really making this kid feel accepted, and it's more diplomatic than I've ever seen her be.

"Right. So I guess you don't recognize these because they're part of the newer security systems below," the golden demon says as they approach one of the panels. "It's surprising that your father would install them here—except we think he's in cahoots with Darkstar." Xerxes beckons the dark feathered demon, and the guy walks over, bending to insert one of his horns in the soft spot on the security panel.

I blink, watching the Prince and the small, fire-colored demon next to him do the same with the other two panels. The doors to each elevator open and Angelo smacks his forehead as he curses under his breath. "Horns and tails work... Fuck, I feel stupid."

The Prince smirks, removing his horn and letting his doors close. "As well you should, Gemini. You and your brother are far too removed from the culture at home. It will make your lives infinitely more diffi-cult if what we all believe is true. You'll be able to fight Luca, but not his allies, and we all need to be prepared for both surface and under-world battles."

"Jasper is correct," the gray demon says as he cracks his neck loudly. "You must learn more about your true home."

"Uh, not to be a jerk, but you guys are in the same situation in reverse," Kit interrupts. "I can only do so much, you know. I have shit to learn, too."

This guy isn't afraid of anything and I kinda dig it. No wonder Rogue likes him.

"You know, I've always wondered why you two never went back there, especially because you went through school *again* up here with us...."

Archie scratches his chin and I have to smile. He's not dumb in the slightest, but he often asks things that are so blunt that people assume he is because of how he looks.

Angelo sighs. "That is a question that requires a lot more time than we have here, Archer. We'll discuss it later, but suffice to say that maintaining appearances based on what age we *appear* to be was important on the surface."

The spunky guy blinks, then nods. "Actually, that makes perfect sense to me. Humans are really focused on how old people look. I'd assume vamps have to move around a lot, too, so they don't get caught out."

"Exactly," I say as I shoot a finger gun at him with a wink. "Plus, we like it up here and Luca hates it down there. Thus, this sus alliance with the old fuckwit who runs your school, I'd bet."

The quiet rainbow demon clears his throat, waiting until we all look at him before he speaks. "Not to interrupt the bonding, but the previous statements about being sitting ducks were right. Yet we're all still standing here. Perhaps we should decide which level we're going to and... go?"

Rogue looks at Angelo and me for a moment before she replies, "I'd guess we need to head straight down to nine, right? That's where the Uber bad guys are, I'd guess."

Jasper nods, then looks at the big guy. "Do you think that's wise? I'm not sure my father would allow anyone to head directly to the highest security zone of his strongholds unless they passed magical tests embedded in his wards. If we do that, we're likely to be identified immediately, right?"

"I believe that to be the case, Prince."

I think about their supposition for a second, then I look at my twin. "We won't seem suspicious if we head straight down. I'm sure Luca and Lola know we were invited. It won't set off alarms if we show up in the shudder zone."

"Maybe that's the best way to handle it, then?" Kit pipes up. "If we start in the middle and work our way down, it might not catch the guys' presence. You guys can pass go and collect two hundred dollars, gathering whatever info you can find as you go. Just don't call attention to us if we get down there."

The kid is smart and by the way those demons are watching him, even the reluctant royal, they're all halfway to falling for him. It's kind of amusing.

I wonder briefly if we all looked like that following Rogue around and realize that we almost certainly did. It makes me grin, and she arches a brow at me. "No worries, Sparkles. I'm pretty sure your new friend is right. But you should exchange information with him so we can keep in contact later. I assume that's what they did when they met the group from the Southern college."

The snort Kit lets out is louder than he expected and he turns bright red. "Um, sorry. Yeah, Jasper and Slash got their info because it was all about royal dick waving. But I'm happy to exchange with Rogue this time. I don't have weird protocols about contacting me, either."

"I bet Morgana *loved* that shit," Rogue says with a smug grin. "She definitely seems like she'd enjoy being talked around as princes and their guards flap their yaps."

"Not at all," Kit says with a mischievous expression. "I like her a lot, too. When the universe isn't being threatened, it might be nice to hang out like normal people."

Rebel's eyes narrow, but our girl shakes her head at him quickly. She leans in, whispering in a stage voice, "Don't mind him. He thinks with the little one before the big one way more often than necessary. That sounds fab, and I'm sure the gargoyle would agree."

"Now that we've settled your party date," the prince drawls sarcastically as he rolls his eyes, "...Salem, deal with the switch for the level they want to start on."

Angelo thinks for a moment, communicating with me wordlessly before he says, "We'll go to nine. The theory seems correct, and I'd like to get this bullshit with our parents over."

The black and white demon moves away from Kit reluctantly, using a horn to activate the elevator at the back of the vestibule for us. As we file over to go in, the guy leans in to murmur. "Good luck, dude. Be careful... I'd hate for Kit Kat's new friend to disappear. He needs friends that aren't us, too. It's good for him."

Man, this one is definitely head over heels; I almost look forward to hearing about whatever this eight person thing is from our girl.

Get Ready

ROGUE

THIS DAMN RIDE to the core of Luca's temporary lair is insane, and even Angelo looks a bit surprised. I guess whatever he's attended before hasn't been this elaborate, and it makes me wonder why this event has been set up so spectacularly. Turning to the demon, I tilt my head as I give him a curious look. "Ang, what is with this meeting? Even you look a bit shocked by the opulence, and there are people being attacked. It's like all this shit is a distraction from something, and I don't think it's the actual meeting part."

He scratches his chin, his eyes darting to Damon before they come back to me. "Honestly, Princess, I've been wondering the same thing. I'm not saying the Apalachins aren't fancy normally, but this seems over the top. The Fae royalty are tricky, but their reps aren't likely to side with people trying to upset the power balance across the realms. That Prince's comments about a rebel faction lead me to believe that maybe this wasn't called for by the actual leadership in Bay City. Someone must have sussed out their protocols and used them to fake the request."

Rebel nods, his expression serious as he adds, "It's something I've been toying with since we met with the folks from the university as well. They came to use underground contacts to peek into the criminal world and find out if there's a problem—no one could have predicted that. Same goes for your sneaky royal heirs—they don't want Hell knowing they're here, either."

"So neither of those groups was lured here, which means their intervention wasn't planned. It foiled a plot that involved the representatives from Faerie." I tap my fingers on my lips as I consider that. "The demons didn't say if they found everyone who should have been in the area that was attacked. They must have busted ass to leave before official security for the event arrived, and likely, Morgana's group did, too."

Damon pulls his phone out, his finger flying over it with impressive speed. He frowns for a moment, then looks up at us. "There isn't a damn thing on the supe-net about the attack. They're keeping it under wraps, which I bet means a lot of memory fiddling. We won't be able to track down witnesses who have accurate memories easily."

"Man, these fuckers all value maintaining appearances more than they do protecting their people. Doing that kind of shit is not only borderline against the treaties, it's, like, counter-intuitive to figuring out what really happened," Archie grumbles. "Why would your people want that?"

I exchange glances with Rebel and we shrug simultaneously. Archie looks puzzled, so I say, "You know we don't interact with them much outside of those who are also Guardians. Speaking with the Daybreak Prince was the most formal conversation I've ever had with someone who's spent most of their life in our former home."

"She's right. I mean, I was older when they brought me here, but like her, my memory is fuzzy in a way that begs the question of whether those almost illegal methods were used on me." He sighs and rakes his hand through his bright green locks. "It would be nice to know more, but we're not the ones to ask, man. We have as much general knowledge as any other Guardian."

A fact I hate with every fiber of my being because knowing more might help me figure out what the hell happened to Reck.

"That doesn't help much, but neither does our lack of knowledge about what's going on below since we came back to the surface after Discordia all those years ago." Angelo cracks his knuckles, his jaw gritted as he ponders for a moment. "I'm sure the shit going on at the core level will be astonishing, even to me. Luca and Lola have never held back when I was present before and this shit is catering to the most scandalous bits of demon culture, even in public view. We should prepare for things we will want to intervene in—but we can't. That goes double for you, Princess."

His warning makes me shudder, but I nod. "Yeah, I figured as much. Most of it will be illegal or really fucking close, which will make Reb and me want to exercise our authority. It won't be easy to fight that ingrained response; they've been drilling it into us for so long it's second nature."

"Fight it, Sparkles. The Society's rules apply in demon territory, but you'd be on your own enforcing them in an underground compound full of the worst people our parents employ or are allied with. It would be foolish to assume that something fucking awful wouldn't happen before your fellow Guardians could break through their security."

Damon looks worried as hell, so I reach over and squeeze his hand. "I promise I'll do my best not to interfere with things that don't involve me. I won't like it and it might make me a bit... difficult, but I will do my best. Reb will too, right?"

"Whatever," he says grumpily. "I'll just memorize their faces for later and we can deal with it after this mess. Sound good?"

Damon shrugs, and Angelo rolls his eyes, but they finally say, "Sounds good."

I'd prefer that to have been more enthusiastic, but they weren't raised to be Society agents like us.

"Glad that's settled, but what about Luca and Lola?" Archie crosses his arms over his broad chest and I lose my train of thought for a moment. "If they don't push everyone's boundaries, I'll eat a puck."

My lips quirk as he scowls. The big guy sees different angles than the twins or Reb and me—it's a good thing because I wasn't even thinking about what the assholes-in-chief might demand. "A good question, Arch. What can they possibly do besides be shitheads, guys?"

The twins share an uneasy look before they turn back to us. Damon ducks his head and Angelo coughs, obviously trying to find his voice. When he finally does, it's very quiet. "As the representatives on the surface and the head of our 'family', they have absolute authority to ask things we may not want to do. Their hold is less on Archie, Reb, and Javier because they don't know you've mated with them. But for you, me, and Damon? It could be uncomfortable."

I squint at him suspiciously. "Uncomfortable how?"

"They could assign us tasks of varying difficulty to prove our allegiance," Damon mumbles. "But that's not really the worst possibility."

"They could make us sit with them and watch the depravity," Angelo adds, then coughs again. "But I think what D is hinting at is that they can demand we confirm the mating in their presence."

What.

"Are you saying they can make us fuck in front of them to prove ourselves?" I blink, then my temper spikes inside of me. I don't care about exhibitionism; I had a room at the bondage club. However, I *do* care about having to perform for their goddamned parents. It's weird, and I will lose my fucking shit if they command it. I'm not supposed to use the wings and dust, but I might do it if they force that shit. The punishment for going outside of my guidelines would be worth taking those perverted fuckers out.

"They could," Damon says softly. "I don't know if they will. More likely, they'll make us watch shit we don't want to. Our parents are sadists, so they prefer to do lasting damage. Violating principles and values does that better than simple humiliation."

"I'm going to need a lot more help keeping my fury in check," I growl as I let go of his hand and wrap my arms around myself. "You guys need to be on your toes."

And the motherfuckers running this show better watch their asses if they cross me—I have people to protect now.

THE DING of the elevator finally reaching its final destination is ominous. We all pause, waiting for the doors to open with grim focus. This won't be pretty, and a brief flicker of hope that my new demon friend headed for the higher levels is doing okay races through me. I didn't get the feeling that we're in danger of being killed here, but I'm not running around with the heirs to the royal throne of Hell sniffing for traitors.

Hurting that kid would set me off, too, so the Gemini and their lackeys need to be careful.

"You okay, Sparkles?" Damon asks as the doors open. "It's game face time, after all."

My expression goes blank and my posture shifts into my usual pose when I'm on Guardian business. He grins a little and I shrug. "Fine like Faewine, little D. Let's get this over with."

Angelo steps out first, holding his arm out, and I take it. I'm not a fan of such gallant throwback stuff, but I assume this is how it's done amongst his kind. Damon falls into place on my other side, leaving the other three to follow behind us. "We'll head straight for wherever our parents are to limit the exposure."

"Thank fuck," Rebel mutters. "I'm getting disgusting vibes already, and we've only taken a few steps into the antechamber."

Looking around, I notice that he's right; it's a match to the room we were in upstairs and there's an enormous set of dark, ominous doors in front of us. This is meant to be intimidating, but it seems clownish to me. Truly terrifying villains don't need the trappings of evil like this—and they look just like everyone else. It's the one thing humans have gotten right with the universe. All this overblown shit means no matter how puffed up the Geminis are... They're not the ones in charge of anything outside of this silly fiefdom, I bet.

"You're thinking pretty hard there, Wheels," Archie murmurs low. "Worried about the view when we do an Aragorn on those doors?"

I snort. "First, I'm not throwing those things open like I arrived at Helm's Deep because it's stupidly unstealthy. Second, I'm *much* prettier than him." Turning to look at him over my shoulder, I wink. "But thanks for seeing me like a warrior princess, babe."

"A *Xena* costume..." Javi breathes and they all stop short, making me almost trip over my feet and crash to the ground. "*That's* the image to hang onto in there."

Fucking dudes, I swear to Mab's merry mischief.

"Okay, fine. If we make it out of this without getting humiliated, tortured, or violated in some way, I'll swing a sword and make all your dreams come true, guys. For now, let's stow the dicks and get this over with."

Rebel smirks at me, his eyes flashing with magic. "And that's a deal, little sis. You will not wiggle out of it now."

I roll my eyes, striding towards the enormous doors with the demon twins in tow. My stepbrother is an asshole; we didn't need a formal bargain cemented for such a silly thing. But he obviously likes the idea, and that alone makes me grin as we enter the vast room. My joy is short-lived as I look around, listening to the cacophony of screams, moans, snarls, and roars echoing off the vaulted ceilings. Everywhere my eyes land, there's something going on that makes me want to heave.

They weren't kidding about the debauchery.

"We should head past that bloody orgy," Angelo says. "I think the path to the highest ranking demons is that way. It feels like the most power is emanating from that direction."

"Agreed," I reply as I breathe through my mouth to avoid the smell coming from the writhing mass of demons and fluids. "And shake a leg, boys. This place smells like death."

Of course, that's because he's likely here fucking a fallen angel or something.

Battlefield

REBEL

Angelo and Damon have been my friends since the Kellys took me in when I was a kid. We never talked about how much older they were than Arch, Javi, and me, nor what their parents' mob got up to. Our recent integration into that part of their lives has opened my eyes to how much they didn't want to discuss the demonic parts of their existence. I don't blame them; while Graciella and Odhran weren't great, this is eye-opening, to say the least.

Especially when I know Angelo's taken the brunt of the responsibilities with this shit to protect D.

Looking around with a grimace, I tune out the moans and groans—whether of pleasure or pain. I'm game for a lot of kinky shit and so are the rest of the guys, but this is pretty extreme. It shouldn't surprise me—supes with a proximity to death like demons, vamps, and their ilk are usually the most twisted beings in the bedroom. That's my experience, at least, and I've heard no different. Ang and D might hold back with our girl, testing her to see where her lines are since this whole 'mated group' thing is new.

"What are you thinking so hard about?" Rogue hisses as she leans into me. "You're making the face."

I roll my eyes, knowing she's probably right. My stepsister has always been able to tell when I'm too far in my head and she swears it's because of a specific expression I make when I'm overthinking. "I was thinking about how none of us have ever ventured into the demon aspect with the twins, and now I'm sort of regretting it."

Her embarrassment filters through our Guardian bond, and I know she agrees. "Yeah, I feel shitty about that, too. They never made a big deal, so I didn't. This shit makes me question why the hell I didn't push it with them because... I feel like a real asshole."

The sound of a cough gets my attention and despite not being able to see well, I turn to look. Angelo is smirking as he shakes his head. "Whatever you two are muttering about regarding us? Don't. When Luca moved us up here, he wasn't as big a deal as he is now. Bay City is the last place we moved to and had to pretend to be much younger than we actually were. Once he consolidated power here, we knew this would be more permanent, and we went looking for actual connections."

Damon hums his agreement, then says, "It was safe to have friends, go to the school, and everything else when we knew he wasn't going anywhere. But we sure as hell didn't want to drag any of you into their web. Demons have a different perspective on the surface dwellers and don't mesh with the major supe factions well because of it. Like the Fae, they prefer to be on visitor passes here and call their own realm home."

"You don't claim Hell—neither of you want to go back there," Rogue points out. "So why stay mum on all this... alternative lifestyle... stuff?"

The echoing scream ahead of us is bone chilling, and we stop as the twins step to the front of the group to survey the area carefully. There are various hot spots of demons and guests fucking or doing what definitely amounts to torture on one another, but nothing that seems dangerous to us. At least, not unless any of them run over here and drag us into their little games. The younger twin pushes his glasses up, squinting as he puts his hand in the air and swishes his tail back and forth.

I have no idea what he's doing, but it's interesting.

"I sense the chaos getting stronger. We're nearing a much bigger concentration of demons. That was only a random echo carried by the architecture down here." He frowns as his expression hardens and his partial shift gets closer to halfway. "The energy is rife with every type of our kind, which means everyone needs to be very cautious. You'll see chaos and vengeance demons like Ang and me, but also pits, drudes, dreamers, Cubi, shadows, fear... They'll all be eager to see how tough your shielding is."

Rogue groans, putting her hands on her face, and I arch a brow. When she removes them, she sighs heavily. "I fucking hate some of those assholes, and these will be the *worst* examples of their genes. Between the team and the club, I've seen my share of demons—not like our boys, mind—but enough to know that I'm going to stab someone if I'm not careful."

Angelo grins, his expression barely concealing his eagerness to see that spectacle. "Princess, if you stab someone, I'll gladly vouch for you when they drag us to the center court. But the sooner we end up in front of my folks, the less intel we can gather from their minions."

"Damn it," she mutters as she kicks the floor in irritation. "I so rarely get to do actual damage. This party sucks more every second we're here."

Javi chuckles, shaking his head as he reaches out to pat Rogue's shoulder. "Don't worry, Sparkles. I'm sure there will be something violent to do, eventually. The odds are against surviving this trip unscathed when our new friends had to fight a fucking orc in Fae territory."

My stepsister's face brightens and she practically beams. "True. Good point, birdie. Someone will attack eventually and I'll get to do my thing for once. Alright, fuckers, let's get moving."

"Only our mate would get so damn excited about being ambushed," Archie says to me as we move again.

I grin back, shrugging. "She's always been bloodthirsty, man. You guys have never seen her in her element, but I have. This will be hot AF and you'll have to hold yourself back—trust me."

It's what I've been doing as her partner in crime for years.

WE WERE much quieter as we approached the first crowded section of the bottom level of Luca's big ass compound. Angelo was accurate in his statement about trying to lie low as we make our way through the crowd of demons and supernaturals gathered around a chalk-drawn ring with a big ass demon in armor fighting an equally dangerous looking Minotaur. The bovine mythical also has on armor, and they're both wielding weapons crusted with fresh blood. My eyes dart around, noting the *pile* of dead bodies in a nearby corner. This little fight club doesn't give a fuck who sees it, much less who's talking about it.

That lack of remorse means the only exit from that circle is victory or death—fabulous.

"Do *not* get drawn into that ring," I mutter to Rogue as she strains to look at the snarling beasts as they clash. "Check the meat sack dump over there."

She turns, making an annoyed huffing sound as she sees the gory evidence of this sport. "Guaranteed, there's someone running book on these."

"The Greed line will have demons working the crowd," Damon says as he moves closer to us. "As you saw with the royals, it could be anyone. The heir looked more like a singer from My Chemical Romance than a revered thief who has served the crown for many centuries. Our kind are very good at blending in when we come into this realm."

"Huh," Rogue says as she looks at him curiously. "I got the impression those guys didn't change anything except getting fancy clothes. Betcha they look exactly like that *all* the time, D. Their littlest member is easier to read than you men realize. At least.... for me."

Frowning, I think about the eight demons for a moment, wondering what she's talking about. I didn't notice anything other than their obvious regal bullshit, though the kid seemed fun. "What does that mean, little sis?"

She gives me a smug smile. "For me to know, Reb. I'm not in the habit of spilling secrets that aren't mine. All of you eejits should be happy about that. I've seen you all wipe out spectacularly over the years. It would be truly humiliating if I started spreading those moments around."

I'd argue, but she's definitely got shit on me, so I'll let that go.

"I thought they were pretty cool, Wheels," Archie says. I turn to look at him, sensing the aura of his cat as he gets closer. His eyes are golden and I know the scent of blood is probably tickling the inner animal. Luckily, his control has always been fairly good—his dads were strict about him learning it very young.

Angelo taps my shoulder, his gaze cutting to a group of demons and what I believe are hybrids standing by the wall. "I'm going to ingratiate myself. Keep them over here, Rebel."

Nodding, I wait until he slips away, then point at the fighters. "That Minotaur isn't just a cow. See the energy around the mace?"

Rogue grabs my arm, pulling it down as she squeezes. "Damn. That fucker is part Harvest, isn't he?"

"Yep. He's got Fae in him, though I don't know how recently in his genetics. Those guys shouldn't be able to wield magic on their own."

Damon studies the way the huge shifter moves for a moment before he asks, "Are you sure? He could have an enchanted weapon he bought. Demis, magicals, and Fae sell them on the black market to species that shouldn't have them all the time. Luca has a dealer; I've seen the invoices."

I arch a brow, his admission getting my attention. "Do you have access to *all* of his books, D?"

The chaos demon nods, not taking his eyes off of the bloody battle as his tail swishes. "Mmhmm. At least, I think I do. He and Lola could have secret ones full of shit I don't know about. I wouldn't put it past the motherfuckers. Ang and I had no idea they've been meeting with malcontents like Darkstar until recently. It makes me question how much they have going on that even my twin is unaware of."

A thought that will keep me up at night, for sure.

"Why would they hide them from you, Damon? If you don't know what they're doing with the shit, it wouldn't spark your scrutiny, right? Seems counterproductive to have to employ two different people to track the stuff. I'd bet they're hiding their corruption in plain sight."

Javier is emanating heat like an oven as he joins us, and I know the phoenix inside of him is probably screeching at the injustice and disrespect for life being shown here. His bird is less demanding than Archie's lion, but that doesn't mean his nature is less vociferous about its desires. Rogue reaches her hand out, resting the free one on his forearm lightly until the fire in his eyes cools.

"I think Javi has a point, don't you, Ang—" Her brows furrow when she realizes the elder twin isn't standing with us anymore and I groan inwardly. "Where the *fuck* is Angelo?"

Hearing the barely suppressed fury in her tone, I murmur, "He's checking out a lead, but we need to let him do it on his own. Calm down and keep quiet—otherwise, we'll draw attention."

"I don't enjoy being in the dark," she says as she flicks her hair over shoulder. A triumphant cry echoes off the walls as the Minotaur claims its victory, tossing the gross demon out of the ring with its horn before strutting around the ring. "And he'd better come back soon, because I don't want to end up on the roster if they're picking new competitors for Sir Beefcake over there."

"Why? Afraid you'd lose?" I snark playfully and she gives me a deadly serious expression.

"No, I'm concerned I'd beat his ass in a split second and we'll all end up in front of the Geminis."

Knowing her, that's a valid concern... more than the others know.

Black Betty

ROGUE

WHILE ANGELO IS off doing his thing, I've been keeping my ears open while my magic sneaks around the crowd. I'm sure Rebel is doing the same, but what I've figured out is that whatever demon is at the top of the 'fight club' pyramid has them spread across the bottom three levels of this nightmare.

I can't be certain, but it sounds like they recruit or kidnap mythical hybrids to train for their matches and set up shop at every big supernatural event in the seven realms when the hosts agree. It makes me want to scream in indignation because I sense that it's probably less voluntary than advertised, but I can't do my Guardian thing here just because some half-baked P.T. Barnum with actual horns is peddling their wares.

I bet those royal dudes are pretty pissed if they've gotten to the seventh level one, though.

My skirt flutters behind me as I keep a small breeze moving under it. It's hot down here—imagine that—and though I'm not wearing a lot, I'd like to avoid being sticky with sweat or soiling this thing because some lead foot asshat stepped on it. I look around in dissatisfaction again, sniffing as I try to identify easily manipulated sources I can pump for information.

"Where do you think you're going?"

The growly voice is my affable lion and I turn to Archie with a grin. "Angelo isn't the only one with the mojo to poke around, buddy. Reb and I have both been trained in interrogation—both friendly and not-so-friendly. We'll find out a lot more if we're *all* working the crowd, not just one of us."

"Perhaps," Archie says as his gaze runs over nearby revelers. "But you know it's dangerous to split up in a place run by the twins' dickhead parents. You can't trust either of them as far as I could chuck them, Wheels. It's becoming really obvious that Ang and D kept the breadth of their depravity under wraps."

Javi snorts as he joins us. "I mean, you can't blame them. And I sure as fuck don't repeat every weird speciesist slur my folks sprinkle our talks with. Why would I? It's embarrassing on my end, but on theirs, it could actually bring bad news to your doors."

I arch a brow at him, letting my knife appear in my palm and spinning it as we lock eyes. "I'm not worried about goons at my door, nor was I before you guys took your heads out of your asses. Just because the Sickos and Mina got me at the bar does *not* mean it's the norm. I've fought off my share of ill-reputed shit heels in my lifetime, and most of the time, Rebel wasn't with me."

They both sigh in relief when my Fae knife disappears into the aether again, and Archie rakes his hand through his hair. "Yeah, we know. It's just... it's hard, you know? We all grew up together, but you were younger, and now that protective feeling is a *new* protective feeling and..."

"That!" Javi says as he points at the lion shifter. "That's exactly it. It's like... double protective now, especially with the 'm word' involved. I'm usually laid back, like Archer, and I'm still feeling it. Which means the twins and Reb have to be damn near losing their shit when things come at you."

Resisting the urge to press my fingertips into my eyes, I suck in a long breath. Intellectually, I understand what they are saying, but emotionally, I want to kick them in their goody bags. Just because they're having *big dude feelings* doesn't make me any less capable than I was before that shit. And treating someone as experienced in this arena as me like crystal will not work. I have to be allowed to do things on my own or I'll end up killing one of them in frustration.

"I get your drift, guys, but... being on a shelf isn't for me. You both know that, or you wouldn't be scrambling to explain. I'm not a damsel; I *save* damsels. That's my actual job when my charge comes into this world and they've been prepping me for it my whole life. All of you will have to put your dicks back in your pants and let me wave mine occasionally, okay?"

They look at one another, obviously lost in my sarcasm, and I roll my eyes. "For fuck's sake, guys. I meant, like, metaphorically. You both know I don't have a dick—though if I did, I'd be hot as fuck still."

It's quiet for a moment and then Archie nods. "Yep. Definitely still would be. But I'm satisfied with you as is, Wheels."

That gives me ideas, but I'm going to keep my mouth closed so I don't ruin the future surprise.

"I agree with him. We fell for *you* all those years ago, not specific features and shit." Javier grins shyly and I tilt my head, filing away that for later as well. The guys surprise me constantly, and even though I'm annoyed about this situation, I can't help but feel squishy about the shit I'm learning about them.

"Well, then we're going to do some re-con of our own, whether my step-bro likes it or not," I say confidently. "He can watch little D while we mingle."

Neither of them looks happy about my declaration, but I hold my arms out and they take them. Walking away from the other two guys, I carefully lead my beaus through the roiling crowd watching the death match. My Fae sense kicks in as I navigate, and I pick up bet runners quickly. I doubt the big boss is anywhere near this mess, so there's probably a middle manager watching the runners to keep them honest. I pretend to fan myself with my hand, using the distracting motion to hide my visual sweep of the area.

When I let the Unseelie fade into my eyes, I can see auras better, which allows me to follow the dark green signature of greed from the small fish to the medium and finally, the biggest one of all.

"The dude in control of this pit is over there," I say to Archie and Javi as we stroll slowly through the throng. "Don't look yet—it'll be obvious—but check out that tall Cubi with the harem of people on the mini-stage in the southwest corner."

Javier squeezes my arm as he replies, "How do you know that?"

I smile as I turn to him, tilting my head like he's said something funny. "Because he should be focused on feeding, and the magic flowing around him should *only* be lust based. It's not, though. The trails of green greed extend from the bet takers to their watchers, then faintly to him. He's not *the* boss, but he's at least in the middle management."

"You think the big boss is even on this level?" Archie asks as he brushes a hair off of my face and looks around. "They can't be everywhere, obviously, but I'd assume this is the big time."

Nodding as I get us moving again, I walk in a non-linear pattern until we're closer to the incubus I suspect of controlling this specific fighting ring. He's beautiful, of course, with aquiline features and a killer smile besides sculpted muscles peeking out of his unbuttoned shirt. The guy's aura reads as more than a demon, so he must be a hybrid of some kind. His clothes are out of date—not quite on trend like some of the rich fucks here, so I assume he doesn't live on the surface full time.

"He's powerful," Javi whispers to me and I feel a hint of his phoenix stretching within him. "And old as fuck."

"Yep," I say as I turn to look up at him, pretending to flirt shamelessly. "Not just from below, either. Not sure what, but it's hard with their kind because they don't mix as much. Plus, he's got the whole pheromones thing going on blast like a middle school kid bathing in Aqua Velva."

Archie winces as he comes up behind me. "Ouch, Wheels. you just dated the shit out of us. Bet a fiver nine out of ten of these chickadees hanging off the Cubi don't have a clue what that meant."

My eyes slide over the fawning women and men at the feet of the demon. Archie's right about how young they are, especially since none of them are hellspawn. There are a few types of Fae, some witches, a couple shifters, and a lone mage. I note the lack of mythicals and demis in his little groupie fest, but they have a much stronger mind blocking ability than the more common supe types.

"You're probably right, babe. Luckily, I'm not trying to impress a bunch of folks who can't keep a half-Cubi out of their heads." Shaking my head, I fight off the urge to break up this nonsense. I doubt they all agreed to be his food source, especially since he's basically ignoring them while he's strengthening his own power. The Guardian in me wants to handle this bullshit, but I know I can't.

Infuriating and I'm going to eventually get vengeance on Luca Gemini for this bullshit... mark my words.

"Calm down, Dragonfly," Javier rumbles as he smiles at me. "We don't want to draw the attention of the bad guys."

He's right, so I close my eyes briefly and push all of my outrage down to my feet until I'm standing on it. Right now, it's more important to keep the picture in mind, especially since I don't want some underling starting a fight. "Okay. I'm good. Now let's get a little closer so we can hear what's being said on that ridiculous platform."

Ever so slowly, the three of us move close enough for our supernatural hearing to allow for whispers and words to carry. The guys stand with me, pretending to flirt and laugh as we listen to the surrounding conversations. It takes a few minutes, but finally, some of the substance flitters through the air.

"... just wait until after the meeting. The Don is bringing all his allies together to plan what will happen at the end of the..."

My eyes narrow as I look at Javi. "That's about Luca. He's gathering people after the Apalachin."

Archie leans in, his lips brushing the shell of my ear. "I heard two women saying that the demons are collecting girls to present at some event later, too. My guess is they've invited some big wigs from Hell to do this plotting thing."

"The royal demons talked about that Games thing, right?" I ask them as I frown. "Maybe this secret after-party/meeting is about whatever they're planning for that. Even Angelo and Damon seemed worried about those happening again."

"I don't know enough about demon shit," Archie admits and Javier nods in agreement. "If something bad is really going on that Luca is in the middle of, it can't be because he wants to rule the underworld. That asshole loves it up here."

Suddenly, Angelo, his twin, and my angry looking step-brother appear in front of us and I groan inwardly. We were just getting the juicy stuff; if they make a big deal out of our defection, it will ruin our cover. None of them looks pleased, but I smile brightly, hoping to clue them into our gambit.

"There you are!" I spin, leaning in to kiss Angelo's lips lightly. "I'm glad you found us."

The elder twin arches his brow, but picks up on my vibe. "Have the boys been treating you well, Princess? Keeping you *safe*?"

Reb's eyes flash at that word and I roll my eyes at him. "Of course they have—not that I need it, silly. I'm very well trained for parties like this."

"I assume there's a reason you guys ditched us?" Damon whispers as he leans in to kiss my cheek. I nod slightly, then turn to bat my lashes at him adoringly. He chuckles, shaking his head. "You're going to be the death of us, Sparkles."

That might be true, but I'm also going to be their salvation—just watch.

Come With Me Now

ARCHER

Rogue can handle herself—not that the two 'alpha' dudes in our new family group get that. Reb and Ang are riding their instincts hard, and I think that's because of their personalities rather than their designation as top-level beings in their species. Obviously, 'alpha' is a shifter thing, and their Fae and demon, but someone who fits that description accurately, they give me a headache. My lion wants to protect her, too, but I know better than to saddle a wild stallion.

We fell for her as a wild girl and that's who she'll always be—I'm sure as fuck not going to change it.

"We didn't really ditch you, man," I say to D with a sheepish expression. "Wheels had a feeling, and we went to check it out. No one was alone, so it wasn't dangerous."

He looks frustrated by my logic, as if he'd like to argue, but knows he can't. Our detour wasn't approved by the group and I'm sure that lit Rebel up once he realized the three of us were gone. But Damon is far more susceptible to reason than Rogue's stepbrother. "Yeah, okay. But you said nothing, and we got worried."

"Not to mention Angelo was pissed as fuck," Reb mutters as he cuts his gaze to our girl, pacifying the elder twin. "He didn't even tell us what he found out because he was too focused on finding you dummies."

Rogue blinks and pulls back from Angelo with a frown. "Then tell us now, baby. We need to know what you found out when you were spying."

The vengeance demon sucks in an annoyed breath, then sighs in acquiescence. "Fine, but don't assume this isn't earning people some red asses later. I don't like finding my mate and my brother *missing* in a place like this, Princess. Remember, I know what kinds of things go on here and how bad it can get."

I rub the back of my neck, giving D an apologetic look when I realize how upset he probably was knowing Angelo was off doing risky shit, then finding Rogue and me gone. "Shit, I'm sorry. But…"

Reb frowns as he glares at me through slitted eyes. "But *what*, Archer?"

"You and Angelo have to let our girl breathe, Reb. She trained with you; you, more than anyone else, know how capable she is. The stupid ambush at the club has made you guys treat her differently than we ever did before—and not just in good ways." I clear my throat, my thoughts gathering steam as I continue. "She's been trying to tell you that one bad incident doesn't make her helpless and you're not listening. Before she was with us, we didn't have a clue where she was or what she was doing every minute of every day, but no one panicked."

My radiant girlfriend practically lights up from the inside as she moves from the grumpy twin to me with a smile so wide it has to hurt. "You, Archer Glaser, are my favorite as of now. Triple points to you, baby, for saying that."

Suck on that assholes—I'm the favorite.

"Damn it," Angelo grumbles as I wrap my arms around Rogue and smirk at the others. "I just can't keep from picturing you how we found you on the ground, Princess. I bet Reb can't, either."

The green-haired Fae nods, his expression stormy. "No, I can't. Nor can I stop feeling that blank moment when your voice stopped, and we had to track you down. It killed something in me to feel you were gone forever."

Pulling back, Rogue looks at them both and then makes a face. "Okay, I get it. But that will not work forever, boys. We are all going to move on from that night by dealing with those responsible. That means *all* of us, and not just you guys playing cowboy. Got it?"

They both nod, and I tilt my head. "So, are you gonna share this hot goss or what, Angelo?"

The elder demon rolls his eyes at me, then drags his lower lip through his teeth as he thinks. "I could hear that Luca's having some sort of secret gathering *after* the big meeting. He's invited folks from below to attend and mingle with 'new talent', according to what the idiots I heard talking said."

"Hey, we heard about that, too," Javier says. "But not the 'new talent' part. However, the Cubi over there isn't high enough in the Lust line to really know much. He's got *power* because he's old, not because he's gifted, I think."

Damon arches a brow at our friend. "How do you know that, Javi?"

"The bird senses his age, but dismisses his magic outside of the feeding. When he does that, I know the person is less threatening than they are projecting." The phoenix looks around for a moment, then murmurs, "There's a lot of that in this outer section, by the way. I've sensed a few strong supes, but not as many as I would expect at the lowest level of this nonsense."

"Agreed." Angelo sighs as he follows Javi's gaze to the beings he's clocked as actually having the ability to be threatening. "We need to get moving. This isn't where we're going to find out the nitty gritty."

Rogue groans as she steps away from me, her gorgeous eyes flashing with annoyance. "I want out of here, so if you think we need to keep going? Let's do it. I'd love to leave for the meeting without once seeing your parents' stupid faces."

Angelo and Damon shrug, unable to argue with that sentiment, and Rebel pinches the bridge of his nose.

I, however, am less hopeful about Rogue's desire being a possibility; my gut says we won't have a choice.

OUR JOURNEY further along the path is filled with demons and supes fucking, plus various tents that I'm pretty sure I do *not* want to know what's going on in. Angelo was adamant that we shouldn't explore the closed-off spaces, and while Rogue challenged him, she ultimately backed down when he said there are things for sale that we don't need to see. I'd prefer the answer to that be 'black market kidneys' rather than people—or worse—but I'm not stupid enough to push the topic. The demon realm is not a place for non-demonic supes and this little territory proves it by one hundred percent.

"You okay, my furry king?" Rogue whispers as she grabs my hand and laces our fingers together.

I like that she's more affectionate than she used to be; the comfort level she's exhibiting with us is promising. Reb hasn't gotten much of it yet, but he's still earning her forgiveness for being such an ass. I don't blame our girl for making him prove that he will not change his mind before she gives everything to him. Rogue's been hurt enough lately and Rebel fucking up would be an absolute disaster.

"I am," I reply as I frown. "I seriously hate this place, though."

She smirks, squeezing my hand comfortingly. "Yeah, it sucks a lot. I guarantee this shit won't go on when the twins take the reins. I mean, maybe some of the normal demon shit, but this... grossness? No fucking way."

"Planning your edicts for when you're the queen of the Gemini?" I ask, and she laughs softly.

"Perhaps."

Her mischievous grin is enchanting, and I want to duck forward to kiss her. I know I can't because we're *trying* to keep up appearances in case we're being watched. But that sucks and I hate it, especially right now. "I second your desire to get the fuck out of here, you know."

"Poor Archie," she whispers, her eyes full of understanding. "This is a bit too much for your taste, huh?"

Giving her a sour look, I snort. "You don't like it anymore than I do, Wheels. You're just better at putting on the mask of indifference because of work."

"You got me, babe. I have to ignore things I'd rather not all the time, so Reb and I don't get in trouble. We're not supposed to mete out justice unless assigned or asked to seek law breakers. It's annoying as fuck to let shit like this go, though."

Damon sidles up to me and mutters, "Plus, it would be a violation of the seven realms' treaties. For all intents and purposes, this is Hell's territory. You know that, Sparkles."

"Ugh," she groans as she rolls her eyes. "I know. Just like all the other places belong to whomever and that sucks, too. I don't get why we have to let these perverts break all the laws of our realm just because they planted a flag and a fence around a section of land, though."

"Because we occasionally have visitors down there or to Faerie or whatever... and we don't want people fucking with them?" The studious twin gives her a reproachful look, and Rogue makes an annoyed sound again. She clearly gets it, but she's irritated, nonetheless. "You're just being pouty because you can't beat the shit out of demons who dearly deserve it down here."

"Bingo," I interject. "Rogue will never be happy on a leash."

Her brow quirks, and she tilts her head. "Archie, however, might enjoy it, methinks."

My eyes widen, and Damon does the same as we all consider that. "*That* is a topic for *much* later," I grumble. "Don't distract us with sex stuff."

"You can distract me with sex stuff," Angelo offers as he winks at Rogue. "Though I suppose this isn't the best spot for it."

Rogue stops, turning to look at the entire group with a stern expression. "I have zero issue with exhibitionism. But... I'd love to avoid doing anything here that could be broadcast all over the seven realms and the fucking supe-net. It squicks me out to imagine your fuckhead parents *watching,*" she says as she wrinkles her nose. "The twins, I mean."

I snort, covering my mouth as I try to contain my amusement at Sariah and any of my dads seeing *that* by mistake. "Fucking shit, Wheels. Luckily, we weren't doing anything with a choking hazard. Man, my mom is so ridiculous that she'd probably yell at me for not taking care of you well enough."

Reb arches a brow. "Then you should up your game, Glaser. If I thought Graciella would—"

"Do. *Not.* Finish. That. Sentence," Rogue says sharply as she slaps a hand to her eyes. "I can't even with you, Rebel Elvis Kelly."

I grin because when Rogue uses full names, she's pissed as hell. That means the emo boy is on the outs and I'm still golden, Ponyboy. That's fantastic. "Okay, so no sexy stuff down in Sticky Surface Land. But I'm gonna be honest, Wheels... that dress doesn't help us stay away from the topic. You look delicious, even when there's bullshit everywhere we look."

Her fingers move to her temples, rubbing lightly as she closes her eyes. "Archie, you're still doing good on points, but I swear to fuck..."

"Don't worry. I'll be good—promise."

Damon shakes his head, and Angelo rolls his eyes, but they also nod. "Us, too."

That leaves Javi and Rebel, only one of whom is a potential issue. Javier winks at our girl, and she smiles, accepting his quiet promise. Her gaze moves to her recalcitrant stepbrother, putting a hand on her hips as she gives him an annoyed huff. "Reb, come on."

He stalks closer, standing within centimeters of her as he replies, "Rogue, I don't want anyone watching anything to do with our family, but unlike the others, I have less certainty about what it will take to get our asses out of here if we're caught. So I promise that I'll fight to the absolute death if I have to, but if there are easier ways to save our bacon, we'll take those before any of us get hurt. Got it?"

If that's not ominous, I don't know what the fuck is.

Hidden Machinations

ROGUE

THE JOURNEY FURTHER INTO 'LEVEL NINE' isn't particularly vomit-worthy, but it's no Sunday in the park with George, either. Demons are definitely loose regarding their boundaries for what they'll enjoy in public, and I spend quite a bit of time just ignoring the things I don't want to see. I'm not judging anyone; I just have no desire to watch the masses get their freak on, whether it's fighting, fucking, feeding, or punishing. The appeal of voyeurism for me is about the people I *want* to watch, not *all* people.

The guys seem similarly inclined, though by virtue of being dudes I catch them peeking sometimes.

Luckily for them, I'm not worried about idle peep shows as we walk past the 'shows'. It means nothing, and I wouldn't want them to ask me to pretend I don't have eyes in the future. It feels like insecurity, and I'm a lot of things, but insecure about my appearance isn't one of them. My little internal traumas have to do with abandonment and betrayal, not comparing myself to other supes and humans.

"Whacha thinking about, Wheels?" Archie asks. His hand lands on my arm and I look up at the easy going shifter fondly. "You had that little wrinkle between your brows that you get when you're really focusing."

Shaking my head at how well he knows me, I chuckle. "Just random shit, Arch. This is a visual buffet of so many vices that I can't help but think it'd be difficult to completely ignore it, even if you want to. I don't know if that's the point, or if it's just that this is bacchanal for the Gemini mob and their guests. I feel like my Guardian impulses are going haywire inside every time I see something that's outside of the lines, and I have to squash it so I don't draw attention."

He blinks, considering it for a moment, then replies, "Does that happen everywhere you go?"

"Hmmm. No, not all the time. I suppose knowing the beings here are probably 'bad guys' makes that more intense. Though, I can't truthfully say if they really are or if I just assume it based on the company they keep." My lips twist and I give him a rueful look. "Species-based assumptions are probably not great, huh? I mean, that Prince and his group seemed okay."

Angelo snorts and shakes his head. "You cannot adopt the Prince of Hell and his caliphate because you like the little one, Princess. I'm pretty sure we're on the money with our assessment of them, but their parents are terrible, and we don't know how much like them the children are. Of course, the current royalty isn't even close to as bad as Luca and his people would be. So that's a complication."

I frown. "I don't know if I've ever been so glad I don't remember nor have ties to Faerie. Their shit is probably as fucked up as Hell's shit. Right?"

Javi, Rebel, and Damon look at me as if I've lost my mind, but the elder twin is the one who answers, "It is, and that's why we're willing to get to know the gargoyle lady's group, too. If Hell's royal court is an eleven on the crazy scale, the people waiting in the wings to conquer the four Fae courts are about twenty. Deities are above that, by the way. A rebellion that involves groups from all the realms and has access to *all* their powers is something we do *not* want to experience. It could fuck up the universe entirely, depending on what their goals are."

"Anggg," I whine as I bump his shoulder with mine. "We're in enough trouble trying to work out what the damn criminals in Bay City are doing. Taking it global is more than I can handle at the moment, especially since I'd really like to avoid telling this to the Councils. They overreact so damn hard when anything gets on their radar."

"They do," Rebel adds as he scratches his chin. "They've always been sure that some big celestial nonsense is going to happen. It's why they track, develop, and monitor lost ones, and why they've all got treaties with the leaders of the other realms."

"We may have to visit other realms or places in this one if this is true," I murmur. "The activity around Morgana's school and nearby, plus whatever the fuck is going on in Hell may need firsthand experience to figure out if we're all right."

Javier glares at me, his expression pinched. "If you say we have to go to Faerie, I'm going to stab myself with a pen. They have *such* ridiculous rules and customs, dragonfly. I don't think you realize how hard it will be to navigate, especially if they think you should already know."

"Guys." We all turn to look at Damon, stopping when he does. He's looking at a large, ornate door a lot like the one we came in after the elevator ride. "Do we want to know what's in there?"

No. Yes. No. Yes. Oh fuck, I don't know, but I'm ready to jump out of my skin.

"Well, the vibes from it are *awful*," Reb remarks. "So I suppose we have to decide if that could be something we *need* to know about or just want to avoid."

Angelo tilts his head, and I have to step back as he shifts to let his horns and tail out. This isn't the full monty , but I think he wants to use his demon side to test the damn thing before we open it. "It's not my parents," he murmurs as his eyes go dark. "But it is full of powerful demons—ones more powerful than Luca has in his gang of goons. I think he's hiding people for the secret meeting there."

"If we open the door, they'll see us," I say, uncertainty making my voice waver. "I don't know if blowing our cover is a good idea. Are they... can you sense what they're doing?"

This time, Damon shifts into half-demon form, and I wait as he makes a disgusted face. "Nothing you want to know about—trust me. I'm not happy *I* know now, Sparkles. It's... well, it's gross and pretty old demon stuff. We should move on."

I consider asking him to elaborate—after all, I'm not a child—but the expression on D's face makes me change my mind. He's actually grossed out and I don't think I want to know what makes a demon that lived in Hell for that long before moving up here squicked out. Sometimes, you can just let shit go. "Okay. Then we should keep going, right?"

The faster we find Luca, the faster we can get the fuck out of Gemini territory and go to the main meeting site.

"Dude, what the actual *fuck* did your asshole father do to build this place?"

I laugh as Archie gripes at the twins. We've been touring the massive level for what feels like hours, though I bet it's been less than one. He's not wrong that it's insanely vast and filled to the brim with so many demons and guests that seeing their perversions has gotten yawn-worthy. I'm barely noticing asses, dicks, or boobs, much less the equipment some are using.

I even missed a crowded table of the horned fuckwits feasting on a dead dragon shifter, and that's hard not to notice.

"Maybe he's not even here," I mutter as I cast my gaze around another room of vices. "Maybe the secret meeting isn't at the end; maybe it's *now*."

Angelo and Damon stop again, turning to look at me like I've revealed the resting place of Jimmy Hoffa. The younger demon pulls his phone out, his fingers flying over it without a word, and his twin groans as he looks at the ceiling. "Seriously?! This is so much sneakier than our parents usually are. I mean, they're demons, but they're so fucking lazy, man. Someone else had to come up with that plan if you're right, Princess."

"Would they listen to anyone else?" Rebel snarks. "I've never known your dad to take anyone's counsel in the past. He'd argue the sky is purple if someone said it's blue, just out of spite."

"Damn it, how did we not think of this earlier?" Archie and Javi flank me as I frown, angry with myself for not suggesting it sooner. I'm usually better at spinning this stuff, but all the surprises we've encountered have me off my game. "I feel like an idiot."

"Then who the fuck are in the closed door rooms? We only analyzed the first one, but there were ten. What do you think Luca and Lola are hiding in them, if not demons who are attending the meeting?"

Angelo shrugs and looks at Javi helplessly. "I don't know. This gambit is so not like him and our mother. They love being splashy and inappropriate in public. Neither has any shame or moral compass, so flaunting their kinks and shit makes them giddy. Not being down here in the worst of the worst has to be *killing* them."

"I think I've figured out the codes."

Rebel walks over to Damon, peering over his shoulder. "Are you on the human dark net?"

"Yeah. There are a *lot* of demon boards there. It helps the crossroad guys strike deals and the vengeance folks like Ang find easy customers. There are more, but since human criminals and supes also hang out there, demons do a brisk business from the non-supe internet. I think I've found codes in some forums that reference 'the circus', which I'm pretty sure is this Apalachin. I also found references to the clowns versus the ringmasters—I think the demons are supposed to be the ringmasters, or maybe the rebel groups...”

Son of a bitch. Now we're going to have to really dig into this global thing.

“Okay, little D. So where is their tent, so to speak?” Archie asks as he looks around. “Is there a portal or some kind of *Hansel & Gretel* thing or...?”

“I'm still looking,” the younger demon says as he stares at the screen, his finger flicking the scroll as he reads quickly. “I haven't figured it out yet.”

“Then we should hang here until you—”

“Well, looky, looky, who's playing hooky?”

My body tenses up at the voice and I have to count to fifty in my head slowly before I turn to face the person who said it. When I do, I see Mina dressed head to toe in tiny leather straps connected by silver rings. There's more of her on display than I've *ever* wanted to see, and that's after sharing a locker room with her for years. Oddly, despite her awkward looking outfit, I'm sure someone else chose, she's not wearing an ounce of her previous glam, nor is her hair coiffed. She looks like she rolled out of bed and donned a silly BDSM suit to fit in, and didn't consider for a moment what looking serious at an important event required.

It's really off-putting, and I don't mean because she made her own choices—I mean that because it makes her stand out as not belonging even more than her ill-fitting cosplay.

“Hello, Mina.” My eyes scan over the other Sickos, most of whom have pretty similar quirks that identify them as supes who normally wouldn't run in this crowd, but want to look like they do. When I hit Winnie, my lips curl into a sneer and I sniff like I've run into something rotten. “Winnifred.”

Mina wraps her arms around Winnie, grinning as she cuddles in. "Doesn't she look *divine*? I have no idea why I never noticed this gorgeous woman before, but as soon as I did, I scooped her up. And her skills? *Top. Notch.*"

Archie, Javi, and Angelo come up behind me, and their energy is full of fury. I can sense their supe sides straining against them, so I hold up my hand to prevent them from causing a worse scene. I'd love to get even with these bitches for their cowardly, sneaky attack at the club, but this isn't the venue for it. Fighting with them rather than finding Luca is a distraction I have no intention of indulging.

I don't even know if that's why they're here taunting me—something that's incredibly possible.

Showdown

JAVIER

WHILE ARCHIE HAS ALWAYS BEEN the most laid back of our band of bros, I'm definitely the calmest in nearly every situation. My bird can be angry and vengeful—don't get me wrong—but together, we're also used to engaging in more long-term, cerebral, or social warfare. That's a common quirk of phoenixes because we're rare, often from ancient and wealthy families, and trained from birth that setting someone on fire is the last resort to accomplish your revenge.

It's lucky for us because all the shorter tempers are going to lose their shit.

"Mina, it's crass to discuss that sort of thing in public," I interject as I rake my eyes up and down her and Rogue's former lover. My gaze flicks briefly to the other Sickos, then back to the first two as if they don't matter in the slightest. "Even here, in demon territory, you're still well beneath the acceptable standards of engagement. I can't tell you how glad I was to hear you'd defected to a more... appropriate team and social circle."

Drawing on the teachings of my parents, I make sure the woman knows I'm looking down my nose at her metaphorically, if not physically. Her eyes flare with anger, and I smirk as the realization hits the nymph next to her. Winnie flushes bright red and looks at the ground, the condescension hitting the mark perfectly for her. Rogue's ex-booty call won't be a problem now, though her new ego feed is fuming so hard she might as well have steam coming out of her ears.

I haven't struck the finishing blow for Mina; no, her delusional narcissism is far too deeply ingrained for one hit to take her down.

"Look, we have places to be," Rogue says, studying her nails with an affected boredom. It's not real; the emotions flooding our bond tell the real story. She's not over the betrayal of her ex-bestie yet, but she sure as hell will not let that bitch know the wound is still raw. "Get out of our way or we'll move you ourselves."

"You can't do that," Mina sneers. "If you do anything to harm me, especially in public, I'll make sure the entire community knows and since I'm *much* more popular and talented than you, you won't be able to find a fan with a microscope. Your career in the Derby will be over, and there's not a damn thing you can do to stop me."

Angelo growls, his demonic tail flicking angrily as he pushes to the front of the group. "Watch it, witch. You're on *my* land, in Gemini territory, and Damon and I are the rightful heirs to the Gemini corporation. Not only do you have powers comparable to TV psychics in this world, but you're insulting our mate."

Mina's eyes widen as she looks at our girl. Rogue looks up from her pretend boredom and shrugs. "What can I say, Mina? You left, and the team has beaten every opponent, I found people who love me, and I'm building my circle of people who aren't using me to prop up their neuroses. Unlike you, I don't need to use fear and intimidation to get people to hang out with me—or to fuck me."

That's our mate—look at her go.

My bird stretches inside of me, spreading his wings as pride ruffles over my soul. He's preening for her, and it makes me grin widely on the outside. "No, you don't, dragonfly. We're all drawn to you because of your good qualities, not because we're scared you'll use the internet to trash our reputations."

"As if anyone could trash some of you anymore than you have yourself," Mina mutters bitterly. "Especially the Kellys."

Now she's got Reb's attention, and that's probably the absolute worst thing she could have done. Not only has he been in love with his stepsister since he was a kid, but he's the least predictable and has the shortest temper of the bunch. The Unseelie Fae practically glows with energy as his magic roars to the surface. His eyes narrowed, Rebel stalks closer to Mina and her now terrified looking brethren.

"Oh, Wilhelmina. Tsk, tsk. Never satisfied with landing your blows and fucking off before the tide turns." His head tilts as his posture changes to that of a predator—cold, calculating, and unforgiving in the hunt for its prey. "I never liked you—not once in the years you were Rogue's supposed friend. Unlike her, I could practically *smell* the rot inside of you. But I let it go, because she felt accepted and happy. But now?"

The smile that comes over his face is bone-chilling, even for him. Rebel's wings unfurl, dark and forbidding against the fiery background of Luca's fake Hellscape. He looks like a punk rock version of Lucifer, despite being Fae rather than a demon. Within seconds, his skin goes from the normal pale color to a blue that looks a little like the Avatar aliens. I haven't seen him do this in the entire time I've known him, but Rogue doesn't look surprised. She doesn't even flinch when his nails grow to almost talon sized and his teeth get sharp as fuck.

Unseelie can be fucking terrifying, and I had no idea just how much he and Rogue keep to themselves about their true forms.

Damon and Angelo fan out, their demon features menacing as they glare at the Sickos behind Mina. The easygoing lion groans and gives Winnie a withering look before he drops his tail and fangs to join in. Everyone is getting ready for battle, but I look at our girl carefully. She's unusually quiet, especially with Rebel ready to lose his shit in public. Normally she'd be coaxing him back from the edge to keep their Society mentors from finding out they're using their extremely dangerous powers in ways not beneficial to supe-kind.

"Dragonfly," I murmur to her. "Are you going to let this happen? Here? Now?"

She sighs heavily, and the emotions in our bond intensify. It's going to be a while before she heals, but it'll never happen if this chick doesn't stop sticking her metaphorical fingers in the wound. "I don't know, Javi. How could it possibly be worse than it is now?"

I arch a brow. "Well, your bosses will be pretty pissed if you let him kill them, especially if we all help him."

Waving her hand, Rogue makes an unconcerned face. "I can deal with that."

Fuck. Her pain goes deeper than I knew, and the expressions on everyone but Reb's faces say they just had the same realization.

"You can't sanction this! I know they put limits on you two freaks; you've told me more than once, you porky pixie!"

My jaw drops when the witch resorts to body shaming. There's no way she doesn't know where *that* wound is after being friends with Rogue for so long. Graciella tortured Rogue over being curvy and while she's more muscled and solid than she is overweight, it plagued her all throughout middle and high school. Reb used to burn off his fury about it in fight clubs and races when we were younger. Derby has helped her in so many ways, which is why we've all been supporting her since she started skating with the Bombers. This is a 'sink your battleship' moment emotionally, and I have no idea what's going to happen now. After all, Reb can strike out at Mina when he couldn't with his adoptive mother.

"We're not pixies," Rebel snarls as his wings flap slowly. He's not spreading the paralytic yet, which is good, but he's awfully close to losing his grip. "You're well aware of that fact, spell sucker."

"Potay-toe, poe-tah-to," the witch replies as her lips curl up. "Trash is trash. That's why your parents had to *buy* you like hookers."

Oh, fuckitty, fuck fuck... not the trafficking thing, too.

As if summoned by the cruel words, Rogue's wings pop free of her shoulders and the iridescent tattoos appear on her body as her humanoid form fades. Her posture goes rigid and the gorgeous, sparkling dragonfly wings on her back flutter quickly with her rising anger. I watch in awe, as even in this fluffy dress, my mate looks fierce as fuck. There's not a single hint of her inner turmoil on the outside as she faces off with the woman who seems determined to keep stabbing the dagger into her back at every turn.

Before she and Reb can attack, the selkie captain of the Sickos steps forward and shakes her head. "No. We're not doing this here, Mina. There are things we need to take care of that are more important than your grudge with your former captain."

"But I—"

Beatrice Janssen stomps in front of Mina, and her teammates follow. That puts them between the ex-friend and us, which is very strategic for heading off the fury of my Fae family members. I jerk my chin at Archie, who looks unsure but nods back. We have to get them out of here while BJ is trying to wrangle the deranged chick she brought on board. After I get Angelo and Damon's attention, we split two per fuming Fae. Archie and Damon take Rogue, grabbing her arms to drag her away while Angelo and I capture Rebel.

There's a lot of cursing and snarling as they're trying to break loose, but it's not optional. If they'd done what they were about to, it would have destroyed all our covert info gathering and completely fucked any hope of figuring out what the hell is going on with the larger community. I agree with anger, and I'd like to slit Mina's throat for the hurt I felt coming from my mate, but now just is *not* the time or place.

Reb is fighting us, but Ang and I finally get him far enough away that we can let go. He moves to push past us, but Angelo stops him with a ring of fire that surrounds us. My bird fluffs its feathers internally, but it doesn't hurt me, so I let it go. "Rebel, you can't. We all want to, but you *know* we can't. At least, not yet."

"It's the same with Luca and Lola, you know," Angelo says, shrugging. "We'd love to fix their bullshit and make the organization less... unsavory. But it has to be the right time, and that hasn't come yet."

"Might soon," he seethes, his blue skin getting darker as his temper flares again. "They've gotta be in cahoots with these bitches and the Stuhlls. I can't imagine how else they'd get down to this level. It required demon intervention, Ang."

"There are no demons on the Sickos, nor can those two disloyal slags manipulate the elevators," I say quietly.

Rebel stops dead, his expression surprised. "I didn't think of that."

"Of course not, man. You were too far gone into rage-land." I grin and look at Angelo's flame cage pointedly. "Rogue's getting the same speech over there, but just because Mina insulted her doesn't mean we have to fuck up our entire lives. We *will* deal with her, but like Ang said, we have to be more strategic."

His sigh is heavy and he murmurs, "She said the worst possible things someone can ever say to her, Javi. Those are bleeding wounds, and that fucking whack job just jabbed her finger in and made it worse. I want to kill the witch and I want to make it so painful that people talk about it for years."

Angelo snorts, snapping his fingers so the flames disappear. "Me, too, bro. But what good will it do to get our revenge now and have you two get thrown in some supe jail like the gargoyle chick we just met, eh? We might not be so lucky and get assigned to run some stupid college. In fact, I'd venture to say some of us will be banished to our original realms, where they'd definitely execute us. How does that fix anything?"

Now we're talking... calm and logical assessments, not overreactions that will end in sorrow.

Magic
ROGUE

Honestly? I have no idea what the hell my 'enemies' are doing consorting with a loose cannon like Mina. She clearly wasn't the person I thought she was during our friendship, and if I look at her behavior objectively, she's a complete looney tune. That makes her a liability and my training would tell me that makes her useless as an asset. Sure, she could be a distraction and possibly do some damage, but long-term? She's as likely to bite the hand that feeds her as to do what you need her to. Her extreme self-absorption and delusions of grandeur based on some mild social media cultishness has rotted her brain.

I don't know when that started, or if it was always there and I ignored the red flags, but it's beyond obvious now.

Unfortunately, knowing those things and dealing with the fallout of her joining more stable 'evils' isn't equivalent. Plus, I haven't had time to heal from the betrayal of trust and absolutely horrid shit she's said and done to me since the split. It makes me vulnerable in ways I feel ashamed of, and I'm not used to that. I'm always the strong one, the one who can shove it down and move on—I learned that at the feet of the Kellys. But her defection, her use of my most deeply held wounds to harm me? I can't escape the destruction inherent in someone you cared about weaponizing your pain for their benefit with gleeful precision.

"Princess, you know she's crazy, right?"

Angelo's soft rumble as we continue on through the stupid demon bullshit makes my shoulders tense. Of course I know that, but my head and my heart aren't on the same wavelength right now. The one ally I had besides Reb for all those years just severed the ties between us with such absolute finality that it left an aching hole in my chest. So I nod, not trusting myself to speak yet.

Yes, it's crazy for your heart to think you could get over having your ass kicked, but it makes up all these wild reasons that it could have been not her fault.

I'm fully aware that this confrontation, filled with purposeful, logically applied stabs into open emotional wounds was *not* caused by any spell or whatever. Mina knew what she was doing and did it publicly enough that everyone around saw and heard her barbs. That's the last straw, and it was meant to reveal my weaknesses and make me even more susceptible to attacks. I don't know if it worked, but knowing her intent changes everything in my fragile internal balance. There's no going back from this, and I have to mourn that—when I have time.

Rebel saves me, snorting as he mutters, "That bitch is on death row; she just doesn't know it yet."

"Well deserved, and it can't come soon enough," Archie says. I blink for a moment, a little surprised by the easy way he says that, but then I remember that despite his laid back attitude, this is the future alpha in the cat shifter pack. His dads are varied by species of cat and personality, but his mom is fierce as fuck. Samara raised him to tread lightly and rip the throat out of someone who threatens your people; it simply hasn't been as obvious as it is right now.

"Guys, we can't do a fucking thing about that cuntmuffin now, so let's drop it, okay?" Damon's rebuke makes my chest loosen up a little, as the more we talk about her, the longer she's living rent-free in my head while my emotions try to stuff her bullshit in a locked box until I'm ready. "We have to be focused on this damn meeting and finding out what's happening at the secret one."

"D's right," I say as we finally reach the elevator at the other end of this enormous level. "Finding that 'circus' place is what's important, and after that, scoping out who invited us and why is the secondary mission. We haven't been attacked nearly enough for it to be about taking us out. If that was the point, BJ wouldn't have stepped in with that nonsense and there would have been more attempts."

"Maybe they don't want to risk doing it in demon territory?" Javier asks, as Angelo uses his tail to activate our ride to the top. "That would track if their parents were part of the conspiracy, as we believe."

"I don't know about that. They're slick; getting it done would be more important than doing it right." Damon looks up from his phone briefly, then shrugs. "I've organized a *lot of clean-up* over the years from the background, and Luca is much less calculating about his vendettas than people think."

Angelo groans as he straightens and shifts his demon features back to normal. "Little D is right. I'm the muscle, so I've seen it firsthand, but he's also the one we called to arrange the work in the aftermath of his insane ideas. He worked with all the crooked law enforcement, politicians, and physical disposal crews."

I give my submissive demon an appreciative grin. "So you have yet another useful skill set that I didn't even know about... Nice."

His face flushes with pleasure and his twin laughs as the elevator doors open. "Man, I just love watching you melt him, Princess. It's both hysterical and perfect every time."

The quieter demon arches a brow, then smirks as he looks at Archie. "I can hold my own on top, too."

Now we all join in the humor as Archie turns almost eggplant in color, muttering, "Shut up, assholes. Don't be haters."

Their antics help calm me and I'm thankful. My body was on high alert from the previous situation, and as we board the stupid carriage, I feel lighter. Moving to my lion's side, I put my lips against his ear. "You're hot as fuck when you're growly with me, but even hotter when D is helping me show you the other side. I love that you two finally admitted what I've known for a long time. And seeing that passion is fucking gorgeous, baby."

His shy smile is my reward and for the first time since we saw my ex-BFF again, I can breathe.

WE STAYED quiet on the trip out of the horror house and to the edge of the demon territory. We walk through the center gardens, avoiding Fae territory for obvious reasons, and when we get to the middle area, I stop and look around. "They have to be hiding their secret meeting place. We know it's not in demon or Fae lands."

"Demons would never agree to the aquatic shifter territory," Angelo says with a sneer. "Not because of water, but the MC that runs it is... definitely beneath them. They could be involved in the bigger picture because that's a lot of expendable minions, but Luca and Lola wouldn't be seen as corpses amongst those dumbasses."

Three down, I suppose.

"The main meeting area that way would be a terrible choice as well. Too much overlapping security sweeps from various clans. Odd visitors from 'out of town' would draw way too much scrutiny," Damon adds. "But nothing on these boards gives enough info to identify the location. Finding it *has* to be tied to some sort of magic because no one comes to these things without protection and staff, but that's the best place for leaks to start. They overestimate their skills and give shit away."

"Clever," Reb says as he rakes his hand through his bright green locks.

"How are we going to find it, then? We don't have a seer, a psychic, or even a fucking palm reader, man."

"But we have Wonder Twins powers, and lots of raw strength," Javi says thoughtfully. "Perhaps if we form a circle and join hands with the demons and Fae at the quarters, then put the shifters in the middle... It might allow us to combine your talents and use us to focus the output. One or all of you might sense the demon magic in areas that aren't Gemini territory?"

"Then we can try to separate it out, line by line, until we find what doesn't fit!" I clap my hands, then grab the phoenix in a tight hug. "Brilliant, babe. Creating a funnel to amplify the two halves of the magical spectrum is really smart. I don't know if it will work, but it's worth a try."

"Hell yes, it is," Archie says as he holds his fist up for a bump. "After that brief trip to fake Hell, I'm not excited about exploring the other lands in our quest to find the bad guys. I don't even want to go to check out the shifters; this shit is way too intense for me."

Rebel nods, looking around to check out the surrounding area for a moment. "We need to make it look like we're doing something *other* than what we are. Perhaps a light glamor, then we'll begin?"

"On it." Closing my eyes, I throw my hands out, waving them at my guys like I'm throwing confetti. When I feel the basic magic take hold, I bob my brows at them. "It'll look like we're praying to whatever from the outside. I used nothing that will survive a deep dive by someone with juice, but it will keep passers-by from nosing into our business."

"Makes sense." I turn to my cuddly lion and he shrugs. "You gotta save the mojo for this big stuff, eh? No use using a nuke to drive a nail."

He's getting much *better at understanding what two-thirds of our family uses—people do not give him enough credit for how smart he is.*

"Exactly. Everyone gets in a circle—Rogue, we take West and East, Ang go north, and Damon is in South. Javi and Arch are in the middle, back to back, looking up. Got it?" My step-brother has switched to an intensely focused magic user now, and there's no point in trying to talk him down until this is done. The others don't work with him like I do, and I'm used to his bossy, matter-of-fact behavior in the field. It's annoying, but it works.

"Alright," I murmur as the outer circle joins hands. "The middle pillars should focus on the sky and open themselves to us. Once we're able to meld together, we'll reach for your power, and then extend it to the grounds little by little. Do *not* break the plane of the circle or let go until we're ready."

The shifters chorus their assent and I turn to look at my magical men. Angelo tilts his head, looking at me in amusement. "Princess, we're waiting for your command. Rebel might think he's in charge, but D and I know better. This isn't a Council mission; this is our family. You're the center of the universe here."

Trying not to preen as Reb scowls darkly, I add points to Ang's total for later. That demon just earned himself a treat for goddamn sure. "Okay. Here we go."

I close my eyes, breathing out slowly as I gather all the power of both my demonic and Fae sides, then start the chant, "*Imbhuaileann na cruinne, bogann an t-aer fós. Ceiltíonn an fhírinne, nochtann an solas. Tá ár gcumhachtaí le chéile, a láithreacht a chruthú dúinn.*"[1]

Magic hits me in the chest like a cannonball, and colors explode in front of my eyes as the raw energy flowing from the twins to Reb and I twine together to form a circle that sizzles with strength.

Damn. We might actually do this; I wasn't really sure it would work.

Find Your Flame

REBEL

WHEN WE CONNECT my whole family together via our shared magic, it's brutal. I expected to be overwhelmed—how could I not when we're putting the strength of so many powerful supes into one strand of energy? But it's much bigger than I expected and my eyes open to look at the woman I've loved since I set foot in this realm. She's a supernova of colors and sparkles mixed with the deep jewel tones of my Unseelie magic and the fiery darkness of the twins' demonic powers. Golden threads from Javier and bright blue threads from Archie join them at a nexus focused solely in front of Rogue.

Much like in life, she's the center of interconnected powers, strengthening and bringing us together simultaneously.

"Damn, boys," she mutters. "I didn't know you had all this hiding from me. No way this is staying hidden from all the gawkers—it's enormous."

I chuckle and shake my head slightly. "Focus, Rogue. Extend the woven threads out to the surrounding area and see if you can find the demonic hotspots. You, Ang, and D have similar signatures, so that will help you scry even without an object."

Usually this sort of thing is *my* role when we're working, but the magic we've assembled doesn't want me to guide it. My step sis needs to sharpen her mind and imagine the landscape as best she can so the feelers will travel along the topography until it reaches our goal. She's had the training for this moment; however, it's simply not one of her higher-tier skills.

But I know she can do it.

"This is insane," Archie mutters. "Shifters don't get to be included in stuff like this often. I've watched you guys do things, but I've never been *part* of it. You know?"

"It's a trip the first time." Javier grimaces and I wonder what kind of stupid shit his parents have forced him to be part of. They're part of the ruling class in this city because of wealth and rarity, so it's not a stretch to believe that people are paying for the use of their feathers in both sketchy and legitimate rituals. The damn things are worth a small fortune, even the tiniest ones. "At least you're not required to cry for it."

"I'm going to murder them." Rogue's grumbling threat is about our phoenix's parents—their tears are even more valuable than the feathers. Obviously, he's been made to create them for profit and it was definitely before he got old enough to fight back. I don't blame her for the desire for vengeance, but we have a *lot* of our enemies on our plate as it is.

"Focus."

She growls at me, but stops talking, and I see her shoulders drop a little as tension seeps out. There's no way she will be able to wield this much power without keeping her mind *only* on guiding it to every nook and cranny of this manufactured portal. It's vast and was created by both magic and technology—I think. It doesn't feel like pure magic, nor does it feel like only some scientific creation that humans would keel over if they knew about. It's a mix, and I wonder who the criminal organizations in this city partner with to create it.

I doubt the Society knows what they're doing with this shit because they aren't invited.

"Does this whole place feel fucking weird to you guys? I didn't notice it until we connected, but the vibe is off." I don't move, but I hope they know I'm addressing everyone but Rogue. "It's not all supernaturally created."

Javier nods, his expression thoughtful. "Yes. I had an odd feeling when we entered, but I attributed it to the variation of species and age ranges here. All the enormous territories and the proliferation of strong beings threw me off, I guess."

"I haven't noticed anything," Archie admits. "But this isn't my forte. My moms and dads are involved in the shifter council, sure, but they don't fuck with the *Lucky Charms* stuff."

Snickering, Damon arches his brow at the lion. "Arch, magic users aren't all leprechauns, you know. Or Fae, obviously. There's a lot of variation in that gift."

"Duh, D," the hockey player says as he rolls his eyes. "But you knew what I meant. Non-mythical shifters are often fearful of magic and the consequences of playing with it. We're more physical and focused on using the body's strength than playing with universal forces and nature."

"This is fascinating, boys. However, I'm not sensing the shit Reb says I should. Do you think they'll be able to cloak it, even with our combined efforts?" Rogue frowns, but doesn't open her eyes again. "I think I was able to locate where the most powerful beings in all the sectors are within them. But there aren't spots where I'd assume the Gemini leaders and their fucking traitors are hiding. What now?"

"You need to try harder," I say firmly. "If you found the highest level folks, you're scratching the surface of what you're capable of without our help. I can do it on my own and so can you. Push the extra flow into that rope of magic—really infuse it before you send out feelers again."

Rogue hates shit she can't do immediately and without a lot of effort; it's the curse of being as smart as she is.

"Reb, that's what you always say." Our girl lets out a grunt and I worry I've pushed her too hard, but she finally sighs. "Okay, that hurt, but maybe I'm getting more traction by weaving it tighter so more energy can be combined."

She has to figure this out; we need to know where that meeting is before it ends.

OUR CIRCLE STAYS CONNECTED LONG ENOUGH to concern me —Rogue is still trying to manipulate our combined powers to find our next stop, but since she didn't develop this skill previously, it's not moving quickly. I'd love to lecture her about that—I definitely told her to stop ignoring the things she couldn't do at first—but for now, my attention is on whether supes who pass by are noticing what we're doing. I think we're still under the cloak we placed, but I have no idea how long that will hold or if it will fade as Rogue continues drawing on us.

"Is it possible they've left to meet? Maybe we're looking in the wrong place."

Archie's question isn't a bad one, and I turn to look at Angelo. He shakes his head, his expression grim. "No, they wouldn't do that. The territory is tied to the power of the Gemini org as a whole and leaving this... pocket portal or whatever... would weaken their ties to it. Luca and Lola *have* to be in this place somewhere."

"Wait!"

We all turn to look at our girl, surprise etched on our faces. She frowns, looking confused, then her eyes open to meet our gaze. "There's a spot that feels... dead. It's not full of magic, nor spirit. Hell, it's like a big icy blotch at the very edge of the area where the groups are going to meet, overlapping with the godly realm's section. I think the amount of energy coming from their shit was masking it at first."

I sigh in relief. I knew she could do this, but I wasn't sure if she could do it before we got caught. Now, we can pull back slowly and head for the place she found with our combined magic instead of standing here like sitting ducks. "Okay, bring the threads back in carefully, then once the whole cord is in front of you, the shifters will unweave their parts. Then the demons will extract, and after that, Rogue and I will recede. It has to be slow and cautious; otherwise, backlash could injure someone."

"You're awfully bossy for not being the one in charge," Angelo says with a smirk. "The Princess is too focused to call you out, bro, but I'm pretty sure she knows how this works."

"Ha. You'd think so, Ang, but our girl *hates* practicing shit she's not good at. It's a continual struggle in training and on our occasional field missions to get her to do the things she needs the most practice with—including this kind of location spell." I grin smugly, then yelp when a bolt of electricity travels down my line to shock me. "I'm telling the truth, woman!"

"Maybe, but you're being a dick. Partners compliment one another, so if you're better at shit, it makes sense for you to do it." Her expression is irritated, but she's obviously still working to pull back all the thickly woven thread with all our magic. "And it's distracting, so shut up."

"Angelo started it," I mutter as I look away. I hate when I get the short end of the stick with the elder demon. The others usually don't best me, but Ang is a master at prodding me until I get myself yelled at. "Gripe at him, why don't you?"

Archie snarls softly. "Guys, cut it out. Wheels is trying to do this shit. If you want to fight, hold it in for the assholes we're looking for."

He's right, of course, but that doesn't mean I have to like it.

"Almost there," Rogue says, stopping the bickering as we turn back to her. "Right about... now."

Her sigh makes me smile because I know she struggled with reeling it back in once she's released it. It's not the hardest part of mental scrying, but it is the most tiring. We probably need to find somewhere with food and drink to refill her before we go charging into any rooms full of nasties. Fae draw strength from the land, but based on what our new friends told us, we definitely do *not* want to pop into the Fae lands. We have to grab some quick energy shit from whatever we can find in the open area in front of the meeting stage.

"As I said before, bring it back slowly, Javi. Arch, follow his lead."

The lion snorts, sucking in a breath as he closes his eyes to visualize what I instructed. He's not really being a dick as much as releasing his worry about Rogue. I know that this is out of his expertise, and it leaves him feeling useless since there's not a need for physical protection at the moment. "You're not my supervisor, Kelly."

Damon chuckles softly. "That's right. You belong to Sparkles and me, baby."

Angelo groans, shutting his eyes as he tilts his head upwards. "You two are fucking killing me, man. Can we all stop with the sexual innuendo until we finish this? I feel like this is a gaggle of clowns bumbling around the center ring. Good thing no one can see or hear us—I think."

Rogue looks tired as she grins. "That's how I *always* feel with you assholes. Let this be a lesson for you." She stops talking for a moment, then shakes her head. "They've got their lines, Reb. The twins are next, then you."

"You know I won't totally be gone, right?" I ask carefully. "There will be a little piece left because we still need to complete the bond. Their pieces are permanent, so when they pull back, what they left is absorbed by the essence inside of you. For me, it will be sort of... free roaming."

Groaning as the line of power recedes into him, Angelo gives me a side-eye. "The Fae are so fucking bizarre, man. I'm not even sure I *want* to know what kind of shit is going to happen when you two actually finish the mating. Every time you tell us a little piece of your lore, I want to put my thumbs in my eye sockets."

I shrug, giving him an unrepentant look. "Demons are pretty weird, too. But you know the ones who trump us all? The fuckers we're about to invade, so get ready for the world to shake and shiver, man."

I don't know how much contact they've had with the godly blessed, but Rogue and I are very aware of how fucking difficult even their demi-progeny can be—and it's no walk in the park.

Another Dimension

ROGUE

THE GUYS ARE somber as we follow the trail towards the main event area. I know Reb and I have dealt with demis before—marginally—but I'm not sure if the others are aware of how insane this is going to be. Everyone knows about deals and bargains with Fae or demons; they don't all have the 'pleasure' of negotiating with the asswipes from the deity realms. Because the humans escalated their mythos to the level they did, the occupants, descendants, and 'adopted' members of that place are insufferably arrogant.

Buying into your own press is something they know all about, just like Mina.

I snort, shaking my head. No need to put *that* idea into the universe. Mina might have an overblown ego, but she doesn't have the power or talent necessary to even catch their eyes. Deities are even known for turning their noses up at infamous supes, until their tales escalate to storybook or mythic levels. She's not more than a bit player in the grand scheme of the internet, much less the entirety of time.

Archie looks at me curiously. "You're amusing yourself again, Wheels. Gotta share."

"I can't until we're not in the open, babe. This place wigs out my magic, especially since we did the whole 'Captain Planet' combine. There's..." I pause, fishing for the words to describe what it feels like. "I've never felt something that gives me a sense that it's been created by so many types of magic combined as well as technology. It's not normal tech, either—humans don't have this. Or at least, not what I sense? It's really hard to explain because it's so incredibly different from what I've ever encountered in the past."

Reb nods, looking over at us. "I didn't feel it before, but the oddness is like a spike of irritation against my Fae magic, too. Like it doesn't belong where nature's magic lives because of the blend."

"The real question is: where is this mysterious tech coming from, if not the humans?" Angelo replies as we get to the lower eastern edge of the main meeting area. "And how are all the organizations represented here accessing it? What's the payoff on either side?"

"Damn, bro. That's the question I had to the letter. Nothing is free, and this is shit wasn't given out of the goodness of someone's heart. It's also been a longstanding agreement—or at least for longer than this year. It came together too quickly to be a new procedure," Damon muses. "And nothing I have on me can identify it, though I plan to snatch some samples and ferret them away for review later."

"Put it on the list of shit we need to figure out or share with the other folks we're hoping to conspire with," I murmur as we follow the outer edge of the demarcation between the meeting space and the adjoining barrier to a territory. "Who's tech is this, where did it come from, and what are they getting for allowing use of it?"

Reb rolls his eyes at me. "Money, lil' sis. No way anyone with tech this advanced is taking anything but fucking money. Look at how grasp-ingly greedy the human tech bros are. Whether this is from their realm —which is doubtful—or any of the others, it's being paid for in cold, hard cash."

I can't deny his logic; the world at large has been a mess for decades because of the dipshit incels who share our realm.

"Okay, so we need people who are good at following the money in their world and ours. Noted," Damon says as he types on his phone. Angelo has his hand on his twin's shoulder to guide him as he stays fixated on the screen and walks, which makes me grin a little. The guys are better at supporting one another than they let on, and I love that. "I can handle our side, but we'll have to sub-contract the other part."

"I love it when plans come together," Archie says with a smirk and everyone groans. "What? I like that show. Shut up."

"Shhh," I cut in as we approach the front edge of the staging area. "We're almost there and I have no idea how we're going to get this secret whatever-the-fuck to recognize us. It's not visible to the naked eye, and we definitely can't do the circle with this many people milling about."

The crews getting the meeting spot ready didn't seem to pay us a bit of attention as we walked through, but that doesn't mean they weren't monitoring us surreptitiously. I'm not sure who or what organization they belong to—or if they're just subcontracted hires. They're obviously not human, though, and I'd prefer not to engage anyone as we search for the place we aren't supposed to know about.

"It's tense here," Javier says suddenly. "My bird can feel the fluctuations. The energy is... very old, but paired with new and strange. Definitely at the right spot, but I can't seem to identify the ancient magic but for a trace of familiarity."

Frowning, I raise my hands to my waist, palms out, and keep my back to the workers behind us. I close my eyes, letting everything fall away so I can connect with my Fae side completely. This isn't something I do often because it's unnecessary, but I might detect what Javi is sensing with the core of my powers. I can feel Rebel brushing against my energy reassuringly; he does this often, and he's just letting me know that he's willing to help if need be.

Everything stills as my magic connects inside and outwardly to nature. Fae have a distinct advantage over other elemental and green magic users because we are deeply connected to it in our realm and the planet recognizes those of the Mother. It's hard to explain to anyone without Fae blood in their veins, so we don't try. We simply use what gifts we have and hope that wherever we go, the realm will accept that connection as the one we came from does.

Basically, I'm begging the magic and nature of this weird hidden pocket to make nice with me and become visible.

After a few moments of coaxing, I find what I need. A thread—oh, so small—that responds to the call of my power. It's thin and reedy because this space we're seeking is very much not created by natural forces. In fact, it is more of a portal to another dimension that resides alongside our own. However, there are elements within it that are answering my pleas and I believe I'll be able to get in... eventually. But who the fuck did this, and why? How is the ability to create portals alongside the human realm a secret?

The questions are important, but I can only focus on following the thread of acceptance I feel. So I let it lead me until I envision a large open space that is *definitely* owned by some sort of magical being. It's set up like it belongs to a witch, with power damn near leaking from the protected circle like it's warning me to back the hell off. I keep my distance, respecting that energy, but since the place it's located in is lush with a forest and plants, I know this is what I will use to help us get inside.

"Give me access," I murmur to myself. "We are not here to damage you."

As if it simply needed to hear that, a tinkling sound gets my attention, so I open my eyes.

In front of us is a glowing door, just waiting for us to walk inside and see this marvel of tech and magic blended—but what happens when we do?

THE DOOR LETS us out not by the wooded witch location, but in an odd small town. There's a main street of small shops, most of which seem closed up, and down the street, what looks to be the area where the housing is. The quiet is unnerving, as this seems like it was a fully functioning place at one point, but is just... shut down. I look over at my guys, shrugging as I gesture toward the other end of the street.

"Fuck if I know where we are, but this is what the damn power trail lead to, and now we have to figure out where the targets are." Rebel looks perturbed, Archie looks unsure, and the others have varying expressions of concern. I roll my eyes at their hesitation. "Look, guys. We said we need to find out what the secret is by locating this place. Now we have, and I don't care if it's sort of creepy. We're going to walk down this road and figure shit out or so help me..."

"Whoa, whoa, Sparkles," Damon says as he comes closer, taking my arm. "No one is saying we shouldn't continue. This place just feels... wrong. It feels like we shouldn't be here because it's unnatural, you know? Hell, it's all of us, so not a single one of our species likes the vibe. Does yours?"

Not even a tiny bit.

But I shrug, forcing myself to be nonchalant. "Maybe not, but that doesn't mean we're going to let that stop us. I thought we came to the stupid Apalachin to fight with the gangs and shit, but this? This is so much bigger—it's like accessing a realm no one knew was here. Isn't that a big fucking deal?"

"Uh, fuck yes, it is," Angelo says as he looks around. "None of the leaders will be happy with this. But perhaps it explains how the various rebel groups are moving around and gathering. If they aren't doing it in their own realms, but here, they won't get caught by spies or snitches or even intelligence groups. Not a single royal or leader or deity is looking for this shit; how could they fight it?"

"Exactly." I tilt my head, looking at my men seriously. "Are you ready to find out who and what this place is hiding? Because I, for one, am *not* comfortable with some mirror realm or whatever hiding a bunch of shit no one knows about."

Rebel nods, joining Damon and me at the front. "Let's get moving before someone realizes we're here. I don't know what kind of magic or tech protects this place, but since we're having a sci-fi *Wizard of Oz* moment, I'd like to get away from the main drag. Ang, take her other arm, and Javi and Arch block the back."

Sighing in annoyance, I let Reb do his pretend general thing. I know this makes him nervous as fuck, and since I'm *trying* to be a good mate/girlfriend, I'm also picking which battles I want to fight. Their overprotective knuckle-dragger shit isn't really a big deal in this context; in fact, it's probably smart. So I don't complain as we walk down the deserted street that was clearly once a hub of activity for the town we're in. It has food, clothing, and other various shops—with pretty recent styles and such. It looks as if the abandonment happened about two to three years ago, based on what I'm seeing as we stroll down the cobblestone thoroughfare.

"Do you think something happened for them to abandon this? Seems pretty nice," I say to Damon.

He shrugs, biting his lip. "I don't know. I don't sense anything that would force them to leave, like spells or hexes; do you?"

"Nope," I reply as I continue scanning. "And I don't see evidence of battles or fighting that would suggest invasion or elimination."

"It's like everyone just picked up and left," Angelo murmurs. "Look ahead at those houses. This shit is pretty fucking nice, but they seem empty as well. Who the hell just leaves a place this well maintained?"

Hell if I know, but it's definitely creeping me out.

Useless

ARCHER

BEING a supernatural in the human world, I didn't think I'd ever find something that was so out of pocket that I'd be as shocked as they are if they find out about us. Like, we're in a world where shifters like me, or demons, or even gods and goddesses are normal.

However, that was before I stepped into some weird science/magic pocket dimension that far exceeds the tech any of us have ever heard of.

"This is wigging me out," I admit as I look at my girl. "Knowing this is out there and even Guardians don't know about? That's fucking scary."

Rebel grimaces, then sighs heavily. "Just because not *all* Guardians know about it doesn't mean some very specific ones don't, nor does it mean the Society is unaware. The levels of secrecy are more stringent than human intelligence and the people at the top constantly decide what should be common knowledge and what should remain in the shadows just like human governments do. Just because their 'constituents' are supes doesn't mean they won't fuck shit up intentionally or unintentionally."

Angelo nods. "That's true even by species level. Consider that we're not telling anyone this shit because we don't trust them—not our families, the Councils, or the Society. They do the same shit on a much higher level."

"I fucking hate this shit," Rogue mutters as she looks at the abandoned township we're walking through. "All the secrets are how whatever is happening can happen. The layers, the clearances, the mistrust? It's why it's very, *very* probable that this has been building for so long that we'll have trouble figuring out the source."

Nodding, I run a hand through my hair, not comforted by their agreement in the slightest. "Exactly my point. Thinking you know the world pretty well and then being hit with this kind of shit sucks balls. What else is out there? Aliens?"

Damon chuckles and bumps his arm, smiling fondly. "Nothing is completely impossible, Arch. No one, and I mean, *no one,* talks about the Ninth Realm. Who the fuck knows if it's space? We could definitely have a *Guardians of the Galaxy* moment."

I blink at my lover, trying to gauge how serious he is. Holding my hand up, I count on my fingers. "Human, Hell, Faerie, Godly, Legendary, ID, Astral... what do you *mean* Nine Realms, D?"

The younger twin shrugs. "There are theories that two more realms exist, but we don't know about them because they didn't come from the same beginnings as the seven. You know the legends of the three and all that shit."

Uh, no, I don't fucking know that!

"Stop scaring him," Rogue says as she grabs my arm and pulls me close to her. "Archie is definitely the kindest, softest heart of all of us. Teasing him will make this even more freaky, D."

But instead of capitulating, Damon pushes his glasses up and makes his 'serious' face. "Sparkles, I'm not teasing him. This is a theory that's been floating for a long time, and a lot of very educated scholars and historians believe it. The Society has deemed it a crackpot theory, of course, but think about what humans say about us. I'm not sure these folks are incorrect about the possibility. I mean, look at this place. Where the hell did anyone get the tech and magic combo recipe to make it? Not from *any* of the known realms, for sure."

"Just what are these 'scientists' saying about the other realms?" Javier asks, curiously. "I'm not on either side of this argument, but I am interested. There's nothing in this damn town and we're heading for the edge soon, so entertain us."

"This is *not* entertaining," I mutter. I'm definitely not going to tell any of these fuckers that being abducted by aliens has been a fear of mine since the first time I saw that damn queen in *Alien* as a kid. "It's dumb,"

Angelo snorts. "Agreed. D has been on this for years, you know. He and his dice-wielding, microscope using, acne infested online friends talk about it. The nerd is strong with that crowd."

"Shut it, Ang," Damon says as he waves his hand at his twin dismissively. "Mock my multi-species nerd groups all you want... I think they're right."

"So spill it," Rogue says with a grin. "I'm game to listen, even if I think it's tin foil hat shit."

"Okay, so the theory is there's a galactic and a primordial realm that are not part of our current world views. They are the very oldest ones, and they represent the first beings who were there as it was created. Primordial is where the myth of the three creators comes from, and that's where they retreated after the mess. Galactic existed alongside the other and comprises space and time very differently. The theory says that the ID realm passes through galactic between the ribbons and primordial is locked tight—no one gets in, though the three could get out if they chose."

"This is supe ghost story shit," Rebel shoots back. "C'mon, D. No *way* there's two no one knows about that have been 'kept top secret' nor are there what I would assume is ass loads of beings in them we've never encountered. It's bullshit, man."

Thinking about it for a moment, I wrinkle my nose as we reach the end of the town's road. "I don't know, guys. If it's possible that all seven realms' bad guys have been plotting together forever and some rando brought them together for a big conspiracy... Doesn't it also seem possible that there's shit out there we don't know about just as big if not bigger?"

"Humans do only know about one of seven," Rogue muses. "Maybe we only know about seven of nine?"

"Do *not* make a Trek joke, D," Angelo cuts in, giving his twin a dark frown. "You just made a huge fucking existential mess of our family, and we have to focus on finding this meeting. I'm going to throttle you if you don't let this go."

That will not help, unfortunately; my mind is racing with possibilities and new fears, no matter what Angelo says.

"This road goes forever," Reb says as he looks around in irritation. "It's just forest and shit. The nature's nice, but... it's not giving me a damn clue as to who or what runs this fucking place."

"Or what it is." Rogue squints into the sunlight, then stops to touch a tree. "Although. I can *feel* real nature. Like this isn't some elaborate illusion, or fake shit. The Fae part of me can sense that it's not unnatural, even though this place may be."

"How is that possible, Wheels?" I ask as we walk again, pushing through the lush forest. "I mean, I don't think you're wrong, but it definitely seems like that should be impossible."

"I have no idea, Arch." She sighs and shakes her head. "And I sure as fuck don't know how the people working with their asshat father found the ones who run this thing. It's not like you can look up 'evil secret tech lords' in a directory."

Damon blinks, then holds his hands up. "But you can. You actually *can*. Though, I'm not sure how it would work using that and being, you know... not human."

That gets Rebel's attention, and he stops our progress to look at D. "Say more."

"Well, there's an entire underground network humans use to get illegal shit done. Rich ones, I mean—like billionaires and criminals and governments and—"

"Those words all mean the same thing," Rogue mutters. "No need to keep going."

"The *point*," D continues, "is that there's an entire piece of the human version of the darknet where they can find that shit. Killers, assassins, thieves, mercenaries, fixers... whatever you need."

I squint at him. "How do *you* know about that?"

"Because the step after that kind of paid shit is finding a crossroads demon, dumbass." Angelo sighs and pinches the bridge of his nose. "Any demon who makes bargains with the desperate knows that while the non-wealthy humans turn to their gods first, the rich idiots turn to criminals. Once that fails, they suddenly find their faith and demons get the next bite at the apple."

"So demons handle all that stuff?" I frown and wrinkle my nose. "That's way more corporate than I'd imagine Hell to be."

Damon laughs. "No, no. Think of it like... venture capital. Demons broker and make sure the deals are followed. The actual work is usually subcontracted out to other demon types or maybe even other supe types. On the surface, you'd end up dealing with folks like Luca if there's a presence in your area. Less populated? A single demon who has that territory."

This entire fucking party is a mind fuck extraordinaire.

"Okay. So you guys have a structure. But you're saying sometimes supernaturals might use the human marketplace or whatever?" Rebel says as he taps his lips. "Especially if they wanted to fly under the Society's radar."

"Yep," Damon says with a grin. "Because if it doesn't need magic, they can just do what they need quickly for a price. Even demons do it if the sub-type they need isn't available and the target isn't a supe."

"Do you think whoever is running this place came from that pool of talent, D?" Angelo looks at his twin, waiting for an answer. When Damon shrugs, he sighs. "I wouldn't put it past Luca or whatever puppeteer is working the bigger picture to use every single resource possible."

"Great. That adds a whole different dimension to this fucking problem." Rogue looks up at the sky, then growls softly. "And it makes everything messier. How the hell do we figure out what human criminals are doing and who might use them?"

"No idea," Damon says ruefully. "But I'm putting it on the list for further research when we're back at the house. That thing is getting monstrous, but I should be able to make progress more quickly when I have all my systems, not just my phone."

"Has anyone considered what we're going to do if we actually *find* anyone here?" I look at Rebel and Angelo, my worry evident on my face. "We have no idea what beings are hiding in this weird Pokeball dimension."

Rogue chuckles and leans in to kiss my cheek. "You're right, Arch, but we have to see if we can find them. It's a wasted opportunity if we don't. Together, we'll be able to handle it."

Maybe, but there's something very unsettling about this place and *the lack of planning for the mission.*

"Archie, you're not usually this freaked out by... well, anything." Javier tilts his head and looks at me as if I've grown a second head. "What's with you?"

I press my lips together and grunt in annoyance. He's right, but I've been sensing weird shit since we stepped into this damn portal or whatever. My lion is unsettled, and I don't know why. It doesn't seem to affect the others, but they aren't full blood shifters. Shifters' animals are just as predatory and primal as real animals; small things can set us off that won't bother them. Even as a mythical, Javi's bird isn't quite the same as my lion.

"This place feels wrong, and I don't like it. Everything is bothering me here and my lion is very edgy. It's making me edgy, and our loosey-goosey approach is making it worse. I'm not criticizing you, mind, it's just—I can't seem to calm the asshole down."

Rogue frowns, walking over to press against me, and looks into my eyes. "Archie, you should have just told us your lion is having problems. Honestly? It's probably sensing things we can't, and we should pay attention to it. You're not just window dressing here, you know."

Before I know it, Damon has stepped up behind me, caging me in with our mate. I feel a light kiss on my shoulder blade and he murmurs, "Sparkles knows what she's talking about, big guy. Not having magic doesn't make you lesser; it gives you a unique skill set. And your lion definitely has good senses; we should listen to it."

Angelo coughs, his lips quirking up. "I'm not going to kiss you, but I agree. You have the best sense of smell, good hearing, and prey tracking senses. We should use that instead of wandering like fools."

When Reb nods, I duck my head. "Thanks, guys. Sorry I didn't—you know."

"No worries, babe." Rogue smiles as she pecks a kiss on my nose. "Now let's get shakin' bacon. Take the lead and let your big kitty help us find the inhabitants of this damn place."

Yes, ma'am.

Fly Away

ROGUE

ARCHIE SHIFTED after he stripped and I've got his clothes folded over my arms as we trudge down this never-ending road in the trees. He pauses occasionally, the huge ass lion tilting its head to listen and sniff about before we're allowed to continue. He keeps looking confused, and *that* worries me more than anything. It's like he smells something he can't identify—which tracks—but also he's hearing things he doesn't know how to quantify.

Put together, it's fucking strange, and it has the hackles on the back of my neck standing up.

By the time we finally see something that looks interesting, I'm ready to throw in the towel. All six of us stand by the enormous iron gates in front of a walled property with a large house set back on a hill. It's not an ostentatious mansion, just a larger home with sprawling land around it. It has tasteful landscaping and foliage, a long drive up to a circle where what looks like some fairly fancy cars are parked. Archie scents the bars, tossing his maned head for a moment as if saying 'no'.

That makes Rebel frown, and he sighs as he says, "Do not touch anything. I'm going to feel out the grounds, but none of you should help. If only one of us gets hit with any magical security, that's better than everyone getting injured. Got it?"

I narrow my eyes at him. "You're not as good with the earth as me. I should be the one doing it."

"I am not arguing about who has better control over the elements, sis. You saw Arch; there's something guarding this damn place, and he doesn't want us hopping a wall because of it."

Angelo holds his hand up, his gaze firm. "I agree with Reb. Even if you're better with earth and fire, he's skilled with air. A scent will work just as well as the connection to the ground. Plus, I'd prefer you remain unharmed, Princess. This motherfucker can get fried; we'll be fine."

"Gee, thanks, Ang," Rebel mutters. He looks at Javi and Damon, who nod their approval. "Five to one, Rogue. I'm the sacrificial lamb this time."

Of course you are; I'm always going to be outvoted, you dick.

But I let him go because I agreed to work as a team, and whether it's weighted against me or not, this was what we decided. Watching closely as my stepbrother approaches the gates, I wait with bated breath to see if forces repel him before he can slip his hands through to touch the ground inside of them. Luckily, nothing surges forward to knock him on his ass, and Rebel reaches between the iron bars to place his palms on the earth inside the barrier.

"I'm not sensing magic," he mutters as he kneels in front of the enormous structure and slides a second hand in between the bars. "Now for the *actual test...*"

The quiet surrounding us is almost deafening as he does his thing, murmuring in our language under his breath. I frown, tilting my head when I realize that despite the 'natural' feel of the trees, foliage, and grass, what I *don't* feel isn't the issue. It's what I don't *hear* that is much stranger. Besides our breath and Reb's muttered chanting, I don't hear a damn thing. No birds or bees or animals… not even far-off sounds of civilization. It's literally like a tomb, but outdoors.

That's definitely fucking out there, and it confirms my thoughts about how manufactured this land is.

"I don't feel magic or threats. There are dogs—two, I think—of a fairly large size, probably guarding the house proper. They aren't outside as far as I can tell, but knowing that doesn't tell me if they can get outside without help. They're certainly trained, and I'd wager as guard dogs."

Damon arches his brow. "How the fuck do you know that?"

"Because I can sense the size by their contact with the earth, and dogs that big aren't usually meant to frolic. They're probably Dobermans or Rottweilers, maybe a Malinois. People who live in big, gated homes with this kind of dog usually train them as protectors." Rebel pulls his hands back and dusts them off quickly as he rises. "It's logic more than anything, D."

Lion Archie throws his head back and makes a loud, pissed off cat sound. I can't say I blame him; I'd like to hop this fence and see who the fuck lives here, but I also don't want to end up having to injure or kill someone's pets. I've got very little worry about having to kill humans or supes to protect myself, but animals are a bridge too far unless I have no choice.

We have a choice right now, and continuing our trek without that bad karma is fine.

"Then we should hit the bricks, man," Javi says as he looks up at the sky, then back at the road. "No reason to waste time here if we aren't going in. It proves people live in this weird pocket despite the abandoned town we came through near the portal."

"Agreed," I say as I nod. "Let's keep going until we find actual beings or the fucking assholes we're hunting down. I don't want to get sidetracked by silly shit."

Rebel rolls his eyes and gestures for LionArchie to lead. "I'm not distracted, simply curious. This is a fairly unguarded abode and relying on two normal dogs tells me the owners aren't afraid of invaders. They know they can defend themselves if need be, but since we don't feel magic..."

"You think they use regular weapons?" I ask as we walk behind the hyper-alert lion again. "Why does that matter?"

Angelo snorts, shaking his head. "If this weird place is run by actual humans, what other monstrosities are they hiding from the supe community? This is well beyond the tech either group professes to have access to. It's beyond what Hell has access to. That's a big deal, Princess."

"Okay." I think about that as we stroll along the wooded path again, biting my lip as I consider the implications. "Having tech way out of line with admitted advances means it could belong to humans—which is bad for everyone in the Earth realm—*or* it means the supposed rebel groups have it, which is bad for *every* realm. Right?"

"Exactly, Dragonfly," Javier murmurs. "The important question is what they plan to do with it, and how big is the scale? Can they make a ton of these little hidey-holes where armies or whatever could be amassed, then deployed? Are they developing them to hold prisoners where no one will ever find them again? The possibilities are grim and endless; it makes my bird restless to consider a cage like this even if it is large. It's not real, and it's definitely worse than a black site."

When you put it that way....

WE FELL quiet after Javier's declaration, and I know it's because we were all thinking about the horrors that *any* group of baddies could inflict with this shit. It's a game changer for all the species, even magical ones, because who knows if it can be paired with that kind of power to make some giant supe Faraday cage? I don't like this one fucking bit, and how it's been created and *hidden* from the officials and agents and all the damned people who should have figured it out —in every realm—is frightening.

I will not say that, though, because none of them have comforting thoughts to share, either.

Archie finally pauses at the edge of the trees, and I notice the light is much brighter beyond his perfectly still pose. We've reached the edge of the odd forest, and he's scoping out the terrain ahead. I walk up beside him, careful to rub my palm over the huge mane so he knows I'm there. No good can come from spooking an apex predator, even if it's your boyfriend inside the furry suit.

"Guys, look at this," I whisper as my eyes rove over the sight in front of me. "What the fuck is this shit?"

Beyond the tree line is a campus of some sort—a very wealthy one. There's a large Gothic style building that might be an admissions or main building with a trickling fountain in front. The road we've been following ends as the cobblestone pavement starts, and the path makes a roundabout around the water feature, then heads east to an open square. It's surrounded by six large buildings that *might* be dorms—but I'm guessing because it feels like this place is a school and it could be damn near anything for all I know. Past those structures, there's another extensive building that could be a gym or athletic center, and behind it, a fancy ass building that might be a church.

"What the actual goddamn fuck is this place?" Rebel says as he joins Archie and me. "It's enormous."

"I know," I reply as I turn to look down the edge of the land, noting it's on a large body of water that flows outward towards a thick group of trees that look as solid as a fucking wall. On the other side of the banks, I see the same deciduous trees we've been walking through, so we might have been able to turn south at some point and see what's in the middle of that forest. "This reminds me of the campuses for the schools overseas we visited. Remember when we were like ten?"

Reb nods, continuing to scan the horizon as his body tenses. "Yeah, a little. I think you're right, though. This is definitely a facility for training or a school or something like that. By the looks of the outside, it's a well funded one, too."

"Not by humans," Damon says as he looks at his phone. His brows are furrowed, and he's scratching his chin as he scrolls with one thumb. "My scanners are fritzing out like crazy, which means whatever beings are housed here, they're not basic meat suits."

"And there are demons here besides us," Angelo adds. When I look at him, I'm surprised to see horns, wings, and a tail adorning his frame. "*Powerful* ones... more powerful than that idiot Darkstar and our father."

Before I can question his statement, Archie shifts back to his bronzed, naked self. I blink, handing him his clothes quickly so I don't get distracted by the sight of his damn muscles. I'm worried, not dead, and he's very appealing to look at without his skivvies on. "Why did you shift?"

"Smells," he says as he pulls on the bottoms first. "There are also shifters here. In fact, if I were a betting cat, I'd say we've got a full house of supes meeting here. Might even be all the baddies in one place."

"We should take them out," Rebel grunts as his wings pop free. "Stop this whole nonsense dead in its tracks."

Yeah, and kill a shit ton of other people who might not be involved, plus we have no idea if the leaders are all here.

"If you scorch the earth without figuring out where the blight is coming from, it will return, and when it does, it will be mutated." I arch a brow at him as I shrug. "We don't know who's in charge or even if they're here. They could rebuild, especially with pocket portals or dimensions or whatever. It's much easier to recruit disenfranchised people since that damn plague the humans didn't get control of."

"Fuck," Reb says as he buries his hands in his hair. "You're right. Balls out, no intel isn't good for keeping the bastards from reappearing somewhere else with even stronger plans. I just hate wasting the proximity."

"If you and Sparkles stay with Archie, perhaps Angelo, Javi and I can use our ability to fly to get closer." Damon pushes up his glasses as he squints at the campus again. "We have faster and less complicated flight mechanics, plus having three of us means we can split the facility into thirds to see what we can find."

"What if they have... air defense...or something?"

Angelo chuckles and winks at me. "Then it will be lucky that we all have magic to avoid being targeted. Stop worrying, Princess."

When in the world's history has saying that ever *helped someone actually stop worrying? A quarter past never, that's when.*

Soldiers

ANGELO

MY TWIN and I let our wings loose first, then Javier does his weird Sailor Moon-esque sparkling transition to his fiery phoenix. Rogue is watching with her mouth hanging open and I chuckle to myself. Because of his ridiculous parents, Javi keeps his bird pretty low-key, and it's probably been a *long* time since she's seen it. The difference between a younger phoenix transforming into a decent looking but not hugely remarkable bird is one thing; an adult in his full glory is something else entirely.

"Morrigan, save me," our girl mutters as Javi glitters up into the sky like a feathered disco ball. "That's so pretty that it *hurts*."

Rebel snorts, rolling his eyes at her. "You are way too easily impressed, lil' sis."

"Oh, yeah. Like I'm the one who almost died on the spot when we met those ice birds a couple of years ago." Her words drip with sarcasm and I look at my old friend curiously, noting the red face he's sporting now.

There's a story I want to hear.

"We can ask about it later, Ang," Damon says as he pushes off, flapping his wings to gain altitude quickly. "We have shit to do right now."

He's right; my twin almost always is. His logical, pragmatic side directly opposes the softness he hides behind it, but Damon is good at switching to 'mission-mode' when need be. I wink at Rogue, then follow him into the sky, splitting off in the direction we agreed on mentally. I'll head to the training building. He's taking the main, and that leaves Javi to cloak himself so he can peep into the dorm-like structure. I would have liked to send Reb to that big monstrosity at the south end, but I'd rather he stay with our girl and Archie, just in case.

"We'll have to check it out at some point, though," I mutter to myself as I bank on a breeze and head for my target. As I get closer to the buildings, I clear my throat and intone, "*Vide modo quid vis videre.*"

That's not a cloaking spell like my phoenix brother, but it will trick the beings in the vicinity enough to keep me off their radar for a bit— I think. Vengeance demons have magic, obviously, but our ability to use it affects the people we're using it *on* more than ourselves. The real question is if the beings who inhabit this fucking place are used to seeing supes or if they go about their days not expecting creatures with preternatural powers to exist.

"Here's hoping," I say as I pull my wings in and descend towards the roof of the immense building. I'm careful to brace myself, letting my dive become a gentle coast when I'm almost there, so I don't make a suspicious 'thump' when my feet touch the surface. It doesn't have windows or a skylight, but when I look closely, it appears it might have a hatch that opens.

Not using that—who knows what I'd drop into?

But it's curious—what are *they* using the hatch for, I wonder? If it really is a training facility, what would create the need for coming in and out of a roof? Certainly not sports, nor regular classes—there's something very sketchy about this place. Shaking my head, I walk slowly so my steps are silent, memorizing the shape and detail of my landing spot. If there's something hidden up here, I'm going to find it; otherwise, I'll take off and try going a level lower.

Nothing stands out up here, which is annoying as hell. It also confirms my belief that the people running this place do *not* expect supes. Seemingly no aerial protection and nothing that trips on the roofs? That means you think nothing with wings might lurk, and you believe there are no *actual threats* anywhere. Otherwise, why the unholy Hell would you have such accessible, unguarded buildings? You wouldn't.

I close my eyes, reaching out to my twin mentally. This works better when we're closer together, but I try to send the vibes I'm getting from this stupid arena, so he knows it's likely not dangerous to land on the dorms. Once I do that, I walk carefully to the edge and take flight again so I can find a good window to peek in. I glide away from the training center, making sure there's enough space for me to circle around and check all the angles first. There are a few tall windows that *might* have a vantage point, but I need to stay away from the lower ones. The mid and ground-level ones are bigger, but I'd end up too exposed, especially in the daylight.

Annoying as fuck, but I'd prefer not to set off alarms until we have an idea what beings use this school.

"Is it possible they only use human-style security?" I wonder as I circle again, trying to decide which one of the windows is best. "If so, there have to be cameras around here somewhere. But none on the outside? So fucking strange."

The house we stopped at definitely had a wall and a gate, plus dogs, but this huge, fancy-ass school or college or whatever is completely unguarded as far as I can tell. It speaks to how confident the admin and staff are—they believe no one will attack, and if they do, the population inside can handle it. Could it be some kind of secret mercenary-type training facility?

No, that only happens in movies, Angelo; don't be ridiculous.

THERE'S nothing like figuring out you're wrong in the most spectacular fucking way.

I've spent the past half hour watching the shit going down inside this damn arena, and to say I'm flabbergasted would be an understatement. The biggest room on the ground level is a wide open space divided into sections—weight training, a fight ring, cardio equipment, and bleachers to watch. Groups of ten to twenty humanoids, many of them bleached blond dudes, have been working their spot in the circuit furiously. I don't know what in the motherfucking shit they are, but they seem to have superhuman speed, strength, and senses.

Five or six more guys are in polos, observing and yelling at the 'students' as they lift, fight, or exercise. Another group of twenty plus humanoids sit in the bleachers, wiping themselves down with small neck towels as they drink from water bottles. They don't look completely spent, but I suppose I am far enough away that I might not be able to tell. None of the groups have many females, and that alone is odd, but the few that are present seem to be more varied than the men.

A lot of them look very *similar to one another in facial features and how they move—another oddity to figure out.*

My phone buzzes in my pocket as I watch the extremely well-trained people continue to work, amazed by how precise and lethal they look even when they're on the treadmills. It's seldom a demon as old as me feels impressed by this sort of thing, but... it's like this damn campus is honing weapons in person form. What for, I couldn't say, but they're doing a damn fine job of creating a goddamn army.

"What?" I whisper into the receiver as I clutch the side of the building with demon claws. "This feels like a bad idea. You guys don't have a *clue* what I'm seeing here. You'd flip your shit, trust me."

Reb huffs, then snaps, "Then *tell me*, asshole. It doesn't help to be mysterious."

"This is definitely a school or whatever, and they're using some sort of super humans to create walking weapons. I think, at least. It might be the influence of superhero movies, but dude, these guys and a handful of women are *bad asses*. They're fast as shit, strong, and they're being taught multiple fighting styles, from what I can see. And I'm only looking at what's happening on the ground floor. Who knows if they have subterranean levels for other shit."

"Are you sure they aren't supes?" Archie says. "That would make a lot more sense, Ang."

"He's right, babe. There's a fuckton of supes who have humanoid forms—demons, Fae, vampires, shifters, sirens, mer-folk... the list is enormous. Not to mention demis and those kinds of jagoffs." Rogue laughs at her own insult and it makes me smile for the first time since I laid eyes on this crap.

"It *could* be any of those, but I haven't seen even one of them change into... anything. Even the ones in the fighting ring aren't shifting or losing glamors when they're getting beaten down. That's pretty high-level shit and I don't think anyone could hide this many of them from the Society and the Councils." Frowning as I lean forward, squinting to see better. "This gym has over a hundred of them, and I assume it's only one section."

Reb goes quiet and when he speaks again, his voice is quiet. "If that's one class full, this campus likely houses hundreds of these super-whatevers."

"Super soldiers," Archie interjects and we all groan. "Like Captain America, dude."

Chuckling, Rogue takes over. "As cool as that would be, I don't think we're dealing with a comic book situation. I don't have a fucking *clue* what it actually is, though. Even if they are humans juiced up some-how, this doesn't have any government or official flags, logos, signs...

nada. It could be some kind of black site, but... I just don't think they could hide it, especially from our kind."

"Then what?" I muse. "Something outside of both the humans *and* the supes? That doesn't exist."

"Angelo, an hour ago, we didn't think some weird in-between dimension where your dad and other dickwaffles could hide existed." Archie's sarcastic drawl isn't meant to be mean, I know, but it wakes me up. The lion is right; acting like this couldn't be something totally out of our sphere is dumb.

"Have you guys heard from Damon or Javi yet?"

Changing the subject will make it easier not to feel like an idiot.

"Javi is in bird form; we will not hear a damn thing until he's done," Rebel grumps. "But yeah, we've heard from D."

"Well?"

He doesn't answer as quickly as I'd like, and this whole thing is making my horns twitch below my skin. "He says the main building looks like offices, and it's hard to see much because of the curtains. A couple of things stand out so far—a top floor that has to be for the person in charge, a fancy receiving room on the ground floor, and an elevator on each floor. That might mean it has lower levels, too."

"I don't like this one bit," I growl softly. "If we were wondering how Lucian, Luca, and whatever other losers are building their movement without being detected, this place is definitely the answer. They could meet here for decades and no one would be any the wiser."

"They probably *have* been, Angelo." Our girl sounds angry, and I don't blame her. As a Guardian, she has to protect her charge when they assign it, and not knowing about a secret hidey-hole full of super soldiers puts them all at risk. "This is a huge deal. Reb and I have to let our handlers know."

"You can't," Archie says and I blink. "Even I know that until we verify who knows about this place already and who doesn't, we can't go around handing over the info. We'd lose our edge if the bad dudes have spies where they shouldn't be, right?"

"Actually, he's spot on." I can almost hear Reb tugging on his hair in irritation and it makes me grin. "We *should* tell them because it's our duty, but we really can't. We'll have to carefully feel around for knowledge of this place when we're at HQ for missions and maneuvers. And we all have to keep this shit locked down to *everyone* except our family —no one else can know. Not parents, not friends... no one."

Well, that's going to suck if Luca and Lola go on one of their paranoid 'everyone's out to get us' phases; hope D's ready for that.

Bad News

THE DISCOVERY of some weird dimension where an army of fucking people is being trained for who-the-fuck-knows-what that we have to keep secret is making every instinct in my body scream. I don't like the guys off flying around to investigate, and I sure as hell don't like the results. Angelo wasn't overly descriptive, but I know by his tone that this was bad. He's not easily ruffled, unlike Reb, and the silence from Damon and Javier is nerve-wracking, too.

I've never been such a nervous Nelly; usually, I'm pretty collected other than when I lose my temper.

Being mated to multiple dudes is making me squishier than I'm comfortable with, and that irritates the fuck out of me. I cross my arms over my chest, looking up at the areas where they're hovering as my mind races through the possibilities. My foot taps as we wait for Damon to say something, anything, and I huff as the anxiety fills my veins. This is fucking torture and I'm about to lose my shit if we don't get news soon.

"Calm down, Wheels," Archie says as he comes up behind me and wraps his big arms around my waist. His cheek presses against my hair as he nuzzles me, likely comforting his animal with the contact.

"They're not newbs just because they didn't have Guardian training. Ang and D are soldiers in their own mob, and Javier is from a species that has to fight poachers at every turn. No one is untrained or lacks the ability to defend themselves."

I sigh, looking at the ground before I answer. His statements are accurate, and I know that, but this damn bond is fucking with my head. "I'm aware, Archie, but..." I rub my chest and frown as I continue. "I had no idea how much mating was going to affect me. When Reb and I are sent on missions, I don't feel like a piece of me is going to go missing if he gets injured. My pulse isn't racing like this... although, I guess it might in the future."

Rebel's gaze is hot on me; I can feel it. His jaw is probably clenching, and he's grinding his teeth like he does when he doesn't want to say something out loud. I know my longtime partner well enough to imagine his reaction without even raising my eyes to see it. He has to know that I'm right and our actual job will be infinitely harder after we bond.

But we're meant to be partners as well, and we will have to deal with it —that's how duo Guardians work.

"Sis, you haven't watched anyone but me handle their shit before. So I get why your bond is rebelling; you don't know what to expect." I look up and his light eyes find mine, the truth shining in them. "I know they can handle themselves or I wouldn't have agreed to stay down here with you two."

"Hey!"

Grinning, Rebel shrugs at Archie. "I didn't say you couldn't, man. They just have advantages you don't have in this arena. You shine one-on-one where your lion can do up close damage. Don't get twisted."

The lion rumbles against my back as some of the tension seeps out of me. I nod, knowing that my stepbrother wouldn't say shit he doesn't believe. He's honest with damn near everyone but himself, and our dance only lasted as long as it did because of societal hang-ups. Otherwise, he would have spoken up a lot sooner, I think. I need to have the faith in him that he has in my mates, and use that to help me get my shit under control. This isn't the time to be vulnerable and soft—it's the time to be harder and sharper, just in case.

I think I've got it locked down now, thanks to Reb's oddly calm reassurance.

Movement from the top sector catches my eye, and I turn in Archie's hold. "Look. Damon's making another circle. Do you think he's striking out or...?"

"I think he's changing angles," Reb says as he looks across the open space. "Whatever he was chasing on the top level ran out and now he's hoping to find something new."

Archie lets go of me and squints over to the south end of the complex. "Looks like Javi is almost done with his recon. He's really hard to see when he's not sparkling like Midas created him, but my cat vision sees the glimmers occasionally."

I wrinkle my nose, still dissatisfied with being on the 'stay put' team, despite our conversation. "This is interminable, by the way. I have no idea how Damon and Javi can be a support team like this. I'm itching like crazy."

"No surprise there," Rebel says with a rueful grin. "You're much more hyper before, during, and after assignments than you realize."

"Shut up. I am not." I shoot him a dirty look as I fluff the damn skirt of this dress out to give my hands something to do. "Besides, you're no better. You can't even behave when I'm driving a twenty-minute circuit in your car, buddy."

"It's my *car*," he grinds out as he glares at me. "I work hard on that damn thing and—"

"Guys, shhh!"

We whirl around to look at the blond hockey player and he shrugs. "There's a lot of people coming out of that main building."

My eyes widen as I whip my head back to look at the entrance. Arch is right; there's a slow trickle of people leaving the building. As they wait, cars are brought around, and some of them get in. I'm not sure where they're going, or even how big this damn dimension is, but I don't see anyone I recognize... yet.

This just got very interesting, and my men better have themselves hidden, or we're all screwed.

"THEY'RE COMING BACK NOW," Rebel says.

I don't stop pacing; in fact, I haven't since we watched Luca and that other demon guy, Lucian, exit the building. They took the same car, pulling away from the building in the long, sleek limo like Very Important People (TM). This entire scene is making my wings itch, and that's never a good sign. "Yeah, I see, Reb."

"Now, Wheels." My feline mate grins a bit, his expression just shy of patronizing. "You can't lose your shit here and now."

"I know."

"Nor can you explode on the guys when they land." My stepbrother is covering a laugh and I want to throttle him. "They'll tell us what they heard and saw one at a time. We can't listen to them talk simultaneously and catch all the info, you know."

Speak for yourself, Fae boy.

Of course, I know he means that he and Archie can't, nor can Javier. I'm pretty sure Damon is as neurodivergent as me, so he might multitask that way, but... Okay, stop. I have to calm the hamster in my brain down before I get so worked up that I won't be able to parse whatever they're saying, anyway.

"Fine, fine. I'm trying, but... who the fuck *are* all those people? I mean, guys... there were *so* many different species that poured out of that door. I saw enough raw power to raze a small village, you know?"

Archie sighs as he comes over and grips my arms loosely. "Rogue."

When he uses my real name, I know the kitty cat is serious. I stay still, trying to shake off the sparkling energy coursing through me. "I know. I need to calm down and go over the details without overreacting. Yes, this is bad and no, we don't know the extent."

"Right. And hey, the whole 'Mina and the Stuhlls' thing doesn't seem like a big deal anymore, right?"

I glare at Rebel, growling softly at his cheek. "Don't be a jackass. The Mina thing is still a big deal because she and her minions are actively trying to harm me. They're not as big as this because it feels like the end of the universe shit, but we can't figure this out if I'm dead, either."

"I think he was trying to distract you, Wheels," Archie says as he shakes his head. "Damn fine job, but here come the others. So maybe... breathe a little, and we'll get through this together, hmm?"

I don't know when he got so fucking Zen, but I could kiss this lion right now.

Blowing out a slow breath, I let his calm flow over me again. My eyes track the two demons headed for us, waiting for them to swoop in and land. I don't see Javi at all until he damn near appears in front of my eyes in a burst of golden beauty. Archie bends to grab his clothes, and the shiny bird transforms into a naked hot guy within seconds.

"Thanks, man," Javier says as he takes the pile from Archie and pulls his pants on. He catches me watching and winks playfully. "Later, Dragonfly. We've got serious shit to discuss, eh?"

"We sure as fuck do," Reb replies as the twins hit the ground and pad over to us. "Especially now that everyone is back."

Angelo grimaces, folding his wings in until they disappear. He watches Damon do the same and then rakes his hand through his dark hair. "This is a clusterfuck."

"Second that." Damon frowns, shaking his head. "That display was practically oozing ancient power. I could feel traces of it from the sky and no one was even trying to intimidate anyone. Those assholes were all just *that* old and powerful."

"So who the fuck were they?" I ask impatiently. "I saw Luca and that other dude you hate. I didn't recognize anyone else from wanted lists or media."

Rebel nods. "I was running the recent files we've gotten at HQ through my head, too, and I didn't know them, either. But yeah, I could tell they aren't people to take lightly."

Damon frowns as he rubs the back of his neck. "That's just it, guys. I didn't recognize any of them, either. The blond man and his...guards, I think... went back inside and I've never seen him before in my life. His face reminded me of something, but nothing from our parents' world. I can't place it."

"Yeah, that's the vibe I got from the idiots in the training arena. Something about them seemed familiar, but I couldn't put my finger on it." Angelo nods his agreement as he moves to kiss my cheek. "And they're dangerous as hell, that's for sure."

"What I saw was similar," Javier cuts in. "A lot of males, some females—many of the males look similar and humanoid, but they don't *move* or act like they're human. They're not shifters, I don't think, because they didn't give off the primal vibe. I think there might be some shifters here somewhere—that I can sense and I'm sure Arch can, too."

"Not from here," the lion grumbles. "We're too far, but I trust you, J-man."

"The other women and men by the door were various types of supes." We look at Damon and he shrugs. "I'm sure of that. I felt nature energy, so maybe magic users, and I definitely saw what I *believe* was a

Fae contingent. They were hooded, though. You saw them get into the Range Rover and head south, right?"

"I don't get why Luca and Lucian headed west like we did, and none of the others went that direction. The other seven cars went south, including that Rover you mentioned." Rebel looks frustrated as he turns in that direction. "What's in that direction? Why are all the others going there and how fucking big *is* this place?"

"All good questions," I murmur. "But I don't think we can answer them today. We need to get back to the stupid party so we can deal with our current issues, before we can deal with the bigger 'world domination' plotters." They give me unimpressed looks and I chuckle, shrugging as I let go of things I definitely can't control right now.

Sometimes, that's all you can do to keep from going completely over the deep end.

Enemies

DAMON

It's a long trudge back to the edge of the ghost town, and I stop my family before they enter it. Gathering my thoughts takes a second, which I can tell frustrates Rebel, but I need the conversation we had to come to a conclusion prior to accessing this gateway.

"The goal is to survive this damned meeting, find out what the Stuhlls are using the Sickos for, and then get home. Once we're no longer trapped in the atmosphere, we can decide how we're going to proceed and what we will share with our new friends, yes?" I turn my gaze on each of them, making sure my voice is firm so the Fae both understand that I'm serious. "Keep your tempers and your mouths under control in there. We want to blend, not cause issues that make our presence noticeable—no matter what."

My twin nods in agreement. "With this discovery, we should avoid Luca's and Lola's eyes as much as possible. They can't know we found out about this... whatever it is... until we're ready to reveal it. That may require some maneuvering when we get home to keep the Gemini organization bindings from interfering if D or I need to attend things, but it's imperative my parents have no idea we're clued in."

"Saying it a hundred times won't make it easier to do," Rogue mutters. "I know repetition is what sinks things in, but after I know what to do, that becomes white noise. I'm not being abrasive, either; Rebel can confirm how my brain works with business shit."

That's helpful, so I tuck it away for later.

"Got it. Is everyone else clear?" I ask. They all nod, and my pulse slows as that acknowledgment settles my anxiety. "Fine. Let's get out of here and finish what we started."

Before something else unexpected finishes us...

As soon as we step out of the portal, I know we made it just in time. It's hidden behind some of the equipment now lining the edge of the stage and we have to carefully make our way out of the maze they created in front of this spot. There are hundreds of various supernaturals milling around the ground floor area like the lawn of a huge concert, and it's easy to recognize many of the faces and groups filling the space. Every organization that has a death grip on Bay City, from mildly gray to pitch black, has their members present and accounted for.

This could be an extremely dangerous gathering if the rules didn't specifically prevent intra-organization violence at these things with their entry spells.

Shooting Angelo a look, I walk over to grab Rogue's hand, and wait until he takes the other before we wade into the mass of criminals, villains, and ne'er-do-wells waiting for our version of the *Legion of Doom* to grace the stage. I assume it will be a big production—the leaders all love feeling important—and the crowd will go bonkers with cheers and jeers as they take their places at the ornate table where their placards are neatly displayed. The podium in the middle will be shared; otherwise, it would create a power imbalance, so I guarantee every one of the asshole alphas, dons, and what have you will speak for at least a few minutes.

"This is insane," Reb grunts. "All these fuckers in one place without a single fight are unimaginable to the people we work for. They believe they're all out for themselves."

Ang snorts, his grin mischievous. "We are, but as humans formed factions, so did every other species. You know that; it's how the Society came together. Obviously, the bad guys have to do the same or they'll be crushed. None of these beings *like* one another, but we know there's strength in numbers."

"Plus, deals to be made," I add. "Demons ply their trade to supes at gatherings like this, as do Fae, magicals, and others. The *Sons* broker deals about the ports. The Stuhlls find new drivers or suckers to bring into their debt... it's how our world works without constant wars."

Rogue makes a face, then grumbles, "It explains why we can't find some targets, and how some lost ones stay invisible when their Guardians are called. They get snatched by your brethren or hunted down through cooperation."

"That doesn't happen all the time, though, right?" Archie says with a frown. "I mean, the lost ones are managed pretty closely."

Both Rebel and Rogue shrug, but it's the former who answers. "We aren't given numbers on that, but from what we're *told*, it's uncommon. I suppose we could be misled as easily as you guys are by your leaders, though. The local Councils can only relay to us what the regional and territory Society folks tell them and up the chain. The highest level of authority could definitely make sure that their narratives are the only ones we know."

Great, now I'm considering the 'good guys' as enemies, too. Anyone who controls the info flow like that can't be trusted for certain.

Archie echoes my thoughts before I can speak. "Shit. The good guys *and* the bad guys might be fucking with us. That sucks ass, dude. We can't trust anyone now."

Rebel arches a brow, his smirk knowing as he nods. "Yeah, that's where I've always lived, man. The circumstances of my placement at the Kellys have always been sketchy, as has her twin's disappearance. That's why I tell no one everything—I know there's rot in the tree that goes all the way to the roots."

"I knew you held back," Rogue murmurs as she squeezes my hand. I think Reb's admission is affecting her and I squeeze back to give her the support she clearly needs. "I'm not mad, but I'm a little hurt, even if I know *why* you did it."

His voice is barely intelligible as he replies, "I'm going to find him, sis. I promise on my life; I will find him for you."

Rogue's eyes widen, and she shakes her head. Her hand is gripping mine hard now and I sense the panic that fills my mate. "Reb, you *can't*. You know we can't. It's forbidden."

Arching a brow, I look between them, then to my twin, who shrugs. My gaze moves to Javier and Archie, noting they both look confused as well. Neither of them has ever mentioned that trying to find Reckoning was somehow not allowed. There's a story we've all been left out of, which doesn't surprise me, but now is not the time to ask for it. I clear my throat, breaking their intense stare, and wave my free hand at our surroundings.

"Not here. Later."

Immediately, Rogue's posture changes, going back to the stiff spined, badass we know and love. Her chin lifts and the air around her fills with confidence as if she simply flipped a switch. Her expression is now the 'game face' she wears while she's on the boards, and the strength flooding our bond must be what she taps when she's competing. "You're right, D. This is not the time or place for that discussion."

Her stepbrother takes the cue, adopting a brash sneer and looser stance as he surveys the crowded field. "Right. Time to work."

It occurs to me that these are the roles they take when they're training or on assignment—Rogue as the intimidating badass and Rebel projecting a lazy, playful attitude meant to disarm their prey. Watching them for a moment, I realize how well it must work; I can see the people around us shifting their attention to her while ignoring him as they move.

Damned impressive, but I didn't really expect otherwise with as hard as they train for their future roles.

"I didn't expect this damn party to be so intense," Javi says as we weave our way through the supes. "Maybe I underestimated it because I stay away from my folks' shit, and I'm not bound to positions like everyone else. Well, except for Archie, though he'll have a role, eventually."

"Not until my dads step down or..." He frowns and I give him a sympathetic look. "Well, if one of them dies, the rest would abdicate, so I'd get the alpha spot. Mom's always said that it was part of the agreement when she discovered her fateds were mixed cats rather than lions."

"They're fine. Don't let that worry you," I say as I see his expression darken. "It will not happen anytime soon."

His handsome features are marred by worry, and I realize Archie is the *only* one of us who would give a shit if one of his parents died. Ang and I would throw a party, Rogue and Reb let go of that illusion as teens, and Javi despises his folks. But Archer Glaser comes from a loving family, with multiple parents who adore every inch of him just as he is. He'll be crushed if anything ever happens to one of them. Luckily, shifters live a damned long time, but still.

We have to make sure he doesn't have to suffer that for as long as possible.

"Speaking of Sariah," Angelo says as we continue milling around. "Do you think there are reps from the Coalition here? There are a *lot* of shifters in this crowd, and I assume that, like the Fae, they're protecting their interests by attending."

"No way," Archie says firmly. "The Coalition of Shifters doesn't work with the gangs and shit. I can't believe they'd send people here—if they even know about this at all."

Rebel frowns, and I wait to see what he's going to say. He knows the same thing I do; any governing body that rejects finding out what their enemies are doing out of principle will eventually be infiltrated and taken over from within. The Coalition has been the 'lawful' collective body of shifters in Bay City for decades; there's zero chance they don't have spies in every organization in town.

"Babe?" Rogue says before Reb can open his mouth. "I adore that you're such a sweet, naïve lion, but that's fucking crazy."

The blond hockey star gives her an offended look. "What do you mean?"

"Everyone in every ruling class has spies in every opposing group everywhere. Yeah, that's vague, but even companies send moles to their competitors so they know what's up. Your assumption is that the Coalition is good, so they do nothing... shall we say, morally gray? But that would be foolish and unrealistic, babe. It would leave them vulnerable. They're not stupid."

Archie stops in place, his eyes cutting to the rest of us before he looks at Rogue again. "Well, fuck, Wheels. I mean... I didn't think about it like that. I'm not cut out for politics like that."

This time, I take the lead, letting go of Rogue's hand to walk over to the upset cat. I place my hand on his broad chest, my smile gentle. "That's okay, Arch. We're your family and some of us are *very* good at that stuff. We'll help you when the time comes. Got it?"

Angelo grins wickedly. "Hell, yeah, we are. We can *totally* be your war council, man. Those shifters won't know what the fuck hit them with us on your side."

"That's lovely, and I'm super touched by our *kumbaya* moment, but we need to focus again," Rebel says as he jerks his head towards the stage. "I think they're going to start."

"How do you know?" I ask curiously.

His response is a Fae-fanged grin as he shrugs. "I can feel it in my bones. Can't you?"

"No, and that's what worries me—unpredictable shit that might fucking kill us." I turn to Rogue, waiting to see if she's sporting the same, and I sigh when she is. "But I suppose we know who's coming first... the Fae fuckers."

This shit is making my horns twitch, and I don't like it one bit.

The Countdown

ROGUE

THE 'STAGE' explodes with a choreographed burst of lights, sound, and smoke, making me blanch in surprise. This isn't a fucking rock concert, and I have no idea why they'd want to startle an army of supes milling around with both enemies and friends. Responses around us range from 'prepared for battle' to 'cringing with pain' as the spectacle continues without missing a beat. My guys automatically step into what I assume is now their formation, encircling me like some incapable damsel, but I hold my tongue.

I can't blame them for being riled with that bullshit going on—it could be a distraction planned to cover many nefarious deeds.

"This is stupid," Javier mutters from his spot on the right. "And I say that coming from a family that sets the luncheon table with full European silver service to this day."

Snorting, I turn to give him an amused look. "Every time I forget how pampered you've been, you say shit like that and I cannot *believe* you're as normal as you are."

"Normal's relative, Wheels. Javi's still the fussiest of the group,"

Archie retorts from the seven o'clock position. "But that doesn't mean we don't love him."

"Aw, Arch." The lash batting purr makes me giggle and the tension I felt after the big televised wrestling opening number recedes. "You'll make me blush."

Rebel turns around, giving us all a stern expression as he grits his teeth. "Pay attention. That was only the opening salvo; people will enter now. We have to keep track of who belongs to what for later on."

He means me, of course, because my memory for visual input is stellar.

We all face the stage again, taking in the spotlights moving side-to-side and the smoke swirling around the proscenium. When the music dies down slightly, a loud, hokey announcer says, "Welllcommmme to the *third* Apalachin of the year, everyone! The leaders of the factions are pleased to host their loyal employees and members, plus any honored guests, vendors, and observers from the other realms."

I suck in a deep breath, realizing this is less like a mafia-style conclave than I thought. The pageantry and breadth of the event is amazing given the short timeframe for setup, and knowing they hold these fairly frequently is concerning. My eyes cut to Angelo, who is frowning in front of me as he watches this bullshit. It seems like he's not familiar with this format and *that* tells me something major has changed from the last one he knew of and now. Is that because of the mysterious entities who created the pocket dimension thing his father popped off to? Too many questions and not a single fucking answer so far; I don't like it.

"Now, to bring out your hosts." The voice pauses for effect and I roll my eyes. "The CEO of Roadrunner Racing, the menacing matron of the mafia... Merrrrrrraaaa Stuhhllllllll!"

Two thoughts fill my brain, overwhelming my ability to keep my face from showing my emotions: one, if this dude doesn't stop that WWE shit, I'm going to lose it and two, what the actual fuck is going on here? Merra Stuhll is striding out onto the stage, waving like the

Queen of England as her tiny legs carry her across the stage. Fennec foxes are small, and she's taller as a shifter, but even with her high heels and long line suit, it's obvious that she's not physically intimidating. That doesn't matter, though, because the sharp-toothed smirk and the glitter of evil in her eyes are enough to make the average supe quake in their boots.

Everyone knows this woman will have you chopped up into bits for looking at her wrong, then serve her crew the leftovers in a chili.

"If anyone could be near her, it wouldn't be hard to take her out within seconds," Reb mutters. "No wonder she's always surrounded by that loser she married and a crew built like brick fucking houses. She might be fast and handy with a weapon, but Merra Stuhll is vulnerable in person."

Archie puts his hand on my shoulder, squeezing before he replies, "Which is why she has to have her dirty work done by others. She's not a threat in person, other than retribution from her goons. Mina and the Sickos were chosen to not only send a message, but to distract us. I see it now, guys. I don't know how to explain it, but there's this... shifter sense that helps your animal make primal decisions. My lion is writing this woman off as we speak—he thinks she's weak."

"Of course he does, babe. He's a *lion*, and that's a miniature fox," Damon chuckles. "I'd be disappointed if he *didn't* write her off."

My handsome jock rumbles in frustration as he thinks. "No, it's not just about a fight, per se. It's... maybe it's the alpha-esque dominance thing? Like, she's all hat, no cattle, as the saying goes. With her minions, she can appear powerful and vicious, like many psychopaths. But my lion knows that deep down, she's weak in body and mind. Her behavior is cultivated to cover her deep flaws, and he's dismissing her."

As Merra rounds the long ass table, I note where she's been seated. She's a big deal in Bay City; as big as the Council or the Shifters Coalition, but her place is closer to the wings of stage right than to the podium. I don't know if that's because she's been downgraded in the criminal infrastructure or if that reflects how powerful the people before her are.

The implication is worrisome, at best.

"And now, our honored guest from Faerie, Julien Goldendash. Fiancé to the Midnight Court royal, Princess Celestine, and born of lineage to the royal security services for the Harvest Court. Our hosts welcome our shadowy trade facilitator, who makes fulfilling your Faerie needs possible!"

Reb's head swivels, looking back to catch my gaze with shock. The Council has been trying to impose sanctions on black market traders from Faerie for as long as we can remember—including those who deal in people. Reck, Reb, and I are *victims* of that supe trafficking, and the fucker helping them do it is next to *two* royal families. No wonder he's able to help smugglers get children, drugs, weapons, and more through the restricted portals. Hearing his family business, I know immediately where the goods are coming through—Harvest.

"Not now, sis," Reb mutters. "That asshole has it coming, but we can't do it now. I promise you we'll circle back, though. He deserves to be thoroughly interrogated by our bosses in the most painful way."

"No shit." My reply is harsh, but as much as Graciella and Odhran were neglectful and occasionally physical, they weren't the worst supes to adopt through this kind of shady shit. And like Reckoning, some have gone missing, some have been killed, and many are fucked up for life. "Put him on our 'blood debt' list, but let me fantasize about helping to peel him like a banana, okay?"

That makes Angelo and Damon rumble with excitement and the other two look at me with wide eyes. I don't have to turn to see their expressions; Javi and Archie are less familiar with my dark side than my stepbrother. The demon recognizes soul scarring, plus they saw me squash the trolls, so they're up to speed. I don't think my shifters will *mind*, but their reactions to my most vicious thoughts are amusing.

Pretty boys with gentle hearts are fun to be in charge of, after all.

The announcer moves on, introducing Axel Finn from the *Sons of the Seven Seas*, a mage named Thornberry from the *Eternal Shadows*, and a dark vampire from the *Sanguine Blade*. Those are all fairly well known 'bad guy' groups in the city, so I tuck their presence away in my expected column. I don't move as I mentally murmur to Rebel *~Think that Julien guy is their Hand of Morrigan rep?~*

~Without a doubt.~

Sighing, I watch the three criminals find their seats, chewing on my lower lip as the outer locations fill and we head towards the middle. The podium is definitely their 'center' and they're telling the crowd where all the groups stand in the broader rankings.

"Gracing us with their presence... Lady Volkov and our *l'Augere* partner, Baulaur Flăcăre. Other than our honored guests and hosts who have crossed realms to be here, they are the ones who traveled the longest distances from the shores of South America and the mountains of eastern Europe."

"Who the fuck is the Lady chick?" Angelo mutters as he frowns. "They didn't attach an organization, nor did they say what the hell she's doing here. I don't like that in the slightest."

Damon shifts at my back as he replies, "I dislike that our fucking father is obviously so high in their hierarchy. We're getting into the power brokers and realms that are less commonly crossed, I believe."

Nodding, as the music changes and the lights dim, I murmur, "Angelo is right. This is *much* worse than Luca scheming or Merra having someone kick my ass. I thought she'd done that because of street racing or maybe even running a book on the Derby. That's really what I thought we'd find out. But this? This is fucking huge and we can't even see all the webs yet."

"Put your hands together for our favorite incorporeal facilitator... Vissi Delice, the revenant from the *Icy Fingers!*"

A chilly breeze covers the entire crowd, and I rub my hands over my biceps. The chill pervades as the skeletal and ripped cloth draped being from the astral realm glides across the stage with glowing eyes. Swallowing hard, I try to shake off the effects of her power, but even as an Unseelie, she's far too close to death for comfort. Archie's warm palm squeezes my shoulder and I have to hold myself back from using one of the guys to regain the heat this bitch has stolen.

I don't want to deal with her or any of her brethren anytime soon.

Once she's settled next to the Volkov woman, the announcer goes on, "Next up, Zeke von Luptin, our honored guest from our partners in The Curators. He's well known throughout popular media for his more commonly used moniker... and he's just as big and bad as the tales claim."

"Yawn." Rebel growls as the huge, muscled wolf shifter comes strutting across the stage. He's from the Legendary realm, so I know that means we're gazing on the one and only Big Bad Wolf from centuries of stories. My stepbrother is never impressed by the storybook or legendary folks—he thinks most of them gained their deity level status when people didn't have the knowledge to discern between things, especially humans. "So what? He's a wolf, and he might have been in a lot of fucking myths, but he's hardly the only one. He's not even the *first* wolf shifter."

"There it is," I say with a small grin. Archie looks at me and I arch a brow. "You're one of his besties and you've never heard him rant about the legendaries being absolute bullshit? Lucky you, big guy. Rebel *hates* that the robed realm gave the big time heroes and muse influencers elevated status and access to that realm."

My stepbrother grunts as the wolf preens his way to his seat. "It's a prize for mediocrity disguised as an award for popularity. What's not to hate?"

"Lotta big words for 'I'm jealous', man," Angelo chuckles. "There aren't a lot of your kind in that land, right? Only Titania?"

"Shut up, Gemini. There are plenty of Fae, but even if there weren't, I wouldn't give a shit."

I think about it for a moment and tilt my head. "I think there's a hybrid named Jack who's a big deal in that realm. Half fairy, half giant, maybe? I remember seeing something on a cable a couple of months ago involving a kidnapping we chose not to get into."

"Ha, ha. You've all had your fun. Now shush until the rest of these fuckers are out here and we find out what they're planning," Rebel grinds out. "Otherwise, I'm turning people over my damn knee when we get home."

I can't decide if that's appealing or not—and I can tell I'm not the only one.

Bad News

REBEL

THE EXPRESSIONS on their faces are priceless—and it's not just my delectable sis looking unsure how much they'd enjoy my threat. I turn back to the stage, hiding the glee it gave me to see every one of my family members except Angelo shiver with anticipation. I know D is experimenting with being a switch with Arch, and that's fun to see... But his suppressed shudder at my words reveals a lot more than intended—as did my bratty woman's and the easygoing phoenix. I think roles in our group might be extremely flexible. Angelo and I should have a chat about it once we're out of this cesspool of corruption. Together, we'd be a perfect team to keep these eager switches in line.

Now I'm getting amped up and I have to picture the worst things I can think of to push it away.

I blow out a breath as the announcer continues his ridiculous call-outs, shaking off my horny thoughts for focus again.

"Next, we have Aetek Qax and Sciron, our honored guests from The Voiceless and Heavenly Plume."

Frowning as no one comes out, I look at my family and they shake their heads. They don't see these honored guests, either.

I'm about to call bullshit and laugh because two *very* important dickheads 'no showed' on Luca and his cronies when a burst of light and smoke on the stage makes me whip my head back to the scene. The light reveals a glowing demigod dressed like a rogue, with a dark smirk on his face. He waves, then blows kisses when a few whackos scream in excitement. By the time he's seated, another dramatic flare of energy and light with a cloud of sparkling dust precedes a tall purple being with tentacles coming from his back like Doc fucking Ock. He's —if that's the right pronoun 'cause I'm not sure—is wearing a weird space-inspired uniform as he strides past the screeching crowd to sit opposite the demi.

This shit is so out of control that I can't even imagine what the hell is going to come next.

"Someone from fucking space?" Rogue whispers in shock. "How damn far... I mean, I can't..."

"No shit," Angelo grunts. "Our father has been really goddamn busy, and I want to know how he's managing it without being caught. He's not sneaky enough for this level of shit, guys. Even Lola is out of her league here, but that doesn't mean they won't pretend they're not."

Damon grins as he adds, "This will be funny. They're obviously going last and they're definitely *not* the most powerful fuckers up there. I'm sure that will rankle some of the immense egos."

Nodding, I cross my arms over my chest as I study the current players and wait for the applause to die down, so the idiot calling the names will continue. As far as Society lore goes, the Galactic and Astral realms are uninterested in this plane. But two of their people are strutting around as guests for this farce, and that means even if the 'good guys' from those places don't give a fuck... their 'bad guys' do. Much of what I'm seeing tonight is contradicting what we learned, and that's why it's been able to grow into a movement of this size.

No one was looking for it.

"Reb, it's okay. We'll figure this out," Rogue murmurs as her hand lands on my shoulder blade. "And we might have allies to help. That's better than nothing, right?"

Sighing, my head drops as I consider her words. They're accurate, but the betrayal of our teachers and leaders is weighing heavily on me. I simply cannot believe that not one seer or psychic or even a fucking card reader had an inkling this was possible. And if they did, why didn't the Society adjust their training? Why put Guardians, agents, and all the other supes in such danger?

"Unless they couldn't say anything," I mutter. "Unless they were bound by the threads of time."

Angelo looks over at me, shooting a finger gun as he says, "Bingo, man."

"Don't say another word out loud," Javier interrupts before I can retort. "Trust me, my parents drilled it into me from the moment I could speak. You have to be insanely cautious about how you discuss the crones lest you change their whims."

"Words have power, and saying them can alter the course. Great," Archie says as he tugs on his blond locks. "When the hell is this guy going to bring the last two seats out so we can *not* be here contemplating the end of the damn world?"

As if he willed it into being, the announcer jerk starts up again. "And now for your most gracious, most benevolent hosts... the sexiest party-throwing demons in town... Luuuuuuuca and Loooolaaaa Gemi-niiiiiiii!"

What the hell? Who is missing from that seat without a damn nameplate?

The entrance music starts up again as the two demons who run the demon mob in Bay City flash big smiles and purposeful peeks at their 'assets' as they use the platform like a runway. Angelo and Damon groan simultaneously as their parents do the cringiest things possible, the latter ducking his head and covering his eyes in surrender. Both of the 'hosts' are behaving more like drunken college kids on spring break than the centuries old beings they are, and I can't blame the twins for wanting to gouge their eyes out.

Rogue moves from my side to Angelo's, looking up at him with an apologetic expression. "It's not weird to dislike seeing your mother dry humping the air as people throw gifts on stage, babe. This is pretty much the nightmare of every adult kid in the known universe."

"For real," Javier says as he shudders. "I can't even allow myself to consider how I was conceived, much less imagine my dad doing pelvic thrusts at screaming crowds."

Archie snorts as he rubs D's back. "My parents are pretty demonstrative, but shifters are touchy-feely, and this? This is more like aging rock star shit than anything else. Your folks have lost their marbles, guys."

"Tell us about it." Angelo growls his response, but it's not for us. His ire is at the gross spectacle his asshole parents are making of themselves because it's forcing him to see things he doesn't want to. "Someone tell me when it's over?"

I chuckle as he claps his hand over his eyes like his brother, accepting that I'm going to have to—

Wait a minute. Who the fuck is that?!

Squinting, I watch a sharp-eyed man with the gait of a predator emerge from backstage and quietly take a seat in the spot with no placard. He *looks* human, but clearly is not, and his strawberry curls are partly held back with a black ribbon. His clothes are from our realm—simple dress pants and an unremarkable blue oxford—and he's wearing thin, oval frames over his eyes. The effect is clearly to make him go unnoticed, to blend into the background with such vibrant supes nearby. But I can sense a threat and whoever the hell this son of a bitch is, he's one of the biggest problems on that platform.

"Rogue. Look at him, not the Geminis."

She heeds my whispers, and I watch as her head tilts. The crowd is still going nuts over the antics of the twins' parents, but my partner and I are watching the real show. Rogue licks her lips, then turns, frowning darkly. "That dude is powerful—enough so that he doesn't give a shit if people know who or what he is or even where he came from."

I grin. "Exactly. That's who we need to identify. The others, especially the guests, are priorities, but that one is the big cheese, sis. He's neck deep in this bullshit; I can feel it in my bones."

Javier makes an odd sound, and we blink. The phoenix flushes, surprise flittering over his features. "Uh, that... that doesn't happen often, guys."

"What does it mean, Javi?" Rogue asks softly.

His features scrunch up and he radiates conflicted emotions as he stares at the stage. "That's... it's one of the things we're not supposed to... Shit."

Uh-oh. We've run into some big species secret for the phoenixes.

Every species has powers and abilities they keep from the public, particularly mythicals. They're the tightest lipped of all, and Javier's parents follow insanely rigid protocols in relation to phoenix and mythical laws. They raised him in that atmosphere and he's never had his loyalties brush against one another quite so profoundly. Or, that's what I think, because I've never seen the guy look like he's going to barf if he finishes a sentence.

"You don't have to tell us if you can't," Damon says from where he's still hiding from the Gemini nonsense. "We'll understand, man."

Rogue moves to the bird shifter, lending her strength to the next of us to have an issue like its second nature. "Damon's right, Javi. If you can't tell us, you can't. No pressure."

Running his hand through his hair, I watch quietly as Javier sorts himself out. He shakes his limbs out like a duck emerging from the water, and it makes me grin. Shifters are always shifters, no matter how human they appear. Once he's settled, my old friend crooks his finger, so we all move as close as Rogue. His expression is serious as he murmurs low, "Several people on that stage have been... dead and brought back."

I blink, giving him a skeptical look. "Well, there's an Astral chick..."

"Not her. They're... I don't know, but it's not the same." Javier rubs his hands on his arms and shakes his head in agitation. The bird is obviously riding him *hard* as he mutters, "It's hard to explain, but you know how we..."

The gesture he makes confuses everyone but the twins. Angelo nods, and Damon snaps his fingers before saying, "Rise from the ashes?"

"Yes." Javi's eyes dart around and I wave my hand to increase the surrounding bubble. It won't stop everything from hearing, but it might muffle what they hear further. "That leaves a mark on you. Phoenixes can sense those marks in one another—how many times you've been born and died is correlated to your power level and place in the flock."

"Okay," Rogue says slowly. "But you can read it in others, too? Like that's what we're not supposed to know?"

My friend taps his nose, looking relieved that he didn't have to voice that information. "Usually it's just someone who was in a bad accident or had a medical issue or whatever, you know? But this? It's not that. The people who have been dead and come back up there... it's not zombies or specters because they're not dead *now*. They are alive, just like my kind—and as far as I know, *only* my kind—can be."

Hol-eee fuck-knuckles.

I bury my hands in my hair, tugging on it in frustration as I process that statement. Javier is saying that not only do we have a glut of combined evil on that fucking stage, we have people who might have conquered death. How much worse can this shit get? Did one of us break a goddamn ancient vase I don't know about?

"Reb, stop." This time my sister is back to me, pulling my face to look directly into her eyes. "Making yourself bald will neither help you drive faster—no matter *what* movies suggest—nor will it fix this giant fucking bomb that just dropped. Take a breath and push it down."

The gentle rebuke helps me swallow the panic that flared up in my heart. Rogue and I have always been able to mirror one another when needed because of our Fae connection. Remembering that helps me calm as I turn back to the upset bird who imparted his big secret. I let out another breath like she said, then reply, "How many, Javier?"

"At least three, but there's one who has done it twice. I've never seen that outside of my kind... not ever."

Just what we needed... three motherfuckers who aren't immortal, but can cheat death.

Money, Money, Money

ROGUE

THE CROWD finally calms as Lola takes her seat and Luca stands behind the podium looking smug as fuck. Being an elder demon, he doesn't tell the remaining chatterboxes to shut up—no, he snaps his fingers and a boom loud enough to rock the Grand Canyon makes everyone cower. It's not quite that bad for me and Reb, and I take note of the species who are also less affected for later. I feel like my brain is downloading a million things a minute at the moment, but I don't want any of it to escape.

We have to build a clear image of what we're up against, especially because it keeps getting worse.

"Good evening, fellow villains of Bay City!"

I make a surreptitious motion of gagging at my stepbrother, and he grins. Luca Gemini has *definitely* drank a metric *ton* of his own Kool-Aid and he thinks he's hot fucking shit. In this arena, he appears to be the big cheese, but that's by design. I'm pretty certain there are beings on that stage who could whip his ass without so much as breaking a sweat. However, they indulge his megalomania by keeping silent. Puzzling, but not much about today has made sense.

"When one or more of our members calls for one of these meetings, the protocols dictate they occur within a specific amount of time and the invitations are handled in the same way they have been for many years. You all received yours, with the requisite quests to locate our gathering, and those of you in front of me were worthy of attendance. For that, you should not be proud—it's your job, and anyone who failed the test is being handled by the cleaning crews."

A gasp echoes through the arena, but I don't see why they're shocked. Gangs are little more humane than human corporations—we're all cogs in their machines, and only those most valuable are kept from the consequences of failure. Even those cherished few will be fed to the scavengers if it benefits the assholes in charge; it's nothing new. My empathy triggers as emotions flood the supes surrounding us, and I frown as I realize some are now mourning family and friends they know they've just lost.

Cruelty is the point and Luca Gemini is feeding off of their misery from his perch on high.

"How did I write him off as a basic criminal with a power trip?" I mutter as I look at Damon. "I really didn't pay attention to what was happening with your family."

Damon shakes his head. "No, Ang and I never talked about it much when you were around. We're not nearly as happy with our future as we like to pretend. But covering it means we can keep anyone else from being sucked in—until now, obviously."

"Do not fret, criminals of Bay City. Anyone who has been taken, sealed their own fate. We do not mourn the inept; we strive to escape their fates." Luca pauses and his eyes flash with the demon inside. "Today we are honored to have not only our esteemed hosts—including myself and my wife—but honored guests in attendance. This gathering is brimming with the most powerful alliances we have made in decades, and we will discuss how this will help us expand our reach far beyond Bay City. *Are you with me?*"

Chaos fills the air, and it ignites the supes in the crowd immediately. Screams, howls, and cheering echo across the venue like a mega-pop star just stepped on stage. A rowdy shifter bumps into me, knocking me off balance and before I can even shove the asshole, Angelo is in front of me snarling a warning. Damon joins him, his eyes dark as he absorbs the power of the influenced supes. Since he is most *definitely* Luca's son, that magic is zooming over his frame like a live wire. I'm annoyed by their manhandling, but I also know D needs me to help him calm before his father senses his presence.

"Damon, it's okay. He was a rude motherfucker, but I'm not hurt." My voice is soft and soothing as I whisper in his ear, but it doesn't stop his horns and tail from emerging. I grimace, knowing the twins aren't supposed to reveal their entire demonic visage if they're not in battle or amongst the family. Looking over at Archie, I motion for him to sandwich the younger twin with me. Once we're pressed to both sides, I murmur, "You aren't him. Don't let this shit get under your skin. I know you can resist him. He's probably doing this to look cool for his stupid guests."

Pulling back, I look into his black eyes, cupping his face as Angelo and the others deal with the mosh pit of bodies losing their shit in Luca's grasp. Damon finally shudders and shakes his head, then looks at me with clarity. "Fuck, Sparkles. He's really laying it on thick. How come you're not...?"

"Mating thing?" Archie suggests as his chin rests on D's shoulder. "That'd be my guess. She's probably more immune to your guys' powers now. Luca's related, soooo..."

It's an excellent point, and he's probably right.

"I think Archie's correct. You know I can do... those things... now. The longer we're mated, the more I might be able to access." I give him a crooked smile. "Which is very helpful to know for later, right? Luca won't be able to wield his power over me effectively. We needed to find that out, so no harm, no foul."

That's when the burst of magic snaps back, and the supes stop clamoring for one another. Luca smirks again, dusting off his lapel as if he's barely even stretching himself to control that many beings at once. I don't have a clue whether that's true, but he's making a big show of it.

"Get this show on the road," Reb growls in irritation. "I've been to cults who spend less time indoctrinating people. This is ridiculous."

"Unfortunately, once the dickheads in charge get a mic, they have to be practically dragged out of the spotlight in every walk of life," Javier says. "It's no different with the 'good guys' meetings, I'd wager."

Reb and I exchange glances, and I laugh. "He's right. Society and Council meetings are interminable. But I'd love to get the fuck out of this dress and not have to worry about every damn person within range for a bit. So I, too, would like these fuckers to get it over with."

"Who is that guy without a name plate? That's been bugging the hell out of me." Archie frowns as he inclines his head a little. "No one has said a word about what his deal is."

"That worries me, too. He *looks* normal—almost human. But I don't think he is, and the others are steering clear of him in a way that is quite sus." I pull out my phone as I step back from Damon, aiming it at the stage. "Pictures of these idiots will help us plot out what we know."

Damon's horns and tail finally recede as he sighs in relief. "I can amend our scatter charts and files with them. Good plan."

"The future of our combined organizations will be profitable for *all* of us... but *only* if we are united. My fellow hosts and I have brokered alliances with like-minded groups across the realms over the past few years; this is the culmination of that long, hard work." Luca stops, looking at the other leaders, then back at the crowd. "It took immense sacrifices by many of our former comrades to secure these partnerships without raising suspicion. In the coming months, your loyalty will be tested by your individual leaders before you may know the bigger picture. However, for now, we will allow each of them to speak to you about their roles."

Hot damn, here we go.

"Julien Goldendash and Baulaur Flăcăre, please rise and address our members."

Luca steps back, waiting for the Fae and the mythical mercenary to stand. When they do, he moves to his seat next to Lola, settling in as they approach the podium. The Seelie taps his jaw with a finger, disregarding the microphone as he gives us all a shit-eating grin. His goldenrod hair and beard make him look like a supermodel, but the real tell is in his dark brown eyes. There's nothing warm about him on the inside—in fact, he's devoid of actual emotion as far as I can tell.

"Hello, Bay City," he says in a smooth baritone. "As your announcer said, I am Julien Goldendash. Before I share my information... *Ó chladach go cladach, ó bhuaic go buaic, ní labhróidh do bheola riamh. Is liomsa mo fhírinne, ní féidir leat a roinnt ar eagla go gcaillfidh tú d'oidhre lómhar. Má bhíonn sibh gann, beidh mo thoil láidir. gach rud a bhfuil grá agat, beidh sé imithe.**"

A burst of magic covers the crowd in pumpkin colored sparkles and I cough as I fight not to inhale. Our group moves together quickly, bending inward to get our faces out of the tricky Fae's bullshit, and I feel the wings of my twins spread over all our backs. Once I can breathe again, I look across our huddle with a dark expression. "That's fucking *illegal*! He can't hex an entire crowd of people to protect his pansy ass!"

"He can and he did," Javier says softly. "Legal or not, there's no way the others weren't complicit. I expect they'll all add their own flair to this temporary block to keep the attending supes from spreading rumors or being bribed."

"Are we affected by that?" I frown as I let my magic flow through me, checking for remnants of foreign bullshit floating around my aura. "I

---

* From shore to shore, from peak to peak, ne'er shall your lips doth speak. My truth is mine, you cannot share lest you lose your precious heir. If ye be barren, my will be strong. everything you hold dear, will be gone.

didn't plan on telling anyone outside of our new friends—maybe—but I don't want to be controlled by some traitorous dickbag, either."

Rebel growls low, his eyes flashing with Unseelie fury. "This will hurt, but I can counter it until we're in a place to remove the damn thing."

Nodding, I clench my fists at my side and look at the others. "You should know that when Reb says it will hurt—he's underselling it. Get ready."

The tension inside our huddle increases as violet streaks of magic shoot out from my stepbrother's fingers, working their way into all six of us. I swallow a scream as his powers flood my system, wrapping around fragments I couldn't see and insulating them. He's basically sealing the hex up in pockets of his own power, but it doesn't feel good, nor does my magic like it. There are matching grimaces on the faces of my other men, and by the time Rebel lets go, even he looks a bit wiped.

"We can stand up now," he says on a pant. "That asshole has to be tapping into the royal bloodline power, by the way. No way he's got that much juice. Probably why he married the princess."

Even in Faerie, women are used by social climbing knobs who want to steal their damn power; it's universal.

"That's a topic for later. He's gonna talk now," Archie rasps as he rubs his palms on his arms.

The wings pull away, and my family rises to our full height again. As I look around, I see the surrounding crowd looking dazed, and I grit my teeth. I don't care if they are all criminals—this is bullshit.

"Now that you're properly prepared, I am delighted to relay that I am the representative from a multi-species organization in Faerie. We are embedded throughout all four courts and facilitate all Fae-Earth realm smuggling. From our addictive concoctions to brutal weapons to alluring creatures and beings, and even intelligence. For the right price, we import your darkest desires." His grin turns wicked as he drops the next bomb. "Thanks to one of the other honored guests, we could demonstrate a *new* product today—did anyone hear about the orc?"

Mother of Odin, the damn thing was proof of concept—they can export enormous deadly creatures to other realms for use as weapons.

We are all screwed now.

Living Dead Girl

ANGELO

THE DECLARATION THAT OUR 'ORC EXPERIENCE' was a planned event makes my blood boil. It was dangerous and stupid to unleash that kind of ruthless being on unsuspecting, random folks. Luckily for the Fae in the marketplace and the royal contingents, there were two groups capable of handling the situation, but if there hadn't been? I have no idea how bad it would have been. The Prince and his caliphate are more than capable of dealing with something that powerful and they had help from a Fae prince—who is likely going to be forced to report the sighting, eventually.

These are the fools Luca is in bed with, and this is only the first idiot to speak—what terrible crap is coming after Goldendash?

"All queries about our new capabilities will run through our distinguished hosts for now. Once your loyalty is proven, you will negotiate with myself and my other colleagues' teams."

The whispers grow to a low hum as Goldendash steps back, giving the podium to Baulaur Flacăre. He's a brute, and I'd lay a fat dime that this guy is a dragon or some sort of hybrid with lizard in the mix. Silence falls as he stares at us all with one eye—the other is covered by a patch—until every single supe shuts their mouth. Once it's dead quiet, a deadly-looking scorpion tail sprouts from behind him, hanging over his shoulder with venom dripping from the end.

"I am Flăcăre of *l'Augere*." His booming voice echoes around us and I look over at Rebel as if to ask if he's ever seen a goddamn manticore in person. My friend shakes his head and we both scowl as we turn back to the man up front. "We are hunters. Our business is tracking, retrieval, capture, and elimination of targets. No other supernatural service has a one hundred percent success rate."

"Bit full of himself, isn't he?" Rogue mutters in a *very* low tone. "I didn't even know these people existed, so their rep can't be *that* good."

Damon winces, rubbing the back of his neck as he replies, "That's because they are so skilled that the good guys don't even know they're operating Sparkles."

Her eyes widen and I'm about to add my two cents when the squeaking of wheels draws us back to the stage. A minion dressed all in black has something chained to a dolly, head bagged, and completely prone as they wheel them out to the proscenium. Whoever this is, I doubt it's a random supe who skimmed from the wrong fucking mob boss. No, this is a big deal, and Luca looks *delighted* to be part of unveiling the surprise.

"Proof of concept for those who might doubt the expertise of *l'Augere*." Baulaur nods at the minion, who whips the bag off of the bound person. A collective gasp ripples through the arena, followed by stunned silence.

The supe in chains doesn't *look* like someone who should be an issue at first glance—unless you know who the asshole really is. Not everyone in this place is old enough to recognize him of course, but those who do, know that this vampire ran rampant through the human world for centuries. He's worn many faces and been called a multitude of apt monikers as he spent his long lifespan killing them under the guise of serial killers.

"The Society and all the Councils have been after this mother fucker since the Dark Ages," Reb hisses. "Every couple of decades he pops up, generating a new legend from the humans under another name... but it's always him. We all know it's always him." The Unseelie tugs at his hair, gritting his teeth to fight off the ingrained urge of Guardians to complete missions they know are open—even if they aren't assigned to them.

Rogue grabs my hand, squeezing hard enough to break my fingers, but I don't pull away. "I've always wondered how he stayed under the radar for so long. I mean, now that we're in the surveillance century, gadding about continents and creating famous killer personas is harder, right? He's had so many names over the centuries. I get why he eludes the humans, but... how has he been eluding the entire super-natural law enforcement community worldwide?"

"And how the actual fuck did *these* guys find him?" Javier says.

Archie hasn't said a word; he's just staring at the stage in shock. I reach over and poke his bicep as I say, "You okay there, buddy?"

He doesn't respond, just continues blinking at the unmasked preda-tor. After a few nerve-wracking moments, he shakes his head as if trying to clear it. "No. I mean, I'm *not* okay. This guy... Somewhere in the family lines of one of my dads is a victim. I grew up hearing stories about my grandpa trying to decipher even one of his personas so he could locate him. I can't fucking *believe* this son of a bitch caught Vlad."

Rogue lets go, moving to our friend quickly. "I didn't know that, Arch."

"No need to mention it. The victim was way back in like... the 70s. It's a half century ago, Wheels. I sure as fuck didn't know them, so I can't be mad about it. Seeing him chained is like your family ghost stories come to life, you know? Bizarre as hell."

"I get it, buddy," Rebel says. "I'd be shocked in your place, too."

Damon and I look at one another, and I sigh. "Well, we both remember most of his lifespan and his crimes. This is a *very* effective marketing tool, much like the orc was. I wonder what—"

The hunter stomps his foot on the stage, and the force of it echoes through the arena. "Now that you have seen what we are capable of... I will sting this miserable fool. He has been approached by many groups, many times throughout his life, and he has denied their requests to stop bringing attention that could reveal our kind to the humans. Both the light and the dark have tried to mediate his madness without success. This is his penance and his final judgement day."

They're going to kill him? On stage?!

Baulaur's tail moves like lightning, striking the chained vamp in the shoulder. A loud moan escapes the elder supe's mouth as pain and the venom from the manticore sink in. "I will let him wither while my colleagues take their places for their own demonstrations. You have been warned about what traitors may face—and that there is nowhere you can hide from *l'Augere.*"

"Anyone know what the hell that is doing to him?" Archie asks as he continues to watch the vampire.

"Draining him very slowly and painfully until he's at his weakest point... then someone will, like, take his head and stake his heart," Javier murmurs. "The venom wouldn't kill a vampire outright, but it will make him regret his choices until someone does."

"Mythicals are fucking vicious," Damon adds. "Especially those who operate outside of the law. I'm not surprised by this display, other than their ability to locate one of the most famous fugitives ten times over. Honestly, if he'd kept one name or close to it, he might have become a storybook."

"True," I reply. "Most of his aliases are modern legends. He fucked up ascending to actual immortality by being too interested in scaring the fuck out of humans."

"Guys... shhh," Rogue says as she turns away from our leonine friend. "Look."

The stage darkens a bit as Baulaur sits down, and two females rise from their chairs. I squint at the one they called 'Lady Volkov' as she follows the revenant introduced as Vissi Delice. I've met no one from the Astral realm—and I can't say I know anyone else who has, either. Luca always said they keep to themselves and handle their business without interacting with the masses. That meant demons, shifters, and all the supes who roam the more traveled realms, of course, but I figured they were just weirdo introverts or snobs.

I was definitely wrong.

"Good evening, ne'er-do-wells of Bay City. My name is Lady Volkov and I represent a faction from this realm that rarely deals with non-humans. My organization has always had strong ties to the supernatural community through our beloved leader, but he has become... short sighted. My like-minded peers and I will take over the organization eventually, and when that happens, the service we provide to your world and the human world will merge into something *much* bigger."

Frowning, I look over at Rebel, who shrugs. He's not aware of their shit, either. It's like Luca and Lola assembled every under the radar villain in existence, then built a flying lair in the swamp to house them. "She's human. This is so many levels of illegal..."

"No shit," Rogue grits out as she stares at the woman who resembles an old school Russian honey-trap from a spy movie. "The urge to deal with her is as strong as it was with Goldenash. I didn't feel it with the manticore because... Vlad deserves to die for his crimes."

"Agreed." The other Fae stares at the stage before he flicks his gaze back to us. "The Astral woman interests me. We're taught very little about the less connected realms like hers. No wonder no one has seen this shit coming—it's tapping resources no one would even consider possible."

"I am Visssiiiii Deeeellllliiiiccccce." A collective chill falls over us as the skeletal woman points herself at the crowd. Bony fingers grasp the podium and the wind kicks up, swirling that icy breeze around until I shiver. "The powers of the *Icy Fingers* are not as tangible as my predecessors. But we are legion, and we can raise things that should not be raised. Your enemies will go mad and armies will be formed should you choose to explore our services."

I've never seen a skull smirk, but there's a first time for everything. Vissi points a single finger at the vampire struggling in his bonds, and his skin wrinkles, pulling tight on his bones. The agonized cries fade as he ages—something his kind should not be able to do—so quickly that he's nothing more than an empty husk. The revenant dips her head, then moves away from the microphone to her seat without another word.

"Holy—"

"There was *nothing* holy about that." Rogue cuts me off and I nod in agreement. "That shit is fucked up. Can you imagine her just... reverse Dorian Grey'ing people all over for money? This is a goddamn disaster."

"I'm more worried about the armies comment," Rebel admits. "I don't know if she's talking about World War Z or just... hell, I don't know. But zombie armies are *never* good."

"If any of you assholes get bitten, you'd better tell someone," Archie warns. "Because I will absolutely set you all on fire if I have to."

I squint at him, my lips curving up. "Arch... are you *afraid* of zombies? You're a fucking *lion,* man."

He socks me in the arm, his expression firm. "I do not. like. things. that are. dead. moving. Leave it at that."

"Okay, but—"

"Angelo, don't bully him," our girl says as she gives everyone but the big scaredy cat an evil glare. "The rest of you be nice, too. Remember how badly Gui creeps us out, even though he's pretty cool? Everyone has fears."

"Giant spiders are real, zombies are *not,*" Javier says, as he chuckles. "That's irrational."

"Uh, all fears are irrational, and according to Bone Lady, zombie armies are a thing." Rogue leans in to stick her tongue out at the phoenix and I sigh.

"At least we're all still having fun as the world flips upside down."

Damon laughs, bumping my shoulder with his. "Bro, if we're only halfway through this nonsense and it's this bad? Laughter is probably the best we can do, so we don't cry. We've always said the worst thing that could happen is Luca getting more power in Hell. It's pretty clear Hell isn't his end game anymore."

My twin is right—and that's much more terrifying than theoretical zombie armies.

Traitor

ROGUE

—

OUR JOKING IS the only way we can cope with so much hidden bullshit being revealed piece by piece before our eyes. Reb and I are the most connected to the Society—the global government that reigns over supernaturals through Councils and reps from most species—and this is beyond shocking to us. It's a major blind spot to find out about from the small-time criminal leaders of one large city in this country. If the training we receive to be Guardians is the same across the globe, then what seems like a slight possibility of missed information becomes much more terrifying.

It's a lot to take in and we don't even know if we can make anyone aware of our discovery—not with this rogue's gallery of embedded assholes on the stage.

"You're frowning, babe," Archie says softly. "We're supposed to look thrilled if people glance at us."

Huffing in annoyance, I paste a fake smile on again as the audience waits for the crew to clean up the remnants of Delice's display. Once it's done, the lights come up again on the stage and two more of the seated villains rise to their feet. This time, it's Eratz Thornberry from the Eternal Shadows and Dmitri Ashenfeld from the Sanguine Blade.

The mage and the vampire stand in front of the podium looking less than impressed with the order of their appearance. Following the revenant's demonstration means they won't look nearly as powerful, but anyone who thinks so is mistaken.

"We deal with these assholes all the time," Rebel says as the two men glare at the audience menacingly. "Their strength isn't in massive individual powers; it's in their numbers and combined capabilities. People look at mages and vampires as 'normal' in our realm, so they don't assume malicious intent until it's too late. Plus, when they form teams, it makes them very difficult to thwart."

I nod, looking at Javi and the twins. "He's right. Since most Guardians work solo unless they are on specialized teams like those tasked with elimination or retrieval, it's dangerous when the criminal elements based here are organized enough for that. We're often honed into more dangerous, capable protectors, but anyone can fall to a coordinated effort."

"Good evening, Bay City," Dmitri rumbles in his thickly accented voice. "My associate and I may not possess powers from the other realms, but we are legion in comparison. Our recruitment efforts over the past three centuries dwarf those of the law-abiding, and we have double agents embedded all over the globe in every walk of life. Our sleepers can be activated for everything from espionage to political aims to eliminations. We are not known to non-supernaturals, nor would anything we do be traced to our groups."

That causes doubtful murmurs to echo over the large group, and the hawk-nosed mage takes over. "We have data to confirm those claims, which is how we were accepted as members of this long-term effort. You will not be privy to that proof until you complete your loyalty tests and are inducted by your leaders. However, once you are, you will vie for the honor of our services."

Eratz looks at us with a confidence that is almost chilling, and then he and Dmitri head back to their seats. I guess they figured if they couldn't perform an awe-inspiring trick like the others, then being supremely arrogant would convey their power. It's not a bad strategy, but it won't gain them customers until they can show that elusive proof. Criminals are distrustful by necessity, and no gang or group will contract to elements they can't verify.

"How much longer is this going to go on?" Javier says, as he looks at the surrounding supes. "Unless they have flashy stuff like the Icy Fingers chick, I think they will lose people soon."

Damon looks up from his phone where he's taking notes again. "Counting the unannounced one, there are four more. I believe they will be guests that produce what is needed, though."

As he finishes, the very attractive dark-haired demi-god and the purple... whatever... stand up and move to the podium. Sciron puts his glowing hands on it, smirking as he looks out at everyone. "Hello, minions! I'm Sciron of the Heavenly Wings, and the very interesting fellow beside me is Aetek Qax from The Voiceless. Aetek speaks over four hundred languages, but since Earth languages are so primitive, he has avoided learning any. That means I'm in charge of talking."

Qax's tentacles shake and I squint until I figure out that he must be laughing at the demi's statement. I guess he *understands* primitive language, then. Sciron must have meant the galactic realm being doesn't physically speak them. Odd distinction, but I don't know that I'd want to come here if I lived in some future tech, less shitty realm. At least, I assume that's what his home is like—a Star Trek-esque high intelligence and evolved place where species aren't dicks like here.

I guess his presence here offering bad shit nixes that idea, though. Damn.

"Aetek and I are only available to the most elite tiers. But if you've dreamed it—in our realms it is likely possible. The Void and Heavenly wings operate on the global and celestial scale—our abilities and projects will impact the very fabric of reality." Sciron makes a ball of sparkling light appear in his palm. It turns into a globe, spinning as it changes the shape of continents and countries, then expands into a galaxy of stars that twinkle. "Regardless of your passing the loyalty test, there are entirely different things you must do to be granted an audience with either of us."

His words garner grumbling that gets louder as the two snots stare into the rapidly darkening night around us. When no one dares to question him, the golden demi and the alien leave the podium. They are quickly replaced by the strawberry blond man who has not been named and Luca, both looking supremely pleased with themselves. I realize they skipped von Luptin, and I'm uncertain why. He looks okay with it as he drums his fingers on the table manically, but who am I to judge?

"Our allies are many, criminals of Bay City, and we are joining something that will transform our world. The gentleman beside me needs no name—however, he is one of the architects of this movement. His reach is beyond that of most groups in our realm, and that allowed him to collect the various representatives you see here together."

Luca pauses, looking out with a determined expression. "Your leaders have agreed for generations that the balance is no longer equivalent. The other side put their fingers on the scale and continue to do so through our own corrupt governments. Our partnership will be the first step to changing that injustice."

Prying my eyes from the two men, I look at my mates, worry etched into my face. "Luca just became a lot more dangerous."

The twins nod, shaking their heads before they reply, "We thought we had time before he went completely batshit."

That time has obviously run out.

When the spectacle on the stage concludes, the big wigs disappear fast enough to leave metaphorical tracks in their wake. Even Luca and Lola go up in a puff of sulfur, which tells me that none of them want to be questioned by their own people. At least, not at the moment, because they have their little playgrounds to go party in for the rest of the night.

I, however, want nothing more than to get the fuck out of this damn place. Turning to Rebel, I blow out a breath of relief. "I don't know if I think that was anticlimactic or completely unhinged because I'm *exhausted*."

He nods, rubbing the back of his neck. "I agree. We've witnessed so many things in such a short time that processing any of it until we've recovered is unlikely. This was... *a lot*."

Angelo and Damon flank me, taking my arms. The elder twin nods at Rebel, his expression dark. "Let's take our mate home, get this fancy stuff off, eat, and discuss everything. If we can avoid any surprises or enemies along the way, that would be great."

"Our luck isn't good enough for our exit to be graceful," I remind him. "But if we're careful, we might not have any battles at least."

Together, we move through the dispersing crowd quickly, leaving the gathering area to walk along the paths we took before. Damon seems to remember the exact route, so I let him guide Angelo and I past the various entry points to the makeshift 'realms'. Javier, Rebel, and Archie are behind us, making sure that no one can sneak up on our family as we head for the portal.

"Damon?" I say as we hustle through the walkway. "Did you get everything?"

He winks at me, his grin knowing. "I believe I did, Sparkles. If I missed something, it's too late now. I have zero desire to stop in *any* of the mini-realms to find out; how about you?"

"Absolutely not." I shudder at the thought. "This has been the longest fucking day ever, and I want to relax for ten seconds without wondering if someone's going to attack."

Angelo pats my arm. "I don't blame you. I've been to events like this in the past, but nothing has ever risen to this level. Luca must have had an entire team of goons working on it twenty-four-seven for the past few weeks. Being with you and the rest of our group kept me away long enough for him to arrange all this shit."

"Well, that and the other 'hosts' probably had a hand in it." I smile at Javier's addition because he has a different viewpoint than the twins, and he often sees things that escape those of us who are geared towards the dark side. "I can't imagine he contributed all the money and labor. From what you've shared, he's far too full of himself to do that."

"You're spot on, Javi. Luca is both extravagant and cheap simultaneously." Damon grins as we approach the mansion we entered at the start of this journey. "He would insist that his partners contribute as much, if not more, than he did, especially if he was instrumental in arranging this whole 'allies' thing. That would explain why we heard nothing about it."

"You *hope* that's why," Angelo grumbles. "Otherwise, we have a big problem because he's cutting us out and we lose all of our access to the bad shit they're planning."

Biting my lip, I look up at Ang. "What if you *aren't* cut out, but he's going to make you go through whatever the hell this 'loyalty' test is? Do you think he'd get rid of his heirs if they fail? Could you fail? What the hell is it, even?"

Rebel snorts. "Sis, I don't think we can answer *any* of those questions based on this stupid meeting."

"Yeah," Damon mutters. "Before this show? I would have said that Luca wouldn't risk it and wouldn't allow us to take part in something that could eliminate Angelo, at the least. But now? These fuckers could be bargaining with other realms to make heirs completely unnecessary. I have no idea what the hell he's thinking."

Angelo grimaces as we enter the mansion and make our way through the rooms until we hit the front door. When we get to it, he puts his hand on the knob, looking at all of us seriously. "D and Rebel have a point. Until proven otherwise, we should assume that even my father might try to eliminate us."

Well, that's just fucking peachy. The entire world might want us dead.

Our House

ARCHER

WHEN I HIT the front porch of our house, I sigh in relief. To be honest, I was a little concerned we'd be followed and attacked, but we made it here without a hitch. Rebel throws open the door, holding it for Rogue and the twins as they hustle inside. Javi and I are the last ones to enter, and I make one hundred percent certain the entire security system is engaged before I take the stairs to my room. The others made beelines for theirs, eager to shed the fancy clothes and get the stench of villainy off themselves.

I'm happy to be stripping, too. That meeting left me feeling filthy as hell just by being in the presence of those assholes.

"Meet downstairs in ten?"

The shouted question comes from Angelo's room, and I chuckle to myself. He's gotta be losing his mind knowing his old man has been slipping this shit past him and D for *decades*. Angelo hates losing control and Damon despises being out of the loop. Both twins have had their world rocked off-kilter pretty hardcore, and so have our Fae family members. Only Javier and I were left out of the 'bosses lying to us forever' club, which means we're the least emotional right now. It's not uncommon for the twins or Rebel to be furious and illogical, but when it includes Rogue, we have to help balance the strain.

"I'll be there!" I yell out my door as I head for a quick shower. As much as I would have enjoyed showering with a plus one or two, this needs to be quick. Running down everything while it's still fresh will help us form a plan—we've been waiting for this damn event and now that it's over, we have to decide how to proceed.

"Got it!"

"Okay!"

Turning on the water as I hear Damon and Javier reply, I test the temperature, then shed my clothes. They land on the floor of the bathroom in a heap, and I kick them away to the bedroom so I can step into scalding hot water. Sighing as it hits me, I wonder why Reb and Rogue didn't answer, though I suppose maybe they were already in their showers. Rogue will *definitely* want to get all the makeup and hair stuff cleaned off as quickly as possible. Our girl can do fancy, but she loves being alfresco more than anything else. She adores hanging out in comfy clothes with her hair out of her face—and it looks just as hot as when she's dolled up.

I'll take my mate anyway I can get her, and I won't utter a word of complaint.

I run through the mechanics of my shower as quickly as I can, getting the grime from being amongst that many people off of my skin. Once I'm done, I step out, wrapping a towel around my waist as I head to my dresser to pull out lounging clothes. Rogue likes when she can see our bodies—even if she won't say so—so I grab a white tank and sweats. Yanking them on without a thought to anything underneath, I look in the mirror. My hair is wet and crazy, so I run my fingers through it until it's not ridiculous.

"Okay, Archie... You don't smell like nasty, sweaty crowds and you're not bound up in dress clothes." I don't talk to myself a lot, but as I stand here looking at my reflection, it feels right. "Your mate and your... boyfriend... are waiting for you. You need food and booze and sex... in whatever order you can get them, because there's serious shit afoot. Focus like you're on the line until you reach the goal."

"Dude, what the fuck?"

Whirling around at the amused tone, I glare at Angelo. "Shut up, man. I'm getting my swagger on."

He snorts, shaking his head at me. "Is this what you do before games?"

"Usually not out loud, but I'm trying something new. Fuck off." My growl isn't really one of anger, but embarrassment, and I want him to take the hint.

"Okay, dude. But it's time to get your ass in gear whether you've got your 'swagger' or not. D and the Fae are already down there waiting." The elder demon smirks, amusement still flittering over his features. "Javier is in the kitchen, unsurprisingly."

I thought I was super fucking quick, but I'm almost the last one. How is that possible?

"Fine, I'm coming," I reply as I step back and walk out of my room to follow him. "But quit ribbing me, Ang. We've all had a bunch of shit thrown at us in the past day—hell, weeks. I'm not the target you want to aim for, not really."

Sighing, he jogs down the stairs in front of me with slumped shoulders. "You're right. I'd like to beat the shit out of a lot of people, but you aren't one of them. We share a mate, we've been friends forever, and you've made my brother happy as shit. I think that means you're on the good list for a while."

My face turns red; I can feel it. "Thanks, man. I mean, I'm just glad it's not... weird for you."

"Uh, it *is* pretty fucking strange, but... how could I possibly miss the affection? My twin and my friend are fucking and it brings them both obvious joy. I'd be a super dick if I took issue with it." Angelo gives me a wicked grin. "Plus, our mate *loves* it, and loves that you two are enjoying yourselves. That's like... a triple play of good shit, you know?"

When he puts it that way, I feel stupid for even asking.

"Luca and Lola would be horrified at how fucking great you two turned out. I'm sure they did their damndest to make you both uber shitheads like them." I grin at the vengeance demon and he turns to bump fists with me when we get to the bottom of the stairs.

"Yeah, it's probably why we were maneuvered around for years while he set that little production up."

We round the corner from the foyer as we move to the kitchen, and the noise coming from it makes my heart thump. My parents formed a large pride together around my mom, and as each sibling was added, the general noise and chaos increased. I thrive in that atmosphere and now that we've won over Rogue, this house finally feels like my home. I have my own pride—different but equally amazing—and the lion inside me is so pleased that I have to stop myself from letting out a roar of triumph.

"What's with the 'grr', Archie?" Rogue says as Angelo and I join the ruckus.

My hand flies to my face and I realize the big cat shifted a little of it while he was preening. "My lion really enjoys having our whole family together in the house. He thinks of this like *my* pride—you know, like my mom has."

Rebel and Rogue share a look, and I know that's because out of all of us, they had the least 'family' atmosphere in their home. Their adoptive parents need to be hung by their toes and bled out, but that's a 'later' idea. We can't deal with Graciella and Odhran when we have total world chaos on the horizon. They're not important enough to worry about *now*. But mark my words, for the way they broke my friend and my mate, I will eventually make them pay.

"I know that feels off to you," I say as I meet Rogue's gaze. "But you'll get used to it."

A beeping on the stove interrupts and Javier says, "I'm cooking, so you need to set the dishes and flatware out. You know the rules, folks. If I make the food and drinks, everything else is on you."

My lips curve up at his firm admonishment. "I'll get the plates if the twins get the other stuff."

"I've got glasses," Rogue jumps in, walking past me with a hip bump. "After all, I'm a lioness now."

Laughing, I shake my head. "Definitely not, babe. But you rule the roost here, and I won't ever say otherwise."

Rebel finally finds his tongue, grunting, "We're not eating at the table, Javi. I know you like shit to be just so, but... we deserve to be comfortable as we digest all this shit. The living room has all our notes and the boards we're pinning things on. It will be easier if we eat there."

The phoenix blinks at his gruff tone and pauses in his chef duties. "Reb, I don't actually give a fuck where we eat. I only insisted on it before, so we'd all eat together. Before Dragonfly moved in, everyone would grab shit and run off. It was the best way to keep us all together with our crazy schedules."

Oh, that sneaky fuck. Maybe phoenixes aren't the most rigid fuckers on the planet after all.

Rogue looks at him, then back at the rest of us, then she snorts. The one snort becomes a laugh, then she devolves into giggles as she clutches her stomach. "I... I can't believe... Javi tricked you all into this whole group thing by acting like the prissy bird you thought he was. And you fell for it..."

That makes Reb scowl darkly, and he strides toward the island. "You are a son of a bitch, King. You could have just said you wanted to eat together."

Turning back to the stove to flip something in a pan, Javier shakes his head. "I did that. But you guys were all on missions to self-destruct or something. Reb was always rushing out to his car. Arch was always at the rink practicing. Damon buried himself in his room and Angelo took off to do whatever Luca wanted. I couldn't get you guys to see that we were sort of... I don't know. Marching in place, maybe?"

I think about what he's saying, trying to be honest with myself. Before the night Mina attacked Rogue, I spent a lot of time at the rink even when there wasn't practice. We went out on the weekends, but during the week? We all headed in different directions except for when Javier was off. We all knew he'd throw an absolute fit if we weren't at the table when he was ready to serve. My friend might be cranky, but he's got us nailed.

"I didn't realize you guys were... not hanging as much?" Rogue says with a frown. "Why? You're all busy, sure, but why did that cause you to live together but drift apart? Why did Javi have to force you all together?"

Rebel dips his chin, looking at the ground. "That's my fault. I couldn't admit how I felt, and that meant we never brought you to this place where we'd built a damn room for you. It must have made us all pull apart to do our own thing, so we could avoid having that conversation."

"Yeah," Angelo agrees. "It did. I wanted to keep Luca away from Damon and I focused on that instead of the fact that I was pissed we didn't follow through with asking you to move in. I couldn't force Rebel to do anything he didn't want to, but I also couldn't help resenting the absence. I think."

Damon nods. "You were always our glue, Sparkles, even as kids. I mean... how many other kids your age had an older group of guys ready to beat down the universe every time someone upset you? Only you, as far as I know, and that's because this was meant to be. All of us, I mean."

She flushes bright pink, swatting at the nearest person—which is me. "You can all stop this shit right now. I won't be able to eat if you don't quit making me mushy, and I definitely won't be able to talk about this bullshit we just endured to make a plan. I have to focus."

That's fine for now, but as soon as that shit's done? Her pretty pink skin is going on display or I'm going to riot in my own house.

Harder, Better, Stronger, Faster

ROGUE

JAVIER WHIPPED the others into shape quickly, and we could settle in the living room with our food. I'm chowing down like I haven't eaten in days, but I bet that's because I spent so much energy being hyper aware and moving around that damn evil fairground while we sleuth'd. The guys are eating just as ravenously, so I guess they worked up an appetite, too. It probably would have been better if we'd eaten while we were there, except I was scared as fuck about being goddamn poisoned.

"You know, we'd eat nothing but takeout if it weren't for you," I say as I smile at the quiet phoenix. "I really appreciate everything you do."

He ducks his head as the smile creeps over his handsome face. "I enjoy it. But I worry you were eating poorly before we moved you into our house."

I chuckle as I spear another bite. "I did okay. Besides, you don't have to fret about it now, right?"

Rebel snickers, shaking his head. "She ate trash unless she was dating people who cooked; I guarantee it. I didn't hang at that apartment, but the whole 'Betty Crocker' thing isn't really our girl's deal."

I throw a potato at him, scowling as they all laugh. "Everyone has unique skill sets, Reb. Mine aren't the traditional female stuff, but I'm definitely the person you want in scrappier situations. Plus, I'm funny as fuck."

"Okay, okay. Enough of that shit," Angelo says as he sips his drink. "Let's get this bullshit over with. I feel like the Apalachin has been a looming specter in our lives for way too long and now it's over. Everything is so much worse, but it's over. Life will move on tomorrow and we have to move with it."

"This is much bigger than we could have imagined, Ang. I don't have a clue how we're going to fight... any of it. Even if Reb and I told our bosses everything? It would still be too big, because they can't guarantee that your dad and all those fuckers from all over don't have plants in the Society. They certainly do in the Councils... that much is blatant."

Damon sets his plate aside, then runs his hand through his hair. "Agreed. There's no way this thing could have been put together in that short of a time without people greasing the wheels on the legitimate side of things. I've never been privy to the ones in the past, but I assume you've heard about that, Ang?"

The elder twin shakes his head. "No. Luca never needed me to work on prep for these, only make appearances. And it wasn't... as elaborate as this, so I couldn't have warned you guys. This is the first one that's been that highly attended and vastly designed. The scale was surprising."

"What do we do, then?" Rebel asks as he leans forward with his elbows on his knees. "We can't tell the good guys, and we can't stop this shit alone. I mean, there's a fucking trike coming, plus Rogue's matches. Regular life will not pause for this because most people don't even know what's coming."

"My matches will be fine, Rebel." I shrug before taking another bite of dinner. "If we follow the protocols you guys set up before this dumb gathering, everyone will be in public places when they are at work or practice. Yes, the race is a huge blind spot and we'll have to deal with that issue as it gets closer. But Archie, Javi, and I are probably going to be okay going to our normal stuff as long as we're accompanied to and from."

That gives them pause, but Archie is the one to state the obvious. "Damon and Ang won't be. At least, they're going to be a lot *less* safe. You and Rebel will be in more danger than usual if the Society assigns you tasks. You'll be fine—theoretically—at training, but not in the field."

"They don't put us in the field often because we're waiting on a charge." Rebel frowns, then continues. "I suppose if they escalate that, it will confirm our fears about moles. Traitors would want to place us in harm's way as much as possible, so someone could do their job for them."

I hadn't considered that, and now my brain is racing with the possibilities.

"Just fucking perfect," I mutter as I grab the fruity thing Javi made me. "Now I'm going to question everyone I see in the building, everyone in the parking lot, and everyone who contacts us. But I guess it's not paranoia if they really are out to get us, right?"

"Truth." Javier bites his lower lip, looking thoughtful for a second. "You know, I'm pretty sure we need to take some people off the board or we'll never be able to function. I'm not saying we need to *kill* them, but we definitely have to prune this shit down a bit."

"Javi's right." The elder demon leans his forearms on his knees, leaning into the circle with a serious expression. "Bit players have to be neutralized or taken out so we can focus on the bigger picture. And we *need* to contact our potential allies to keep communication open."

Setting my plate aside, I rise and stretch up on my toes to work out my now tense muscles. "I suppose the easiest target is Mina and the Sickos. I think they'll abandon her in a New York minute, if we can make her look bad enough. It won't matter that they 'stole her' or even that she's working for the Stuhlls if she gets a crap ton of negative attention."

Damon snaps his fingers. "We need footage. Cameras are everywhere in Bay City, but they're not always aimed at what they think they are. Because we have to stay separate from the humans, the Council sends teams to enchant them to not be able to see supernatural occurrences, don't they?"

I blink, a slow smile spreading over my face. "Yes. Guardians and agents who... wash out... are assigned to preventative duties in their home cities. They get menial tasks like that so they can stay active, but not be directly responsible for others' lives."

"Wash out?" Archie asks in confusion. "What's that mean?"

Reb makes a face, but after a moment, he figures out what to say. "They may fail training assessments too many times. Or they lose a partner or a mate and can't function properly anymore. Sometimes it's a lost one we retrieve but they never actually emerge with any actual powers, so we're stuck with them. It's a toss-up and depending on what their issue is, they are assigned different things."

"You want to tap *rejects* to help us?" Javier says and we all stare at him. His face flushes bright red; it's not normal for him to be so callous. "I'm sorry, but I just... It's our family's safety, you know? It makes me a little heated."

Archie claps him on the shoulder, smiling wryly. "I get it, dude. I'm pretty laid back unless it's this and that's odd for me, too. But I think D was suggesting he work with them on getting the feeds or whatever from their tech. That would, um... possibly have stuff no one is looking at, yeah? Because it's the humans' stuff?"

"Exactly right, baby," Damon says with a firm nod. "Council surveillance folks don't monitor the human stuff after they do the enchantments because they aren't monitoring our neighborhoods or businesses, etc. They might question them if something terrible went down, but otherwise? They assume it's not our problem."

Very isolationist of us, I know, but humans are more likely to discover us and commit genocide than live peacefully, so I guess that's fair.

BARELY AN HOUR LATER, Damon has contacted both the 'Human Interaction and Supernatural Secrecy Team' *and* gotten access to their systems to dig. I didn't think it would work without an official request, but apparently, computer guys of all stripes have a 'code'. The team was happy to provide him with the access to help him hunt down a girl who may have been involved in an attack outside a human club. Obviously, that's not actually what we're looking for, but it worked.

"How did the owners of our favorite dive get a pass to run in *their* territory, anyway?" Damon asks as his fingers fly over the keyboard of his chunky laptop. "We're not supposed to operate supe-only places in human land."

"I don't know," I admit. "I've heard whispers that they bought the place when one of the old gangs had control of the area. That group was cleared out and there was immediate gentrification—it just sort of... happened? But again, that's a rumor and I don't trust Winnie's version of the story for shit. She's obviously a scheming bitch looking for the most powerful sugar momma she can find."

"Agreed. She's a wh—"

I glare at Rebel scathingly. "Absolutely *not*. I don't care if she's promiscuous; I certainly was. I also don't actually care if she's someone who wants to have a 'benefactor' in that way except that it's *Mina*. We will not shame someone for sex work or their sex life in this house—not on my watch. I'm shaming her two-faced, evil villain sucking bullshit, nothing more."

My stepbrother groans, throwing himself backward in his seat with a growl. "You have *so* many rules, little sis. It's exhausting."

"You need them, Rebel Kelly, if you think you can act like an asshole about legitimate life choices in my presence."

"Hot."

Our heads whip around to see Archie smirking. "I see it now. The fighting thing? It's because it makes you guys get riled and horny. When you were pretending you really hated one another, it seemed stupid and proud. But now? It's like... watching two idiots fight their lust on a TV show."

"They call that 'enemies to lovers', I think," Javier adds. "The appeal is pretty obvious when you two snipe, I'm afraid."

Traitors—they're all fucking traitors. Rebuking Rebel is not hot, nor is it... appealing.

"Whatever. She's still a pain in my ass."

"Making it hard to focus," Damon sing-songs as he continues clicking and clacking in his chair. "If you want me to find and capture incriminating stuff, there are *some* parts of it that are not automated."

My brow furrows as I tilt my head. "I thought this was about the club. Isn't that how this convo got started?"

"Maybe, but I've expanded across the city. I believe we can catch her and the Sickos doing shit everywhere, which might be troublesome enough to back them off." Damon looks up, his grin wicked. "The internet may have made your ex-best friend a minor star, but *I* can make her untouchable if we find the right footage."

"Now *that* was hot," I say with a big grin as I look at little D. "Like super fucking hot."

Archie gets up, grabbing his plate and mine to take them to the kitchen. When he comes back, he plops down at Damon's feet and leans against his legs. "I whole-heartedly agree. D getting vengeance is pretty sexy, and seeing you that happy for even a second is even better. I'm all for this plan."

"Then let's get it over with," Angelo growls. "If we get other computers, can we make this go faster? Everyone has a laptop. We can all pitch in if you tell us what to do, bro. I'd like this evening to have a happy ending *before* the sun comes up."

Yet again, a statement I'm totally on board with.

Searching

DAMON

Before they went to grab the tech, Javi made sure everyone bussed their plates, and the kitchen got cleaned up. That was good for me because it allowed me to contemplate how I would use the extra help once they were ready. Movies and TV seem to show people just jumping into a situation like this and being uber-successful, but in reality, non-computer people are rarely so easily led in a digital effort. Even if they're pretty good with tech, they are *not* versed in the areas of the web you'll need to surf to find truly hidden or illicit shit.

So I'm making a quick list of targets to search for, how to enter and leave the deeper levels of the web through the ports I'm creating, and what to watch for that would indicate a problem. I know my family is good at sensing real life baddies and issues, but they are *not* trained for doing so in the online arena. I don't want to be set back because someone chased a rabbit into a trap by mistake. Reconfiguring and cleaning out the house network, devices, and fuck knows what else would be time consuming and annoying. I have fairly decent proto-cols set up, but there are more skilled hackers out there, both in human and supe worlds.

I'm not eager to fight one off while we're trying to duck actual killers and criminals.

Online Search List Assignments:

Rogue- contact new friends and relay information carefully about the channel that D is setting up on the dark web for communication.

Rebel- search for dark web activity in re: gambling, cheating, theories, predictions for the trike. Looking to see if it's being fixed.

Angelo- search information on Society, Councils, realms, and various rumors about big names, especially any from the Apalachin.

Javi- search information/theories, etc. on weird happenings around the supe and the human world as other new friends suggested. Check across realms and the globe.

Archie- search information referencing Luca, Lola, and any other demons we suspect are involved in Hell or new goings on there. Can't be Angelo, as it could trail back. (hopefully not if we're good.)

That should do it. I have a lot of other things I'm looking for, but since I'm better versed in our tasks, I don't want those assigned to anyone else. Sighing as I go back to roaming the digital landscape setting up trackers and spiders, I wait for the others to come back with their devices. We'll have to load the right software first, then I will have to teach them a few things about how to actually *do* what I need them to in order for their efforts to be fruitful. That won't take too long, I don't think, because they aren't useless, just not hackers or IT pros.

If this works, it might cut some of my workload in half—at least, for now.

"No response from either side, yet," Rogue says as she watches the screen in front of her. "But I got the chat rooms set up. I'm doing a little research on them while I wait, so I'm not idle. I see why you and Ang were surprised by the demons, though. Their rep is solidly *against* what they presented in the elevator lobby."

Angelo snorts. "It would have to be or their parents would have had them killed eons ago. Keeping their true aims hidden amongst expected behavior is what's kept them alive. Or... so I assume."

"The little one isn't talked about *anywhere*—which might be why they hovered around *him* so carefully." Rogue frowns as she looks at the laptop, her fingers flying over the keys in an impressive display of skill. There's something odd about the way she emphasizes the words, but perhaps she has a theory she isn't ready to share.

I take a sip of my drink, pondering that for a moment before I decide against asking. If she's not ready to disclose, she's not ready. I get that; I'm often slower to share than the others because I'm still weighing options. "Well, make sure you're navigating *all* the likely places. It seemed like he was new and I agree they were both cautious about us being near him *and* indulgent with his snark. I wouldn't have anticipated it from the royal caliphate."

Rebel holds a finger up, and we all turn to look at him. "It may just be that he's the center of their circle, like Rogue is ours. I noticed the family we met from the university formed the exact same kind of ring around the hybrid woman. She didn't need it, but they were obviously protective. It might be mating behavior."

"It's true that multi-mated groups, even inter-species ones, gather around a central figure that brings them together." Javier scratches his chin as he thinks. "It's an instinct that is almost unavoidable, even if the fateds aren't thrilled about being connected. The dragon in the college group seemed to resent his position in it, which confirms my theory."

Rogue laughs, shaking her head. "Man, I feel for her with a dragon mate fighting the bond. It was bad enough that Rebel was stubborn as hell, but a *dragon*? That's like... the most stubborn mythical on the planet. They're fiercely loyal once they accept things, but until then? It's a nightmare. We've seen some fight the Guardian bond, and it's not pretty."

"The Guardian bond?" I ask curiously. "You guys don't talk about how you were... selected. How does it work?"

Rebel sighs and our woman shushes him, waving her hand dismissively. "We're not *supposed* to talk about this stuff, which is why we don't. But since I'm mated to most of you... It works a *lot* like the mating bond, so I assume that someone with a great deal of power enticed the primordial sisters to do the magic required for it. It's something that awakens with your powers; you just know and if you're not in an enclave, the Society finds you. They place you with families in places with the needed support until you're of age."

"There's a ritual that identifies your current charge *or* reveals that they are not born yet. Unemerged supes are given their Guardian very quickly—usually someone at or around the same age, so they blend in. That Guardian follows them until they emerge, then brings them to the local Council to have the ritual completed. Then they are trained, and either released or inducted, depending on their talents and favorability for agent/member status."

I look at Rebel, noting that despite looking pained about relaying that information, he's following Rogue's lead on this. "Members are those who aren't suitable for 'agent' status, whatever that is."

"Yes," Rogue says firmly. "They have voting rights, knowledge of our world and leaders, but no duties besides managing their powers and our secrecy. It's a label that declares them not useful in any Society efforts amongst various places in the realms."

Archie frowns, tilting his head. "That's for everyone, right? Like we're all technically *members*, but only the supes capable of providing bene-fits to the groups are inducted, right?"

"Yep. That's why your mom and dads are inducted, so are Javier's, but *not* ours. Graciella and Odhran are useless." Rogue looks extremely pleased at that statement, and I don't blame her. Those two treated her, her twin, and Rebel like accessories guaranteed to give them access to things they've never deserved. "They have nothing to offer, not enough dough, *and* they traded in Reck, which didn't go over well. But unemerged supes are different and their rules are very strict."

Angelo looks up again, his brows furrowed. "I don't know that I've ever met one, honestly. They don't advertise it to the public. I've never met lost ones that test as 'forever human', either. The rumors Luca used to use as bedtime horrors say those poor orphans get sold to some insane human organization to train as criminals."

"I've never heard it confirmed," Rebel grimaces and shudders. "But it's been tossed around in the Council ranks. Before you ask, Rogue confirmed Reck had powers from his early childhood. So that's *not* where he went if it's true. He was very weak, though, as far as we've been told."

"I can't remember it." Rogue's whisper is heart-breaking, and I rub my hand on my chest. "I remember most of our childhood before he went away, and I have vague memories of them being weak, but... I don't know if that's because it was repeated over and over until I believed it. They wanted me to accept Reb and forget Reck. That's how they trained me—or tried to."

Those fucking people deserve to be auctioned off to a death dealer, and I'd do it myself if she'd let me.

"We'll find him someday. You know we will, sis. Just keep believing, and don't let anyone discourage you." Rebel's expression is full of barely contained fury as he watches her nod, and then goes back to her screen quietly.

"The point is that they deal with the lost ones differently, and no one is sure if it's ethical or not," I say. Rebel sighs as he nods. "I guess no realm's leaders are *all* good, huh?"

"No beings *anywhere* are all good because that's subjective." Archie rakes his hand through his hair as he slumps in the chair. "What is determined as 'good', 'fair', or 'right' in every realm is going to be different. Their mores and values may not match our own. I mean, look at how the demon thing was set up in the portal. Sure, that's the 'evil' criminals, but... you guys didn't seem surprised or bothered by those events other than thinking about your parents being involved. Demon culture is not Fae culture or shifter culture or even surface culture... you know?"

I do know, and he's usually spot on with that.

"Yeah, it is. To be fair, regular demon culture is also varied from *that* mess. However, Hell's accepted norms would not be the same as up here, even though there are demons up here and hybrids of other types down there." Angelo wrinkles his nose as he makes a face. "Everyone in the more traffic-filled realms has mixed pretty thoroughly now. The ones from others are still homogenous, I think."

Rogue sighs, slamming her laptop shut for a moment to pinch the bridge of her nose. She looks frustrated, and my eyes dart to the others while hers are closed. I'm hoping one of them might have an idea what's eating her.

"Sis, I know finding out the other realms have this new travel method that could be how they have trafficked beings for a long time is hard. And it makes finding Reck seem even more impossible," Rebel says quietly. "But we haven't located him yet because we weren't looking in the realms that don't cross here as much. Now we have more places to check for him; that's a good thing."

Her breath escapes in a slow hiss as she lets it out, and her eyes finally open to meet ours. "I know all of that logically, but I haven't processed the possibilities yet. We were so focused at the meeting that it didn't really *hit* me until now that he could have been sent to a lot more infinitely large places to do... whatever. It could have been good or bad or straight up abusive, you know? It's just hard to process."

"We could distract you," Archie says with a grin. "I mean, some of these things can run without us sitting at the keys. And we planned to have a six-way celebration, anyway. Some orgasms might help you take your mind off of things we can't possibly control."

Angelo grins, shutting his computer as well. "I vote for that. We can check this shit out after we clean up."

Matching nods from Javi and Reb make her bite her lip until she looks at me. "Do you think that will be okay? Everything will run while we have fun?"

Oh, my beautiful, sparkly mate... it most definitely will.

Control

ROGUE

WITHIN MOMENTS of me putting my laptop aside, all five of them are converging on me like hungry sharks. I roll to my feet, stretching my limbs one by one to loosen myself up. "Now, boys... you know I will not allow you to take charge completely. Wipe those smirks off your faces."

Angelo and Rebel stand firm in their alphahole postures, but my statement has little D, Archie, and Javier looking flustered. Between the five of them, I know who will submit and who is going to require more finesse, so that's expected. Arching a brow at the more domi-nant pair, I tilt my head as they pause in front of me with their arms crossed over their chests.

"You know how this works, Princess," Ang says in a dark rumble. "No changing the rhythm mid-song."

Rebel nods, but his case is less firm than the vengeance demon's, based on time and experience together. "I agree with Angelo. Let us take the reins; it will feel so much better."

I enjoy negotiations like this, which he doesn't quite get yet.

"Perhaps I allow you two to direct me while I direct the others?" My lips curve up tantalizingly as I stretch up on my toes again, emphasizing the small tank and shorts I'm clad in. "Would that work out for you?"

Stalking closer, Reb stands nose-to-nose with me. "You're a brat and a half, lil' sis."

"Nope, just not the usual easily led Bambi-eyes, *bro*," I shoot back as my hands land on my hips. "I'm a woman who knows what she wants and how she wants it. Is that going to be a problem?"

He shakes his head slowly. "Nope. Angelo and I can handle it. Right, man?"

The dark-haired demon laughs huskily as he meets my eyes. "I think we can, especially if she gets to split the difference with the others. Everyone wins."

"I'm cool with it," Archie says as he sheds his shirt. "Tell me where I fit, babe. I just wanna be included."

He's such a submissive, and he never realized it until now—and I love it.

Javi and Damon nod, tugging off their shirts as well as they move into the middle of the room. There's a *lot* of delicious muscle and skin on display right now, which makes my body hum with excitement. I wiggle my shoulders as the wings I keep inside itch to be set free. That's not an option at the moment, though I know deep inside that once Rebel and I complete the bond, I won't be able to fight off the natural instincts of either of my supernatural sides. Both the Unseelie and the Cubi will want to make their marks across the entire group, claiming them as belonging to every part of me.

"Your turn," Angelo says as he gestures to my shirt. "Set the sisters free, Princess. Show us your sparkle."

Reaching down, I tug the small tank up slowly, teasing them because I can. Reb growls a little, but that's okay; if he wants to do something about it, he can. I finally pull it over my head and toss it aside, padding away from my stepbrother to get closer to the men sprawled on the floor. Archie pats a spot in the middle, his eyes filled with the golden threads of his lion.

"Come on down, Wheels. Those fuckers can share, even if they're in charge of us." His sexy grin draws me in, so I drop to my knees among them, then look over my shoulder at the two Doms.

"He's right, you know. You can share like big boys."

Angelo walks into the circle, smirking darkly. "We can. So tell them what to do before your mouth is too full to manage it."

Shiver.

"Javi, help Archie get undressed. Splay him out for Damon, then come back so you can touch me while I take care of Angelo." I grin to myself, knowing I'll enjoy watching that and sucking the demon off simultaneously.

"And what about me?" Reb gives me a challenging look as he joins Ang. "What do I get?"

"That's not up to me, according to you, *bro*." I retort. His eyes darken and he chuckles as he adjusts himself in his pants. "I suggest you figure out what you want."

I settle in, ignoring his dangerous glare as I watch Javier push Archie onto his back. He's careful to wait for the blond hockey player to lift his hips to remove his sweats, tugging them down the perfectly toned legs slowly. Once his golden skin is revealed, I lick my lips as Damon moves to his other side, dipping his head to kiss the eager athlete.

"Very nice," I mumble as my nipples harden. "Soooo pretty."

Before I can continue, Angelo's hand tugs my face to the side, his hard dick bobbing a little as it waits for my attention. I wink up at him then slide my lips around the tip, toying with it until he groans loudly. "Stop fucking around, Princess."

If you say so, buddy.

In a distinctly bratty fashion, I swallow him down quickly, letting him deep into my throat. That makes him shudder, so I grab his hip bones to hold on as I start a fast rhythm. Rebel is behind me in an instant, his fingers sliding roughly through the wetness of my cunt. That was supposed to be Javi's job, but if he wants to do it, I'm not going to complain. As long as I'm being touched, I'm happy as fuck.

Speaking of the gorgeous phoenix, my eyes cut over to see him very gently following Damon's hands on Archie with my own. If Ang wasn't fucking my mouth, I'd grin in satisfaction at the sight. I knew he leaned that direction, and with Damon taking charge of him and Archie, I get to see sexy as fuck things while the other two are monopolizing me.

A sharp crack on my ass brings me back to reality, and I make a muffled sound of protest as Reb's hand marks my skin. He chuckles wickedly, obviously unconcerned, and I bob over Angelo harder. Drool is escaping from the side of my mouth, but I don't care. I'm going to make this demon come so I can wrestle my fucking stepbrother's ass to the ground. Another slap, this time on the other side, stings with the force of his hand.

I can't admit I like it or he wins and I'll be damned if that's going to happen.

"She must like it," Angelo says smugly. "Every time you give her a slap, the vibration from her moans vibrates over me even if they aren't audible."

That makes Reb unleash another firm slap, and I scrape my teeth over the demon in response. Angelo clearly likes it, though, because his thrusts speed up, so I let my Fae fangs descend. They draw blood and I taste it in my mouth, but that doesn't stop him. Tucking that tidbit away for later, I continue sucking and licking as he slams into my mouth. My gaze cuts to the side, and the sight of Damon and Javi teasing Archie with light touches on his frame makes my pussy clench.

A flood of arousal escapes, leaking down my thighs as I see him straining not to move as his thick dick twitches.

"You enjoy watching them torture Arch like we're doing to you, hmm?" Reb's hand grabs the ponytail I pulled my hair back into, tugging on it firmly. "And you *love* having your ass blistered while you service Angelo. I had *no idea* how much fun you were going to be, sis."

My lashes flutter as he and Angelo push and pull me back and forth between them. Reb isn't giving me what I need—no, he's merely alternating smacks and light touches on my soaked cunt while the elder demon fucks my face. But the delicious edging is accomplishing his goal; it has my climax swelling and ebbing over and over as he mutters his dirty shit. Archie is being similarly edged nearby, so the scents of his arousal, mine, and all of theirs have combined to make a musky, primally satisfying smell that pushes me even further into pleasure.

It's the scent of mine—*my family, my mates, my personal clan of powerful men—something I never thought I'd have.*

That thought makes me shudder from head to toe, and I realize that I'm so close to climax that it's going to be hard to keep it at bay. I push that information mentally across the Fae bond I have with Rebel, since I can't speak while I'm getting face fucked by Angelo. His hands on my face and Rebel's in my hair prevent me from pulling away and my stepbrother needs to know that I'm going to come whether he approves or not.

"Oh, you're close enough that you can't hold it, hmm?" he purrs from behind me. His fingers are sliding through the mess between my legs and back to my ass tantalizingly. One finger traces my hole, making me whimper around Ang's cock, and his snarl deepens.

"For the love of Hecate, Rebel, fucking do it. Her mouth is so hot and wet that every time she moans it's like a goddamn vibrating toy. *I will not hold* out much longer, you jackass."

If I weren't being railed so hard, I'd try to smile around the enormous dick in my mouth, but *c'est la vie*. Instead, I redouble my efforts, scraping and sucking and drooling all over myself as I work to push Angelo over the edge so he can demand I orgasm as well. My body's like one big raw nerve demanding to be plucked, so I *need* him to give permission.

"Patience, my winged friend," Rebel says with amusement coloring his tone. "She can hold out, and so can you. It's all about control and release now, right?"

I'd punch him in the nose for his superior tone if I could, but my brain loses that desire when he slips his thumb into my ass. I moan again, pushing my hips back into his hand as I pray for him to use the rest of those damn fingers to fuck me. The need for something inside of me is building pressure so intense in my lower half that I'm ready to cry.

"That's my girl," Angelo croons as he continues holding onto me and shoving his cock down my throat. "Look at how fucking gorgeous you are. I love when you're strong and shine like a shooting star, Princess, but this? This glimpse of submission, small as it is, is sheer perfection. Only we get to see you like this—no one else. And it makes you that much stronger, that much more powerful, because you hold the keys."

Rebel makes a strangled sound, his voice even raspier now. "Oh, she liked that, Ang. And because her body can admit what her mouth can't, I'm going to give her what she so desperately wants."

His fingers—all four of them—slam roughly inside of me and this time, the scream I let loose isn't in my head. It echoes around Angelo's cock and out into the room. Every one of them makes a primal sound in response; I've triggered the animals and demons and Fae they have locked within, as they are in human form. My fingers dig into the elder twin's legs as I hold on, meeting his fast thrusts with even more zeal while pushing back into Rebel's fingers eagerly as rhythm speeds.

"That's it, Princess. Keep fucking yourself on Reb's fingers while I come down your throat. Get ready... it's happening.... *nowwwwww*."

With that snarl of pleasure, Angelo's dick hits the back of my throat hard and I feel the hot cum spurt into my mouth as his orgasm takes him.

Now, if only Rebel would fucking release me, I'll be ready to fuck them both into the goddamn carpet.

Mount Everest

JAVIER

Of all the things I expected tonight, being sent to torture Archie wasn't on the list. Obviously, he's hot as fuck because of his workouts and sporty shit. I hadn't missed that fact, but given that I was sure Damon had a crush on him, that might go nowhere? I simply didn't put this on my list of possibilities. Rogue storming into our bedrooms broke open *all* the dams in our group and now I'm following the lead of a guy that I *thought* preferred being topped as we make the huge, hunky hockey player squirm and whine.

Life is really fucking surreal right now.

One thing I'm certain of is that Archer Levi Glaser is going to turn out to be a power bottom. He's not someone you'd think that about because of his appearance, but I saw him with D last time, and I can almost taste the submission in the air now. Not all bottoms are subs, mind, but Archie is one hundred percent both. It's intoxicating, even for someone like me who's comfortable switching and being Vers. My eyes flick up to Damon's waiting to see what he wants me to do next —I don't want to overstep, but the sounds of Reb and Angelo making our mate come are driving me *crazy*.

"Javi... run upstairs and grab the box from Rogue's room. I think we should try something."

His voice is rough, but firm, and I scramble to my feet to obey. Damon has learned a *lot* from his older twin, it seems, even if he never made use of it until now. "Yes, sir!"

That gets me a dark look and sends me running through the living room to the stairs. It only takes a moment to run up them, locate the treasure box he wants, and damn near trip myself getting back down to the family room. I hold it up for Damon, grinning as he takes it and jerks his head toward the side of Archie I was on before. I'm not sure what he's going to dig out of the thing, but I'm intrigued as hell.

I enjoy the addition of toys and devices greatly—they're some of the best teammates.

D sits back on his heels, placing the box on the ground as he roots through it. My eyes move to the flush peeking through the tanned muscle of Archie's body as his chest rises and falls. The lion swallows hard as he watches the demon sift through the stuff, his dick twitching and leaking at the tip.

"Fuck, guys... I'm so... Fuuuuuuuck."

His groans are sexy and throaty in that raspy big cat way, making me shift as I kneel beside him. "What are you looking for, Damon?"

The demon holds up a sparkling chain that links two nipple clamps with a wicked grin. "These. He's very sensitive and I think this will enhance everything so beautifully." He looks down at the cat shifter pointedly before he says, "Do you consent to a little torture, pet?"

Okay, I'm not one for that level of play, but the way he said 'pet' made my cock jump like a gymnast.

Archie's eyes roll back in his head and his hips wriggle a bit before he nods. D makes a *tsk* sound, and the hockey player corrects his mistake quickly. "Yes... yes, sir?"

"Perfect," Damon replies as he looks over at me. "Take this one and I do the other, little birdie."

I suck in a breath, his moniker triggering the desire to please him immediately. Grabbing the clamp, I lean down and attach it to his right nipple. The moan and his full body shudder tell me our prone friend likes it, especially when Damon puts the other one on and his hips buck. "He definitely likes it, Sir."

Damon smirks as he tugs on the chain, pulling both at the same time, and Archie bites his puffy lower lip adorably as he whines. That sound is fucking delicious, and I know it has to turn the demon on as much as it did me. "Good boy, Archie. You're doing so well. Perhaps... a reward?"

His blond head bobs, and his eyes flutter closed. I didn't notice how long his lashes are before, or that he has such a perfectly golden boy feature set, but now? I realize that D and I are torturing the pristine example of an athlete until he's ready to beg. It's a heady feeling for guys like us, especially since we're not the ones you expect to control this hulking dude.

"Okay, Javi... what do *you* think Archie needs? Tell me what you'd like to reward him with."

Sneaky... that's a gift to both of us.

I pretend to think while Archie pants, looking over his form. "I think his dick deserves attention; don't you? Maybe just a little?"

"Very good, little birdie. Go ahead," D practically purrs. I move to get closer and he shakes his head. "No, wait. Strip first, *then* give him his reward."

Nodding, I shuck my pants, then move back into position by the lion's hips. "Hands or mouth, sir?"

Damon sits back on his haunches again, head tilted as he takes a beat. "Hands for now, but carefully. He can't come yet, and I don't want him to lose control."

"That's gonna be difficult," Archie pants softly. "You two are driving me *wild*, sir."

"Ah, but you want to be a good kitty cat, yes? Make me pleased?" Archie nods emphatically and Damon grins. "Then hold back until you're given permission, pet. You can do it."

I wait for him to come back to me, and when he nods, I scoot close enough to wrap a fist around the large, pulsing red cock head to squeeze. The moan is louder this time, and it drowns out the sound of Rogue and the others nearby as I slide my fist down his length. I work him slowly, keeping my gaze on how each touch gets a different reaction—he's so responsive and I believe him that he's teetering on the edge. A drop of pre-cum drips from his tip and I lick my lips. His scent is delicious and I bet he'll taste good, too.

If Damon allows it—this is his mini-scene, and I'm at the mercy of his whims as well.

"Go ahead, Javi. Taste how needy he is."

The words have barely crossed his lips when I dip my head to eagerly lick the droplet off. Archie shudders, and I slip my mouth over the head to suckle gently. I was right about his taste; now it paired with the scent of his arousal is making my balls ache. I lift off of him, then pull back and close my eyes as I savor the experience. Damon rumbles across from me, and I'm still letting the pleasure arc through me as he does something that draws more moans out of the hockey player.

"I'm ready to fuck him now," Damon says, and my eyes pop open. "I'd like to watch him suck you while I do it, though. Would you both enjoy that?"

Archie nods again, then clears his throat to answer. "Yes, sir. I w-want that. Definitely."

I'm shocked to hear it, but my eyes skate from his to Damon's to make sure they're both okay. "Um, yes. Yes, that would be... um, yes."

I sound like a fucking idiot, but I really didn't expect this to ever happen.

Damon smiles, obviously pleased by our responses, then turns to the chest to pull out the lube. "Excellent. On your knees like a good boy, Archie, and Javi, you'll be in front."

I've never seen a guy as big as Archer move that fast, but within seconds, he's rolled over and positioned himself exactly as D instructed. It has to be the cat in him—he was graceful as hell doing such an awkward move. "Damn, man. You're flexible."

Archie looks up at me, his blue eyes threaded with the gold of the lion inside. "Flexible and hungry, Javi. Get in place while D gets me ready... I *need* to come, and I want to do it while I'm filled by you both."

"That's exactly what you'll get," Damon says as he sheds his pants and the smell of fruity-scented lube fills the air. "But you don't get it until *I* say, so behave."

The sound of his palm cracking on flesh makes me chuckle softly, especially when Archie lets out another long, dark groan. "Uh-oh. He likes a good spanking, too, sir."

"I'm wondering if we all do," Damon mutters, and I laugh. His hand slips off of Archie's hips, and our friend jolts as the demon works his fingers in to prepare him. "But I definitely know he likes this a helluva lot. More than any of us but our mate, I think."

Chuckling softly, I move closer, but not close enough for Archie to disobey. "I actually thought that as well, sir. Our big, muscular athlete is the happiest bottom I know—in my opinion."

Damon nods, placing his hand on the lion's other hip. "I agree, little birdie. He's so damn responsive, and he just *writhes* when you play with his tight hole."

"Guysssss..."

I laugh again, looking at the demon in control of this threesome for permission. "He's definitely ready to pop, sir. Can I help him?"

"You may."

This time, I move within range of Archie's mouth and it closes over my throbbing dick immediately. My hand drops to bury in his blond locks, a moan of pleasure escaping me as he figures out how to take all of me in. I know he's inexperienced with this, but his eagerness makes up for it. Archie is licking and sucking as he bobs carefully over my dick, his teeth scraping occasionally in a delicious, sharp pain that makes my balls tighten.

"Good boy," Damon says as he flexes long clawed nails into the lion's hip. "Very good. Make him moan and whine like I do you. I'm going to pound your ass hard enough to make you choke on him. Would you like that, kitty cat?"

Shit, I would; how could Archie not?

The dirty talk makes our captive shifter groan around my shaft, and it vibrates over me. "Oh, he wants that, sir. He really wants it badly."

I watch as Damon's demon emerges, his horns and wings sprouting quickly, as he removes his fingers and grips both of Archie's hips. "Good, because he's going to get it. You should hold on."

Before he can line up, I grab onto Archie's shoulder with my other hand. I'm guiding him by his hair already, but he's clearly enjoying it. I don't want to overwhelm him, though, and if DemonDamon gets a bit too wild, I can pull back. "I'm ready, sir."

As soon as I speak, Damon spears the lion shifter with his cock, his hips slamming into him hard enough to push my dick further into his throat. "Fuuuuck, yeahhhhh..."

Our spit-roasted lover makes a sound that is strangled by me, and I chuckle softly as I feel another fang scrape. "You're doing good, Arch. Breathe through your nose and don't worry about drooling."

That gets me a pleased grunt from our Domming demon, and he pulls back, then pounds into Archie again. Soon, the push and pull between us is working like a machine, and the ecstasy is thrumming through me like molten lava. I lose myself in the feel of his hot mouth and the thrusts that bring him back, then down to the root of my dick as Damon fucks him.

"Motherfucker," I whisper as I tug on Archie's hair gently and he moans louder. "This is fucking perfect; holy fuck, D."

"There are ways it can be better, but that would require our girl to be over here, too," he growls. "But that's just more icing on the cake, little birdie."

Shuddering as he fills my head with even more sexy images, I feel my cock swell until it almost hurts. "Gonna need to come, sir. Our fuck toy probably needs it, too."

Damon licks his demonic fangs, bobbing his brows at me as his tail whips around behind him. "Then come we shall... Archie... you have permission..."

I watch as he leans forward and sinks his teeth into the lion's back and it pushes me over the edge, the sensation intense enough to almost knock me off balance.

This family thing is the best goddamn thing ever and no one will ever convince me otherwise.

Fuck The Police

ROGUE

—

WE WERE ALL COMPLETELY SHREDDED after the mini-orgy in the living room, and I'm ashamed to say that I let Damon and Reb handle getting everyone aftercare and cleaned up. Javi promised to have cleaners come in during the day today, and I found myself grateful yet again that I'm now functioning in a unit.

Having others who help with shit is more useful than I would have predicted—but then, I was used to taking care of myself.

Shaking my head as I finish my cool-down laps as my other teammates leave the track one by one, I think about what any of them would say if they heard I was giving up control to anyone. It would be a shock to their systems; I never allow that, whether it's in my team or my personal life. Rainbow Smite is known for being fair, tough, and having impeccably high standards that she only asks because she also meets them. They've seen me float from casual relationships to hookup to friends with bennies over and over throughout the years. I've made it crystal clear that I wasn't looking for anything serious outside of my baller derby team, and my occasional stints at the club.

"Things change, Rogue, even you," I mutter to myself as I glide over the hardwood slowly. "The Fates make it impossible to say you'll 'never' do shit, and they laugh when they prove you wrong. This family thing is proof of that."

"Hey, Rogue, where the hell were you this weekend?" Betsy Sue skates over to me, her eyes curious as she moves alongside me. Anita and Melanie join in, followed by Drusilla, and they all look at me expectantly as we move in unison without trying.

I'm not telling my teammates things that could put them in danger, so I shrug. "Off with Reb and the boys causing trouble. Why?"

"You didn't show at the bar or the club; we wondered," Anita replies as she switches to skating backwards so she can face me. "It's weird for you to be totally incognito, woman."

She's right, but that doesn't mean I'm going to give up more information.

"We're not married, dude. I can do things not at the same place with the same people all the time. Don't be weird."

Drusilla snorts, shaking her head as she joins Anita. They're all surrounding me now, and it feels irritatingly like a coordinated 'gang up'. "Come on, tell us. We all share shit, or we did before that ho left for the Sickos. Now you're closed up like a clam."

"That's not a shock, Dru," I growl low. "She betrayed us, betrayed *me*, and she was my closest, oldest friend and teammate. I'm not real eager to give *anyone* access to my private life with her spreading lies and rumors all over the fucking world like some deranged Hilton sibling."

"Yeah, that makes sense," Melanie says softly. "Mina burned us all, but you really got screwed. She's got this obsession with destroying you by playing the victim, and it's... Well, *I* think it's downright pathological. Like, why can't she just move on? The damage is done, and you've left her alone unless she confronts you directly. What's with the stalking?"

You're telling me, girl.

I sigh, spinning in a circle once to see them all, then following the pack again. "I don't know. It's not like I'm attempting to challenge her stupid culty team or even bad mouth her—when I definitely could. I know her deepest, darkest secrets and fears; she knows that. Pushing me could lead to my releasing that kind of receipt shit, yet she just continues to press my buttons. I don't get it."

Anita tsks, looking thoughtful. "Mutually assured destruction should keep her at bay, but it isn't. That's really fucking psycho, Rogue. She doesn't seem to care that you could easily ruin her rep globally, and even if her cult doesn't believe it, everyone else will when they see your proof. I agree that it's just bizarre that she doesn't shift her focus."

"I don't have an answer for that, ladies." I point at the two skating backwards, twirling my finger to indicate that they should switch with the forward-facing ones behind me. "All I know is that with the Sickos —and whoever is funding them—behind her, she's gotten way more aggressive and reckless. Beating me down in a place where one of them died was foolish and wasteful."

"Very wasteful," Drusilla repeats as she moves around me to her new position. "It hurt their team as she was pretty talented."

"Bringing Winnie into it was dumb as fuck." Betsy Sue frowns as she replaces Dru. "That draws lines in the bar and local hangouts that we don't need in shifter spots. It has to be fucking with business because you weren't the only one not there this weekend. It was deader than a raft full of corpses in the Amazon."

That's probably because of the Apalachin, but again—they don't need to know.

"Maybe there were other events out of town or something," I mumble.

Anita cackles. "That we weren't invited to? Hardly."

The rest of them join in, and normally, I'd agree. The Derby teams are always invited to big shit, especially because large sponsors are also our sponsors half the time. They like the talent to mingle with the normal folks. But this time, they're mistaken, and it's because they aren't involved in any of the criminal shit in Bay City.

"Whatever the reason, maybe it will be better this weekend." Melanie looks hopeful, and I smile back at her. She's gentler in personality than most of us Bombers, but she's fast and good. "Then we can all hang again, like usual."

I nod, not really committing since I have no idea what I'll be doing once the guys and I figure out the various shit we're focused on this week. "Perhaps so. It'd be fun to let loose a bit before the next match next weekend."

Oddly, I mean that, but I'm also not ready to guarantee my presence until I know if we're going to end up sleuthing.

ONCE PRACTICE IS OVER, I head outside, looking for my 'shadow of the day'. Rebel is leaning against the hood of his car with a smirk, and I roll my eyes at him. "Man, you guys are so damned serious about this shit. I'm not in danger at the rink amongst my longtime team."

"Since your ex-bestie was one of them until a few weeks ago, I'm still going with a big 'no' on being here without someone close enough to step in, little sis."

Not that again.

"You can't keep using that," I hiss as I stomp over to him with my bag full of gear that needs to be cleaned. Shoving it into his hands, I yank the car door open. "When we come out as mated, it will be really fucking jarring, and I'd like not to draw *that* kind of attention to myself."

"Ashamed of me?" he asks with a raised brow.

Growling softly, I shake my head. "Obviously *not*, but I do *not* want to have that specific slur thrown at us. We aren't related by blood, and we're not really brother and sister. It's a piece of paper that we don't even know is legal, given Graciella's bullshit. But people will be assholes regardless, and no matter how cute you think it is, I'd rather not have that added to my list of sins along with the rest."

Rebel tosses my bag into the trunk, then moves to get in on his side. "Look, Kiandra. We know people are going to be dicks no matter what because of that very topic, plus the poly aspect. You and Arch are well known; Javi and the twins are high-powered. We cannot escape their scrutiny, so why not have fun with it?"

He's got a point, but I refuse to let him win.

"Whatever," I reply as he guns the engine and peels out as if we're on the starting line. "Stop that! We'll get pulled over. Cops aren't part of the plan, either, dummy."

His lips curve up, and he shrugs carelessly. "I'd love to see them catch me, babe. You and I both know that whatever they have under the hood can't compete."

"But we have to pick up Archie. He'll be waiting, and I don't want him alone either, if you're so damned worried." I cross my arms over his chest, and he makes a face at me. "I'm right, and you know it. Be less ridiculous, Reb."

Despite not getting an answer, I feel him slow down as we hit the highway. Traffic isn't great, but he's good at weaving in and out of it like a pro. It takes a good fifteen minutes more than it should to arrive at the arena in the end—something that makes me tense. I don't completely believe that we're unsafe in every single place on earth, but the mating bonds in my gut have a field day when they worry my mates might be in danger. It's a difficult balance, especially since I definitely cannot tell Rebel yet.

As we exit the expressway, my eyes widen when the arena's parking lot —which should be nearly empty on non-game days—is packed to the gills. There are emergency vehicles, lights, sirens, and press vans everywhere. Gasping softly, I reach over and grip Reb's arm lightly as he grimaces.

"What the fuck is this?" he snarls as he whips into the lot and heads for the barriers near the entrance. "And why isn't there anything coming over the chats?"

I pull my phone out, swiping it open quickly, but he's correct. Not one word in our group chat, nor anything else, that would alert us to a problem with Archie. "Damn it. Nothing."

Rebel parks, hopping out and slamming his door as he rounds the car to open my door. I don't have time to tease him about the knightly behavior because as soon as I'm out, a police officer comes striding over with a stern expression on his face.

"No parking!" he barks, and I groan. I really fucking hate most canine shifters; Anita is an exception to the rule. They're territorial and over-bearing, but they also have just as much dislike for Fae. "Take your bullshit fake racer somewhere else, rich kid. You can film your TikTok at the edge like all the other morons."

My temper flares, and I hunker down, crossing my arms over my chest as I give the guy an acid glare. "We're not *influencers*, Officer. Rebel and I are official Guardians, emissaries of the Council by induction, and we're related to someone inside that building. Tell us what the hell is going on and watch your fucking tone."

The mutt winces at the word 'Guardian' and I know I'm going to win. Agents, Guardians, and other Council official employees are well above local law enforcement, though some more than the others. He knows we can make a phone call and have his ass on traffic duty at the worst intersection in Bay City with very little effort. "Fuck, I hate your lot."

"Fae? Guardians? People who can read?" Rebel snarks as he mimics my posture. "There are so *many* choices I could list."

That doesn't help a bit, and for a second, I think the damn dog is going to dig his heels in, too. "Look, man. My partner can be an ass, but that doesn't negate your protocol here. We outrank you, *and* we're family. I'd prefer not to derail your career because you're being a pain, but I will if you make me."

"Freya, give me patience," the officer says as he turns on his heel to head for the barrier. "Come on, then. You can deal with the fallout if it comes. I won't forget your names or this bullshit. You screw something up and I'm throwing your asses under the bus so fast you won't be able to see the blur as I move."

Rebel laughs this time, letting me go first as we follow. "As if you could even come *close* to our speed, you flea-bitten ding-dong. I'd say in your dreams, but even there you're so slow you're almost not moving. Take us to our family and stop with the empty threats."

This is going to be special—I can feel it in my bones.

Bad Boys

ARCHER

THIS SHIT is like being invaded by a foreign nation—the supe division of the local cops has flooded the arena, and ever since, a slow trickle of feds and Society fucks have followed. I don't get why this is such an enormous deal, either.

Badger Brisco is volatile even on the best of days—he'd been sent to the lockers for a reason and probably stomped off to pout.

"Listen up, all of you!" Coach towers over us, a perk of Yeti shifter heritage, his expression serious as he stares at the entire team before him. "I want cooperation with all the officials here—no exceptions. Brisco is a pain in the ass, and I know he's got beef with some of you, but he's Thunder, through and through. That means until we prove otherwise, we assume he's been taken against his will."

I have to cover my snort at that directive. The guy was bleeding when he left the ice; I saw it. He picked a fight with a third-stringer who accused him of fucking his wife—something it's likely Badger did— and when he got sent packing, it dribbled all the way back to our room. Notifying all these damn cops and shit was premature, if you ask me. That shithead is probably hiding in a dive bar slamming back cognac as if it's his last day on earth as we speak.

"But Coach—"

Oh, rookie mistake, Evans. Even when he's incorrect, you don't correct Hokesh.

"*Did I ask for your opinion or concerns? No!* We are not a sewing circle, nor a slumber party, gentlemen." I wince, knowing Rogue would have my coach's misogynistic balls in her back pocket within seconds. "I gave an order, and I expect it to be followed without question. *Do you understand?*"

"Yes, Coach!"

The resounding reply is familiar and easy to fall into, even when we disagree. Hokesh is skilled and connected, but so old school that it's painful to be in his presence sometimes. Unfortunately, even supe sports leagues aren't yet full of enlightened people, so you have to choose between success and preference sometimes. Though if I'm totally honest, that choice doesn't occur to a lot of the players or staff to start with, so I'm a bit of an oddball, anyway.

I push to my feet, heading over to my locker to strip off the gear so I can get in the 'interview' line for all the damned officers in this building. They wanted to speak to each of us alone, but luckily, my prickly coach could get them to agree that we could change before meeting with them. That seems dumb if they think any of us had shit to do with Brisco fucking off—like, wouldn't there be evidence to look for? However, I'm not a fool, so I didn't say that thought; I wanted out of this sweaty shit as much as the others.

It's not my job to help cops, especially not in Bay City, where they're five to one bought and paid for.

"I don't know why we're bothering with this circus," Alexandre grumbles from his spot next to me. "Everyone here knows Old Badger is off doing shots off a hooker by now. No one 'kidnapped' that asshole; we can't even get rid of him when we want to."

Snickering, I nod at the grizzly. "I know what you mean, man. I think this is a waste of time, too."

One of the newer recruits leans over from the locker to my left. "I heard they did it because there were others."

"Other what?" I retort as I clean myself up. "Other assholes who stomp off to pout? Not on this team."

"No," the guy says, and I arch a brow at him, waiting. "Other athletes who have disappeared or worse."

Frowning as I tug on sweats, I look at Alex and some of my other teammates, who shrug. "Where did you hear that, rook?"

"On the news, duh. First, there was that big college player killed in the South. Then, there were a bunch of players in amateur leagues in the Northwest who got injured in that accident. And now there're missing players here."

I press my lips together and then shake my head. "Look, dude. I think you're connecting dots that don't go together. It's weird, but it's not like... a conspiracy."

The ginger-haired kangaroo shifter shrugs at me. "We don't have time for me to lay out a bulletin board with strings on it for you, Glaser. But anyone with pattern recognition can see that there's something fucking weird going on, and it's definitely connected to sports, large supe enclaves, and a myriad of other shit."

"Okay, buddy. Just remember to take that tin foil hat off when you put on your helmet," I reply before I wink at the other guys. "Otherwise, you'll cook your noggin."

"Meatheads," he mutters in annoyance, as he finishes tying his shoes. "Keep your heads in the sand if you want, but I'm sure as hell lobbying for more security in this place."

"Good luck with that," Alex mutters. "We can't even get catered lunches."

Laughing as I finish putting on my clothes, I wait until the new kid leaves with his bag slung over his shoulder. "Man, he's gonna be a trip if he lasts. We've never had a conspiracy theorist before."

"It'll be fun as hell to mess with him."

I shoot a finger gun at Alex in agreement, then pick up my shit. "Alright, gents... I'm going out there to get this over with. I have much more important shit to do than to sit around waiting for Badger to pop his head up and laugh at us for being worried."

Like finding my mates and my family, so they're not freaking out about the ridiculous shit going on in the arena.

THE TALL, elegant-looking swan shifter looks at me with a doubtful expression. "And you claim you saw nothing after Mr. Brisco headed off of the ice?"

I roll my eyes, sighing in annoyance. "For the third fucking time, no. We lined up to run a play again, and since Badger isn't exactly known for keeping his temper, I thought nothing of his grand exit. I don't think you're going to find *anyone* who was surprised that he left to sulk when Coach sent him packing."

Her partner is some kind of cat shifter, but I think he might be a hybrid. He keeps looking at me as if he's trying to dig through my brain, but that will not work. Reb has made sure all of us know how to block those mindfuckers out, and the second I clocked his gaze, I set my shields before I even sat down.

"You're awfully calm about this," the feline detective says. "Aren't you worried about your teammate? Others are."

Snorting, I shake my head. "No. As I said, Badger is known for his fits of pique. If people are worried, it's because they don't know him and haven't been on the team long enough to witness his random binges when he gets spanked."

Detective Birdwoman—or whatever her name is—writes something on her notepad, making sure I see her keeping it from my view. I guess that's supposed to intimidate me, but she must not have researched who I am. This is not the first time I've been interviewed by law enforcement at various levels, and it won't be the last. Hanging around Rebel with his street racing and growing up with the guys, I gave my mother lots of gray hair getting hauled in but never charged with anything. My dads basically started rochambeau'ing for the punishment of coming to get me when I was in middle school.

"Fine. You think he's gone off to lick his wounds. I hear you." Detective Cat Guy leans back in his chair, crossing his arms over his chest. "Why was there a blood trail, then?"

"Because he and Smitty got in a rumble over Badger fucking his wife. Again, that's nothing new and leads to problems all the time. Coach should axe him, but he's too damn good, and his contract is ridiculous. *Allegedly*."

They look at one another, then at the window to the office like it's two-way. It's not just that the blinds are drawn, but I suppose they have some friends from other agencies listening in from the outside. There's a knock on the glass, and I roll my eyes up to the ceiling in supplication. I've watched enough TV and movies that I'm sure it means that they're tagging in another motherfucker who will ask me the same shit in a different order.

The door opens, and an austere-looking guy with a jokey-looking dude comes in, nodding at the detectives. They pull chairs up to the table, the less serious-looking one sitting on his backwards as he leans on the top of it.

Oh, good... they're trying 'good cop', 'bad cop' with me.

"I'm Agent Raskin, and this is my partner, Agent Barcec. We're from—"

"You're Sibbies. It's pretty obvious." I blow out a breath and stare at them before pointing to serious guy first, then his partner. "Minotaur. Griffin. Got it."

They look surprised, but Raskin nods. "You're correct. I don't meet many supes who can identify mythicals so easily."

"Dude, you guys *suck* at interview prep. My mom and dads are big in the Shifter Council here. I've grown up meeting damn near every kind of shifter possible, plus my best friends are—"

That's when the door bangs open, breaking the frame as it slams against the wall. Standing in the wreckage is Rogue, her eyes full of fury and outrage. Rebel and the others are behind her; I can smell them. My face splits into a huge grin as I relax in my chair while the asshole cops and feds scowl.

"Has he been offered his Council rep?" Rebel's expression is just as angry as my girl's, and I have to swallow a chuckle.

"This is just an interview... He doesn't need one." Swan Cop looks annoyed as she tilts her head. "Who are you?"

"I am Rogue Kelly and this is my partner, Rebel. We're Guardians and friends of Archer Glaser." I can almost see the anger emanating from her as she steps into the room like an Amazon warrior. "He is no longer answering questions, and if you're going to charge him, do it now. Once I report your negligence to the Society and the Chief, your asses are *toast*."

"I don't think so, pretty lady," the griffin drawls as he winks. "We're Sibbies; we don't play by local rules."

"You play by the Council and the Society's rules or you're out of a job," Damon says as he makes his way around Reb. "As an heir to the demon rep in the city, I'm well-versed in the protocols, even at your level."

The Sibbies look at one another as Angelo joins his twin, and Javier follows. Their gazes cut to the local yokel detectives, then the Minotaur says, "We were told this was cleared with everyone. A famous player is missing, and—"

"Someone important always throws up a flag, right?" Rogue scoffs as she rolls her eyes. "Well, I don't know this player, but I know Archie. He's one of the most honest shifters in the damn city, and if he told you shit before we got here, he's not lying. Why are you ganging up on him?"

"We don't have to share evidence—"

Rebel holds up his hands, magic glowing on his fingertips as he makes a soft 'shh' sound. "Stop talking. You're only making this worse. Rogue and I have been trained for longer than you've been busting bad guys. We had to learn every procedure and every permutation of laws in this city, state, and country for our jobs. You can absolutely tell us why you've tag-teamed our friend."

The griffin sighs, then shrugs at his partner before turning back to us. "Because there were physical evidence markers that dispute the 'walked off on his own theory', including fur, fibers, and other indicators that Brisco was snatched."

I tilt my head as I realize. "And you think it ties to all the other shit going on around the country; that's why you're here."

"How do you know about that?" Raskin barks angrily.

Now I've stepped in it, and I bet that snarky little shit is nowhere to be found when I relay what he said in the locker room—just fucking great.

Show Them

ROGUE

THIS IS *why Society agents* hate *dealing with Sibbies or any other fucking agencies—they're such dipshits.*

I cut Archie off before he makes this worse by arching a brow at Raskin. Staying quiet until he backs down, I keep my triumphant grin to myself. "My partner and I know many things that you probably believe we should not. However, our clearance is much higher than anyone in this building, and if you force us to call in a rep from *our* employers, it will not go well for you."

Barcec frowns, looking at me, then Reb, then back at Archie. "I don't see how that's relevant."

Rebel snorts, his temper simmering in the air like a slow-burning blaze. "Because Archer isn't just our friend—his dads are on the Shifter Council. We've invoked for him twice, which has been ignored, and when our superiors or his family find that out? You're all going to be busted back to fucking Wichita or some other Podunk town far away. He's too humble to flaunt his stature or his fame in your face, so I will. Stop trying to make fetch happen before you end up on the wrong side of some powerful people."

"You never said 'lawyer'; you just said he was done talking," Raskin pleads weakly. His posture says he knows he fucked up now, and I grin broadly as his failure seeps into his bones. "We're only trying to understand your missing teammate, Mr. Glaser. Seems to me you'd want to help."

I hold up my hand before the lion responds. "He does and he will. However, it will not be here or now. Unless you're charging him, we're walking out of here with our friend. We can have his attorney contact the station, so he can come in and give a formal statement. Your tactic might fly with people who aren't savvy and don't know how dangerous it is to answer questions without representation, but Archer is not one of them."

They look at one another, communicating silently for a moment before Raskin turns back to us. "He's free to go. But if we don't hear from you, Mr. Glaser, we *will* come looking."

Archie lets out a breath of relief, then salutes the Fed. "Aye, aye, Agent Asshat!"

"We're not pirates," Barcec mutters grumpily.

I roll my eyes, offering Archie my hand, and he rises as he takes it. "You should know that we will have to report our contact with you and the locals. Guardians are required to report every enforcement community interaction, even if it's minimal. That helps the Society monitor how our names are mentioned in your systems and prevent us from being exposed to anyone who should not know. Keep that in mind when you file things, agents."

Raskin nods, but I know he's pissed. He was ready to go off when he got back to his desk, whether it was in his report, to his co-workers, or even to his boss. My warning has him reconsidering that, and that's why I said it. Guardians—with or without charges—must be kept under wraps until they have fulfilled their duties. Even after their charges can go on sans monitoring, they are re-assigned to rapid response teams to assist in bigger problems. Revealing our identities is like burning a human spy's cover, and the Society would come down on those assholes like a ton of bricks.

"Come on, guys," I say to the twins, Reb, and Javi. "It's time for Arch to get his stuff and for us to get out of here without the press seeing. We don't need to be on the six o'clock news."

Archie and Javi go first, then the demons, and before we exit, both Rebel and I give the Feds one last challenging look before we follow.

Putting the fear of our highest bosses into the growly Minotaur is a good thing—he's the most likely to fuck us over for an easy solve.

As we walk down the hallway to the locker room, I whisper to Archie. "Do you really need anything here? I'd like to avoid more cops if possible. They're looking to pin this on someone quickly and get it off their plates."

"Nah. I can come back another time, or wait until the next practice," he says as his gaze moves to the guard in front of the door. "Let's make our way to the back and get out of here."

"Ang, you and D go out the front and get the cars. Bring them around back as inconspicuously as you can, and I'll get him in there," Reb says as he tosses his keys to the elder demon. "I don't know how you fuckers got here so fast, or what you had to leave to show up, but I appreciate it."

Javi winks and then shrugs. "I got Dragonfly's text. She must have been *very* surreptitious about it as you guys pulled up. It gave me enough time to call these two, who picked me up and... perhaps cheated a bit to get here in time."

My eyes widen, and I smack Damon's arm. "You're not supposed to use that kind of magic where the humans can see it!"

He chuckles, then fist-bumps his brother. "Trust me, they didn't see *shit*. That's how fast we were going."

Goddess save me from men and their reckless bullshit, I fucking swear.

The twins got the cars to the loading area fairly quickly, and before I knew it, we were sneaking around the police barriers with ease. Archie pointed out the service entrances used by players avoiding the press—not what they're there for, but that's jocks for you—and we even got away from the arena without a tail. I was worried for a few minutes when I saw an older sedan behind us for a few blocks; however, Reb and Ang revved up their engines to ditch it within minutes. I'm not sure it was a cop or even a reporter, but there's no use courting disaster by ignoring something obvious.

"Archie, is Badger really the type to fuck off without notice if he's mad?"

The lion nods, sighing heavily. "Dude is the *least* chill person I've ever met, including you, Reb."

I snicker as my stepbrother mutters under his breath then turns back to my mate. "So he *could* have done that this time. Maybe he did, and someone planted evidence to frame the players. Badger himself could have done it, I suppose."

"Uh, no. Badger is *not* the 'think ahead and plot' type, Wheels. He's the 'accidentally kill someone in a blind rage' kind of guy. He definitely wouldn't think that many steps ahead."

Rebel licks his tongue as he races through the streets, obviously considering Archie's info. "Mmm. Well, if he's not that bright and very hair-trigger, maybe he *was* kidnapped, but not for anything connected to the other shit. Yeah, the idiot Feds reacted when we mentioned it, but that doesn't mean this actually *is* connected. Chaos and butterfly wings, you know?"

"I don't know if chaos theory *or* Occam's Razor is going to help us on this one, Reb." I bite my lower lip, spinning the pieces in my head as I try to make a full picture. "I guess we're lucky Badger wasn't lying in a pool of his own blood like our new friends' rival was."

At the mention of Morgana, Archie beams at me. "There's a lot of 'arctic' big guys in hockey, obviously, because they're suited to it. But that kid was scouted pretty intensely before State U picked him up. He could have had his pick of supe unis; I looked it up."

I didn't know that.

Giving him a curious look, I tilt my head. "When?"

"I'm not *always* on the ice when I'm here, Wheels. Sometimes the other strings are doing things, sometimes I'm in the box, sometimes I'm watching the plays... Coach likes to make sure we're well-rounded."

I arch a brow, my lips curved up in amusement. "How is playing on your phone making you 'well-rounded'?"

"It's not." He chuckles and shrugs. "I was having trouble focusing today; it happens. To keep him from noticing, I was pretending to look at stuff on my phone, then at the ice. That's how I made time to check on the surface half of our loose alliance."

"What else did you find?" Reb asks as he heads onto the highway, accelerating quickly.

My cuddly lion shrugs. "The stuff about the Dean lady and her chopping off her ex's head—but that's old news by now. Gotta say I admire a chick who has the stones to face a dragon with a broadsword alone and come out on top."

"Stones, ha," I snicker as he grins proudly. "But you're right—we've faced various dragons, and they're not to be trifled with. Morgana comprises two very strong mythicals, but that was insanely risky and super impressive."

"Agreed," Rebel says as he passes a semi and then hits the gas again. "What about the others? The professor and the student?"

Archie shrugs. "I didn't remember their names, honestly. The kid caught my attention because he could play against me someday, you know? And the dragon-slayer woman is hard to forget."

Pressing my fingers to my eyes, I groan. "How on *earth* could you forget the fucking Prince and *heir* to the entire Fae court, babe?"

He blinks. "I dunno. I don't much care what they're doing over in Sparkle Land, Rogue. The only faeries I give a shit about are in this car giving me a hard time after a very rough day."

"Don't be a drama queen, Arch." Reb looks over his shoulder, then back at the road. "Royalty isn't a big deal for some things, especially in this realm, but that guy is a *big deal*, even to non-Fae. There are four courts, and someday he'll be in charge of one. That's like being in charge of a quarter of this planet, man."

"He's not *my* king, so I don't give a fuck," Archie says stubbornly. "Well, except that he seems to be on our side and since we saw assholes from his realm in the bad guy roll call... I guess that's important."

"It is," I reply without thinking. "We will need lots of strong supes from all over if this becomes an out-and-out war. The more elite the bloodline, the higher powered the Fae will be. A prince of Daybreak is an enormous ally."

Archie frowns. "But you guys are really powerful, especially you, Wheels."

"I'm a hybrid nobody, and my power isn't really normal."

Rebel grunts, shifting as he changes lanes. "I've got juice, man, but you haven't seen shit until you see what royals can do. Rogue is right about her shit, though. No one has a clue why she is the way she is. Since Graciella and Odhran won't spill on how they got us, we don't know how to trace her line. She might have some distant relatives who are distantly related to low-level royals or something. We just don't know."

"The hybrid thing is so weird," the lion mutters, and I smack his arm hard. "Ow! I don't mean like that, babe. I mean... the old rules said species and realms couldn't crossbreed, which led to this huge amount of abandoned, possibly supernatural kids popping up all over. They put together an entire government and infrastructure to deal with it, but all it did was highlight that the realms and species were doing whatever the fuck they wanted, law be damned. It's like... equal and opposite reactions, you know?"

"I'm not sure Newton has anything to do with gods and shifters and Fae fucking, but okay." Rebel snorts as he turns off the expressway to head toward our home. "Supes do not differ from humans in some ways, man. Tell them they can't do something and they'll do it harder."

"Plus, people fuck up. They get drunk or high, and jump someone. The Fates meddle in shit. There's so many ways that the stupid law could go wrong, and it did." I shrug, sighing as I lean back in my seat. "Somewhere a Fae and a Cubi had a fling, and Reck and I were made. The gap between that and how my asshole adoptive folks got us is a black hole. No one's been able to answer that question anymore than where they sent him before they got Rebel."

I frown, trying not to let thinking about my real twin cloud my day.

Even if I swear that someday, I will find out what happened to him and take my vengeance on everyone involved.

Down To Hell

REBEL

—

ARCH WASN'T wrong to say that all the old farts meddling in who can love whom and how supes can express that, but it just underlines the fact that we may be more 'evolved' than humans in some senses, but in others? We're identical. Our elders thought they could pass down edicts that would control normal instincts to preserve their power, and it didn't fucking work. In fact, it only made a *bigger* mess that required this intricate system to fix the problem *they* caused with their bigotry.

Absolutely ridiculous, when you really think about—all these aban-doned kids all over the planet because beings didn't want anyone to know they broke the law that now has to protect the products of that criminality.

Protecting those kids is what Guardians do, and Rogue and I will eventually be called to ours. I think it's a noble calling—much better than random-ass jobs people do just for a paycheck. However, that will not be relevant at all if all this garbage leads to a multi-realm war. I'd put hard cash on a lot of these fuckers who are in the evil factions being from the same families and groups that enacted those stupid-ass laws. It's always the jackasses who want to tell everyone how they should live that are crawling around in the muck to get their way.

"Reb? Are you getting out of the car or do you live there now?"

I blink at Rogue's teasing, realizing that I've been sitting here like a fool while I pondered. "I'm coming. Just got lost in thought for a moment."

"It's easy to do when the world is exploding every damn time we turn around," she says with a wink. "But I figured you wouldn't want to miss throwing your weight around as we discuss this shit inside."

Hopping out, I follow my step-sis into the house my friends and I claimed as our own before we even knew we were building a home that needed to include her. It does now, which improves it a thousandfold, but I think Angelo should figure out how to buy it from Luca before that ownership becomes an issue. It didn't matter as much prior to finding out who he's aligning with, but now it *definitely* does. We can always move, but I find myself oddly attached to the 'first time' memories we've recently created here.

Who knew a bit of happiness would bring out the simp in me? I sure as fuck didn't.

Rogue deactivates the security quickly, yanking the door open and stalking inside as Archie and I trail behind. I hear D and the others pull into the drive as we head for the living room and the door closes, which lifts a weight off my chest. I know they aren't likely to have been stopped, but the amount of shit going down every time we're separated is making me paranoid. I know we can't stay together all the time; it's not logistically possible. But the uptick in bullshit happening to our fam when we're not in force isn't a coincidence. I just don't know why we're the ones who keep stepping in it.

"I'm going up to change," Archie says as he does an about-face. "I know I did at the arena, but I can't shake off the disgusting feeling of those dickheads interrogating me. I have to swap clothes or something. It's making my skin crawl."

Once he's up the stairs, Rogue gives me a worried look. "Archie's more sensitive than us, Reb. So are D and Javi. We have to join with Angelo to protect them—this constant assault will harden them, and I don't want that."

"Me neither, sis," I reply with a sigh. "They're not innocent, but they've all been kept from the real harshness the three of us have seen in our work. But I also know that we may not preserve that innocence forever with the current atmosphere. Damon has learned more about his dad's perversions and crooked dealings in this past month than Ang ever wanted him to. Arch and Javi are going to be exposed to bad things despite their parents doing their damnedest to keep them naïve. We can't control that."

She snorts and tugs her hair out of the scrunchie. "We don't have to speed it up, either."

"True, but *not* telling them things will leave them vulnerable." I tilt my head as I shrug. "Today was one of those moments, and you know it. Archie felt safe in the arena because he had less knowledge of the world than he should. He thought being in a public place where well-known athletes practice and the team has security would be fine if he was escorted. You and I know from experience that *nowhere* is safe depending on who and what is out to get you."

"Stop being so smart, damn it."

I chuckle as I kick off my shoes and head for my chair, flopping into it. "I know; it's not my forte. But we all need to be smarter right now because we have no idea what framing, killing, or kidnapping a bunch of sports stars gets *anyone*. It doesn't make sense."

"Could these be test runs?"

We both look over at the entryway to the living room where the rest of our family stands. Damon was the one who spoke, and that doesn't surprise me at all. His mind is constantly whirring like a supercomputer, and he sees patterns no one else does.

Rogue beams at him proudly as she nods. "I think it's possible. If there are teams being built to hit more important folks—higher in the food chain—they could practice on celebs."

"It could be about sports gambling," Angelo says. "The Stuhlls run it here in Bay City, but they could partner with sister organizations across the country to fix games."

"Also possible," I muse as they join us. "Merra has long wanted to take her show on the road to conquer more cities like the human mobs did."

Javier snorts. "Reb, you know as well as the rest of us that Vegas was a fairytale. Supes have owned that town since it was built. We just let the humans spin their tales."

"Yeah, but they did spread across the nation in other ways—and not just the Omerta ones. Many mobs have criss-crossed the US over the years, just different from what the masses think." I frown, considering another possibility. "It also could be completely unrelated to this mess. Chaos theory and all—especially if Hell is putting pressure on demons to broker more deals to feed the coffers because of those Games you guys were talking about."

Angelo leans forward, his forearms on his knees as he grins. "Hell is *always* pressuring brokers for more deals, man. The Games don't need that cheddar to run. However, the royals like having as much debt as possible in case they need to mobilize for some reason. Being worried that a new coup will follow this iteration as it did the last is a damn good reason to up quotas."

"Of course, it could be *all* of that," Archie says as he pads in, freshly washed and changed yet again. "Hell could be pressuring the sales folk, which leads to the evil rebels upping their test phase, and part of that is people like Merra pushing to expand their territories. Like, it could all be a giant spider web of doom, man."

Damn, he's on point today.

"It very well could be," Angelo says thoughtfully. "Usually the simplest stuff is the answer, but with all those factions and special guests meeting at the Apalachin? It allows groups to mingle and create more complex interconnected plots. We don't know what the fuckers on the stage discussed in their weird portal meeting. That could have been one big project management session."

Rogue sprawls out on the floor on her back, looking up at the ceiling in annoyance. "That's just fucking great. There's no way we can figure out what all these assholes are doing simultaneously, especially across nine goddamn realms."

"But we have friends who might help," Javier offers. "The group from State U and the demon royals aren't fully in the 'trust circle', but I got the impression that they aren't crazy about the idea of multi-realm warfare. I wonder if D could work with whoever does tech for their groups to create some sort of... hub... that we can share info in?"

Damon scratches his chin as he considers it. "I'd need their help to build it. It has to be available here and in Hell, possibly other places as well, and it needs to be magically and physically secure. We can't put a damn thing on it until we've crash-tested damn near every kind of attack. Otherwise, we're all risking more than just bad PR. With the right eyes on our shit, we could be executed for treason or speed up the whole 'Project Multiverse' bullshit these asswads are planning."

"Execution would be less painful if so," Angelo mutters. "There is no world in which Luca or Darkstar should be in charge of enormous masses of beings—be it Hell or here. That's a recipe for disaster I can't even contemplate."

"You guys never mentioned that guy," Rogue says as she lolls her head over to look at the twins. "You just used to disappear for summers and come back looking older and pissier."

I chuckle at the accuracy of her remark. Angelo and Damon attending *Discordia* was never a topic their friends could broach, but we could see the changes in them when they returned after each span of time they were gone. "She's right, dude. You guys hated that place with a passion, but we know nothing about it."

"What's to know?" Damon says with a shrug. "It's an all-male college for demons in Hell that accepts all the royals and rich kids. There's a sister school for the women—Brimstone Academy—and a reform school for the ones whose parents can't control them."

Rogue frowns at him. "Where do the *non-rich, non-criminal* demons go to college?"

Angelo shrugs. "Blackmoor, Izaulrelts, or if they're really unlucky, Zexrerarth. They're all over Hell, and usually the demons from the area stay within their lands. No one really pays attention to those schools, though."

I arch a brow. "Has it not occurred to you that the 'poor demon' schools are probably very fertile grounds for recruiting? I imagine this Darkstar guy wouldn't go himself, but I bet he has people on his payroll finding the right teens and younger demons who are easily manipulated and angry at their station. That's sort of how rebellions work, Ang."

He blinks, then looks at Damon, who shrugs. "I guess I didn't consider it at all—which means you're probably spot on, Reb. D and I aren't even into that 'who's richer/more powerful' BS that most of the demons at Discordia are. We stayed away from politics and kept our heads down so we could graduate as fast as possible and be back here full time. But our classmates? They were absolutely *consumed* by wealth, ties to the court, and all that shit."

"No one gives a shit about the 'working class' of Hell at all unless they're failing at their jobs," Damon adds. "They're not, like, punished for existing like humans here seem determined to do. But they're also not really given opportunities to change their station."

"Which means they're ripe for plucking by the right megalomaniacal asshat like your old Headmaster, hmm?" Rogue says as she sits up. "I mean, the guy looked like he dropped out of a stupid fantasy movie where the villain runs a school and abuses the students. He reeked of dictator-wannabe."

"Yeah, that's old Lucian in a nutshell," Angelo says with a sigh. "And Luca's not much better, so the two of them very likely have some pissed off-lower-demon-to-rebel pipeline set up. I don't know how we're going to confirm that, though. The royals can't go anywhere *near* the places you'd need to, in order to figure that out. They're far too recognizable, and they'd be in a lot of danger. Plus, they probably had to get a pass approved to come to this meeting. It burned a lot of capital, I bet."

"But they're rich, right?" Javi says. "They've got more."

"Not money capital. *Political* capital," Damon corrects him. "Most demons don't come here but for work and such, and the royals *never* come to the surface. I'd bet the prince had to ask Daddy for permission. Funny if you think about it, but that probably cost him something dearly to get. So no, I doubt they can work out going to the main areas in Hell where the commoners live."

"Great. Then how do we figure out if that's what your dad and his bestie are doing?" I ask.

Angelo sighs, looking extremely unhappy. "We'll have to go there ourselves. D and I can come and go as we please now that we've graduated. We can bring guests."

A trip to Hell wasn't on my bingo card this year, either, but it's not exactly been a picnic so far, anyway.

Killing Time

ROGUE

THE MOOD WAS SOMBER for the rest of the night, and by the time we all retired to my room to sleep, I was exhausted. No one thinks a little jaunt to Hell will be a fun vacay, but nothing else we spit-balled seemed like it would be as effective. The real question is how we schedule it and keep our absence off the radar of those damn cops and the Gemini capo. Javi and Archie's parents won't be hard to put off with a fib; Graciella and Odhran couldn't give less of a shit where we are. But the twins are definitely monitored, and Luca will know when they pass through the gateway, according to Damon.

"Demon crap is so complicated," Archie says as we drive to the grocery. "Why would they have a system that tattles on their own people for coming and going from their realm? Is there some exciting new stuff down there they think is going to draw undesirables?"

"The better question is, who does Hell find undesirable?" I reply with a grin. "But I get what you mean. It's pretty controlling for a place populated by demons and their ilk. Maybe that has something to do with the fear of rebellion the royals mentioned?"

"A valid fear, as far as we've seen." Archie whips off the highway exit, heading for the retail area. "Luckily for us, the traffic wasn't absolute shit this morning, huh?"

I nod, looking around. Bay City *seems* like a perfect place to live, but that's like a lot of things in life that are gorgeous on the outside and rotting on the inside. "True. And I know Reb and the twins hated for us to go alone—even together—but they had commitments. Javier had to get the restaurant open for lunch. And I needed to be out of the house before I went crazy. I hate knowing all the things we need to do and not being able to actually *do* any of them."

Archie chuckles as he pulls into the parking lot of the organic mega-mart. "You've never been good at waiting, Wheels. A woman of action —that's part of why you're so captivating."

I give him a wry look as I put my hand on the door handle. "Flattery will get you everywhere, but not right now. I want to attack this pantry list Javi made for us with surgical precision. Getting it done will help me settle a bit."

"Then let's hit it, babe," he says as he opens his door. I laugh and do the same, getting out and meeting the handsome hockey player by the trunk. He pulls out the reusable bags Javi and Damon insisted we bring, and we head into the store together.

Sometimes, the simplest things make you feel like everything will be okay.

ARCHIE PUSHES the cart through the produce section, wrinkling his nose as he watches me pick out the things Javier requested. "How do you know what to do to make sure it's good? Is this like that 'make a towel a hat' thing women just seem to know how to do?"

I blink at him for a moment and then roll my eyes. "For fuck's sake, Archie. I would have thought someone as progressive as Sariah would teach her son this shit."

He looks confused for a moment, scratching his chin as he looks at the tomatoes. "About produce?"

Good to know that I'm right; even mothers her age are still neglecting to make dudes functional in the world without a female.

"Yes, Archie. I mean, most girls are taught by some female in their life to do the 'traditionally female' stuff like pick out produce, braid hair, do laundry, use makeup... I suppose it's getting better now that our parents' generation is getting older and the next one is raising less gender-focused kids. But... it's shit we're usually taught without anyone asking for it." I sigh, holding up the fruit for him to see. "You have to get a firm one, and which type you pick depends on what you're using it for."

"I'm gonna learn all this shit just to break the norms, then. Fuck that shit."

The lion isn't joking. No, he follows me to every item I have to get in this section, asking how he knows if this fruit or veggie is ripe, over-ripe, or bad. He asks about cutting imperfections, and what kinds of dishes Javi might be using them for. By the end of that part of the list, I'm actually enjoying his curiosity, and as we move to the bakery, I give him an amused look.

"Want to know how we pick out bread and stuff now, too?"

Archie snorts. "Hell yes, I do. No way that flaming featherhead is having an edge over me just because he works with food. I want to know it all."

"Okay, but people are going to look at us like we're insane," I warn him. "We still have a lot of shopping to do."

"As if I give a shit what people think." He scoffs as he picks up a French bread loaf, and I point to the date stamp. Once he checks it out, I nod for him to add it to the cart. "Besides, it's stupid to act like guys don't have to eat. I mean, sure we can order out, and we have Javier to help us with that, but why shouldn't dudes learn this, too?"

"Archie Glaser, your mama raised you right even if she missed how to pick out food." I lean in, kissing his lips lightly. "And I like that you want to learn stuff, even if you don't have to. You're pretty enlightened for a sportsball lunkhead."

He wrinkles his nose at me, and I laugh as he grabs my hips to pull me close. "I'm the most enlightened athlete you'll ever meet, Wheels, and you should be grateful every day that I had so many dads who adored my mom. I watched them treat her better than most ladies get in their lifetimes—every day. I won't stand for you getting any less."

Shit. Be still, my black heart.

"You know I love you, right?" I murmur against his lips. I'm not ashamed of that sentence, but I also have no idea who might be watching us. Archie is famous—at least, in sports circles—and the last thing I need is—

"Hey, Jack... look, it's Glaser!"

Of course there's some puck-loving guys running around the grocery right now. That's exactly my luck, and that they're now jabbering loudly nearby is further insult to injury. Archie pulls away, his lips curved up in an apologetic grin. He turns on his heel, looking over at the blatant fans to wave.

"You caught me, guys. A growing player has to eat, too."

I move to the cart, hoping to keep their attention off of me if I just very slowly push it away to continue working on the list. Unfortunately, yet again, I don't get what they want as the first guy calls out to stop me.

"Where are you going, pretty lady? No one knew the Mane Event had a girl!"

Wincing to myself, I gather all my patience up and turn the buggy so I can force a smile at his fanboy. "He doesn't. I'm just a very good friend."

It sucks to do that, but the scrutiny it would bring if these idiots spouted it off on some podcast or blog would make everything even worse. We have enough to worry about without puck bunnies all over town losing their minds. Archie presses his lips together, and I know he's fighting the urge to correct me because his lion demands it. It's no picnic for me either, but it's the best choice for now.

"I wish I had hotties in short shorts and tanks built like you to stand that close to who were *'just friends'*," the second guy says before he guffaws.

This will not go well; the question is whether it's me or Archie who teaches them a lesson.

"That's very... generous of you to say," I reply with an even tighter smile. "Archie is my stepbrother's best friend. We grew up together."

The two men elbow one another, laughing and practically confirming evolution as they clown around. Archie rubs the back of his neck, and I can tell he's embarrassed, but doesn't want to piss off his supporters. When they finally stop hooting, I give the supposedly adult men an unimpressed look.

"Is there something humorous about that?"

"Well..."

Archie frowns, crossing his arms over his broad chest. "Well, what, gentlemen?"

The first joker shrugs and says, "You were waiting until she wasn't jailbait, eh, man? I don't blame you. This chick is hotter than fuck."

I barely realize he's moved before Archie has the disgusting fool by the collar of his shirt, holding him aloft as he snarls. His tail has popped out, and it's swishing angrily as he shakes the guy. His friend looks terrified, so I give him a look that dares him to move. I think he's going to try running for a split second, but the guy pisses himself.

Oh, I love when I don't even have to lift a finger.

"That is no way to speak to a woman, you shitheel," Archie growls as he gives the dude another shake. "First... gross as fuck. Predators like you should be locked in Blackwater before you get old enough to hurt anyone. Second, no one looked at her like that *ever*. My best friend and the rest of us would have beaten them within an inch of their lives... even if it was one of us."

His words make me smile, but it's only for a moment as I go back to keeping the dangling jackass's friend from getting security. "He's telling the truth, you know. They were my protectors, and people like you are why girls need them."

"Get his wallet out, Rogue. Damon can do a little recon on whether this fucker has done anything that will take him out of the dating pool. I don't like letting him go with a warning when he suggests something vile." Archie jerks his head at the man he's holding, and I walk over to fish it out as instructed.

"Butch Lockland." My mate nods, and I put the wallet back, careful to barely touch the asshole as I do so. Once I'm done with him, I stalk over to the scaredy-cat. "Now, you, buddy. Give it to me because I'm not getting anywhere near your... mess."

"Please... I'm only here with him. I didn't do anything," the piss-drenched dude says as he hands me the requested wallet. "Don't come after me. We won't tell anyone; I swear."

"Dude, no one is coming after you themselves," Archie grunts. "We're going to check you out, and if you're just gross idiots in public, you'll be fine. If you've done anything to suggest that wasn't just a disgusting joke? We'll give info to the right people and make sure you're dealt with *legally*. I'm a hockey player, not a fucking vigilante."

Chuckling as I look at the ID, I shake my head. "Stanley Hammersmith."

"Excellent." Archie lowers the guy to the ground and gives him a fangy smile. "Now, gentlemen... I'm going to let you go once you apologize to my good friend, Rogue. But you should worry—our friend Damon *will* find any dirt you're trying to hide."

The dangled one swallows hard, nodding, and his buddy joins in. They stammer apologies, and I shrug when Archie waits for me to accept. As much as men like that make my skin crawl, Archie's caveman bullshit was hot. I'd like them to be gone as soon as possible so I can tell him just how hot it was, even if I didn't need his protection.

"Get lost, dickheads."

I watch them scramble and give my lion a slow grin. "You're sexy when you're growly, Archie."

Even though I would prefer to defend myself.

Bad News

ANGELO

"I HEARD you and your brother were in attendance, but I didn't see you." Luca looks at me from behind his enormous desk with a frown. "Your mother and I were quite disappointed."

As if you weren't busy facilitating some sort of inter-realm rebellion, Dad.

But I don't say that. I need Luca to believe I'm not really aware of what he's doing in the background, so my family and anyone else we can assemble can work to prevent it. Instead, I shrug. "We were enjoying the delights of the Apalachin, Luca. You, of all people, know how much there is to sample."

My lie makes him beam like a proud papa—something he's never been for a second in his long life—and he shuffles some papers before he responds. "I suppose I can't blame you for wanting to introduce your brother to the finer things in demon life. He's been buried behind those screens for so long, that I wondered about him. Your mother and I want *lots* of heirs running around eventually, which means you and he have to get started with that 'rescue' you've decided to share."

It takes a lot of effort, but I suppress the shiver his words make run up my spine. I don't enjoy his talking about our mate like that, and I like his assumption that we're using her as a broodmare even less. Rogue isn't the type of woman to settle down and pop out little demon hybrids to fulfill Luca's imperial dreams. Hell, our *mother* isn't even that type—she simply gave him what he wanted quickly enough that he left her alone after that. Once D and I were born, she handed us off to the staff, and they both continued their adulterous bullshit on their own.

That's probably what he thinks Damon and I are doing by picking our girl—gross.

"Rogue escorted us, and we brought our other friends as well. It was an eye-opening adventure." Hopefully, that's vague enough for him to interpret it however he wants, and he won't demand details I would *never* be willing to give. Luca has no business in my goddamn bedroom or my mate's preferences, nor does my conniving mother.

Luca beams again, then picks up another sheaf of paper. "Excellent. You and Damon will have our family expanding in no time. Once you produce heirs, you'll figure out how that's supposed to work. Your mother and I did very quickly, and it's been enviable for centuries."

I hold back my sneer, schooling my features as my theory of what he alluded to is proven on the nose. Neither of my parents gives a shit about anything other than themselves, and this 'revolution' thing they're part of is no doubt as self-serving as possible. I'm not sure *why* they'd want anything to do with being part of the ruling class of Hell other than the title; they're both damn near allergic to actual work. From what I understand, the current courts and leaders actually do shit besides sit on their asses and amass wealth. They're not *good* leaders, but they are working ones, and my folks do more pretending to work than they actually accomplish.

It's puzzling as fuck.

"Why did you ask to see us?" I venture casually as he moves more things around the desk in an impression of someone who is busy.

"Usually your requests are for events or because there's a job that needs to be done."

Luca's eyes narrow, and he studies me carefully for a moment. This is a dangerous time; I'm well aware. When he hasn't decided if I'm being a smart ass or loyal, there's a brief interlude where he might continue or launch into his favorite forms of punishment for mouthing off. I got lucky today, so he must be focused on whatever he wants. He sniffs, then looks around the room. "And *where* is your brother? I demanded his attendance as well."

"Lola stopped him as I came in," I shrug, hoping that won't set us back to his temper getting the best of him. "She's probably still fussing over him."

"That woman coddles him far too much; it's why he's not fit to rule without you."

Again, a statement worthy of a disbelieving scoff. Lola *despises* D for being 'weak' as much as Luca does. She simply shows it differently and pretends to protect him from Luca to make the staff and anyone in view think *she's* the loving parent. She doesn't give a hairy rat's ass about either of us, except for elevating her status as the paragon of demon motherhood and mob boss's wife. The fact that Luca doesn't see it tells you just how much he pays attention to anything she does.

"I could call him in?" I offer blandly.

"No, I'll deal with this." Luca presses a button on the intercom on his desk, then bellows, "Damon, get your spineless tail in here before I send someone less pleasant to fetch you!"

My teeth grit as he knocks my brother for absolutely nothing, assuming he's hiding rather than appeasing our faux-grasping mother. D never hides from Luca, but I often leave him out purposefully to protect him. However, I've never given my father the impression that he's not along for the ride because of that—I always make sure he has an assignment to cover for it. Luca is just being a dick because he *can* and he *enjoys* it.

Damon wanders in a few seconds later, his face a mask of indifference. "Sorry, Luca. Lola was asking me about our stay at the Apalachin. I apologize for being late."

That's a convo I need to hear about when we're far away from this place.

"As you should be," Luca says, then pushes back from his desk slightly. "I have jobs for you two, and I expect them to be done thoroughly, quickly, and with the utmost discretion. Do you understand?"

I blink, then nod automatically. "Of course. What do you require?"

Smiling with pleasure at my quick acquiescence, Luca puts his hands on the edge of the desk. "I need Damon to build a database and application system for a membership we're going to offer later this year. I've had someone draw up the specifications to ensure the proper security, questions, and vetting mechanisms are listed. You will build this within the next three weeks and come back for a meeting where we can 'test' it. Once it's verified, I will provide details on launching the program. Is that clear?"

Damon frowns for a second, then asks, "Is the person who made your list of requirements tech-inclined? If I don't have the right information at the beginning, I could make very time-consuming mistakes in the foundational build."

Luca doesn't know shit about technological stuff, so that's a well-worded and fair question.

But our father admits no faults, so his face reddens and he slams his fist on the desk. "Of course it is! I didn't come up with it myself; I was given the specifics by those who are experts in the field. How dare you question my competency!"

Stepping closer to the enormous piece of furniture, I hold up my hands placatingly. "Luca, wait. D was only confirming that he has the necessary tools to complete your assignment within the time slot and do it right the first time. He doesn't want to fail you, right, bro?"

My twin nods, then pushes up his glasses. "Correct, Ang."

I feel his simmering rage at being dressed down for clarifying something like a good employee, but he's doing a great job of hiding it. Turning back to Luca, I ask, "What is my job?"

Our father sucks in breath through his nose, then cracks his neck as if we're the most irritating thing he's ever experienced. I highly doubt that, but whatever gets him through the day. Finally, he says, "Once your brother builds and launches this successfully, you will be in charge of setting and completing interviews for the members in the 'round two' live portion of the vetting. There will be a small panel of interviewers, and your unique skill set will be perfect for leading them in verifying the authenticity of those beings."

I frown, trying to puzzle out what the fuck Luca is doing until it dawns on me.

We're setting up a pre-qualification for supernaturals to join their goddamn rebellion as discussed at the Apalachin—and I'm the fucking interrogator.

When Luca lets us leave, Lola is nowhere to be found. I let out a sigh of relief as we pass through the living area, the sitting room, and the foyer without being accosted. This visit troubles me in ways I can't discuss yet, and I have no idea how we're going to finagle it so it hurts rather than helps him without giving away our disloyalty.

"Always good to see them," Damon murmurs for whatever surveillance is listening. We got used to making sure we said and did the right things in every section of our house the moment we moved to the surface. We realized even as younger demons that our parents would punish us for any perceived slight, and stroking their egos helped keep their ping-ponging moods from smacking into us unexpectedly.

"Yep. I can't wait to get to work on the stuff Luca gave us. His trust is one of the best things he's ever given us besides our names."

Seriously, it's always this corny, and it never fails to work.

Damon and I open the front door, leaving quickly and heading to the car we came in. We took mine this time, so we knew for certain that we could outrun something if we needed to. Since the event, our family has been watching every shadow for enemies. It's not really paranoia, per se, because we know Mina, the Sickos, possibly the Stuhlls, my own mob, and now the damn cops may have people tailing us. We can't *stop* doing normal shit, but this knowledge forces us to revamp every procedure and protocol when some new fucking threat comes up. It's bullshit, and I hate it with a passion.

I peel out of the drive, maneuvering the car down the long drive and onto the private road that leads to their mansion. Once we're far enough away from their neighborhood and speeding along the highway, I turn to my twin. "You know what that shit is, right?"

"Of course I fucking do, Ang. I'm not stupid," he replies irritably. "I risked my ass in there to ask my question because I was already trying to figure out how to leave backdoors open so I can monitor it without being seen."

"You'd have full developer access, though," I say as my brows furrow. "Why does that matter?"

"Because if Luca has people who know what they're doing, they can see what I'm doing in the logs with admin access. Hell, for all I know, his experts are techno-mages. Building a secret door will keep my spying on things away from their prying eyes—*if* I'm good enough to hide it correctly. If he just made up some stuff with his friends, who have zero technical aptitude for it, then I don't have to figure that shit out. Get it?"

I don't, but I nod. "Okay. That's probably as close to understanding what you're doing as I'll get, bro, but I see your point. You had to know what kind of people would examine and spy on you as you built this thing."

"Yep," he replies. "But my part isn't really the shitty one, and we both know it. Fuck knows who he's giving you on this 'team', and you'll be expected to push the limits of the applicants who make it to your interviews until they break. That's what he wants, you know."

"I know."

"Are you okay with that?"

I give him a disbelieving expression. "D, I do that shit for him all the time. And we know the people joining this 'club' or whatever are no goddamn angels, especially if they make it to round two. It's not like I'm clubbing baby seals."

"True." He's quiet for a moment as I navigate toward our next stop, which is the gateway office for the portal. "But I also know that Luca will pick people with far fewer morals than you to assist. And that might actually bother you."

That's the one thing bothering me since our asshat father gave us these assignments, but I was hoping he wouldn't catch on, damn it.

Guess we're all going to be worried about this when everyone hears about it—Rogue is gonna be pissed.

Thunderstruck

ROGUE

—

Luckily, the rest of the shopping was without incident. Archie texted one of his dads—the one who handles his agent-type stuff— about the standoff before we left the parking lot. I marvel for a moment at how fortunate he is that the response he got was quick, supportive, and ready to act on his behalf. My adoptive parents would have lectured me about behavior that invites trouble and left me to flail about on my own. That's why when Mina started taking off online, she could wrangle and maximize it—she had the support I didn't. It's also why I wasn't able to jump in and vie for that spot; she had resources I didn't.

Not that she'd admit it for a fucking second, of course.

Archie, however, has definitely had that and more the entire time we were growing up. He's got a fierce as fuck mom and five snarly dads who have made sure his dreams can come true. I don't begrudge him that; I just... I'm glad I have a more stable environment now, even if bad shit keeps happening to us. The guys forming a family with me are the closest thing I've had to real bonding since they sent Reck away when I was a kid. I didn't realize how much I needed this, and now I'm determined not to let it slip through my fingers.

"You look more upset than me, Wheels. I deal with dumb shit with fans all the time. It could be worse."

My head whips around, and I gape at Archie. "That is *not* okay, babe. If someone acted like that at the derby matches, both teams would give them an ass-whooping that would make us all disqualified."

My new mate shrugs, looking uncomfortable for a moment before he replies. "And you absolutely should, but... things change when you're at the level of fame and pay we're at on pro teams. It's hard to say, but we become... less than human to some people. Either we're a product that is lauded for performance or harangued for failure... or we're an object people obsess over, aspire to be, or want to fantasize about. There are a lot of things you have to make split-second decisions on, while weighing massive public consequences for whatever you choose."

Wrinkling my nose, I sigh. "I suppose it comes from all directions, too, right? Like fans, coaches, agents, owners, and everything in between?"

"Hell yes, babe. Throw in social media and multiple species? It can get scary as fuck, even if you're a big strong dude like me." He looks uncomfortable for a second before he says, "I've had to decide whether I wanted to lose a fanbase, a sponsorship, or even whether I could realistically defend myself without being accused of harming a much smaller female. Women can be... worse than men in some ways, especially because of size difference and societal expectations."

I work hard to get a grip on my rage at that sentiment, mostly because I don't want to re-traumatize my gentle giant.

"People are way too comfortable with not being popped in the mouth," I mutter instead. "I promise that once we're able to be public? I will one hundred and fifty thousand percent knock some bitch's block off if she rolls up on you." Grinning broadly, I bob my brows. "And you'll never have to worry about it again when the word spreads that you have a feral mate who has zero fucks to give about all those trappings."

"My dad will be happy to hear that he and my other dad will handle your PR nightmares when we tell them," Archie says as he chuckles. "The two of them are the most put-upon members of the family anyway because they do my stuff and have actual clients. It's a *lot*, and my mom gets on them all the time for being too plugged in."

"She'll be happy to know I'm jamming for you, then," I say as I lean back in my seat. "I bet it will even make her feel *less* worried about you when you're at away stuff if *all* of us travel with you."

The lion thinks about it for a moment and then nods. "Probably so. Reb has a quick temper and little patience for fools. The twins are known for viciousness, and Javi is the voice of reason. Sariah would likely say that's a perfect combination of talents to keep me in line."

I feel better now that the haunted look on his face has disappeared. Despite being serious about how fervently the derby teams would protect one another, I know that many players at his level are on their own. It's not that the team doesn't support one another; it's simply that there are way too many angles and people with their hands in the pockets of the players and teams. That sucks, and I'd *never* want to be in that position, but I'll sure as hell keep Archie from getting manhandled while he's living his dream.

Of course, we may not have to worry about any of that if the rebels get their way and end up in some gross alternative universe where the villains run everything.

WE'RE ALMOST home when a storm closes in on us, seeming to appear out of nowhere. Archie is navigating the roads well, but my senses are *definitely* tripped. Scenting the air, I look around the landscape as it whizzes by carefully. The energy in the air is tickling over my arms, and I don't know what it is, but I just have a gut feeling that something about the weather is off.

Turning to him, I murmur, "Do you feel that?"

"Yep," he says quietly. "Have you contacted Reb yet? He should drop shit at the garage and get his sparkly ass here. I've been trying to pretend I don't smell it so I reveal nothing to anyone watching, but something is coming."

I nod, sliding into my mental link with my stepbrother. *~Archie and I are about twenty miles from the compound, and there's weird shit afoot at the Circle K. Either Ted's landing a phone booth or we stepped onto a set for a new Greek mythology movie, but the weather is not normal. Get your ass here and bring the others.~*

Rebel growls in annoyance in my mind. *~You could have ordered groceries in. This is what I was worried about, Kiandra.~*

~Stop using my real name, Cosmo Caspian.~ I grin to myself as I use his true name; I don't normally do that, but I'm tired of him scolding me with it like a child. Archie looks at me in confusion, and I shake it off before I say, "Rebel is being his usual charming self. But I think he's going to gather the troops. The question is, will they get here before all hell breaks loose?"

"I don't know, Wheels, but if the storm keeps getting worse, I won't have a choice but to pull off."

My eyes focus on the road ahead, noting the lack of visibility as the rain gets worse. "This isn't normal, but to most humans, it would seem like a freak storm. That's been planned, I think."

"Definitely. Since it didn't start until we were within a short distance on back roads to our house, I think whoever or whatever is doing this knew when it would be most strategically advantageous to hit. That screams stalking or tracing us somehow."

I slap my palm on my forehead. "We were so upset about the fans that we didn't check for devices on the car."

"Son of a bitch," he growls, and I know Rebel is going to read us the riot act. That's basic security shit, and the rattling experience inside *could* have been planned to distract us. "Reb's gonna pitch a hissy; you know that, right?"

"Oh, I do," I say as I keep my eyes on the road behind us in the mirror. There's no one there, but that doesn't mean shit when the people after you have supernatural assholes at their disposal. However, at the very least, I'll see if someone is sneaking up from behind so Archie can correct his trajectory.

The storm picks up; the wind pushes against the small, speedy car we're in, and I hold on to the hand grips as we race down the road. If we get to the edge of the barrier Damon has, it will trip the alarms, and that will transmit distress signals to various places. I could turn it off, obviously, but I'm not sure I want to, given that someone with elemental or nature-based powers is stirring this shit up. I'm never a fan of calling the authorities rather than handling it ourselves, but this time? Maybe there's wisdom in letting that shit bring down the flood of demons who will be alerted when the twins' compound is breached.

Of course, that only works if the goddamn demons aren't part of this shit, but there's no way to know that right now.

"We're close, but if it keeps going like it is, we're not gonna make it." Archie's hands are tight on the wheel as he maneuvers through the water and debris flying. "It's picking up as we get closer, and I feel like that's on purpose. Someone doesn't want us to get inside our walls, Wheels."

Sitting up taller, I look over my shoulder at the blackness in the sky behind the car. It's time for me to break out the Guardian shit, even if that's not technically within the rules. I put my hands on the roof of the car, using the metal outside to conduct my magic so it rises into the sky. Faint traces of pink and purple sparkles zing around, searching for the source of the storm at my direction. My tattoos glow from head to toe as I connect to nature itself, hoping to find friendly forces that might combat the magic seeking us.

"What the hell?" Archie says, and I shake my head. "Are you like... glowing in the dark?!"

"Yes, now shhhh!" I scold him quickly, not wanting his chatter to disrupt my concentration. I'm good at this, but I'm also in a car going ninety in a rainstorm that I know isn't normal. My focus has to be on finding the caster or supe doing this, not on answering him. Archie hasn't been around as much when Reb and I do our thing, so he's probably shocked, but this isn't the time. "I have to figure out what the fuck is going on so I know how to prepare to fight."

"Prepare to fight... Fucking shit, Rogue, it's a storm. How are you going to—"

"Shh!" I say again as my magic whirls around the growing tempest outside the car. "Whatever this is, it's not one person. There's interwoven powers joined. It's a group."

"I'd hope so," he mutters. "One person who could do this is insane."

"But not at all out of the realm of possibility, especially with the other realm fuckers we saw at the meeting," I grit out. "However, I truly don't think we drew the attention required to put us on their list for an attack this soon and this... public."

Archie goes quiet again as I continue searching until a crack of lightning damn near hits the car, and he has to skid off of it to get out of the way. My head hits the ceiling of the car, and I curse loudly as we thump over grass and field, then come to a stop in a completely open-air area. We're sitting ducks here, but I'd wager that bullshit just fucked up our getaway. I turn to look at him, making sure he's not injured, but all I see is the lion bleeding into his eyes as fury takes over.

"Are you okay?" I ask as I rub my head gingerly.

"I'm going to fucking kill someone."

"Well, that makes two of us, and hopefully, whoever it is arrives before my temper gets the best of me."

I may be dangerous when I'm angry, but when someone threatens the people I love, I turn lethal—whether it's legal or not.

Fight Back

DAMON

"Shit, shit, shit!"

I look over at my twin as he slams his palm on the dash of the car hard enough to pop the fucking airbag. "What the hell, Ang?"

"Nothing ever goes smoothly in this town," he growls as he turns to me with the demon in his eyes. "Put the pedal to the metal, bro. I'll have to throw a portal ahead and hope to fuck it's strong enough to get the car *and* us through."

That's not something we normally do, and he's already done it once this week; he shouldn't try it again.

"Why? What the fuck is going on?"

Angelo cracks his neck and then his fingers as he stares at the road ahead with intensity. "Rogue and Arch have some sort of unnatural weather shit building on the road to the house. They're fairly certain it's an attack, and they won't make it to the secure perimeter in time."

"Motherfucking Belial's dirty bib..." I mutter as I hit the gas hard and the car shoots forward like a rocket. "I'm tired of this shit. Tell me how to help you make this portal stable. You'll need it since you're doing it a second time."

My twin sucks in a deep breath and holds his hands out, chanting in Latin under his breath as the demon takes control. I watch for a moment, then let my demon rise so my tail pops out to hold the steering wheel. Once the car is stable, I lift my hands and mimic my brother as the color of my magic blends with his to rip the fabric of reality ahead of us.

Fuck, I hope this works.

THE ENGINE REVS as we appear on the road that runs from the main area where our house is located to the entrance to our private drive. I feel shaky and shocked that we managed it, and Angelo looks paler, but unharmed. That kind of transport is a *lot* when you don't do it often, and we do not, simply to avoid common mistakes that lead to human bullshit. Our father makes it crystal clear he won't bother with be-spelling or wiping the minds of folks who see things they shouldn't, because he doesn't want the Council breathing down his neck. Angelo and I give a shit if innocent people are murdered, so we err on the side of caution with this sort of display. That saves others, but makes us rusty at magic that requires consistent training.

Like portalling two people and an entire fucking car way the fuck across town.

"Step on it, D," Angelo says in a raspy voice. "We have to get there before whatever is coming traps them. I know our girl can fight like a champ, but Archie is less violent and not trained to do battle the same way she is. He's her weak spot."

I love that he doesn't say the man Rogue and I share *is* weak, but that his lack of training weakens her. It's Angelo's way of admitting how fucking strong she is, but also how deeply she cares for the people she loves—enough for it to be a chink in the armor. He's also not making Arch sound bad for not being a warrior like him, Reb, Rogue, and to a small extent, me.

"Do you think Rebel contacted Javier, too? That's another question mark in a fight, you know."

"I'm sure he did." Angelo frowns as we fly toward the house, his eyes on the road to watch for our mate and Arch's car. "He's definitely one of the soft ones, too, but phoenixes are born to do other things in battle, Damon. The big concern I have is if he does his thing in front of Rogue; she's never seen that before, and we have. She might be distracted enough to get injured."

"He can't exactly yell, 'I'm going to immolate myself to destroy everyone; don't worry, I'll be back' across the fight, Ang." I smirk a bit, trying to use humor to take the edge off the worry shooting through my body. "It wouldn't be very stealthy. He should have told her when they mated; the dumbass has had a million chances since then, too."

"None of us has been raised to talk about emotions, strengths, and weaknesses with others except for our fluffy lion. You know that. He's the only one with sane parents and non-whacked expectations of him."

Angelo might be blunt, but he's very insightful when he chooses to be.

"Yeah, but we should do better about overcoming that crap so we aren't blindsided like this. That's especially important when you think about how huge this is—holy *fuck!*"

The massive storm system in the sky wasn't as apparent as it is now, and I almost drove right into a tree that's been ripped from the ground. Swerving around it, I speed up, my gut telling me that tree isn't the only thing that got beaten by the howling wind.

"D, there's a car off the road up there."

I squint, then floor it even harder—as if that will help—shifting as the car pushes to the limit. "It's Archie's car; no question."

"I can't see it well enough to—"

"Ang, don't be a dipshit! Of *course* it's their car!" My frustration leaks out of me as I chastise my brother, and I know that it's because I'm worried about my people. This fucking attack, whoever it is, targeted the two most important people to me right now, and I'm ready to let every part of me burst free and rip something to goddamn pieces.

"Hey, bro... keep it calm, man."

How the fuck am I supposed to do that when people I care about are in danger? For that matter, how is he?

"Angelo, you're the one with the temper. How are you controlling this shit?" I grunt as I maneuver around a flying bit of debris. "I don't get it."

"Because I'm saving my rage for whatever or whomever is doing this. Wrecking the goddamn car will not hurt them—only us. Let it simmer, but keep it reined in until we get to the battle."

I forget how much more thoroughly he's trained for this type of shit than me, and of course, he's on the nose. I need my demon to keep its fury intact, so I can unleash when we get to the scene. "I'll try. This isn't my normal M.O., and I'm struggling."

Luckily for us, we get to the car that's off the road within a few moments, and I whip onto the edge, cutting the engine as I look over at my twin. "Change once we're outside?"

"Oh, fuck, yeah," he growls with a toothy grin. "Bring it all out, little bro. We're going to kick some motherfucking supe ass when we find them."

"I don't like that we can't even *see* them," I murmur with my hand on the door. "If they've been taken, I'm going to lose my everloving shit."

"Then that's what you do."

We push the doors open simultaneously, fighting the wind and the pouring rain to get out of the car. I round the front, and then let the chaos flow through me. Wings, horns, armored skin... it all erupts to join my tail in a symphony of hellfire and anger. This form is reserved for demons only or family events and one other circumstance—bloodletting. I rarely transform this completely, but my demon is triumphant when I let him have control of us. My head swivels to look at my larger and similarly terrifying-looking twin as I growl, "Let's go."

Together, we flap our wings and push off the ground to take to the air. It's not easy, but demon wings are made to fly through the horrors of Hell and beyond, so we have an advantage many winged shifters do not. Our strength and ability are comparable to dragons or other mythicals with the magic of the caster species imbued in our veins—it's a double threat that most don't plan for. Swooping over the grassy field, we head to the darkest spot where the storm's fury is opaque.

That has to be where our family is.

"Are Reb or Javi here yet?" I yell over the din, and Angelo shakes his head as he points to a spot where we may crash through the barrier of nature's wrath. "See you on the other side!"

Entry into the eye of the storm is physically painful despite my demonic armor, and I dive toward the ground to get a better grip. Once I see Angelo, we fight our way through the flying objects and duck small bolts of electricity as we search for Archie and Rogue. The eye is bigger than it looks on the outside, which is a definite sign that this is *not* a normal weather occurrence. It's almost like a portal, but to my knowledge, we didn't leave the plane or location we entered at.

"Fuck these assholes," Angelo snarls as he raises a hand and bashes a huge tree limb heading right for us. "Pulling *Wizard of Oz* shit on the outskirts of Bay City when anyone could fucking see it. They're getting bolder, D."

"Or more desperate," I call back as I dart around a rock formation I almost missed. "This is too obvious for people to pretend it didn't happen. The Council will have explaining to do."

I nod as I stomp through the gusts attempting to keep me from what I think is the absolute center. "Big time. This is news-report level shit."

When we finally dodge and swat our way to the middle, my eyes widen as I see Rogue in full Unseelie form blasting the everloving shit out of a nebulous form. The thing is laughing at her, its tone mocking as she keeps Archie behind her in his lion shift. He's much, much bigger than he normally is, and I assume that's because he's tapped into his mate bond to increase his size well past 'Narnia' level to mythological size.

"Hot damn, this is a party!" Angelo shouts before he lets out a demonic roar and grows three sizes bigger until he's *almost* fully trans-formed. His warning gets Rogue's attention, and she gives him a gnarly, knife-toothed grin that makes me stumble a step. "Get him, Princess! Rip a chunk off this fucker."

Rogue goes back to shooting sparkly energy at the shrouded enemy, and Archie throws his head back to roar an answer to my twin. I take a deep breath, closing my eyes as chaos emanates from my pores. I feel the effects immediately, even without seeing them. Lightning and objects are sent off target or into boomerang motions that go back to the being attacking them. I grin to myself, knowing Angelo will sense my powers and avoid them as he launches his own volley.

A loud boom echoes through the space, shaking the ground and making me dig my clawed feet into the ground to hold on. That would be Ang releasing a blast of vengeful fury big enough to level a small hill, and Rogue's delighted laughter tells me he hit his target. I push more chaotic energy into the atmosphere, and open my eyes as it rolls off of me in small waves. The attacker's cover is showing spots where the magic is waning, and if we continue fighting, we're going to reveal it, eventually.

"Keep hitting it," I yell to my mate and my twin. "I see tears in the shielding! If we uncover its true form, we can figure out how to fucking defeat it!"

Angelo winks at me and then takes off running as a huge, flaming Hellfire sword appears in his hands. He runs right into the cloudy enemy space, slashing and hacking at the magical barrier like a madman. Rogue watches for a moment, then her terrifying Unseelie visage looks pleased—especially when her Fae blade appears in her clawed hands.

I'd almost forgotten about her enchanted 'Mary Poppins' weaponry—too bad for this son of a bitch, because that thing is going to hurt.

Aftermath

ROGUE

Once I have my blade in my hand, I feel a million times better. I've had this weapon since I can remember—as most Fae do—and having it in my hand feels like a home I don't remember. Charging forward, I ignore the calls from my men as I dodge the twins' hellfire and magic. I know Rebel will be here soon; I can feel him approaching with my other mate as they fly toward this stupid storm. It's covering something more nefarious, which will make it easier to hide the supernatural shit, but I don't know when that will break containment—it could be when I'm able to sink my blade into the blob I'm headed for.

"Reb will be here soon!" I scream at the twins, hoping they will hear me over the laughter and howling wind. "I'm going to stab this motherfucker until it looks like a sieve."

My path to the fucker causing this isn't easy—debris and magic are coming at me from every angle, and I have to duck and roll multiple times to gain ground. I suppose that means whatever or whoever is behind this knows that I'm a great deal more deadly in this form, especially once my weapon has been called. That's not a big secret about Fae, of course, so it doesn't help me figure out who is throwing lightning bolts at me like they're going out of style.

"What in the name of Mab is going on here?!"

I grunt to myself as Rebel announces his arrival via a booming shout that echoes through the entire eye of the storm. "Always so dramatic," I mutter as I duck a huge electrically charged bolt of magic. "Men need attention so badly they can't even fight villains without everyone watching."

That's unlike me, obviously, because I'm getting closer to the blob through speed and skill. It's trying to kick my ass and send me rocketing back to my starting point, but it's failing. I'm going to make it, and perhaps Reb being ridiculous will distract my target long enough to get a good stab in its protective shell. If that happens, I'll let his bullshit entrance go when we're done.

"Stop strutting and do something, dickhead," Angelo yells at my stepbrother, and I chuckle. "We've been fighting this since we got here, and Arch is doing his best, but we need more magical backup."

A loud shriek sounds out, and I look up for a second to see Javier in full phoenix form, resplendent and golden as he flies into the center to join my men. He's bigger this time, and I wonder if that's because he knows what's going on or just because the storm is so big. He dives for the murky enemy I'm headed for, his cries angry enough to shatter glass, and I know I have to follow suit.

"Good thing I'm almost there, you impulsive jackass," I say as I push myself to run faster to meet him. "Not like you should have waited for instructions or a better opening or anything."

Honestly, I expected this from Rebel, not my gentle, submissive birdie.

"Javi," I yell over the noise of battle and weather. "I'm coming, just slow down a little so we can strike from opposite sides!" I'm not sure if the phoenix gets it but I'm hoping it does. We mated, but he's so secretive about his animal—like all of his kind—that I don't know as much as I should about his powers.

"Rogue, get out of the way," Rebel shouts as I'm almost within reach. I ignore him, feeling my muscles and meat burn even in Unseelie form as I try to make it in time to join Javier in his first strike. "Damn it, get out of there, sis!"

I don't get why he's acting like I can't handle this shit; we've fought together many times on missions. Sure, this thing is unknown, but that's not new, either. "Fuck off, Reb! I'm helping Javi. Why are you guys staying so damn far away?"

"He's going to—"

Then, a blast of magic and bright light explodes in the air above the blob, and I realize that I have definitely girl-bossed too close to the sun.

That is, if my gentle phoenix is the sun and his purposeful implosion knocking me clear across the fucking eye in a crumpled heap is girl-bossing.

WHEN MY EYES OPEN, I suck in big gasps of air trying to fill my lungs in panic. It takes a few moments for me to get my damn scrambled brain to reboot, and when I do, I sit up like a jolt has gone through me.

Javier.

Ignoring the aches and pains of being that close to what felt like a damn nuclear explosion and hitting the ground at Mach eleven, I push to my feet and stagger back towards the direction I *think* I came from. I'm not firing on all cylinders yet, but I'll be damned if that's going to stop me from finding out what happened to the sweet birdie. My bones feel like they're still knitting—and they probably are—and my muscles are screaming with effort as I squint through blurred vision on my way to the blast zone. I'm tingling with pain and fear as I shuffle like the Walking Dead, but I don't care; I *can't* care about that.

I have to know what happened, and I have to—

A sob wrenches in my throat as I grit my jaw and continue my agonizingly slow progress over the debris-filled terrain. I bite it back, knowing I don't have time for grief or any other emotion. If Javi is gone, I have to get to my other mates and Reb next. I don't hear anyone, and that sends the terror into overdrive, but I press on. Rogue Kelly is a survivor and a fighter; that's how I made it through my stupid childhood and losing Reck. It's how I'll get through this and take my vengeance on whoever did this, if my men are gone.

There is nothing in this realm like the unfiltered rage of an Unseelie when they begin a rampage, and I will show those motherfucking rebels what that looks like without prejudice.

"Come on," I whisper to myself as I feel the shaking in my limbs. "It can't be much further. You are strong enough to make it, and you will handle this. I won't allow their deaths to be in vain. Just. Keep. Going. Rogue."

It takes longer than I'd prefer to reach the spot where the pedestal was —I can tell by the big-ass smoking hole in the ground—and my hand flies to my mouth when I only see debris there. My breath comes in heaves as I double over, trying not to let the panic that's making my balance wobble drop me to my knees.

"No, no, no, no..."

He can't be gone; he just *can't*. We had so little time together, and our family was forming so nicely, and the bond was—

Wait.

I blink rapidly as my mind latches onto something, and I have to swallow hard to focus on it. Licking my lips, I use every ounce of my being to push away the anxiety and negative emotions, shutting them in an imaginary box. The aura around me settles slowly as I go from completely open emotionally to shut down like I usually am in battle. It takes several moments of letting that ice slide through me before my mind gets sharper, clearer, and able to process what has happened without the pesky feeling muddling it up.

"Javier is a phoenix. Phoenixes have many, many lives." The revelation makes me pop upright, and my eyes fly wide as I look at the hole full of debris and weird goo and fuck knows what else. "Get your ass in there and see if you're right."

Talking to myself is all I have at the moment—that and the minuscule sliver of hope my brain just gave me. So I stagger over and drop to the ground, sitting on the edge of the hole so I can slide into it. I'm definitely not spry enough to do anything more *yet*, but my healing will eventually get me back to speed. Shucking all those damn feelings will help it along, I think. My body needs all my energy to recover now, and this redirects my magic to the physical needs.

Yeah, it's also easier; I'll deal with that shit later.

As I reach the bottom of the crater, I find my balance and then glance around. I have no idea what that neon ectoplasm stuff is, and I don't really want to touch it. But it's covering a lot of the bigger pieces of pedestal and tornado detritus, so I'll have to. Making a face, I summon my blade. Using it to shift the pieces that look like they've been drenched by Vigo the Carpathian is safer than using my hands. I can't waste magic on moving things when I'm trying to heal up.

"Okay, Rogue. Where to start?" My eyes land on a large glittering shard, and I frown. "That seems like it's a good place. Didn't even *see* a fucking crystal or whatever."

Carefully, I pick my way around and over things to get to the jagged gem-thing. It doesn't *feel* like it's going to shock me or fight back, so I nudge it with the tip of my blade. When I'm not sent reeling by a spell, I breathe a sigh of relief. This time, I dig the blade into the ground below the damn thing and try to use it to leverage the crystal away from whatever it's covering. It finally pops free after a few tries, and I tilt my head at the iridescent slime under it.

What the actual fuck is that?

Again, I'm not touching things I can't identify, so I move on from the new goo to a spot where there are shiny pieces shattered nearby. I feel like an archaeologist or something, hunting clues in the wreckage of a civilization long dead as I follow the splintered metallic bits along a trail to a huge chunk of stone. My brows furrow as I dig the blade in again, putting my entire body into the lever this time until it finally gives.

A loud shriek echoes through the air, and my heart almost stops in my chest as it reveals a tiny, very dirty, ugly-looking baby bird.

Holy shit on a shingle, is this...?

Leaning down, I reach out to pick up the damn thing and suddenly, I feel the bond snap back into place like a rubber band from a slingshot. It aches for a moment, and I can hardly catch my breath as it settles into place, but once it does? The trembles stop and my soul feels like it's knitting a tiny bit. I look down at the hatchling, chuckling as I realize Javier knew he'd reform, and that's why he did what he did. I suppose the others did as well, which is why Reb was so fucking intent on calling me away from the blob thingy. However, I'm going to kick every single *one* of their asses hard enough to send them back to their births when I get my hands on them. This fucking scared a few decades off my life, even if I'm likely going to outlast the damn planet at this point.

"Okay, little guy. For now, you get a pass. I don't know how long it will take for you to go from a gross-looking naked thing to the Javier I know, but trust me, once you do? Your ass is grass, and I'm a goddamn lawnmower. Got it?"

The bird makes an indignant shrieking sound, and I wince. That *kills* my Fae hearing, and I'm going to have a bad time until it can make noises other than screeches. This feels more like a punishment for *me* than for the fuckers who whipped up this storm, but I don't have time to focus on that indignity. I have to get out of this hole and go find the others.

One down, four to go...

Wake Up

ANGELO

I'VE NEVER BEEN this close to Javi doing his thing before, and I never want to be again. I feel like I've been cast down to Hell and summoned anew. Every inch of my body aches, and I can barely expand my chest to breathe. Demons are hard to injure mortally, but we have pain points. Apparently, the nuclear winter-level blast of a phoenix imploding is one of those fucking things that can knock us out of commission.

Who knew?

The silence is eerie as I work to pry my eyes open. It's not working well, and that makes me nervous as fuck. Damon is my twin, but his power status is lower than mine. He's got to be doing worse, and I have no clue what this shit did to Arch, Reb, or Rogue. There's no sound but for the low ringing and buzz in my head, so I can't get a fix on their status with my other senses while I fight my eyelids. Having Javi do his thing solved one problem, but it may have created a multitude of others.

Suddenly, the air around me changes and the energy gets more frenetic. I think that means someone is getting closer. Growling weakly, I order my eyes to open again, and my frustration mounts when they don't obey. This is ridiculous, and if I need to draw on the small well of re-formed power I have left right now, I will. But I'll be damned if I'm going to lie here and not know if that's an enemy approaching.

"Angelo!"

I think my breath comes out in a soft whoosh as I hear Rogue's voice and realize that freaky sensation is her. My senses are totally overwhelmed, it seems, by the blast, and I'm not registering shit very well. I definitely should have known my *mate* was coming, not a combatant. "Mmmmmmnnuughhhh."

That was eloquent. I guess talking is out for a bit as well.

"Oooookay, then," Rogue says, and a loud screech lances my ears. She must have found bitty Javi, and I'm sure that's going to be a long, angry conversation once this nightmare is over. "Angelo is alive and seems to struggle with moving or talking."

"Nnnnghhgghhh," I groan, trying to help but failing. This sucks, and I'm definitely putting D on figuring out if there's some sort of shielding we should have done before our friend went ashes to ashes. I never want to feel like this again, and I sure as fuck don't want to scare our girl like this. I can't see her, of course, but I *hear* the strain in her voice.

"Right. So, Ang, you're not doing so hot, but you're *stable*, which means I have to take this piece of fried fucking chicken with me to check on someone else. I don't know how I'm all mobile and shit when I was closest, but that's a question for later. I've gotta know if everyone is breathing first, you know? Just... hang tight, okay?" She reaches down and squeezes my hand gently, and it takes everything in me not to wince in pain.

She doesn't need to feel any guiltier than she already does.

"I'm gonna give you a tiny sip of this and, um... well, it might help. I don't know if this works like it does for Reb and me, but you are my mate, and I can't just do nothing. So don't be grossed out, and if it doesn't work, then I'll know when I get to Damon. Got it?"

I can't answer, but I hope she knows I'm agreeing. I'd trust Rogue with anything she asked, and if she thinks that whatever she's doing will help, then I'm in. After a moment, I feel skin against my mouth, and my lips are pushed apart by her fingers. Slowly, a floral-tasting liquid drips onto my tongue. I realize it has to be her blood, and it makes my demon fight to the surface. He's keen to consume her essence again, whether it works to heal me or not.

As it runs down my throat, I feel a low hum spread across my chest. The magic in her blood *might* actually work the way she'd hoped. I let myself relax as my demon practically purrs in approval; no one told me that imbibing my mate's blood would calm him this thoroughly. I suppose it could be because they didn't know—Luca and Lola are *not* fated, so they likely have no idea. They didn't allow the staff who helped raise us in their frequent absence to teach us about lore and legend, either. Damon will be just as shocked when he figures it out.

I know he's alive, by the way; the twin bond is as strong as the mate one, and I would feel the empty spot where he should be inside of me.

Unfortunately, I can't share that information because our sweet little birdie blew me almost to Hell and back. But Rogue's magic is doing something, and if it keeps working, I might be able to speak soon. The knives in my throat are dulling, and the weight of my limbs is slowly becoming less burdensome. If she has enough power to continue for a bit longer, the effects will free me from the silent, motionless prison— I think.

"Ang, come on, man. Wake up and bully me. Make me tell you that you don't control me anywhere but the bedroom. *Please*," Rogue whispers, her voice raw and pleading. It makes pain lance through me, but this is an emotional ache because I'm here but I can't convey it to her. "You know I love you, you colossal idiot. I've loved your stupid, smirky face and uppity attitude since we were kids, and it was too weird and scary to admit. Just... respond or something, 'cause I have no idea what I'd do if you were confined to a machine or stasis or whatever the fuck they do to demons who won't wake up."

She's terrified; I feel it in the surrounding air. Rogue isn't one to admit that sort of thing out loud, and this is as close as she'll get to it, but my lack of reply in any form is wigging her out. I think I grit my teeth and gather whatever energy is reforming internally at the agonizing rate. Preparing myself mentally for it not to work, I throw all of that into opening my eyes and mouth. Shock fills me when it works, and I groan softly as my blurry vision lands on her leaning over me.

Holy shit, I did it.

"Angelo! You're... You're really conscious. Sort of. I mean, enough for me to verify you aren't in a goddamn coma or something. That was a sound, and I think you can see me. If you can see me, even a little, try to blink or moan again."

That's asking a lot, but I do what she says, and my eyes are the ones who obey. Rogue is still blurry; the images haven't merged entirely yet, but her blood is also dripping one fat drop at a time in my throat. I suppose she's keeping it that slow, so she's able to save enough for everyone who needs it. However, I think I'd be moving along faster if she weren't. My impatience aside, I'm lucky to be this healed as it is, and that she's so damn mobile and spry is a fucking miracle. Reb is going to answer for this shit when we're all back to normal; that is for damn sure.

"Good, good. Okay, I want to stay here so badly, Ang, but I have to move on to the next person. I've got Javi bundled close, and I'm going to *murder* you all for that surprise, but we need to go check on our fam. Stay here and just... breathe. Let the magic and time work on you, okay? I know you'd fight me if you could, so I'm taking advantage of the fact that you can't. You'll have to forgive me for it later." Her wrist moves away from my mouth, and I see her dip down before I feel her lips on mine, then she's gone.

That little brat—I'll get her for this later, even if I know she's right.

ONCE ROGUE HAS LEFT ME, I'm stuck lying here as I wait for my body to catch up with the injection of healing her blood gave me. Piece by piece, I feel my lips and mouth regain the ability to move, and then the rest of my face. My vision finally clears up so that I can see the blue sky above us, and I hear faint movement nearby. I would have expected my limbs to free up first, but it seems like my senses are the beginning of the process.

It's fucking weird that my demonic magic took such a hit when Javi let loose.

"That might be a clue," I slur to myself as I impatiently await my body's range of motion to return. "The blob thing could have been destroyed, but sent out... something?"

My head flops to the side, tired from even the small amount of thought and puzzling I did. Whatever the actual cause of my non-ambulatory state, it's damn powerful and laser-focused. I think if the effects of the implosion had rocketed out far and wide, we might have ambulances or more damn Guardians here. With the event so close to our property, it might have even drawn some of my father's minions to the site.

"The fact that no one has appeared makes it feel even more suspicious. I wonder if this was the only attack or if there were more test runs in Bay City—or even in other places."

Considering how big the conspiracy is supposed to be, I bet there were other incidents in other places. I can't imagine it would be useful to only hit this town when a multi-location strike to test the defenses would give the rebels more data. But then, I'm not the one in charge, and I have no damn idea if they have a *good* strategist running this shit or a nepotism one. That would make a difference, and it might also give us an opening when we head down to Hell to poke around.

After all, Hell is preparing for the first Caliphate Games in centuries, and the bigwigs in every arena have to be busy as beaver demons getting ready. That kind of realm-wide event would generate lots of revenue in the cities, on the intranet, in merchandising and food sales, gambling... There's very little enterprise down there that wouldn't see a serious spike as those damn things head towards their beginning.

Lucian Darkstar has to be shitting his pants with glee over this; it endangers the royals and opens a path to the throne.

I blow out a slow breath, pleased when every inch of my frame doesn't scream in pain. Rogue's plan is working incredibly well, and hopefully, she's moved on to my twin, Arch, and her stepbrother. It will take a while for Javier to run through his growth cycle, but I'm sure she'll figure something out for when we go on our clue hunting trip. I don't want to leave him behind in that vulnerable state, but taking him along has its challenges as well.

"Angelo! I feel you getting better. Try to move!"

Rogue's voice is strained, and I react blindly. My palms push flat to the ground, and I'm lifting myself to a sitting position before I know it. It hurts like hell, and every inch of me is fighting the movement. There was *definitely* something left behind to keep us weak and helpless, which makes every one of my internal alarms go off.

This battle isn't over, and we played our trump card too quickly.

Lean On Me

ROGUE

DAMON IS CLOSE TO ANGELO, so he's easy to locate. He's projecting his injured state onto everything around him—not that he knows it—but even in shock, chaos demons can't stop radiating their own brand of metaphysical static. I find him curled around himself, shivering, eyes wide and blank like he's watching three movies at once and they're all terrifying. I have to duck random objects and debris that seem to be under his control, but his demonic power working better than his twin's is promising.

"You're not dead. Get your ass up." D doesn't blink, and I look over my shoulder to see that Angelo has finally pushed himself to his knees, "If you're done with your nap, get over here," I yell.

My sarcasm is helping me keep my fury about my injured mates at bay, so they'll have to deal with it for now.

He flips me off but lurches over, dragging a leg. Once he's close, I gesture at his twin. Angelo sighs, peels back Damon's eyelid, and hocks a mouthful of black blood directly into the corner of his eye. His twin spasms, arches, then sucks in a breath and rolls to his side. Ang flops on the ground to rest, allowing D to press against him for strength as his body processes the infusion.

"That was disgusting, and I had no idea it was what you were going to do," I grumble. Damon clutches at Angelo and tries to shrink into his shadow, and the elder twin shrugs.

"I had blood there, and I didn't have to reopen something. It was convenient."

"Men." The look on my face conveys my opinion of that method, but I lean down to slice the cut on my wrist open again with one of my nails. Holding that against D's lips for a moment, I drip my essence into his mouth as well, hoping the combination will speed this up.

I don't like the aura of this crater, and I want out of it as fast as possible.

"Something's wrong," Angelo says, his voice a rough whisper now. "The pedestal must have had a spell to obfuscate healing if it was a destroyer. That's why this is so slow; it's still draining us. At least, I think. D would be a much better person to explain it, but he's not lucid yet."

"Great," I say, because obviously nothing can be as simple as blowing up the villain. I rock on my heels, weighing my options. Tiny Bird Javi has stopped biting me through my shirt and is now trying to escape as I ponder. I resist the urge to throw him—after all, he *did* neglect to tell me his plan—and clutch the small phoenix more tightly against my chest.

"We need to get Archie," Damon mumbles as the wheels in my head turn. "Weakest link. Easiest to target."

"Welcome back, little D," I say as I look down at him in relief. "You're right, but I seem to be the only one who was left with enough mojo to get around. Your brother had to crawl over here, and I'm not even telling you how he shared blood for healing."

"Not the spit thing again?" The younger twin shudders and closes his eyes. "Ang, you're so gross."

Angelo shoots back a retort, but I'm distracted by analyzing the shit surrounding us more closely. The blob I believed to be our enemy is gone, and the pedestal is in ruins, but I can feel the power through the soles of my feet. We didn't *kill* it with Javier's sacrifice; we merely fucked up it's focus and physical manifestation. That means Angelo is probably correct that a reverse spell or enchantment on the thing that we blew into marble chunks is why we're having a bitch of a time getting ourselves back to semi-normal.

"Why do you look so pissy, Princess?" Angelo asks, bringing me back to their demon puppy pile on the ground.

I glare at him, not ready for him to be cute yet. "The next person who keeps a tactical nuke-level ability secret from me gets to walk home in a mayonnaise jar," I respond.

My comment was definitely heard and understood by the bald baby bird. He makes a noise that pierces my eardrums and I squeeze him a bit tighter on purpose until he squawks again. "That meant you, Angry Birdie, but also the rest of these clowns. Don't be salty."

"Understood," D and Ang chime in together.

I suppose being healed enough to do the 'twin thing' should make me happy, but it doesn't.

IT TAKES a bit for the two of them to regain enough power and energy to move, but once they finally can, we head around the crater's lip. Damon faceplants into a splintered chunk of what used to be an electrical pole, and I have to rush forward to flip him over. I'd prefer him not to ruin his pretty face, but I'm more concerned about him vibrating at a frequency I can feel in my teeth.

"Nice one, bro. Very graceful."

D growls softly as I help him to his feet again and he wipes the blood off his face. "This is why I hate being in the field, you know. I'm strong, but my skills are meant to be used up close. And sometimes if I'm having trouble controlling the chaos, it boomerangs back at me... like it just did."

"You tripped. It's fine. No need to be dramatic, babe," I reply with a shrug, but it comes out a bit harsher than I intended. He looks at me sadly, like I confirmed that he's not useful, and my insides twist. I turn, jostling the baby bird Javi against my stomach, and grab Damon by the chin.

This calls for a more dominant approach because he's feeling so out of control; he needs me *to be in charge instead.*

"Little D, you're important behind a computer and lots of places, but you belong with us in the field, too." His eyes sweep to the ground and I give him a crooked smile until he meets my gaze again. "I know no one ever let you be in charge, nor did they want you to fight, and that was Angelo's mistake. You can and will do this, especially since Archie and Javier will be looking for you to be the person for them that I'm being for you right now."

He blinks, then rubs the back of his neck with his hand as he flushes. "Maybe not Javi yet. He's still ridiculous looking."

That gets another squawk and I sigh. "I'm going to make you carry him soon. This is... just not in my wheelhouse."

Angelo looks at me as D's face brightens, but his color stays pale and I nod. He slashes his wrist again, letting the black trickle out and shoves it at his brother. "You need more, little brother. Take some and then some more from Rogue before she adds to your punishment list for later."

I snort when Damon does exactly as he's told without complaint, then provide my silvery blood as another power source when Ang is done.The combined hit works—Damon's cheeks go from ashy to bruised-rose. He coughs and clutches his stomach as he recovers, but the electricity that got him seems to be gone when he raises back to his full height.

"He's fine," Angelo says, voice raspy. "Just a bit more juice than he could handle in this state. Probably made him so emotional, too."

"I'm gonna pull your spine out through your nostril if you don't quit minimizing this shit," I inform him. "We're all seriously injured and someone is either watching or waiting for the right moment to try to finish the job. It's not the time to be a pain in the ass, Ang."

He snorts. "Just wait until we find Reb. He'll piss you off even more, I bet."

"Yeah, but I'm *used* to his bullshit. This situation with you and Javi and D? This isn't normal for me and I'm doing everything I can to... hold it together. Help me out."

"I don't want to fit in a mayo jar, so I'm behaving," Damon says helpfully. Javi makes a loud screeching sound in agreement and I throw my hands up in annoyance. Luckily, D walks closer and holds his hands out. "You're probably right about me holding onto the bird for a bit. Your nerves are too frayed for it."

"The noises are *killing* my ears," I mutter as I hand bald bird Javi over to the younger demon. I frown, my eyes narrowed as the bird quietly snuggles against him. "Are they meant to scare away Fae, I wonder? That sound doesn't seem to affect you guys as much as me."

The demon twins shrug and I sigh. "Whatever, let's keep going. Damon was right about Archie and I'm itching to find him and my snarky-ass stepbrother."

"He should be close," Damon says. "I can sort of feel... something? I just don't know what."

We move slowly, shuffling like a gang of injured supes hoping not to keel over. It takes longer than it should and that irks me, but we don't have a choice but to work with what's available—our broken ass bodies. As we climb over some more chunks of stuff, Damon lets us know that Javi's finally figured out how to sprout feathers, but it's going to take a bit before the naked ugly bird look goes away. That's probably a guess, but I appreciate him telling us. Naked Angry Bird is a bit freaky and I'm glad it's not going to be his form for days on end.

"This wasn't random, you know." Angelo's assertion isn't news to me, but I'm glad someone else is saying it out loud.

"I got that memo when we figured out that this thing was programmed to keep us weak—it *clearly* knew we had someone with Javier's ability to implode and reform, unlike me."

"You want us to believe that you had no idea phoenixes catch fire and turn to ash then rebirth?" Angelo says, his eyebrows up as he gives me a doubtful look. "I know we didn't tell you it was going to be a tactical option, but come on, Princess. You *knew* Javier's people had the ability. It's not a big leap for enemies to know it, too."

"Don't be a smartass," I warn. "My patience today is stretched about as thin as it can go. But *yes*, I knew phoenixes did... something then fire then ashes. I just... I never really got my hands around seeing it used in battle. Their kind keeps so much from everyone so they won't be hunted by humans and magic users alike, especially in recent years after those stupid books and movies. People were going to make phoenix shifters *extinct* if they didn't do something, the Council said."

My bones itch with a rage I'm barely keeping under my skin. Whoever sent the blue nebula freak knew exactly who we were, and exactly where to find us—less than a mile from our very fortified house where we were vulnerable. Not only that, but Javier blew up, the twins are injured, and the other two of my mates are a question mark at the moment. I'm overloaded as hell, and I can't even process my own damn injuries.

It's a lot and I think I'm handling it better than most would.

We're almost on the other side of the blast zone when Damon jerks his chin at Angelo. "Do you think Luca knew they were setting a trap?"

Angelo goes still. For a second, I see hesitation, but I know that's not about thinking either of his parents are above that shit. "No," he says quietly. "He would've sent someone from our own organization because he's cheap. But he also wouldn't have done it right after we left his place. It's too obvious and he's smarter than that."

"You sure?" Damon's voice is almost gentle. He's far less connected to those two dipshits who birthed them and it's not hard to see it when you're looking closely. "Mom was pretty angry."

"She's all bluster and no bomb. You know that," Angelo says, his face a mask of indifference. "Plus, she wouldn't want to be forced to provide new heirs. It would cut into her 'me' time if she had to fuck Luca again." He shrugs as if that doesn't matter, which is weirdly sad. "If he wanted us dead, he'd have plans in place for the new heirs. He doesn't."

I don't trust the Hell's mob boss logic, but I know Angelo does. "Then who do we think sent this lovely little treat?"

Damon waves his hand to get my attention. "The pedestal was old and weird—definitely not made or enchanted locally. It came from another realm, probably. There were runes on it that don't correspond to the supe languages I'm familiar with, so that rules out Faerie, Hell, and the normal stuff."

"Deities?" Angelo muses. "Could be."

I roll my eyes. "The gods don't care about any of us unless we make ourselves a problem."

My mate smirks, looking at me. "You don't think we're doing just that?"

I bare my teeth at him with a growl. "Not in a way they'd notice yet. Deities rarely come when the stakes are this low. We haven't done shit besides hear that plan and I thought we did a good job of staying stealthy at the meeting."

There's a rustle ahead, and for a split second, my heart stops. We may be getting close to our target.

"Archie's fine," I say out loud, not letting any doubt creep in. "Shifters are hard to kill for a reason, and Reb's like a bad case of the clap... We're never getting rid of him."

I'm trying to make this hunt for their bodies easier on all of us, obviously.

In the pit of my stomach, I know none of us are fine. The finite rules of this realm and how we deal with the other ones are changing. If this attack was meant for us, then the next round will be even worse because they know we're going to try to stop this bigger conspiracy. The problem is... I don't know *how* they would have figured it out. We've kept everything very close to the vest since the meeting, yet in the span of a day Archie was accused of murder and now we've been blown up.

Not good odds at all.

Survivor

ARCHER

I AWAKEN from my trip to La-La land hard—not dramatically, with a white light or a tunnel—just the hot sting of grit in my gums and a hunk of rock stapling me to the smoking lip of the blast crater. My right shoulder's definitely fucked and the left side of my ribcage is numb enough to tell me I've got serious problems internally.

Fuck, I'm never getting near Javi at zero dark thirty again.

I try to pull in air, but I get half a lungful of dust and something that tastes like copper, battery-acid, and someone else's skin. I cough, and a loogie slimes down my chin that I know has to be tinted with blood. My ears are ringing so hard it makes me think of the time that bruiser from Echo Lake Prep knocked me into the barrier so hard I didn't wake up for a week.

Hockey is brutal, especially in the supe leagues, and I've been banged up good plenty of times in my long career. This might take the cake, though, because I'm so fucking weak that I don't think I can help myself out of this jam. My body tries to shift—automatically, the way you flinch when a door slams—so I can start healing. Instead, everything seizes up, refusing the command. It's like something is saying, 'Human form only, motherfucker' before laughing maniacally.

That's not normal, and it's bad fucking juju.

Since I can't move or transform, I try yelling. My mate's name only comes out a splintered croak, which won't do shit for me if she isn't nearby. I know she can't be close, though, because we were close to the blast center when—

Javier blew up...fuck.

The memory of his golden wings in the blue sky, then him screeching in fury, and then the blast. No way anything survives that direct hit, not even a cockroach, when a phoenix does its thing. We *should* be safe here from whatever baddie we were fighting, but I'm less concerned about that than what happened after I blacked out.

I flex my fingers. The tremor in my hands says I'm running on fumes power-wise, but not zero. I can't hear anything over the buzzing in my ears, so I take inventory of myself. My clothes are shredded from the shift,so I'm naked as a jaybird. I think my left knee is pointing the wrong direction, but let's table that for now. The debris pinning me is a chunk of enormous tree, or maybe the spine of a hellbeast, but either way it's big enough that I can't lift it without shifting. There's no way I don't have broken ribs and internal bleeding, plus my throat is too raw to make noise.

I am stuck here until someone comes for me—no question.

There's no sign of Rogue, Angelo, Damon, or even Rebel and his snarky bullshit yet. Usually I'd smell them before I saw them, but the only scent here is overcooked meat and the weird blue-sugar stink of whatever that pedestal was leaking. I need to figure out what the fuck that smell is later; maybe D can help? I guess that only applies if everyone has *survived* this bullshit, and I can't confirm that right now because I'm *fucking trapped* like a bug on display.

My lungs panic as I realize how compressed I am. The logical part of me says, 'Archie, you're not buried, you're just pressed flat.' However, the other part of me that got stuck in a fridge at the dump as a kid is screaming, 'If you don't shift, you die here.' Childhood trauma is funny like that, showing up to taunt me when I have far worse problems than a truly shitty choice of hide-n-go-seek spots with the guys. I got through those five hours, but damned if I ever purposefully put myself in tiny, tight spaces again if I had the choice.

Rogue's face pops into my mind, flickering like a movie of her emotions: smug, snide, pouting, caught off-guard, unsure... If she died, I'd know it, right? That's how my parents' stories about bonded mates go—once you're mated, you always know. That piece of your soul that you exchange is magical and if the link is broken, it lances you with pain for the rest of your days because it cannot find its match.

I don't feel that pain, so it can't be broken. Right?

But I'm not Fae, and she's not a shifter, so I don't know if those tales apply cross-species as well as they do between different animals of our kind. My dads and mom are all varied cat shifters, and they definitely have it, but that doesn't mean my bond is the same. Plus, I did things to link to Damon and he's a demon and that's... a whole different ball game. I think I'd know if he was gone, too, and I don't feel like that.

I try to call out again, my voice scraping the bottom of my throat. "Rogue. Damon. Fucking—somebody, answer before I lose it."

It's embarrassing, but panic makes everyone feel weak as a baby.

No answer except the steady, wet drip from my side, which is probably important. However, since I can't get my hand in there to check it, I have to focus on other shit. I can move my neck enough to see that the crater is maybe a couple miles across, glowing blue at the center, and rimmed in upended debris and crispy grass. If I really strain, I think I see where all the chunks of that stupid pedestal are, but that doesn't help me. It was constructed somewhere definitely *not here*, and neither Rogue nor I recognized the markings on it.

I dig my nails into the ground instead just to remind myself I still have hands that work. The dirt here is melted and full of hard glassy bits, which means the explosion must have been hot as fuck. I grab a small shard and press it into my palm and squeeze, letting the sharp, new pain ground me. That's something I learned in years of playing elite tier sports, by the way. Old pain will eventually fade into a hum and you can ignore it, but that's dangerous. New pain will bring the focus back and you can keep yourself conscious until help arrives.

Modern day gladiators in silly costumes playing for modern-day Romans greedily consuming their feasts, I guess.

Yikes. I got a bit philosophical there, so the glass thing worked. It's better than letting the other pain lull me into another blackout, or thinking about Javi exploding into ashes to save our bacon. I can't process how that works logically, and this is the first I've ever seen it, so my brain doesn't want to wrap around him turning from a fun bartender to a pile of fireplace detritus. Javier could be a little tightly wound at times because of his folks, but once he was in our pack, he was in. And my parents always taught me that you die for your pride —that's why the lioness is so fierce, like my mom.

Oh, she's gonna hide us all when she finds out about this shit. Sariah does not *play when it comes to taking stupid risks.*

After all, she was the one who led the search team who found me in that fridge and she scared the piss out of me, Reb, Javi, Angelo, and Damon *for life*. No one wanted to cross her by doing something stupid like that again, and trust me, we did a lot of stupid shit. We just tried to keep on the other side of the 'Sariah will come for us' line when we did it.

I close my eyes, resting as I cough a laugh. The darkness behind my lids is comforting for a moment, then I see more movies of my mate and my friend playing behind my lids. I have to pry them open again because I can't... I just *cannot watch* that when I don't know where they are or how injured they might be or if anyone is dead.

What if the thing that hit us is still out there, just waiting for the slow ones to drag themselves upright so it can finish the job? Given that I *should* be able to shift, and I *should* have started to heal by now, it's very possible. Something has to be preventing it, and I'll be damned if I know what, but it's making us sitting ducks.

I try to twist my arm under the slab. My muscles bunch and shake, but it's like being zip-tied by some cartoonish assassin for a torture session. I taste bile in my mouth as the pain lances through me and I have to swallow it back. Shifters shouldn't be able to bleed to death like this, but I definitely could if I don't get out from under this thing and away from whatever is keeping my supernatural abilities from working.

This is the shittiest death ever, by the way—pinned under some broken wood like a weak human and conscious enough to know what's going to happen if I don't get help. The alpha-guy vibes in me are taking a real beating with this and even if I don't die, I might perish from embarrassment if this gets out in the news. I don't really care about that shit, but it'll fuck up my sports rep for sure.

Of course, I could close my eyes and just drift off, see what's on the other side. It would hurt less; I think. But I hear my mother's voice, as loud and clear as if she were squatting beside me in the dirt. 'Glasers are not built to give in, Archer. The world might look at us as if we don't belong and we should hide who we are—don't let it win'. She always said it with a snarl and flash of sharp teeth because she meant it.

My mother and fathers endured a lot of criticism when they were younger about our pride because it's made up of so many different kinds of cats—and led by the female without compunction. It made lots of kids and adults be shitty to me and the other kids, but Sariah told us we were put here to thrive on our terms, not to fold at the first sign of adversity

I imagine her here, licking her thumb and swiping the blood off my jaw, telling me to 'Get up and find your pride, boy'. I want to tell her I'm trying, but something is physically preventing me from just powering through. But she's not here and I can't really say much anyway, so I mutter what I think is "I'm sorry, Mom."

Another spasm of pain rockets through me, and it feels like something important is getting ready to quit. For a second, the world tilts and I see blue light dancing in the cracks of the crater. I see Damon at the rim, or maybe it's Angelo, sprinting toward me, yelling something I can't hear. Relief spikes in me so strongly that it almost knocks me out.

They're alive. Rogue is probably with them.

If I can hold out another minute, they'll dig me up. Maybe we'll even make it home. I hang on to that thought because my family being okay is enough for me to push through.

I clamp my jaw, and press the glass shard deeper into my palm so the new pain brings me back. My folks' stories weren't wrong—I'd feel it if she died. I'd be hollow, but instead, there's a thin thread keeping me tethered.

The mate link is real and she's alive, so I can't leave yet.

I whisper her name, like a prayer, and wait for the world to come back and get me.

The 30th

ROGUE

My boots leave sunken holes in the scorched mud, every step a squelch of hot, chemical-scented soup. Smoke and magic hang so thick you could wring them out and light them on fire all over again. Damon has baby phoenix Javi cradled to his chest in a nest of his shredded shirt, and it is exactly as grotesque and adorable as it sounds: patchy red and gold featherlets, crumpled wings, beak wide in a silent wail. Javi's eyes glint with feral intelligence, but his body's stuck on 'freshly microwaved chicken nugget'.

It's more than a little on the nose.

Angelo's behind us scanning the haze like someone's going to pop up and shoot us from the bushes. Which is fair, because if I were the bad guy, I'd wait till the heroes were hunched over a casualty, then finish them with a coup de grâce they didn't see coming. I'm trying not to think about how I'm supposed to be the steel backbone, but every five steps I want to curl up and let the ash bury me.

We finally found Archie after not hearing anything during our ten-minute walk around the edge of this damn crater. There's a tree trunk, snapped and sharp-edged, pressing him flat to the earth like he's been pinned by an angry god. For a split second I see the lion inside of him

—all gold and sinew and pride—but it's not real. Right now, he's just a guy, naked and caked in blood and ash, his chest hitching in little hiccup-y gasps. One leg's flopped at the wrong angle, shin looking like a broken hockey stick, and his arm's half-shoved under the wood with an ugly bend just above the wrist.

Damon makes an infuriated noise—a half-demonic growl, half-sob that tells me he's in the same pit of rage I am about this motherfucker hurting our boy.

"Don't—" Archie says, teeth clenched but voice light, "—don't panic. This is absolutely the dumbest position I've ever woken up in, and it hurts like hell, but I'm going to be okay."

Always a joker, this one.

My body moves before my head does, knees squelching into the muck beside him. There's blood everywhere, leaking from under the trunk and seeping into the ground like it's watering the soil. I reach for his shoulder—the intact one—and find it fever-hot, skin trembling under my fingers.

"He's going to slip into shock, guys. We have to do something—*now.*"

Damon moves quickly, despite the phoenix tucked under one arm like a football. "We've gotta lift it. On three, we—"

Angelo interrupts, shaking his head. "He's not shifted yet, bro. If we lift it and there are things we cannot see underneath, he could bleed it. Think, D. I know that he might also get compression syndrome, but we have to handle this like supernaturals, not humans. Shifting is a requirement before we touch anything."

That's the scary part: Archie's stuck in normal meat and bone. No lion, no healing—just the slow collapse of every system he's got if we don't defeat that damn enchantment from the pedestal. He's joking with us, but we don't have a lot of time to get this done or we could definitely lose him.

"Have we all had enough time to recover so we can donate?" I ask as I look at the twins, my eyes tired and worried.

Damon's eyes flick to mine, demon black but wet with unshed tears. "We're all getting hammered by that fucking spell, but a shifter has to heal first in their animal. We have to try because I'll be damned if I'm going to lose the guy I've liked my entire life and finally had the guts to show it in this stupid field."

The bird in his arms gives a wheezing squeal, which is hilarious except for how unfunny this all is. I know Javi did what they thought would work, but they were so fucking *unstrategic* about it and now we're paying the price.

I want to strangle them, but that's taken a big backseat to wanting them all to live through this day.

"Guys, I'm going to be okay, but you have to work together," Archie groans, every syllable a test of will. He shudders a bit, and I know that took a lot out of him. His leg is what keeps drawing my eyes and while it's not the worst injury, it's the one that makes me worried the game he loves will be out of his future even if he survives.

Unless...

I squeeze his hand and give the twins a determined look. "We have to reset the leg before the shift so it heals correctly. Archie, if you don't want to puke, keep those baby blues on me, okay?"

His eyes meet mine, so full of trust it nearly floors me.

"Ready?" I ask, and he nods as he grits his teeth. I let go of his hand, moving down to his lower body and getting into position. I've seen this done before by healers when Guardians are hurt, but this will be the first time I've done it myself. Hopefully, I don't fuck it up.

"Hit me," Archie says, and when I wrench his lower leg with both hands, the sound of screams almost does me in. This is a compound fracture for sure, and we have to get this shit dealt with so he doesn't end up permanently injured.

Damon frowns, but he looks thoughtful. "Maybe we should try the wood again."

"We *can't*, bro. We've been over this," Angelo says with an annoyed growl. "How is that you're brilliant and this has made you absolutely unable to think straight?"

"He could have a concussion," I blink as I look up at the gentler twin in concern. "I mean, he didn't seem like it but this is pointing to worse than it seemed head injury. That's not good, Ang."

Despite the hoarseness from his screams, Archie gasps, "Guys, listen. I know you want to help. But you gotta do it together." He coughs, which is all blood and spit, and I put a hand to his cheek because it's the only thing I can think to do. "Take a minute and come together before I pass out."

For a second we all freeze except Javier who lets out an ungodly screech that makes my eyes feel like bleeding.

"I'm sorry," Damon mutters, and there's something genuinely broken in it. "I keep... I keep screwing this up because I'm too upset to be logical."

I surprise myself by not saying anything snarky. Instead, I give D an exhausted, but understanding smile. Angelo kicks a stone, and it skitters into the blast crater as he processes our friend's words.

Archie's voice is softer now. "Rogue, come closer?"

He's looking at me the way people look at old wedding photographs, and I feel myself blush all the way to my hairline. I lean in, waiting to see what he wants only me to hear.

"Little more," he whispers, and when our faces are inches apart he says, "You're scared. You hide it behind all that 'I'm tough' crap, but I know you. When you're terrified, you slice up everyone around you, just so you don't have to feel it yourself. You get mean because you care too much, and you'd rather be hated than see anyone hurt. Especially the people you..." He stops, sucking in a breath that sounds like it's tearing his ribs apart. "You don't have to do that—not with us."

The words hit me like a punch in the teeth, and I flinch. I'm about to retort, but the look in his eyes is so painfully gentle that I can't. I just stare back, and the lump in my throat is bigger than my pride.

Holy Dr. Beardo, the half-dead funny man is right.

"It's gonna matter," Archie says, barely above a whisper, "when you find Rebel. He's gonna be hurting, too, and if you go in sharp you'll just slice him open more. Please, Rogue. For me."

I never cry in front of people, but my face is suddenly wet. Archie's hand squeezes mine, and I bite my lower lip to keep from making a sound as I think about his statement. "Okay," I finally say. "I'll try. But you have to *not die*, first."

He grins, and blood slips between his teeth. "Deal."

It takes longer than I want to get my face back together, but once I do, I wipe the snot and sweat with my palm and look up at the two other idiots I call family. Damon and Angelo are hovering close enough I can see the lines of worry drawn across their faces.

"So," I say, voice thick, "if I'm an asshole again, you have to tell me. Like, immediately."

Angelo blinks. Damon almost laughs. "Archie gets his ribcage collapsed and still manages to psychoanalyze you in under a minute," Damon says. "He's gonna be insufferable about this."

"Yeah, well, he's earned it," I mutter, and then, before I can lose my nerve, I dig my thumb into my own forearm, where the skin is already puckered with half-healed scratches from earlier. "This is the solution that worked for you guys and we need to try it here even if his injuries are much worse."

Blood wells up, silvery and floral scented as it drips from the cut. I let a couple of dribbles run, then I close my eyes and push the recovering magic in me into the air surrounding us. It's not a lot, especially for me, but I'm hoping that both breathing me in and getting the essence will combine to turn this naked hockey player into a lion.

"We do this together, right?" I say.

Damon just nods, baring his own wrist and dragging a thumbnail across it to reveal his obsidian blood. Angelo follows, less showy, a neat slice at his fingertip, but the blood's just as thick and dark. For a second we're a fucked-up communion table, demons and sinners pouring blood into the purest of us all to heal him.

Archie's eyes are open but glassy as I tilt his chin up and let my blood drip onto his tongue. Damon adds his, slow and deliberate, and then Angelo, all three types mixing in the hollow of Archie's mouth. Blood magic isn't clean— even with me in the mix—it smells like burnt sugar and old pennies, tastes like the first lick of a flowery battery, I'd guess.

It's not pretty like in the movies, but it's ancient and powerful, which we need right now.

Nothing happens at first. If anything, Archie looks worse—his skin mottles, lips going a sick shade of blue. The blood drains from his face, and for a split second I think maybe we're just speeding up the process of death.

Damon's hands start to shake. "It's not enough. He needs more. If he can't shift, he's going to die. No one is coming to help—not after all this time."

I grab the younger twin's face and shake it hard enough that his teeth knock. "Hey. Don't you tap out on me now, D. If we lose Archie, we'll all suffer. I know you're struggling here, but put your back into it and *believe.*"

The bird in Damon's arm makes a strangled trilling sound, and before anyone can react, the phoenix sticks its nugget head out and yanks one of the few feathers it's grown out with a squawk. It falls onto Archie's face, covering his eyes and there's a flash—hot blue, then orange, then something pure white—and the bird's fire lances into Archie like a defibrillator.

"Motherfucker," I murmur in awe.

Archie jerks, back arching off the ground, and then he makes a garbled sound. It's not human—it's a lion straining to roar, but lacking the ability to do it yet. The trunk cracks as his body expands, splintering apart, and in the next second, we have to scramble back before the wood's been tossed three meters by a set of paws the size of dinner plates.

I'm still kneeling, my jaw unhinged, watching bones knit, muscle balloon under shredded skin, fur explode in a ruff around his head like the sun rising after a goddamn hurricane.

He's huge, and beautiful, and most importantly—not dead.

The lion limps forward, then collapses, with its head in my lap. Damon sniffles, which is both deeply embarrassing and also kind of touching. The guys are going to give him hell about it, though.

That is until Angelo wipes his own eyes with his forearm, then grunts, "Told you he'd make it."

Javier, still a lump of bird, responds by trying to wiggle out of Damon's arms. When he's given freedom, Javi curls up on the lion's back and tucks his head under his own wing, obviously unconcerned by his plucked chicken look. Archie's tail gives a feeble swish, and then the world settles again, just us, the mud, and the promise of one last impossible thing to do.

I bury my face in Archie's mane, which smells like fire and copper and home, and whisper, "Don't ever scare us like that again."

He rumbles, which I choose to interpret as "Deal."

We sit there in the ruined field, blood and magic on our hands, knowing full well there's one more family member out here. He's alone and probably hurting, so we'll have to get up and do this again in a few minutes.

But for now, we all need a moment to appreciate that Archie is going to be okay and that we survived.

We're Not Gonna Take It

DAMON

Archie has to rest for a while before he can move. He peels himself off the caked earth by degrees, and his leonine body is definitely still fighting the injuries. I watch the change, carefully monitoring him for signs that we're outpacing what he can handle. He had it worse than Ang and me, and we were more crumpled than Rogue. But he shakes his mane a little as if clearing his head, and I breathe a sigh of relief.

There's a rainbow of wounds—a few scabbed, some healing, others open but not bleeding—on him, but the worst have knitted enough to ease my panic. I see the bad one is working hard at his ribs, ugly until it's completely reformed. Javier, still a mostly bald baby phoenix, is clinging for dear life with clutchy little claws, looking like the world's ugliest decoration.

I give a low whistle. "Are you going to make it, baby?"

Lion Archie answers by sneezing—a wet explosion that flattens a patch of grass as he rumbles. Javier chirps his outraged response at my disbelief, his head too big for his tiny, half-plucked body.

Okay, the damn shifters don't like me questioning them; got it.

Rogue finally says, "That's the most annoying newborn I've ever met —and I don't like human kids, either."

Her voice is empty and flat, but she's not losing it anymore, so that's a win. There's blood dried on her face—definitely not all hers—but her eyes are locked on the horizon, the far edge of the crater where the fight went down. She's looking for Rebel now that Arch is out of the woods, and she can't focus on anything else until we locate him.

Archie gives a low, impatient growl as he watches our mate. He's ready to help her, and so am I. Rogue being this worried is affecting all of us because we're mated, and what she needs is her grouchy stepbrother that she's likely regretting her last words to. She needs to not to be comparing this to losing her twin and feeling helpless.

We have to help her and ourselves find the last piece of our family even if it's painful.

Angelo limps over to her, his face a mess of bruises and smeared glittery blood. The silence hangs around us as we prepare for the search, secretly hoping that Rebel won't be worse than Archie. But there should be noise here—sirens, cops, fire, Rebel's moans, demons, whatever—and it's still quiet as a tomb.

"Weird, isn't it? That no one from any side or group has noticed this shit yet?" Angelo says. He looks at me, his left eye swollen shut. "You'd think there'd be cleanup crews by now."

"It's not over," I say. "Maybe no one is sending people because the area is… not suitable? Fuck, I don't know, Ang. We've been over this."

"Yeah, but it's still creeping me out, bro. This is next-level shit, and even after we find Reb, I have no idea where we go from there. You know?"

"We keep moving," Rogue says as she starts forward. "That's all we can do with something this big and this complex. Take it in chunks; knock a piece off the board one at a time. I'd bet it's what *they're* doing —whoever they are."

The shifted version of Archie paces beside her, with Bird Javi making this sad little rasp every third step. Angelo walks behind them, and I take up the rear, keeping an eye out for movement, threats, residuals. Every sense is on high alert as we search for our brother and her future mate.

He's not dead; Rogue would know.

But it doesn't feel like Rebel's here either, and that makes me paranoid. Even as we find the impact site where Javi's fireball big enough to torch a city block took out the pedestal, it's just a patch of scorched earth and glittering shards. The ground is smoking, and that viscous goop from the blob is everywhere. There's no body under the rubble or lying in the open; it's only the traces of the explosion.

"He's not here," Rogue whispers.

"Maybe he—" Angelo can't finish, and I don't blame him.

Rogue's legs give out, and she hits the ground hard. Her knees are in the ash, and her hands are braced to hold herself up. She's not crying, because she never cries, but I can see the fracture run through her. It's her fault for surviving, just like it was her fault when they sent Reckoning away.

Archie paws at the edges of the circle, his ears flat and tail lashing. Javier hops off and immediately face plants, then rights himself with a huffy shake. He pecks at a shiny spot, then screeches.

I squint at what the naked bird is trying to show me. Something in the debris and ash is weird... in fact, it's something that shouldn't be here: Fae dust. I scan the horizon, then the sky, then the dirt. No sign of him flying, but his wings were out again for sure. The only other thing is the goop, spreading slowly from the impact like an oil stain.

"I don't think he was... evaporated or whatever, guys," I say slowly. "There's Fae dust on *top* of the debris here. If it was let out only before the blast, it would only be under stuff. This is... fresh."

Angelo frowns as he comes over to where the animals and I are investigating. "You're right, D."

Rogue shakes her head. "He can't just be missing; I'd feel it. I'd know." Her fingers dig into the earth as she shudders. "Unless—"

"Unless he's in a place even you can't reach," Angelo finishes. "Then he wouldn't feel *dead*, but he wouldn't feel *here*, either."

I crouch, sifting through the dust to find a clue of who might have done this: a smell, a trace, or a piece of something that doesn't belong will work. Archie's nose is sharper as he noses around, but even he looks stumped. It's like someone could completely hide their presence in defiance of all principles of evidence and magical tenets simultaneously.

Who the fuck can do that shit?

Rogue's wings flicker into existence, shuddering in the afternoon sun, and I know she's losing her temper. She's burning magic she needs, but she doesn't care. Her posture is rigid, determined, and she looks like a death goddess as she surveys the entire crater with fury in her aura.

"Whoever this is," she growls, "will pay, and I am *not* cheap in vengeance. I am fucking *tired* of this shit, and especially of people stealing my goddamn men."

Angelo cracks his knuckles, his own wings unfurling. "Agreed, Princess. Injuring our people, stealing our family? That's an affront to us, and to everything else we're connected to. The Geminis, the Guardians, the phoenixes... hell, even the shifters."

I hold up a hand. "Not that we can tell any of those damn organizations because we don't know who to trust. Sparkles is right; we have to get our pound of flesh and rescue Rebel ourselves."

No one wants to admit it, but we're on our own with this.

Javier creeps up and tries to climb Rogue's leg. She stoops down to pick him up, and I join her, locked in a silent circle as we all come to grips with what I said. I'm the one who breaks the silence first, because if I don't, Rogue's going to disintegrate right here in this ash-pit and take the rest of us with her. She's running on rage, but there's a splinter in her, twisting deeper by the minute.

"Can you feel the Guardian link at all? Is it—" I don't want to say, like Reckoning, but she knows what I mean.

Rogue draws in air like she's prepping for a punch. Her wings flicker—half in, half out, a riot of sparkling dragonfly-like shadows. She closes her eyes and goes quiet as she tries again.

I hate making her do this, but we need to be sure.

Angelo paces like a caged wolf, his wings ruffling. Archie sits curled tight around his body as he watches. Even Javier, haphazard lump of feathers that he is, goes quiet.

Finally, my mate opens her eyes. They're dry, but not okay. "I can't feel him through any bonds, even Fae-based ones. There's no..." She's searching for the right word, and struggling as she rasps, "He's not *gone*, just...absent."

"So he's not dead," I say, my voice still raw.

"No," Rogue says. "He's not here, but he's not dead." She looks at me, and there's hope and a terrifying fury behind her eyes. "I didn't think there was anyone who could hide Fae from one another like that, especially ones with bonds in place via their magics."

I don't have to fake the shudder. "I mean, we have no idea what all those new realm fuckers can do. And we were so separate from the real world in that pocket realm that the bad guys didn't know we were there. We think that's how the people are trafficking supes like Reck, right? They're taking them through portals like that one that disappear and allow them to get anywhere in any realm."

Angelo runs a hand through his hair, his expression thoughtful. "Then he's been kidnapped and taken to another realm, while we were all knocked out cold. Seems weird it'd be him, right? Two demon heirs, an oft-hunted mythical, and a hybrid Fae Guardian available, but they take Rebel? I mean, even Archie's parents are on the Shifter Council. Reb had the *least* hostage value of everyone."

"Not to us," Rogue says through gritted teeth. "If they were aiming at us, he'd be important even without all those fancy designations."

"And less likely to draw *outside* attention when he goes missing, especially if Rogue doesn't tell their handler," I add. "Kind of a brilliant strategy, now that I think about it."

Rogue actually smiles at that—knife-thin, but a genuine smile. "I hate this shit," she says. "But if he's alive, we can work with that. We can figure out where and rescue his ass."

"Then we need clues," I say, getting practical.

Rogue looks at the ground. "That's all that's left," she says, gesturing at the shimmer in the dust and the dark slicks of goop. "This is all we have to go on, guys. We have to gather some of it up and get it back home so Damon can do... science things."

"We've been blown to shit, Princess," Angelo points out. "We don't exactly have evidence kits like on a TV show."

"Maybe not," Rogue says. "But we have whatever is on us, and what's in Archie's car. We'll use that to collect shit as best we can."

Javier hops off her shoulder and struts in a little circle around her boots, then looks up expectantly. I could swear the damn bird is listening, but I have no idea if that's possible.

I pull out my phone, which is half melted. "No way this does anything useful. Sorry, Sparkles."

"Then take off the scraps of your shirts and wipe up some stuff. We can take those back, analyze everything, and then we let D do his lab thing. Angelo, you're walking the best of everyone, so you should go check the car for anything we can use to get this stuff back or contact help."

"Yay for me," Angelo mutters, then flashes her a grin. "Don't worry. I'm going. Maybe Arch has some water and shit, too. We all look damn near desiccated with dehydration, injuries, and magic depletion."

Rogue's brain is firing again; you can see it in the set of her jaw. "If you find a phone, we'll send for some of your demon minions, guys. We don't give them the authentic story, but if they show, then we can get a ride to the gates of the house at least. That will keep us from having to stagger around until we get there."

"Are we sure that Luca isn't involved?" I ask tentatively. "We definitely can't fight off a gang of our own dudes in this shape."

Rogue hesitates, but then nods. "I think this one is above his pay grade. We were right before when we said he wouldn't be dumb enough to arrange it right after you guys left his house."

I strip the remains of my shirt off as she instructed. "We need something to store this. Get a move on, bro."

Angelo sighs and gives us a little wave as he heads out of the crater and towards the field where we entered the area.

Javier lets out a peep, and she bends to stroke his head. When she straightens, she looks at me carefully. "Are you holding up okay now?"

I want to tell her no, that my ribs feel like popcorn and my head's still swimming from the hit I took, but I just nod.

She moves closer, laying her head on my shoulder gently. "We can't let them see us bleed. It gives them the idea that we're weak, Damon."

I stand up straighter, even though it hurts, chuckling a bit. "We didn't really have a choice before, Sparkles. No magic or shifting to staunch it."

"You know what I meant." Rogue lifts her head, then starts using the fabric I give her to collect the goop residue. I follow her lead with the sparkly dust, and together we scrape up as much as we can.

By the time Angelo gets back—miracle of miracles, with an intact lunchbox and a half-empty bottle of water—we've got a small stash of samples. This should be enough to test and maybe trace their origins.

"Are you ready to head towards civilization now?" he asks. "I found the CB in Arch's trunk from racing, so I could get some signal and send out a blast for help."

Rogue just starts walking. I fall into step beside her, and for the first time since the blast, it feels like we're going to get through this. We just had to get our heads right and our bodies able to function—now we can meet this bullshit head-on.

"What's the plan after this?" Angelo asks as he looks at the lion and the small bird trotting along beside us.

"We get home. Then we get him back," Rogue replies firmly. "That is *all* we have on the plate right now."

"Do we start in Hell?" I ask curiously. "We had to do a lot of dancing to get that approved, and Luca will be suspicious if we don't visit for at least a day."

"Probably," she says in a sigh. "I really dislike the idea of going there, but the testing is a 'Hail Mary' and we all know it. There aren't references of stuff from some of those realms because their people never come here. We may find that none of that is from here, but not be able to identify where it came from. Then it will be a process of elimination."

The sun's setting by the time we get to the car to wait for whoever is coming from Angelo's SOS call. I glance at Rogue. Her mask is back in place, but under the armor, I see her heart. Rebel is integral to who she is, and without him, she's aching. Despite that vulnerability, she's showing an emotion that surprises me. It's not hope or anger; it's something worse: certainty.

Rogue Kelly is going to bring Rebel home, or she's going to die trying— that I know without a shadow of a doubt.

Abracadabra

ROGUE

I'VE BEEN SHOT, stabbed, and once broke my foot in three places while running from a half-crazed 'lost one' sent after Reb and me in the tunnels under Bay City. That was years ago, and it still didn't hurt as much as this shit does.

Never, not once, have I been as furious as I am now, squished in the back seat of a rumbling van with Damon and a full-grown lion who keeps growling grumpily at every bump. I'm pressed against the window, trying to convince myself that holding myself upright is not a sign of weakness, while Damon is cataloguing his injuries out loud.

He's doing it to keep his mind off of Rebel, so I let it go.

"Seven lacerations, two likely require sutures. Bruising on the left flank. My pinky's probably dislocated, but the flexion's improving. Rogue, how's the arm?"

I flex my right hand. The tendons pull tight, bright white lines beneath blood and a layer of charred, sticky stuff from the blast site.

"More functional than everyone else," I say. I glare at the side of his head. "How's your shoulder?"

He shrugs and I nod, figuring the blood sharing did enough healing on us to make the serious stuff go away.

In the driver's seat, one of Angelo's lackeys tries not to stare at the lion in the rearview. The other rides shotgun, looking increasingly nervous to be headed to their boss' house. They keep their mouths shut and drive like they've got something to prove. The only words out of either of them were 'Everybody in,' and now there's just the hum of the engine, Archie's tail-licking, and the newborn shrieks of baby phoenix Javier in my arms.

Javi doesn't look like even an actual bird yet, not with his pinkish see-through skin and those black pinprick eyes. I don't think anyone expected him to be palm-sized, angry, and already trying to peck Damon's thumb off. But his sacrifice kept us alive, and bought time to heal, so I won't complain—at least, not right now.

Angelo rides shotgun in the other car—a blacked-out luxury SUV, which left with us at the scene of the explosion, but peeled ahead on our way to the drive. He texted to say the house was secure, the gates locked, and Florissa had been called for a house visit. Florissa isn't my favorite witchy healer, especially because she charges triple for after-midnight calls and always smells like a ton of herbs and oils that irritate my Fae side.

Beggars can't be choosers, though, so I'll suck it up.

"Do you think we'll be able to find him?" Damon whispers. I stare through the window, watching the scenery go by as I try *not* to think about my missing stepbrother.

"We have to." I shake my head as I mutter, "I won't survive losing someone else, D."

Archie makes a low rumble that vibrates through my bones. He's in pain—but staying in animal form is helping with that. With Rebel gone, we're all on edge, and our leonine companion is no exception. I turn to pat his mane gently, and his big tongue swipes over my palm, making me shudder.

"Stay cool, dude. We're almost there. Once that flighty spell slinger gets here, you can shift back and she'll finish the job."

"Almost there," says the driver. He winds down the private street that leads to the enormous gates of our mansion, stopping for a moment as they open to allow us entry. I shudder to think how much more protection Damon will add after this fucking attack so close to our home, but I don't blame him.

The first lackey hops out, opens the sliding door. "Out you go," he says, and when Archie growls, he adds, "I'm sure they have a nice juicy steak inside for you."

We do, but he's going to eat regular food once the healer fixes him.

Archie ducks his head as he backs out of the back and leaps to the ground. Once he's at the side of the van, I push the door open and step out with Javier cradled against me, then Damon follows me. My eyes dart around the drive, checking every angle to make sure someone isn't lurking there hoping to take us out completely. I know better, but the stress of the weather bullshit has me jumpy.

I catch a whiff of something acrid and realize it's me. My shirt's torn, one sleeve blackened and melted into a kind of dreadlock at my bicep. Most of my wounds are already closing, but my skin is red and puckered in places. I think of Rebel's face the last time I saw him and I lock it down behind my eyes.

I don't have time for fear or grief right now.

Angelo's standing by the garage door, tapping at his phone. His own blood is wiped away, but there's a smear on his collar and an edge to his voice when he says, "Are you okay, Princess?"

He asks only me. The others can walk it off, but me, he's treating me like I'm made of crystal when I saved all their asses. Go figure. "Is Florissa on her way? I don't want to wait if she's running a fucking tab that will make my eyes water."

"On her way," he says. "I want her to look at Archie first. If he shifts back before his insides re-align, he'll fuck everything up. She has to make sure all the bones and shit are in the right places."

The lion lifts his head and sniffs the air. There's a long second, where I think Archie's going to leap at Angelo and maul him for the insult. Instead, he yawns and lumbers toward the house.

That's my cinnamon roll boy, alright.

Nodding at the door, I take Damon's arm. "Let's get in there and wash this crap off. I'm tired of being covered in debris."

We follow the path Archie took, letting Angelo dismiss their goons on his own. I don't settle until I hear the door close behind him and Damon makes a beeline for the control panel of his military-grade security system. Once everything is secure, I let out a sigh of relief. Now I can try to calm my jangling nerves enough to think straight.

Angelo pulls me aside, head tilted as he says, "We have ten, maybe fifteen minutes, before the healer gets here. Do you have the evidence we collected?"

I fish the bundle from the dirty car towels I'm holding Javier in. The various bags and papers holding the goop, dirt, dust, and other things we thought might be important are inside of a plastic grocery bag. He takes it, heading for the wall of the living room and pulling a painting aside to reveal a safe. I had no idea that was there, but I'm glad for it.

"You can't possibly think Florissa is a suspect if she's coming here," I say quietly.

He doesn't look back at me, just shoves the bag inside of the safe. "I think we have to behave as if anyone could be a suspect in Bay City right now. We saw that damn line-up at the meeting, and how did people know you and Arch were headed after the arena?"

"Lots of people there are being questioned, and law enforcement types, too," I reply as I consider his question. "But I don't think that's really where the leak happened. This is bigger than cops on the Stuhlls' payroll or Mina tattling to someone. Other realms bigger, and I have no idea what those people are capable of—not really."

Angelo nods, looking concerned. "Exactly. So, this is going in here until Damon has what he needs to analyze it. It could be the key to finding him, Princess."

We stand in the living room with blood and muck covering us, neither one wanting to say the thing we're both thinking: If we don't get Rebel back, we'll turn this city inside out.

Archie pads over, leaving flecks of blood and a trail of fur across the office floor. Damon's behind him, chasing him with rags as he tries to get the cat to be still so he can clean him up. The sight makes me grin a little, and Javi squawks a warning as Archie gets too close.

"Do we have a plan yet?" Damon asks.

I look at Angelo. "Sort of. The evidence is locked up, and Florissa is on her way to heal us."

Damon nods. "Okay. That's a start."

The lion slumps to the floor in front of the couch, its breath coming fast. I sit next to him, stroking his ears lightly. "You'll be all good soon, babe. Just keep hanging on, and we'll get you patched up." He snorts, and I chuckle softly. "I know you aren't used to staying an animal this long."

"It's better for him, though. He heals faster, and the injuries don't drain his energy as easily."

"I know," I say as I continue petting my poor hockey player. "But it's shitty that he can't talk with us and stuff. I'm sure he wants to tear his mane off because he can't communicate."

"Well, he's a talker," Angelo says with a smirk. "This is his punishment for some prank he pulled, I'm sure."

The lion huffs, and I chuckle again.

Anything to keep from thinking about Rebel.

"I'm going to go get cleaned up, guys," I finally say. Keeping baby

Javier close, I kiss both twins on the cheek before I go. "Keep an eye on him until the Worst Witch arrives."

At least if I'm clean, I won't leave behind a stinky corpse if she hexes me for being salty with her.

WHEN I COME BACK DOWNSTAIRS, the beeps from the alarm tell me that the healer has finally arrived. Damon buzzes her in, and I settle on the couch with my clean towel-wrapped phoenix mate on my lap. He wouldn't let me leave him on the bed while I showered, so I had to put him on the sink to stop the screeching that made my ears ring. He's on the naughty list for sure, but I won't mind if he gives Florissa hell.

The doorbell rings, and I hear the jingling of bracelets outside. Angelo goes to open it, and Florissa steps in, all patchouli and power, her hair wild around her face. I have to bite my tongue as she surveys the scene: my lion mate bleeding on the floor, me with exposed wounds and a reborn bird in my lap, Damon limping in from the kitchen with water, and Angelo trying to pretend he's an immaculate host despite his appearance.

"I charge extra for healing that begins in animal form, you know," she says.

Of fucking course she does—this is why Fae human magic users don't get along very well.

"Fine," Damon says as he sits next to Archie. "Just get it done."

Florissa breezes past, laying out her materials on the floor as she kneels near big kitty Archie. Her incantations sound like French and Latin and some other language I don't recognize. I watch as she rubs some greenish ointment into his fur and chants, her voice low and rhyth-mic. The smell alone makes my vision swim. After five minutes, Archie's eyes go glassy. Florissa turns to us, wiping her hands on a rag.

"He'll sleep this off," she says. "Then, when he wakes, he'll be in human form again and healed well enough to resume normal activity. I've made certain that all the internal injuries are addressed."

"Thank you," I murmur as I look at my mate. I mean that, because no matter how greedy the witch is nor how much I dislike her, she just kept Archie from being in pain. That deserves respect and gratitude.

She sizes me up, her eyes sharp as they roam over me. "Your turn, girlie. I didn't think I'd be doing this with you again so soon. Someone may have put a bad mark next to your name, you know."

Yeah, I've considered that, but I'm not telling her.

I comply, sitting Javi aside as I move closer to the witch. Damon turns away as I pull my shirt off, which is both sweet and unnecessary. Florissa pokes at my burns and cuts and then rubs paste on them that stings like hell. "You heal fast, but at least one of these might scar. Did you share power to keep everyone from dying? Your aura feels much weaker than it should."

"I didn't have a choice," I mutter. "I couldn't just let them all die."

"Understood, but that took its toll. You know the saying about magic and prices... It doesn't mean what humans think it does. It means the universe demands balance, and scars may be yours."

"I'll decorate them with ink and wear them with pride as always." I smirk at her and the witch sighs like I'm the most trying person she's ever met.

"Fae are infuriating." She cleans up, packs her bag, and pauses before leaving. "Do you know what caused the burns? Because it looks like phoenix fire and you seem to have an ugly naked bird."

"Coincidence," Damon says with a shrug. "That's Rogue's new familiar."

Florissa rolls her eyes. "Fine. If you want to lie, I can't stop you. I'd recommend contacting its family to find out what you need to do to speed its growth and keep it healthy. There's little to no information available outside of their groups on the care of reborn mythical birds."

My stomach drops—I didn't even think about that.

Angelo nods at the witch. "I appreciate the suggestion. Your payment will arrive through the usual method shortly. Don't stray too far from your phone, just in case."

"You two don't need me, but you knew that," she says as she heads for the door. "Your kind are impenetrable once your magic flows again."

My gaze narrows as I look at Damon and Angelo, who both look sheepish. They didn't want to admit that only Archie and I needed her, and I'm honestly too damn tired to fight about it.

Once she's gone and the cameras show her exiting the gates, I drop onto the couch again, sprawling out with baby Javi. "You heard her. Call his damn parents, Ang. Damon, you deal with getting equipment here to analyze our evidence."

"What are you going to do?" D asks curiously.

"I'm going to take a goddamn nap with the menagerie. Don't wake me until you have what we need."

I think I've earned it after all this shit.

In The Dark Of The Night

REBEL

Nothing like waking up with a probable concussion and half a pound of ash in your mouth.

My tongue feels like it's full of gravel, and my eyes are crusted shut. For a minute, I try to remember what day it is and what the fuck happened, but it comes rushing back pretty quickly. I taste blood mixed with something musty and ancient, like I ate a fucking mummy or something. My shoulder cracks against the wet stone and sends a current of pain all the way to my ass. I have to do a more thorough inventory before I attempt moving, or I might make shit even worse than they are now.

I lie still with my gross eyes closed, assessing damage piece by piece. Both legs and arms: attached, but numb, which means pain is coming, eventually. The left side of my face is pressed to something damp and fuzzy. If it's moss, fine, but if it's a dead rat, that'll fit the mood for today. My body feels like a deep, solid bruise, but everything seems to be in one piece.

I'm not sure if I should be grateful or pissed.

Memory seeps back in, like water working its way through a plugged drain. There was a flash—a sound that ate all other sounds, then… nothing. That part doesn't track because I've survived bigger explosions. Javi's implosion couldn't be worse than being too close to six pounds of TATP, right?

But if I'm alive, so is everyone else. Unless, of course, this is the Fae limbo area where we get sent to new bodies because we can't really die —which would just be embarrassing. I'm too highly trained to end up here because a phoenix did its thing and blew up a magical pedestal. I'll never live it down.

It's time to open my eyes. One lid peels back after some convincing, but there's nothing to see except darkness and a faint shimmering gray stone. I drag in a breath and nearly cough up a lung. The air is heavy, damp, stinking of rotted wood and that sourness you get in old root cellars.

"Rogue?" My voice is a fistful of sandpaper. "Archie? Damon?" I hesitate, then say, "Angelo? Javier?"

My voice echoes off the walls, just barely, which means the space is bigger than a coffin but not by much. It sounds like my voice has been smothered with a wet towel. The silence that follows is eerie, and I growl softly under my breath when nothing responds. I'm definitely somewhere soundproof or alone.

I'm not sure which option is worse yet, so I'll try again.

I try again, louder this time. "Time to make some noise!"

Nothing.

My heart beats faster as panic grows in my chest, but I smother it with a curse. I have no idea what it looks like when a phoenix dies and comes back—maybe Javi's gone all the way molten and needs to reconstitute from a pile of carbon. Maybe it takes hours, or days, or a fucking century.

What about the others? I repeat the names, just in my head this time, one after the other like a litany, hoping the words will shape the dark into something familiar. Rogue is always first—if she's alive, she'll be furious, and if she's furious, nothing in this world or the next will stop her from burning it all down to find whoever's left.

The back of my throat closes up. I don't want to think about 'if' and 'left'. That's not a useful direction.

I try to reach for her, not with words, but with that channel that runs straight through our bones. If Rogue is somewhere in range, even if she's locked in another goddamn hole, she'd feel me or I'd feel her response. I fumble for that thread, my breath gone shallow, and get... nothing.

Dead air, silence...like the world's been unplugged.

Fear doesn't suit me, but it skates across my skin, anyway. Either she's dead or I'm dead, which is unlikely based on what I remember of the battle. Maybe the concussion is worse than I thought, and I'm hallucinating this whole thing. Or I could be in a coma, like in that shitty ending to *Lost*, and I'm imagining all of this because my brain is a lazy-ass writer.

I spit on the floor. This can't be the limbo-esque space; there's too much pain, dirt, and my own goddamn sweat in the air. The world is still here, so somebody's captured me. Honestly, that's a feat in and of itself, and I almost have to admire the motherfucker... almost.

My head spins like a loaded roulette wheel as I push myself to my knees, and I gag. The ceiling is low, maybe two feet above my skull. I reach up and smack my palm flat against it to feel slimy, cold stone. I stretch my legs as far as they'll go and hit another wall there. The wall at my head is rough and flakes under my fingernails.

A cave? A grave? Who the fuck knows?

I consider screaming, but decide against it. Instead, I talk, just to keep my voice from vanishing. "Gotta hand it to whoever did this—points for creativity. Last time I got kidnapped, there was at least a mattress." I snicker, but the humor tastes sour. "But this is good—old-school, even. I respect the classics."

They've stripped me down to the bare minimum, so I won't find much help in my pockets. I have a torn, dirty undershirt, boxers, and my left sock, which is deeply insulting. No phone, no weapons, and I'm not sure if calling my Fae blade will work if this place is magically enhanced. If I had a knife, I could start carving tally marks or shank myself out of boredom, but even that's denied.

For a while, I sit here fuming while I try to slow my pulse. I inventory the rest of my injuries, including bruised ribs, swelling over my eyebrow, and a cracked molar. I dig at it with my tongue until the metallic taste gets overwhelming. Maybe it's dumb to worry about a tooth when you're locked in a stone coffin, but I've never been good at focusing without Rogue around.

She balances out my natural tendency to jump from thing to thing as I think.

I try the Fae link again, this time pushing with every bit of magic I have at the moment. The effort leaves me sweating, but it's like screaming into a void. Something is actively blocking us, which means this wasn't a simple snatch-and-grab. Our attackers planned to take us out, and when that didn't work, they adapted quickly by kidnapping one of us. Plus, they're powerful enough to make sure no one can trace a line right back to me.

That's some serious firepower, so it wasn't Luca or those idiot Stuhll goons led by Rogue's shitty ex.

I punch the wall, just to see if it'll budge. All it does is split my knuckles and smear a red streak across the stone. I lick the silvery blood away; no use wasting it. Rogue would say I'm posturing—that I knew that wouldn't work and did it, anyway. She'd be right, as usual, but that doesn't mean that getting some of my fury at this situation out doesn't help clear my brain a bit.

My eyes are slowly adjusting to the dark here, but there's nothing to see. I count seconds, lose track, start again. I try humming, first a pop song, then a drinking song, then just a single note until my voice cracks. There's no feedback, no sign that anyone is listening—not even a rat.

There's a reason they say people lose their minds in solitary, and I can bet you a hot fiver it has to do with neurodiversity.

For a second, I think I hear water, but it's probably just the blood in my ears. My mind flips through possibilities of what this place is as I whistle. It could be an underground bunker, dungeon, abandoned subway, or root cellar. But none of that fits because who kidnaps a known *Guardian* and puts them in a wet rock closet unless they have a death wish? Rogue and I aren't *actively* watching our charge, but we're active in the Society, and it's no secret. It's asking for more trouble than it's worth.

I force myself to lie back down, pressing my spine into the cold ground. The contact helps somehow because physical touch is real. While my mind wants to panic, I keep it pinned to reality through pure stubbornness. If I'm alive, then there's a way out. It may take time, but someone will come for me. I just have to keep my shit together until they do.

"Sis," I mutter again, softer this time. "Don't be dead. I need you to be alive so you can tear whoever did this to shreds, preferably with your teeth."

If she were here, she'd roll her eyes and say I'm being dramatic.

Even if I have to drag myself over broken glass and through three dimensions of hell, I make a promise to myself to do whatever it takes to get out. I grip the floor as if it's an anchor and let the anger settle in.

Fear is useless, but rage—rage I can work with.

I close my eyes and wait for whatever comes next.

Time is weird down here. I measure it in heartbeats and the way my body aches more or less depending on whether I'm awake or drifting. Sometimes I shout myself hoarse, to see if anything echoes differently, but mostly I let the silence fill up the gaps in my skull.

The thing is, there's no guard, no torture, not even a taunting voice on the other side of the wall. It's almost offensive, being kidnapped and then left alone.

Do they think I'm going to go insane and off myself? Sorry, but I'm not wired that way.

I spend a while sitting with my back to the cold stone, legs outstretched, face tilted up to where the ceiling is so close I can smell the mineral sweat weeping from it. I talk to myself, sometimes I talk to Rogue, and sometimes to whatever god or goddess might be listening. Occasionally, I even talk to my captors, just in case they have a camera or spell working to watch me.

"So this is it? You grab me out of a crowd, throw me in a hole, and just... forget about me? Not even a ransom note?" I sigh, annoyed, and pick at the crust on my busted knuckle. "If you're trying to break my spirit, you're going to be sorely disappointed."

Little rituals help me keep from going crazy. I count my fingers and toes, flex my limbs, see if anything new has snapped or gone numb. I run through a mental checklist of every person who has the resources to pull off a stunt like this.

But I can't stop coming back to my stepsister. She's been my favorite person in this realm since they brought me here, and not just because of our link or our partnership for the Society. The memory of her is so sharp I can smell it, and it's both torture and bliss. If she's gone, then I'll go down swinging to avenge her because mating with her was going to be the best moment of my goddamn life.

I won't have mercy on anyone who takes that from me.

Eventually, I get bored enough to theorize again. This isn't about ransom or revenge because they could have taken *any of* my family left alive for that. Whoever locked me up wants me neutralized specifically, even though my absence will activate the other Guardians the second they find out. That's attention they shouldn't want to swing in their direction. It's a tremendous risk for their bosses on high to take notice of the shit going down in Bay City at the moment.

So why pick me when it would make everything worse?

Sighing, I put myself in the place of our mysterious enemies. When we thought this might be about the mob goons, it made sense that if you can't take down my little sis directly; you go after her crew. Take us off the board and maybe she hesitates or falls apart. That opens the door for them to get a hold of her when she's not paying attention, and it's a plan someone as simple-minded as Mina would think is a banger.

But that stupid bitch doesn't have the juice for this, nor does she know my girl well enough to realize that it wouldn't happen that way, either. Rogue in the Derby is not the same as Rogue, the Unseelie Fae hybrid Guardian, which is who you get when you touch the people she cares about. Mina has no idea how much power my sis hides, especially since she lost Reck. If the jailers had a single clue about what she's going to do to them, they'd let me head for the darkest realm they can gain entry to as fast as possible.

They had better options for kidnapping if all they wanted was money or leverage on shit in Bay City without bringing a raging Fae or the Society, too. Archie is pure shifter royalty; all of his parents are on the Council. Sariah would arrange a ransom without batting an eye. Javi's a wild card—once he went up in flames, his parents would take great offense at his having to reveal his magic in public. They wouldn't like that Rogue and the rest of us were involved, but if these dickwads had taken their reformed son, the Phoenix Consortiums would have bought his freedom.

Damon and Angelo not being targets makes sense even though their sketchy-ass parents didn't do this. The two of them are too ancient and too connected across the realms to make their disappearance not launch a demonic hunt. There hasn't been one of those on the surface in so long that they were probably in college, and that's a long goddamn time.

The only thing that makes any sense is that I'm bait, and unfortunately, I can't warn anyone about it.

Straight To Hell

ROGUE

THE FIRST THING I notice is a burning weight across my chest. I know in the back alleyways of my mind that I'm not dead—if this were the transition period, I wouldn't be sweating this much.

Unless I'm coming back inside a trusty fur sauna—which, based on my life choices, is plausible.

Attempting to lift my arms, I find my right shoulder entirely buried under something both heavy and golden. It's either the world's most realistic weighted blanket, or—yeah, it's definitely lion fur. I attempt to inhale and come up with cat dander, a trickle of my drool, and the faint scent of spicy demons. My left cheek is plastered to something smooth and warm and definitely breathing. I'm pinned by Lion Archie and surrounded by demons on either side; no wonder I'm roasting.

I crack one eyelid and grimace when the sun spears through the narrow slat of the blackout curtains. Squinting bleatily, I realize that the blanket pinning my other side is a pair of demon wings. One's folded neatly; the other is flopped over the lion's rump, twitching slightly in sleep. If I squirm even a centimeter, it'll probably whack me in the face.

"Shit," I croak. My throat is a sand trap, and I frown as I assimilate the rest of my surroundings.

Above my head, there's a hellish, piercing baby screech. Not a baby human, obviously; I don't know many infants who sound like a blender hitting a kazoo. The noise makes the lion rumble like a discontented diesel engine, and dig its chin deeper into my solar plexus.

Thanks, Archie. Didn't need that rib, anyway.

It all comes back: the attack, Rebel's abduction, our injuries, and the fuzzy memory of passing out on the sofa. I must've been black-bagged in my house because now I'm upstairs, sandwiched between two demons and an apex predator, with a baby phoenix screaming on the bed frame. My hands are tangled in Archie's mane, and I'm pretty sure I'm drooling into Damon's bicep. The small mercy is that my legs aren't tangled up with anyone's but my own, and I might be able to get out of this air fryer via the bottom of the pile.

I wiggle my fingers experimentally. There's no numbness, no ache—actually, the deep soreness that had been chewing through my magic reserves is gone. I feel like a person again. My head is clear, and if I can just unpin myself, I might even stand up successfully.

"Unnnngh," I say, in case anyone wants to register my distress.

The demon wing twitches in answer, flicking my ear like it's bored with my suffering. I try a more targeted approach: I nudge Damon in the ribs with a pointy elbow. He doesn't wake up, but he snorts and mumbles, "Five more minutes," like a petulant teenager.

Even in sleep, he's adorable, but I have to get out of here.

I try the other demon. "Angelo," I whisper, aiming for the exposed bit of his neck not covered by lion mane. No answer, but his tail flicks, then wraps around my ankle. He's not even awake, and he's already being a possessive dick.

Above us, the baby bird goes off again—louder, this time and my ears *demand* that I stop that sound. I wriggle my head out from between the demon and the lion, craning to get a look.

Perched atop the bed's wrought iron headboard, Javier looks less like a gross featherless chicken and more like an angry, downy fireball. He's got one tiny talon wrapped around the bar, and his little beak is gaping in a war cry. Every time he screams, he horks a smoldering little ember into the air. By my count, the bedspread is seconds from spontaneous combustion.

I try again to wake Damon, this time with a slightly harder jab. "Hey. Wake up. Javi's about to torch the sheets."

"Do not care," Damon slurs, then his arm slinks tighter around my waist, pulling me closer. "Let it burn."

I shift back against the lion, which is also now making an annoyed grumble. Archie's breath is heavy and hot, and when he opens a single gold eye, it takes a second for the light of recognition to flicker. Then he blinks, remembers he's a person inside there, and flops his tail off the bed, nearly taking out Javier.

"Off," I hiss, shoving at the wall of fur.

Archie ignores me, instead doing the world's slowest, most deliberate stretch, like a two hundred pound house cat. His ass end rises, then collapses, and the rest of him follows in an avalanche of muscle. There's a moment when I get a truly intimate view of lion anatomy I never needed, and then he's rolled away enough that I can peel myself up.

So. Fucking. Weird.

My tank top is soaked in sweat and lion drool, so the minute he moves, I scramble upright. Kneeling on the mattress, I massage feeling back into my arms as I scramble out of the oven made of my mates.

"Did we decide to have a sleepover and not wake me? What day is it, even?" I mutter as I look around.

The lion gives me a side-eye, then a full-body shake. Its mane explodes in a halo of gold, and a few tufts of fur drift lazily to the floor. Damon finally rolls onto his back, wings stretching and flexing, his eyes still closed. Angelo is the last to wake, but when he does, he's grinning like a wolf with a mouthful of canary.

"You're finally awake," Ang says, his tone sleep-rough, but his dark eyes bright. "We were starting to take bets when that would happen."

I stare at him, incredulous. "I passed out on the couch for a nap. How the hell did I get up here and again, what damn day is it?"

Damon grins, cracking one eyelid. "It took us a bit to figure out, but I guess you went full 'Fae-sleep'. According to my research, nothing short of a direct hit from a howitzer was going to wake you in that state. We debated throwing you in the tub, but decided waterboarding was unnecessary after the shit we just went through."

"Hilarious—also, don't ever do that. Fae-sleep is no joke and if you had awakened me early, I might have tested all our immunity to death." I pick at a clump of lion fur that's gotten stuck under my bra strap.

Angelo shrugs. "Morning-ish, two days after the blast? We've been up and down, getting shit done, but you were out cold and Arch refused to shift until you were awake. We just...let you recharge while Javi grew and the big kitty guarded you both."

I blink at them, letting the fact that I went into the sleep after the attack settle in. The last time I did that was when the Kellys sent Reck away, and I was asleep for two months. I woke one day to an empty house and a new kind of emptiness that I never wanted to feel again.

But here I am, coming out of it with Reb gone and our mating indefinitely postponed.

A fresh peal of baby phoenix rage shatters my brooding. I reach out and grab Javier mid-flap as he comes off the headboard like a comet, talons raking air. Once he's in my hands he settles, staring up at me with coal-bright eyes. He's warm—no, he's hot, like holding a bread roll straight from the oven. His down is prickly and there's a fleck of ash on his beak.

"You're looking better," I say, stroking his head with a finger. He bites me, but gently.

Archie, still in lion form, sniffs at the bird and makes a grumbling purr. He's probably thinking about breakfast and a tiny angry bird that he can't eat isn't exactly a good thing.

"Okay. Now that everyone's awake, someone explain why Archie is still a lion?" I ask, waving a hand at the cat, whose only response is to yawn so wide I can see down his throat.

Damon props himself up, his wings tucking behind him. "We don't know, but he just refused to go human again with you out. I tried to coax him, but he just huffed at me."

Angelo snorts. "He gave the Dom voice a try and pouted when it didn't work. Don't let him fool you into thinking he just let it go."

I sigh, reaching down to ruffle Archie's mane lightly. "Fine. Did anything else important happen while I was out?"

Damon and Angelo exchange a look. Angelo looks at me without his usual smirk. "We had a call with Javi's parents. The Kings and their phoenix consortium are not happy about Javier going boom. It took forever to get them to give us the info on what we needed to do to help him. They wanted to come take him away, but his screeches seemed to talk them out of it. Maybe they understand that loud shit."

Angelo leans forward, voice dropping. "They also don't know who snatched Rebel. That wasn't easy to get out of them, either—both that they'd heard he was missing *and* the shit for taking care of our feathered friend."

Lion Archie makes a noise that could be a huff, or a laugh, or just a reminder that he has teeth.

My chest is tight as I think about my stepbrother, but at least I'm not weak anymore. I squeeze Javier, who squirms, then settles. "Okay," I say. "Well, we're on our own because if the Kings have heard about Reb, then my handlers have, and no one's come calling, I assume."

Ang's smile is back, sharp and a little dangerous. "We're better without all those windbags, anyway, Princess. No rules, no guidelines —just our family working together to find him and take whoever the fuck snatched him out."

I slide off the bed, legs wobbly, and land with a squawk. Javier flaps in my hands, but I manage to keep him from launching. "First things first... I need food and Fae energy coffee. Hell, we all need our versions of that to be able to focus on getting him back."

It's a dysfunctional pack without Reb, but right now, it's all I have.

THE KITCHEN IS COOLER than the bedroom, and not just because I'm not covered in animals and demons. I shuffle to the coffee pot while the others trail behind. Javi rides my shoulder, a little ember shed every time he flicks a wing, singing holes in my tank top. His claws are digging into my skin, but somehow, it doesn't hurt as much as it should and the pain sharpens my mind.

I do enjoy a slice of it occasionally, and this fills that gap nicely.

Archie pads in after us still in lion form, his huge head ducked and eyes fixed on the tile. Damon and Angelo head for the stove and the cabinets to get the food cooking and the table set. There's a weird domestication in all this that comforts me a bit as I try not to think about Rebel being tortured or hurt somewhere.

I pour four mugs of their fancy-ass rich people coffee and add Fae energy potion to mine. Damon pours sugar in his until it's barely coffee at all. Angelo spikes his with something from a flask that definitely isn't Kahlua, and Archie just sniffs at us as we caffeinate.

Glaring at the big feline, I ask, "Are you planning to spend the rest of your life as a throw rug, or do you want to use words again?"

He blinks at me, then at the others, his tail thumping the floor.

Damon leans forward, chin propped on his hands, and says, "You'll have to use the 'boss lady' command again, I fear."

"The boss lady command?" I echo, and the nerdy twin grins at me.

"Alpha. Princess. Girl boss. Pick your poison," he says.

"*Never* 'girl boss', D, or I'll make you suffer in non-fun ways. Fine, I'll do it." I roll my eyes and growl at the lion, "Shift. *Now.*"

There's a ripple in the air and the hum of magic. Archie's fur contracts, shudders, and then collapses inward. For a second he's a fuzzball, then a heap of muscle, and then he's Archer Glaser again— all six plus feet of blond bruiser—bare-assed in the kitchen and completely unbothered. His body is still mapped with the fresh pink scars from the explosion, but all the wounds are closed, the bruises gone.

Thank fuck for that.

He stretches up on his toes, and for a second I'm not the only one admiring the spectacle. Damon gives a low whistle and Archie actually purrs, the sound weird in his human form. Grinning, our no longer feline friend flexes his arms behind his head.

"That's more like it," he says, and gives me a salute. "Good to see you awake, Wheels. Looking hot as always."

I try to ignore the heat crawling up my neck. "Get some damn clothes, puck boy, and then you'll get your coffee and food."

He winks, loping off to the laundry alcove.

The rest of us watch him go, and Damon says, "You know he only listens to you, right? At least, the lion part. The human is a good boy for me, but that cat is allll you, Sparkles."

"If he wants to be a good boy, he needs to listen to both of us in all forms," I say as I sip my brew. "Otherwise, he's being a brat and that's completely different."

Javi starts pecking at my earlobe. I reach up and rub the soft down behind his head, and for the first time all morning he stops squawking. "He's getting less hideous," I say.

Angelo goes to the counter and returns with a small wire perch, complete with a plastic tray for droppings. "They told us we need these in every room so he doesn't shit on the furniture," he explains, setting it up beside my place at the table. "The nest his parents demanded in the bedroom went ignored because he wanted to be with all of us, so hopefully this isn't a wash, too."

I snort. "The Kings don't know their son very well, do they? He was never going to leave the rest of us for some birdy bed."

Angelo shrugs, pours himself more coffee. "New offspring stay in the nest until they're grown, according to them. But our Javi marches to the beat of his own drum, and I hope that means he'll grow faster than they suggested as well."

I look at Javi, who seems to be mulling this over. "No offense, but I think he'd rather incinerate shit his parents suggest rather than use it. He's not fond of their 'traditions' and elitist shit."

"Exactly," Damon says, lifting his mug. "Which is why he fits right in with us, because only Archie doesn't hate his parents. The rest of us hope they all fuck off into eternity."

Javier hops onto the perch, then glares at us all, daring us to say something. I guess he realizes that he shouldn't be at the table while we eat, but isn't happy about it.

Archie comes back in, t-shirt stretched tight across his chest and his shorts hanging so low it's barely decent. He pours half a box of cereal into a mixing bowl and starts shoveling it in, stopping only to chug a liter of milk straight from the carton.

I guess that's one way to start refilling your tank, but it's an infinitely male one.

Nursing my coffee, I watch my new family. Damon and Angelo quietly making our breakfast, their wings folded tight to their backs as they work. Archie eating like he's fueling up for a prize fight, while Javi grooms himself on the perch.

For a second it almost feels safe, but that's not reality, especially with Rebel missing. I clear my throat. "D, if I've been out for two days, you should have some results. What's the story with the blast site evidence?"

The younger twin doesn't answer right away. Instead he takes a long, slow sip, then sets his mug down and folds his hands in front of him. "The samples we brought home are weird. Whoever did this has access to some heavy, old-school shit."

"How old-school?" I ask.

"Like Astral, Legendary, Godly, or Galactic realms old-school. None of this is found in the known ones according to our analysis."

"You're not joking?" I say hopefully, despite knowing he wouldn't do that with Reb waiting for our rescue. "It's really not even Fae or dragon or whatever?"

Damon shakes his head. "I wish. The residue didn't react to anything I tested. Whatever they used to make the crystal, the pedestal, and the blob, it's not from this world."

Archie stops mid-chew, his head tilted curiously. "What does that mean for us?"

Angelo leans forward, resting his arms on the table. "It means whoever took Rebel knew what they were doing, and it means they wanted us to know it."

I set my mug down, fingers tapping the rim. "They're trying to get us to make a mistake. Taking him and finding this stuff was certain to stop our current progress, right?"

Damon nods. "That's their game, but we don't have to play by their rules."

The room goes quiet for a second, the only sound is the ticking of the wall clock and the soft scratch of Javi's claws on his perch.

It feels awful, but I know what we need to do.

I take a deep breath and push back from the table. "We have to go to Hell without Rebel. This is a distraction and they knew we'd derail our plans to go if they snatched one of us."

"Are you okay with that?" Angelo asks, cocking a brow. "Leaving him while we take a short hike to my homeland to sleuth?"

I glance at Javi, who's watching me with unblinking eyes. "No, but I'm not okay with Javier being a baby bird or Archie almost dying, either. I didn't ever want to go into Fae-sleep again, nor do I want to inform Luca and Lola that they most *certainly* have a leak in their house."

Damon stands, his wings flexing as he frowns. "We're *telling* them?"

"We have to. That's how they knew to hit us and why it was so sudden and in public," I say. "This was meant to keep us away from Hell; I feel it in my gut."

Archie grins. "We should definitely disappoint whoever the fuck it is. They could have fucked up my whole career with that shit. I'm lucky to be mated to a bunch of badasses with magical blood."

"Focus, babe," Damon says as he winks at him. "We can't get distracted again now that we're going down there. People from the other realms don't get how different Hell is from here or Faerie. It's... worse than Luca's funhouse at the Apalachin, but also... oddly familiar in some ways?"

"Let's get moving then," I say as I look at my men seriously. "We need to get in, snoop around, see our new friends and exchange info, then get out. Rebel is waiting for us—somewhere."

The devil may have gone to Georgia, but my family is going the opposite direction—and we're up for any challenge they throw at us.

READ the bonus here

Preorder book three here

Get a Secret Bonus Scene!

For a secret bonus scene, *click the link below, sign up for my newsletter, and get your freebie.*

Get your bonus scene here!

Reviews, Print, and Merchandise

If you have enjoyed this story, please review it.
It helps other readers find my work,
which helps me as an indie author.

Thank you!

Reviews are appreciated on the following platforms

TikTok
Instagram
Facebook
Bookbub
StoryGraph
Threads
Goodreads
Amazon

To purchase print copies or merchandise, go to The Worlds of
Cassandra Featherstone

World & Pronunciation Guide

CHARACTERS

Rogue Olive Kelly (roh-g AH-live kei-lee) adopted by Graciella and Odhran Kelly; Guardian partnered with foster step-brother Rebel; her real brother Reckoning was sold off when they were kids; roller derby captain for Babe City Bombers; secret racing star with Rebel; half Unseelie Fae and half succubus; her dragonfly-like wings have fatal fairy dust;

Nicknames: Princess, little Sis, Wheels, *zuccherino*, *Kiandra Ormanda* (Fae name), Rainbow Smite, Skates, Dragonfly, Sparkles, *mi alma*.

Rebel Elvis Kelly (reb-uhl ell-viss kei-lee) street racing star; step-brother and co-Guardian with Rogue; been in love with Rogue since puberty; adopted by Graciella and Odhran Kelly after they sold Reckoning off, Unseelie Fae; his bird-like wings have a paralytic fairy dust;

Nicknames: Reb.

Graciella Kelly (gray-see-ell-uh key-lee) adoptive mother of Rogue, Rebel, and Reckoning; Society adjacent, looking to move up; wealthy social climber; sold Reckoning off to someone mysterious when the twins were young; dislikes Rogue; witch

Odhran Kelly (or-ahn kel-lee) adoptive father of Rogue, Rebel, and Reckoning; Society adjacent, looking to move up; lets Graciella do whatever she wants; brownie

Javier Emil King (hav-e-air ee-mieel king) one of Reb's best friends; bartender; phoenix from old, snooty money; also in love with Rogue; submissive.

Nicknames: Javi, J, birdy.

Archer Levi Glaser (ar-chur lee-vy glazer) plays for hockey team; sports star; from large pride family; lion shifter; mother has a harem of various cat shifter dads; also in love with Rogue; huge flirt

Nicknames: Archie.

Angelo Gemini *(ang-el-OH gem-in-eye)* twin to Damon; one of the heirs to Gemini Mafia; father is an evil dick; mother isn't much better; Dom; demon; also in love with Rogue; bat wings; vengeance demon.

Nicknames: Ang.

Damon Gemini *(day-mon gem-in-eye)* twin to Angelo, demon; submissive; mother isn't much better; also in love with Rogue; chaos demons; horns, angel wings;

Nicknames: D, little D, good boy.

Mina (mee-nuh) Rogue's ex-BFF; social media maven; leaves the Babe City Bombers to join the rival team; arranges for Rogue to be beaten up, witch with low powers,

Winnie (win-nee) bartender, dated Rogue; nymph

Merra Stuhll (mare-uh STUH-ll) fennec fox shifter and wife of the rhino shifter; really runs the Mob instead of her husband,

Nicknames: Queen Bitch.

Beatrice Janssen (Bee-uh-triss jan-sen) captain of Silver City Sickos, selkie

Nicknames: Holly Go Bite Me, BJ.

Florissa (floor-iss-uh) hippie healer witch Rebel takes Rogue to

Apollonia (ap-uh-loan-nee-uh) one of the Sickos, put in a permanent vegetative state during the fight behind the bar by Rogue

Luca Gemini (loo-cuh gem-in-eye)head of the Gemini mob; Angelo and Damon's father.

Basil (baz-uhl) Bay City's ancient caladrius healer

Samara Glaser (suh-mare-uh glay-zer) Archie's mom; mated to a harem of big cats; lioness.

Benton Glaser (ben-ton glay-zer) Archie's dad; puma shifter; works at the docks where the Ligeia Chorus runs things

Forest Glaser (for-est glay-zer) Archie's dad; leopard shifter; works at the casino uptown owned by the Gemini Mob

Saber Glaser (say-buhr glay-zer) Archie's dad; panther shifter; works at the bank rumored to be run by the Magus Consortium

Bramble Glaser (bram-bull glay-zer) Archie's dad; tiger shifter; works at the hospital owned by the Phoenix Foundation

Harley Glaser (har-lee glay-zer) Archie's dad; lion shifter; leader on the local Council

Betsy Sue (bet-see soo) siren; on the Babe City Bombers

Nicknames: Intoxiskate

Drusilla Banks (droo-sill-uh banks) cougar; member of Babe City Bombers

Anita (uh-nee-tuh) wolf shifter; member of Babe City Bombers

Mugs, Dingus, and Vern (dooshbags) dumb smelly trolls who attack Rogue at rave

Sariah Templeton (suh-ry-uh temple-ton) Roadrunner Racing's manager; cobra shifter

Melanie (mell-uh-nee) unicorn shifter, member of the Babe City Bombers; replaces Mina

Nicknames: Interstella

Vinnie the Tooth Stuhll loan shark

Esmerelda King (ez-mer-el-duh king) Javi's mother; phoenix

Diego King (dee-eg-o king)Javi's father; phoenix

Guillermo (gee-air-mo) brown recluse spider shifter; tailor to Geminis; ancient as hell

Laurel (laurel) racoon shifter; assistant to Guillermo

Cheshmak (cheh-ss-mack) mean demon at the Gemini party; succubus

Abbott Remington (ab-butt rem-ing-ton) criminologist from the Sibbies; past lover of Rogue's; nerdy Sphinx shifter

Tracer Finn (tray-ser Fi-nn)one of the heirs apparent to the *Sons of the Seven Seas* gang; kraken; Slade's brother.

LOCATIONS AND TITLES

The Rink- Home of the Babe City Bombers, Rogue's roller derby team

Babe City Bombers- Rogues' roller derby team

Silver City Sickos- rival team Mina joins; cheaters.

Roadrunner Racing- street racing team run by the Stuhll Mob, Reb races for them sometimes; Rogue pretends to be Reb and races for them occasionally.

Bay City Thunder- hockey team Archie plays for

Drop Kick Mollies- derby team from Mounty Cove, all human but criminals

The Banshees- a supe band that plays at raves

Rogue's apartment- where Rogue lives

The Guys' House- owned by the Geminis, where Damon, Javier, Angelo, Rebel, and Archie live

Florissa's house- where she runs an underground healing clinic

Emerald Lotus- restaurant where Javier works; a fave of Rogue's

Blackmoor Academy- reform school for bad supes

Discordia University- demon university, also a place to send bad hybrids

The Ramble- supernatural penitentiary

Hell- the underworld where demons and demon hybrids typically live.

Stalk Cassandra Featherstone in the Dark Corners of the Web

JOIN MY FACEBOOK GROUP AND FOLLOW ME EVERYWHERE!

WANT MORE?

SIGN UP FOR MY BI-WEEKLY MANIFESTO FOR A FREE SERIES SAMPLER:

Join my Ream as a FREE follower or exclusive subscriber to get access to cover reveals, WIPs, Serial Stories, and personal chats from me!

KILLER QUEEN

Morgana

Looking around the campus with a critical eye, it isn't hard to notice the differences between the campus of Swallowtail and State U. The major difference is age, of course, but even secondary schools overseas are unlike the blatant marketing machines that are American universities. State U doesn't resemble the colleges I've seen in American movies or on TV, though much of that is the Society's doing.

However, banners, statues, plaques, signs, and even architecture are emblazoned with the school's motto—*Honoris. Veritas. Potentia*—as if constant reminders will enforce the virtues it extols. *That* differs from the places in Europe I attended or worked in.

"Getting used to the sales aspect of education here won't be your biggest challenge and you know it," I mutter to myself.

When the outcome of my trial led to a guilty sentence, I didn't expect the punishment they handed down. Instead of being jailed for the murder of my ex, they decreed I would replace him as the Dean at State U. I wasn't the only one who disagreed with my purgatory—the vote on the High Council was split down the middle until a mysterious figure cast a vote in favor of my exile. They summarily dismissed me from Swallowtail Academy and sent me home to pack my shit for a journey overseas to the nest of corruption created by the man I thought I would marry.

Not only am I the youngest Dean to ever hold the title, but I'm the only hybrid to head one of the Society's schools.

Placing me at the helm of the crown jewel of their American institutions made their unorthodox punishment even more bizarre, but I've never believed the group that guides our kind to be infallible. The irony of replacing the being responsible for all the university's current issues with the fiancee who killed him hasn't eluded me. It's like my penance for not blowing the whistle on him instead of taking my vengeance in blood.

They did not impress hard line elders with the eventual outcome, but that had to be expected. Some supernaturals don't believe in the young being given positions of power, especially when that young candidate is also a woman and a hybrid. Given that I believe Magnus had cronies at various levels of government he was paying off, some of them must be worried I'll expose them to prove I was right to remove him from this world. Either way, the assholes who are screaming I'll ruin their precious programs and reputation haven't shut up since I left the trial chamber.

Let them whine about their outdated, elitist standards. I'll show them.

I turn away from the greenery of the campus, leaving the balcony to take a seat at the enormous desk in my overly plush office. Knowing the way parents and donors behave in this country, I assume every inch of this space has been purchased not by the college, but by donors who had 'one little request' for my ex. Magnus Corona was well-known in academic circles for milking the wealthy Americans until they ran dry, but his lack of ethics couldn't go on forever. My greedy, dragon lover went on the lam after a series of scandals involving kickbacks, illegal sponsorships, sports, and sexual harassment. The last one is why I hunted him down and eventually watched the last breaths he took on this planet with vengeful glee.

I'll start looking for a decorator immediately. If it's not in the budget, my trust fund will cover it.

Like most lost ones, they left me on the doorstep of a very talented witch and her gargoyle mate. I never found my 'real' parents, but growing up on Swallowtail's campus was not a burden. It was different when my adoptive parents were professors there—three hundred years brings a lot of changes. When I graduated, I attended Oxford and came back to work there in administration because I missed the old buildings and libraries.

That's the gargoyle in me, I know.

My adoptive mother is blind—except for the gift of future sight. Being a beautiful, blind witch couldn't have been easy when she was teaching, but she met my father in college and they've been together ever since. When they graduated, they came back to Swallowtail to teach. Eventually, she became the head of the Witchcraft & Wizardry department at the Finishing School and my father was the chair of the Physical Education & Training program. Over the years, my mother's gifts made their investments and ventures fruitful enough to retire while they could still enjoy it. They live on a small island in the

Mediterranean where supes of their caliber like to soak up the good life.

Once I get settled here, I might invite them to come tour the campus. My father would particularly enjoy the Gothic structure of the buildings; they were constructed to evoke the feeling of Oxford and he loves those old buildings. I give the picture of them on my cherry wood desk a half smile and sigh when I realize it's going to be awhile before I can extend that invitation.

First, I have to figure out how to get this ship back on course. Loyalty divides the staff; the students are due to arrive in two weeks, and I have a lot of house cleaning to do within these hallowed walls. It's going to ruffle feathers to do the things that are necessary to keep our supernatural accreditation *and* our human sports certification. I'll have to let some staff go, shuffle departments and assignments, and bring in new people to monitor certain aspects of the college's accounting to satisfy all the requirements we need to meet by the end of the semester.

State U has never been forced to toe the line quite as closely as we must now, and that is all because of Magnus Corona's lack of scruples and inability to think without his dick.

Not that any of his adoring fans will believe it for a second—and that is the rock I'll have to push up the hill for the foreseeable future.

"They'll have to get on board or get the fuck out," I say as I compare the list of coaches, trainers, and support staff for the football team. "I don't have a choice and neither do they."

When I finally finish going over the massive budget for the major boys' teams, my brain is damn near fried. I cannot fathom how colleges here justify the expenditures of these programs compared to the paltry sums I saw on the balance sheets for academic programs. Americans truly have lost their focus on education, and it doesn't surprise me at all that Magnus could manipulate this to his advantage.

There's so many discretionary funds and black holes in the books that I'll have to find someone much more numerically inclined than myself to help me wade through this shit.

It's almost like it left room for loopholes and nefarious deeds.

Pushing to my feet, I rise from the high-backed leather chair and slip my shoes back on. I've been at this for hours and because I don't have office staff, no one was there to remind me I should eat or take a break. I had to fire everyone who worked in Magnus' immediate circle—both out of principle and necessity. I can't prove they knew what he was doing, nor that any of them would try to harm me as retribution, but I'm also not stupid enough to let someone with loyalty to my ex pour my goddamn coffee.

Coffee.

The word makes my blood hum and I know it's time to find sustenance—particularly caffeine. I locate my phone on the massive desk and slip it into the pocket of my suit pants. My appearance has been a topic of gossip on campus since I arrived—social media is a terrible curse when you're in the spotlight, even if it's for the right reasons. I've seen staff and alumni commenting on the 'uptight murdering bitch' strutting around campus dressed like someone from the *Addams Family* as if their vitriol isn't public when they post on Facebook.

My lips curve as I look down at the bespoke Tom Ford suit, Zegna tie, and Louboutin heels. Dressing the part has always been a theme of mine, but Magnus preferred the 'rumpled academic' look. He allowed the staff to run around looking like grad students and that will soon end. If they hate me for looking sharp compared to my frumpy ex, they're going to hate the new dress code when it rolls out in a week. I will not go as far as the Society schools did at home or in other countries, but I refuse to have the press haunting our grounds while taking pictures of grubby looking professors and coaches for their rags.

If this is the crown jewel, it needs more polishing than the Council realizes.

Before I go out, I shake my purple and black curls out of the messy bun, letting my hair settle over my shoulders. A quick check with the selfie mode on my phone tells me my makeup doesn't need to be freshened—thank hell—so I close the camera and put on my sunglasses to keep my sensitive eyes from the waning sun.

I'll need the State U app to find a place that's out of the way. I open it and cringe—the damn thing is hideous in form and function. I make a mental note to interview app designers and web developers; the website has to be as poorly maintained as this bullshit. Yet again, I marvel at the level of incompetence men can show without consequence. It finally loads the map and I scroll around until I find a coffee shop on the edge of campus. I don't want to go to a break room or the food court—there will be far too many eyes on me and I'd like to relax.

Noting the landmarks around the shop, I walk out onto the balcony and touch the amulet at my neck. My wings spring free, sprouting through the suit without a single tear, and I leap into the air. Catching a wind shear, I glide to the far end of the commons, then bank to the right towards the arts building. They nestled the little beanery I identified between the theater and the gallery, so I pull my wings back to descend slowly as I approach.

When I land, the magic of my mother's amulet helps me slip my appendages back in gracefully and walk towards the door without missing a beat. I open the door, take off my sunglasses, and stride in with confidence. I'm not here to throw my weight around, but I can't let anyone see me sweat, either. I look at the menu board before I lower my gaze to see the barista behind the counter.

Holy. Mother. Forking. Shit.

The guy behind the counter is beautiful, and I don't say that lightly. His long blond hair is pulled back in a ponytail, but somehow, it doesn't look douchey. Paired with his patrician features and thin silver framed lenses, he projects the air of a student, but not a new one. My guess is a grad or doctoral student and this is his side hustle. The muscled forearms and powerful hands tell me he's not just a bookworm, so I ponder what discipline this lithe, gorgeous supe is studying. When I finally drag my eyes back to his, the aqua color of his is mesmerizing.

"Can I take your order, ma'am?"

Yikes. That destroyed my brief fantasy.

"Um, yes, sorry. It's been a long day. I'd like a triple espresso and a club sandwich, please." I feel my cheeks heating not because I was staring—he's got to be used to it—but because I got caught checking out one of the students.

It's not forbidden at State U, but I am the murdering bitch with ice in her veins that's here to destroy everything the university stands for. Or, so the article in the *State U Review* said last night. There's no way this gorgeous coffee-serving man doesn't recognize me and I'm sure I'll get an earful about my evil ways once he's done making my order. In fact, I should continue watching to make sure he doesn't mess with my food for revenge.

Yeah, that's why I want to watch him.

"I don't blame you for coming here. It's not one of the campus hot spots. Mostly we get professors, arts kids, and the occasional normie who wants to hide from the masses."

I blink, realizing he's nailed my reason for choosing this shop without even trying. "I think it's rather cozy."

"You don't have to pretend, Dean LeCiel." His pretty eyes meet mine again and I feel that heat creeping up my spine. "I'm aware of how contentious your appointment was. It doesn't bother me, honestly. I've been a student through much of your ex's reign and since the music department was of little concern to him, I don't have any allegiance to the former administration."

Definitely a doctoral candidate. His thesis is probably massive.

Covering my mouth as the unintended double meaning of my words occurs to me, I wait until the urge to giggle like a teenager fades. It would be extremely unprofessional of me to comment on his... attributes... especially since that kind of bullshit helped bring Magnus down. Of course, that doesn't mean I'm not wondering now...

"Dean? Hello?" The hot barista is waving his hand as he looks at me curiously.

"I'm sorry to be so rude. I didn't catch your name?"

There we go. That sounded totally normal.

"I'm Slade," he replies with a slow smile.

That doesn't surprise me in the slightest, and I wonder if he might be part Fae. Not giving me his real name is part and parcel with them, and so is the ethereal beauty. "You may call me Morgana when I am here. I think titles are dreadfully stuffy, but..."

"Set boundaries early because you have mutinies to deal with."

Frowning, I tilt my head. "You aren't reading me with magic, are you, Slade? Even during my ex's time, that kind of invasion of privacy wasn't allowed."

"No, no!" He stops making the sandwich and gives me a sheepish look. "I inferred it. I mean, I don't run with the undergrads or the popular crowds, but I hear things. It wasn't hard to figure out that you're at the hole in the wall shop so you don't have to be on stage while you eat or that you're going to make big changes because of all the charges against the former dean."

I nod, observing him. "I believe you, though I probably shouldn't. Betrayal hides in obvious places; I'm living proof of that."

His features look sharper as he smirks. "There are those of us who don't believe what you did was unjustified, Morgana. Living here at State U will provide you with plenty of evidence to give the Council that will mitigate your actions."

"That's both my desire and my deepest fear, Slade. There's only so much bad PR this place can take before the Council shuts it down and moves on."

A coffee cup and a plate with my sandwich slide across the counter as he murmurs, "You'll have to decide if that's what you want when the time comes."

"I know."

Get it on Kindle Unlimited

Get Season Two on Vella

LOSER

Kat

The little blue icon on my app has been glaring at me all day, but I'm too damn nervous to open it. Everyone at Woodlawn High has been buzzing all day with their notifications and the squeals of joy and moans of despair were too much for me to take. My anxiety is through the roof—this is the moment I've been waiting for since middle school, but I can't seem to force myself to bite the billet and check.

Maybe it's because I don't have the support system most of my classmates have?

That's probably true, given I've always been a loner and I don't fit into any specific 'caste' here. It's hard to make friends when you get shuffled from foster home to foster home over the years. I've rarely stayed anywhere long enough to make a friend, much less a group of them.

I'm not delinquent or anything—the families I've been placed with just return me like a pair of pants that doesn't fit after a year or so. The caseworkers click their tongues sympathetically and hunt down a new placement, but I've never been given a reason *why* people don't want me around. One lady said I must be born under a bad sign and hell if I knew what that meant other than I'm not good enough to keep around.

It would be different, almost understandable, if I misbehaved or got bad grades. But I don't—I'm always in the top five percent of my class and I do everything I'm asked. I don't even lord my smarts over the other kids or adults. Being presentable and unassuming was something I adapted long ago to improve my probability of staying in a home long term.

Unfortunately, it never worked and though I should be a shoo-in for scholarships and acceptances galore, I can't bring myself to be rejected yet again.

So I wait for the last bell of the day, slinging my bag over my shoulder and trudging home to the latest in my temporary housing. I can't even contemplate looking at the possible heartache waiting for me in the college application system WHS insisted we use. The fear is too great and despite knowing I'll be on my own for good at the end of this year, I'm unable to risk the pain.

I hate being this way.

My court mandated therapist says it's some sort of attachment disorder that's common in foster kids, but I think that's bullshit. The problem isn't *me* not forming attachments; it's asshole adults not forming one to me. Being left at a safe haven in a fucking basket as a baby wasn't because *I* did anything wrong—again, fucking adults couldn't handle their commitments.

As usual, I arrive home to an empty house. There are two other kids who live here—Bryce and Blake—but they're at football practice. Of course, the Jamesons *love* them; they get to strut around at games because their strays are the stars of the team. I'm not mistreated, but I'm definitely an afterthought. Both of my 'parents' are still at work, so I drop my bag on the couch and head for the kitchen to get a snack:

Don't get me wrong. I *could* have been placed in far worse homes than any of the seven I've been in since elementary school. None of the ex-fosters starved, beat, molested, or abused me. They were all decent folks with jobs and houses that weren't hellholes, but they never liked me.

I have no idea why. I tried to be everything they wanted.

But when the end of each school year came, I was handed in like a textbook and off I went to some group home until the next contestant stepped up. It baffled everyone, not just me, but that's what happened every single time.

Sighing, I pull some fruit out of the fridge and grab a soda. I have homework to do and if I want to have time to work on my stories, I'll need to get it done before the house is full of people at dinner time. Bryce and Blake will have gotten messages about their applications, too, and I'd bet my pinkie toe those idiots got into some big sports school. Brett and Allison will be oozing happiness for them and I don't know if I'll be able to keep food down if I have to admit my failure when they ask.

Being eighteen sucks ass.

After I grab my books and tablet, I head down to the den. I have to give my current parents credit; they set up a very nice workspace for us to study in the converted basement. By the time they took me in, the Jamesons created a cozy room down here where the three of us could relax and do our work for school without being interrupted. It might have been more for the boys than me, but I appreciated it all the same. Desks, a couch, big chairs, and bookshelves fill the space, making it almost seem like our mini-library. They even put a small fridge for drinks and snacks in case we had to be up late to cram.

It's my favorite place in the entire house and I spend most of my time here.

I sink into the huge armchair, putting my drink and snack on the side table. It only takes a few minutes to arrange myself in the soft cushions and I pause to tug my headphones out of my pocket. Music always soothes my jagged edges and I need it to stay focused on the bullshit AP Calculus I need to keep my average up in. My course load is heavy, but I applied to tough colleges. I wouldn't have a chance to get in, especially on a scholarship, if I wasn't taking equally challenging classes in comparison to all the prep school kids.

As always, the sounds of Vivaldi carry me away as I scrawl equations on my screen and before long, thoughts of the blue notification completely fade away.

"Kat!"

The shouts barely register as I continue working on the problem set, gnawing on my lower lip in concentration.

"Jesus fuck, where is she? I could eat a hippo!"

"Kat!"

Thumping followed by what could pass for a stampede of elephants jerks me out of my math filled trance when Bryce and Blake come down the stairs. They smell as bad as the aforementioned pachyderm's cage, so they must have rushed home right after practice. The blond twins glare at me as if I'm the offending element despite being sweaty and covered in dirt and grass stains.

This doesn't bode well.

Usually, they're tired and hungry after practices so I'm used to cranky ass boys, but tonight, there's a light to their faces. That had to mean they've gotten their letters and dinner will be a gush fest in honor of their perfection. I'm going to need all of my strength to fake smile and nod as Brett and Allison fawn over them.

I don't begrudge them their success—not really. They work hard and play even harder on the field. It's not their fault they're the American dream teens and I'm the nerdy basement troll no one wants. But it's awfully hard living in the shadow of their bright light, especially when I'm no less intelligent or talented.

"I'm finishing the AP Calc, guys. What do you want?"

They roll their eyes at me before Blake scoffs. "It's not due until Monday. You're so hyper."

Duh. I take anxiety meds, douchebag; of course I'm 'hyper.'

"I can only be who I am, Blake." That earns me a snort from Bryce and I know it's because he thinks that's the problem. "Is dinner ready?"

"Almost. Get upstairs and set the table so we can shower—Brett's orders." Blake grins smugly.

The two of them seem to always arrange it so chores get passed to me for some half-assed reason and this is no exception. Sighing, I put my stuff aside, fully intending to hide down here after the dinner mess is cleaned up. Likely by me, but like I said, I could definitely live in worse foster homes so I let it go. Doing some chores isn't worth risking the group home for the last few months of my high school career.

They take off running up the stairs and I wait for them to disappear before I follow suit. My phone is tucked in my pocket and I feel like it's a stone of shame I have to bear. I know once the adults make over the twins' success, they will remember me, and I'll be forced to find out what disappointment lies in wait for me. The dread weighs on me, but I head into the sunny kitchen and pick up the pre-prepared pile of plates, silverware, and napkins on the counter.

Allison looks up from the stove and gives me a half-smile, nodding as I take the dishes into the dining room. Like I said, no one is mean or horrid, they just seem...obligated. After a while, it makes it hard to waste time trying to be bright and sunny. Being reserved makes it a hell of a lot easier not to feel rebuffed when they don't pay attention to you regardless.

"Make sure you include champagne glasses for your dad and I!" she calls from the other room.

The twins definitely got acceptance somewhere big. Brett must have gotten the bubbly on the way home.

Once I set the table, I return to help Allison bring out the roast and sides. I'm a little amazed at her efficiency when it comes to getting the housework done while working full time, but I suppose it's something people with real parents get taught as they grow up. My home life has been so fractured that I haven't learned how to cook more than very basic shit from YouTube videos. That may be a problem after graduation, but I've never felt comfortable enough to ask Allison if she'd teach me. I'm sure she would try, but it doesn't feel right.

"How was school, Kat?"

I look over my shoulder, seeing Brett in the entry to the dining room. He's already changed from work and smiling, but I see the distraction in his eyes. He's waiting for the boys to come down. "It was fine. I've got a Calc test at the end of the week. I'll be studying a lot to get ready."

"Good, good. No matter what happens with applications, keeping your grades up will ensure no one pulls any offers," he says.

Those words aren't for me. They are for the two wet haired boys who just appeared behind him.

"Kat's too much of a geek to ever let her grades slip, Dad," Blake says as he pushes past his brother and drops into his usual chair at the table. "Grab me a Powerade since you're in the kitchen, mouse!"

Both Brett and Bryce stare at me and I turn around, heading to the fridge despite the fact that I was *not* closer than the other twin. Out of habit, I take two of the drinks and a soda for myself. I've been here long enough to know Bryce will send me back to get him one as well. It would feel like typical sibling stuff, but for some reason, I just *know* they do it to fuck with me. I have no idea why I feel that way, but trusting my gut has been the one thing that helped me get through all the upheaval in my life over the years. It's a good gauge for knowing when I'll get booted or if people are being earnest in their reactions.

The therapist says that's some sort of trauma induced early trigger warning shit, by the way.

After I hand out the drinks, I sit down on my side of the table and we wait for Allison to come out. Brett is at his seat at the far end of the table and the twins are punching each other as they look at something on their phones. I know where this is all going but I drop my gaze to the table, swallowing the coppery taste of fear as it courses through my body.

I'm going to be exposed and there's nothing I can do to stop it.

Read the first three episodes free on Kindle Vella: https://www.amazon.com/kindle-vella/story/B0BSTMB1X3

JUST A GIRL

Delores

Sighing, I look around my bedroom at the posters and decorations covering my walls. My obsession with pop music, musical theater, and high school rom-coms sickens my parents. They would prefer me to be into heavy metal and horror movies like the other kids my age.

Being the only child in a family as prominent as mine is difficult when you don't fit the mold. My parents—like their parents and all my friends' parents—are apex predators. Preds rule our world, and the division between us and prey is so severe that we regulate them to a completely different echelon of society. Prey shifters are weak and beneath our lofty abilities. The ruling class of elite predator families stretches back generations, and they've evolved into a bunch of assholes who only care about succession and greed.

My animal has not manifested yet, but it will soon enough. Luckily for me, none of my friends have manifested their inner animals, either. I'm part of the in-crowd at school, and my boyfriend, Todd, is the most popular guy in my class. While he and I aren't officially engaged yet, we've talked about it enough that I know it's only a matter of time before he puts a ring on my finger. I should be on top of the world, but I can't help but feel like my life just doesn't fit me the way it's supposed to.

Every teenager wishes their life was different, but I dream of becoming an entirely different person. Not inside, mind, because I'm pretty comfortable with who I am. I don't want to be part of this legacy, this society, or even this family. They are all focused on competing to be the richest, the deadliest, or the most powerful, and I want no part of it.

I walked over to my closet and pulled out the outfit that I had chosen for my tour of Apex Academy. My mother hired her personal designers to create a custom school uniform for today and expects me to present the 'appropriate' image of the sole heir to a Council seat.

I hate having to pretend to be like them because I'm nothing like them.

Regardless, I pull on the short, pink pleated skirt, three quarter length sleeve blouse, knee socks, and Mary Janes that comprise the uniform for my exclusive private high school. Since I'm using a 'college visit' day to tour the Academy, I'm expected to represent Shifter Secondary as well.

Shifter Secondary is the most exclusive high school for unmanifested shifter teens on the East Coast. Unfortunately for me, it was not my parents' first choice for my education. They hoped I'd follow in their footsteps by choosing to force my animal to emerge early. If I had done that, I could have attended *Apex Academy Lower School.*

I didn't have the stomach to use my body in that manner at fourteen.

Their heirs followed my lead, which made my mother and father furious and their hoity-toity council colleagues angry. My closest friends, the Heathers, also refused to force their animals to emerge, as did Todd and his friends. That was the first time the adults in our circle decided I was a bad influence. After that, I had to toe the line at every turn, ensuring that I followed all the strict rules and regulations that govern the heirs to council seats.

Everywhere I went, I had to dress in a manner befitting the next Drew to sit at the table. They forced me to take dance lessons, piano lessons, diction lessons, and other more humiliating tutorials to prepare for the day that I became a true predator. In our society, teenagers have no say in how we prepare for our animals to emerge.

Your parents make all the decisions, choose your friends, choose your mates, and decide every detail of your life down to what you eat every single day. At least, that's how it is in my family, because my mother is from the old world.

She came over from Slovenia when she was incredibly young and met my father on the society fundraiser circuit. Her idea of preparing her daughter for the future involves lessons in makeup, clothing, jewelry, and on how to keep your mate satisfied. Lucille is completely unconcerned about whether I end up happy, only that I attend to my council seat and my husband's *needs.*

Once I get dressed, I grab my vintage Vuitton bag and peek at the mirror for a last check before I head downstairs. I tuck my perfectly highlighted blonde tresses behind my ears, and the smokey eye and winged liner are on point with this year's fashion trends. I apply a quick swipe of cherry red lip gloss and open my mouth, inspecting my teeth to make sure they are pearly white. Even though once I develop threatening incisors or sharp fangs, something will inevitably cover them in blood, my parents want my smile to look like a toothpaste commercial.

It's all such utter bullshit.

I take a deep breath and turn on my heel, heading for the door. I can already hear my parents yelling in a Scotch and vodka induced rage in the drawing room. It's only eleven thirty in the morning, for Hera's sake.

Lucille and Bruno don't fuck around with cocktail hour. They are nicely sauced by ten a.m. every day, without exception. I can't remember a time when my parents didn't get drunk off their asses at an event or party, much less in our 'home'. They liquor up and fight until they part for the day, and then start again once they arrive home from their daily commitments.

I brace for the barrage of criticism my mother will subject me to when I cross the threshold. Closing my eyes, I whisper words of encouragement to myself via lyrics to some of my favorite songs, desperately trying to hype myself up before she can tear me down.

"Delores! I hear you breathing at the top of the stairs, darling. Come down this instant and let your father and I inspect your presentation."

My mother's purr *sounds* friendly, but believe me, it's not. I roll my eyes as I make my way down the stairs, knowing my mother won't hesitate to send one of the staff if I don't acquiesce to her command. Most of their staff would gleefully jizz themselves with being chosen to drag me downstairs for inspection.

At this time of day, the only servant in the drawing room will be Matilda—my ex-nanny turned personal assistant—and that request would test her loyalties. As the only person in my household who has my back, I don't want to put her in that position, so I answer. "Yes, Lucille. I'm on my way."

I'm not allowed to refer to her as 'mother' because it makes her feel old. 'Lucille' is always what I've called the woman who supposedly gave birth to me. I'd be tempted to disbelieve we shared any DNA at all if it weren't for our similar bone structure. She's about as nurturing as a rattlesnake, and if it weren't for Matilda, I might have died as a child. If the kitchen staff whispers are accurate, I have to accept that my mother neglected to feed me much of the time.

"You coddle her far too much, Lucille," my father growls. "As the heir to our family seat, Delores will come without being instructed to do so. We will not tolerate her insolence after her animal emerges. She will behave as I command or suffer the consequences."

The last of Bruno's rant echoes off the marble walls of the foyer as I step onto the hideously expensive, endangered teak floor. Schooling my features into the mask of indifference I wear whenever I have to deal with them, I enter their den of drunken fights with my spine steeled for an emotional assault.

"I apologize for my tardiness, Father. I only wished to perfect the image I will present during my tour of Apex Academy. I realize it is imperative I impress the Headmistress and her staff."

The humanoid features of his face shift seamlessly, and the hungry crocodile inside of him gives me a toothy smirk. "You will impress them, daughter, or so help me... I'll send you to Bloodstone Isle."

My stomach drops like a stone as I barely suppress a shiver.

Bloodstone Isle is a reformatory school. It's surrounded by spells and enchantments to prevent students from escaping—a feat that has only happened once in its one thousand years of existence. The most feared cat group in the shifter world—the Khan ambush—runs the school, and they're rumored to consume errant students when the Council allows it.

It's the threat both rich and poor shifter parents used to keep their children in line. Wealthy parents like mine use it as a method of controlling any heirs that refuse to conform to the rigid structure of our society. Predators don't value the lives of those who are weak, and they label heirs who refuse to take their rightful place at the top of the food chain weak. Everyone knows Bloodstone is full of criminals, miscreants, and psychos, and even they don't seem to survive.

Bloodstone is a death sentence—pure and simple.

"Y-yes, Father. I understand," I croak out. As if the pressure of touring my new school isn't enough, now I worry the Dean will relay something to my parents that gets me shipped off to Death Island.

"Bruno, darling, if you scare her, she'll frown. That causes wrinkles. Delores, chin up and smile for us."

Swallowing the lump in my throat, I flash my mother my brightest smile. Her blood-red lips curve, and her leopard fangs burst free as she all but purrs. "I will not have you sullying the family name, Delores. It's bad enough that your education gave you ideas about your value beyond breeding stock. You will take the seat on the Council when it is time, but the husband we select will control the business—as nature intended. Do you hear me?"

My eyes narrow briefly, and for what is possibly the millionth time this week alone, I nod at my mother to appease her temper. "Yes, Lucille."

"Excellent!" The leopard fades as she claps her hands. "Matilda!"

The tiny woman steps up, her eyes wide behind her glasses. She's a pred, but the smaller size of hawk shifters puts her in the servant class. I believe she genuinely lives in fear of one or both of my parents deciding to eat her. "Yes, madam?"

"Fetch Bruiser. He will accompany Delores to the academy for her tour. Tell him to take the Escalade—it won't do for her to arrive in a tiny car—it will draw attention to her extra weight. We must make an impression."

Matilda nods, and I feel the fear radiating from her, and I don't blame her. Bruiser is one of my parents' bodyguards and our frequent chauffeur. He's a Komodo dragon shifter and the house staff are terrified of him. It's hard not to be, given that he prefers to play with his food, then eat it after it's dead. The kitchen crew believes he 'handled' the gardener that looked too long at my mother when I was ten. He disappeared without a trace.

Once Matilda scurries away, I watch my parents drink and bicker about their plans for the day. Bruno is going golfing with a congressman, and Lucille is going to the spa. We all know that both outings will include stops at the homes of their current pieces of ass for a quickie, but no one talks about it. The appearance of the loving couple has to be maintained, although neither of them has slept in the same room since I was a baby.

They don't give a damn about fidelity; I learned that at an early age. Children often discover things they shouldn't because of adults discount their ability to understand the conversations happening around them.

I stopped keeping track of who they're boning long ago, because I'd need an assistant to keep the affairs straight.

While my parents' marriage is a sham, I remind myself that my boyfriend, Todd, isn't like them. Yes, his parents only own half the live entertainment industry, but my father allows me to see Todd. The other parents will force the Heathers to accept an arranged betrothal, and I'm grateful I'm lucky enough to have found the perfect match on my own as my high school sweetheart.

"Delores, Bruiser is ready to escort you to Apex. He's pulling the car around now," the hawk shifter says softly.

Snapping out of my reverie, I smile at the trembling woman. Bruiser must have scared the living hell out of her. For no other reason than it amused him, I'm sure. He's as much a brute as his name implies, and I don't look forward to riding alone to the academy with him.

Something about that shifter gives me the creeps...

MAGIC

1. Worlds collide, the air still moves.
     The truth hides,
     The light reveals.
     Our powers combine, their presence it proves.

Cassandra Featherstone has channeled her lifelong passion for writing into a flourishing career, a journey that started when she first grasped a pencil as a gifted child with ADHD.

Her debut novel, born during the solitude of COVID lockdown in March 2020, draws on a tapestry of personal encounters and insights that resonate deeply with her readers.

An international bestseller, Cassandra has topped Amazon charts in categories such as LGBT Anthologies, LGBTQ+ Mystery, and Bisexual Romance, among others. Her works navigate the complexities of bullying, PTSD, body dysmorphia, mental health struggles, personal reinvention, and the empowerment of claiming one's own space. Importantly, Cassandra offers a thoughtful and respectful portrayal of LGBTQIA+ relationships, subtly reflecting her own connection with the community through her narratives.

Her literary repertoire spans sci-fi fantasy, urban fantasy, paranormal, and comedic genres in academy whychoose settings, with a strong commitment to portraying consensual, safe, and accurately depicted BDSM and kink lifestyles. Her books are an invitation to explore transformative stories that are both inclusive and engaging.

Often affectionately called 'The Muppet' for her wacky theater kid personality, she resides in the Midwest with her tech-savvy husband, their creatively inclined college student, a literary-minded dog, and four scheming cats.

READ MORE AT CASSANDRA'S WEBSITE OR HER FACE-BOOK PAGE. SIGN UP FOR EXCLUSIVE CONTENT AND UPDATES HERE.

FIND HER ON ANY OF THE SOCIAL MEDIA BELOW AS SHE *LOVES* TO CHAT AND *NEVER* SLEEPS!

Come Out & Prey

Let Us Prey

In Prey We Trust

TRANSLATIONS OF THE APEX ACADEMY CAPERS SERIES

Come Out & Prey (German)

Let Us Prey (German)

In Prey Trust (German)

DISCORDIA UNIVERSITY

Veiled Flame (Book One)

Quiet Burn (Book Two)

Zero Spark (Book Three)

TBA Title (Book Four)

AUDIO OF THE DISCORDIA UNIVERSITY SERIES

Veiled Flame (Book One)

Quiet Burn (Book Two)

SECRETS OF STATE U

Blood on the Ice (Book One)

Suspicions on the Stage (Book Two)

Fatality on the Field (Book Three)

FAETAL ATTRACTION

Hell on Wheels (Book One)

Jammer in the Box (Book Two)

TBA Title (Book Three)

F.E.A.R. ACADEMY

Failed State (Book One)

Trigger Protocol (Book Two)

VILLAINS & VIXENS

Bloodthirsty (Book One)

Ruthless (Book Two)

Wicked (Book Three)

AUDIO OF THE VILLAINS & VIXENS SERIES

Bloodthirsty

Ruthless

TRIANGLES & TRIBULATIONS

Hoist the Flag (PQ)

Yo-Ho Holes (Book One)

CHILDREN OF THE MOON- WITH SERENITY RAYNE

New Moon Rising (Book One)

Waxing Crescent (Book Two)

Waxing Gibbous (Book Three)

Samhain Secrets (Novella 3.5)

Full Moon (Book Four)

Waning Gibbous (Book Five)

Waning Crescent (Book Six)

RISE OF THE RESISTANCE

Ream Exclusive Prequels

Hooked on a Feline (Book One)

Peacock Me Like A Hurricane

Love The Way You Lion (Book Three)

TBA Title (Book Four)

REAM SERIALS

Secrets of State U

Discordia University

Faetal Attraction

Rise of the Resistance

F.E.A.R. Academy

ANTHOLOGIES

Unwritten

Shifters Unleashed

Jingle My Balls

Love is in the Air

Silent Night

Snowed In

All Hallows Eve